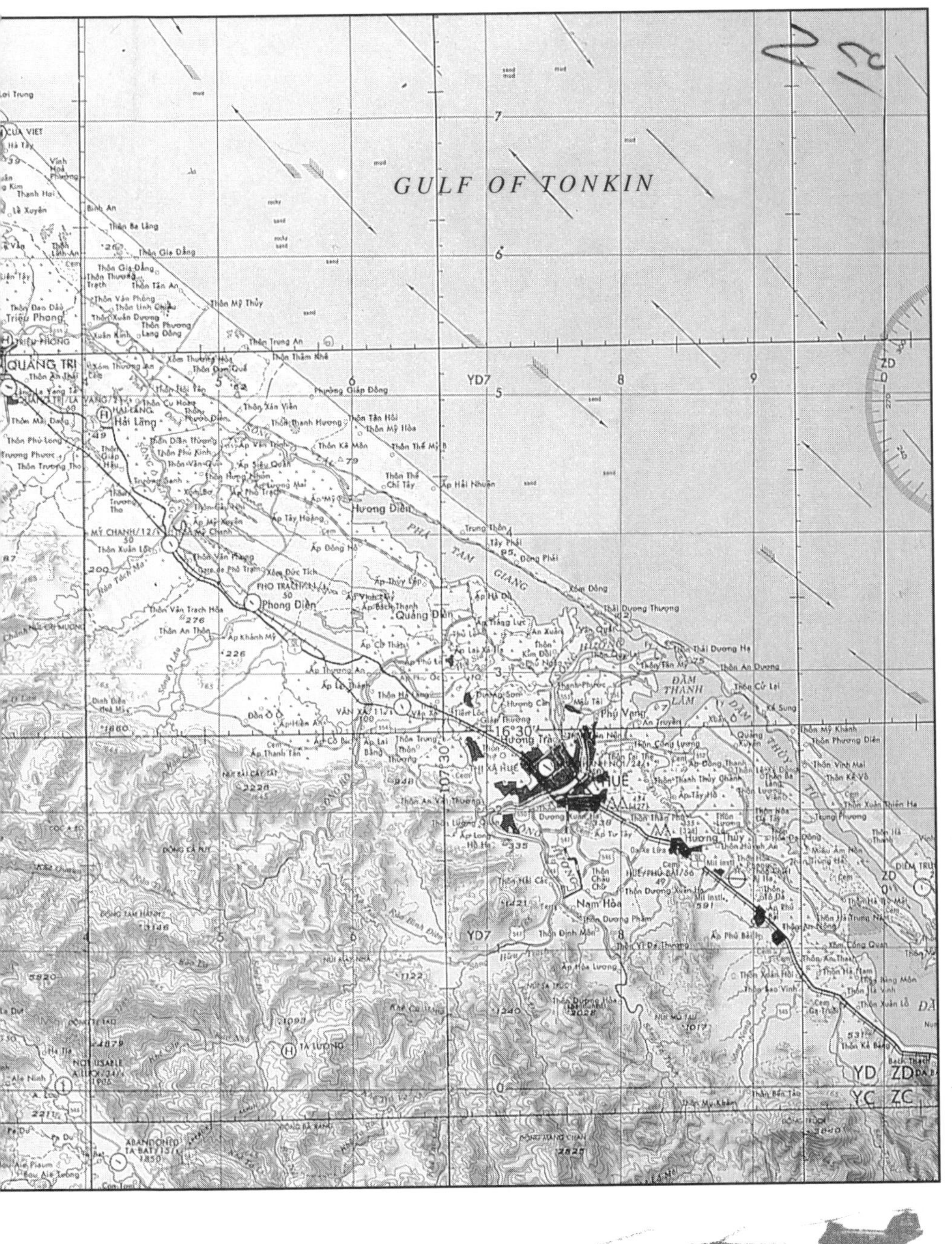
GULF OF TONKIN
QUANG TRI
Triệu Phong
Hải Lăng
Phong Điền
Quảng Điền
Hương Điền
PHÁ TAM GIANG
ĐẦM THANH LAM
Phú Vang
Hương Trà
HUẾ
Hương Thủy
Nam Hòa
YD7
16°30'
107°30'
Thôn Thái Dương Thượng
Thôn Thái Dương Hạ
Thôn An Dương
Thôn Cự Lại
Thôn Mỹ Khánh
Thôn Phương Diên
Thôn Vinh Mai
Thôn Kế Võ
HUẾ/PHÚ BÀI/56
TA LUONG
NOT USABLE
ABANDONED
YD ZD
YC ZC

D1164788

RANDOLPH E. CREW

A KILLING SHADOW

A NOVEL

Semper fi,
Randy Crew

ARTEC PUBLISHING

First Edition

Publisher's Cataloging-in-Publication Data

Crew, Randolph E., 1944—
A Killing Shadow

1. Fathers and sons — Fiction. 2. Military helicopters — Fiction. 3. United States Marine Corps — Aviation —Fiction. 4. Vietnamese Conflict, 1961-1975 — Fiction. I. Title.

Library of Congress Catalog Card Number: 96-84959

Published by Artec Publishing
POB 25103, Greenville, SC 29616
864-288-2111

PRINTED IN THE UNITED STATES OF AMERICA

10 9 8 7 6 5 4 3 2 1

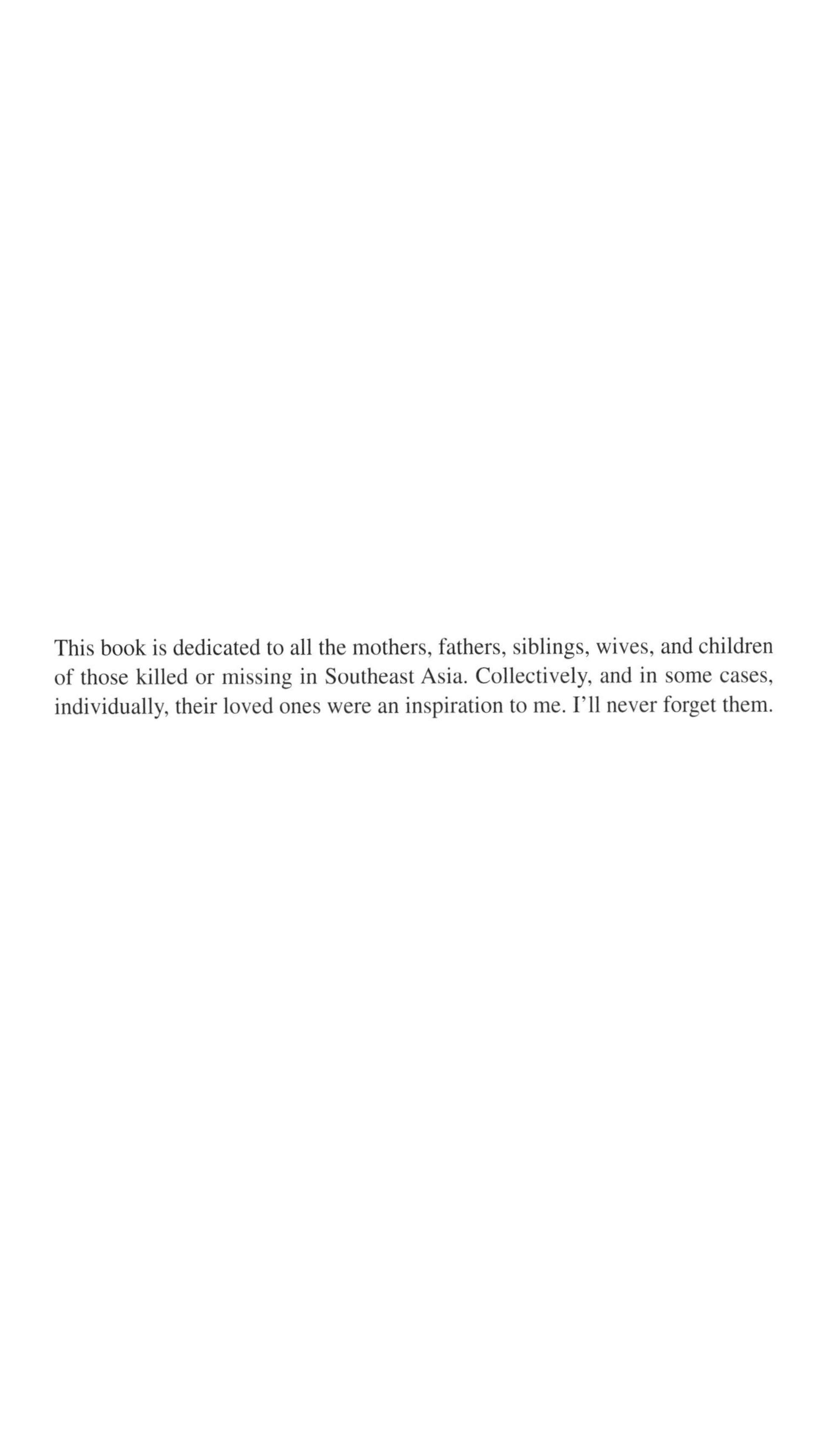

This book is dedicated to all the mothers, fathers, siblings, wives, and children of those killed or missing in Southeast Asia. Collectively, and in some cases, individually, their loved ones were an inspiration to me. I'll never forget them.

Table of Contents

Table of Contents (cont'd)

"Greatness of name in the father
oft-times overwhelms the son;
they stand too near one another.
The shadow kills the growth."

– Ben Jonson (1573-1637)

A KILLING SHADOW

BOOK ONE

Prologue

In my family, the beach trip is the beginning and ending of all things important. My memory starts there, all of us flying down the highway, our '50 Chevrolet riding high on the asphalt.

On the back seat, cheeks in her hands, spit in her eye, my little sister would crouch across from me. In front, smiling, my mother would wave to people on their porches or at their mailboxes. Behind the wheel, my stern-faced father, only days short of leaving for Korea, would be in command—ever committed to the mission, ever the Marine fighter pilot.

Beside that two-lane highway from Havelock, North Carolina, to the beach at Morehead City, lay a flying field. The field wasn't much: an overgrown cow pasture with a wide strip of close-cut grass; a weathered old barn beside the strip; an airplane beside the barn. I enjoyed the beach, but the flying field was where I wanted to go. I wanted to go flying with my father.

On those trips, watching out my window, I'd see the faded orange windsock on the top of the barn first, then the sagging roof, then the peeling white sign on the side of the barn boasting, "Flying Lessons, Aircraft Rental, Small Engine Repair." I'd be on the rounded corner of the seat by then, my face outside the car, eyes squeezed against the wind, hands on the door panel. Finally the little yellow airplane would appear and I'd wrinkle up in a smile, bounce on the seat, and squeeze my hands into fists. Alone out there in the sun, its tail hidden in the grass among the crickets and grasshoppers, its wings tied to the ground, the airplane would flicker by behind flashing fence posts—waves of heat blurring its shape, and I'd want to say something; I'd want to ask my father to take me flying in that airplane. But I didn't. I knew what he'd say.

My father, like all fighter pilots, flew real airplanes—fast, death-dealing airplanes. He didn't pay anybody to fly anything. I heard him tell my mother one time, "Only wimps would fly something that slow, that yellow, and pay good money for it." Low-slow-and-yellow was not his style. Besides, when it was time to go to the beach, we went to the beach. That was the mission. That's what we did.

My mother, who my father referred to on those trips as "Evelyn the Cruiser," never cared about the airfield either, or even where we were going or why. She was just glad to get away from our two-bedroom oven, to cruise. On the road at sixty miles an hour, windows down, her flowered scarf dancing in the wind, her tanned arm resting on a folded towel over the glossy black paint of the door panel, she just liked to go, to roll, to hear the tires sing to the passing trees. A window fan in every room of the house couldn't cool you like a two-lane country blacktop at a mile-a-minute.

My little sister Sally, her blonde hair tied in pink ribbons, intense brown eyes, just wanted to get there. She didn't care about the flying field or the yellow airplane or the singing tires. She didn't even enjoy the wind in the windows. Trapped in the back seat with me, forced to sit still and be quiet, the beach trip, or any trip, was simply pain to her. I didn't like my role any more than she did, but it was either keep her quiet or deal with my father. At least my sister enjoyed herself after we got there. Given enough space, she could have a good time.

My name is Ross, and good times don't come that easy for me. As far back as middle school, Sally has described me as "strong, silent, and boring." Compared to her, I guess I am.

Back in June, 1969, after four years of college, a commission, and two years of training, I was transferred to Vietnam, to a Marine air base near a beach. There, along with Bill, Rod, Walt, and twenty other first lieutenants, none of them boring, I was paid to fly Huey gunships.

The Huey gunship wasn't fast—the air rushed in the windows at barely 120 miles an hour, two-miles-a-minute. But it wasn't yellow, and like any "death-dealing" air machine, it was armed to the teeth.

Had my father finished his tour in Korea, had he not crashed and died there, I think he would have been proud of the aircraft I flew in Vietnam. I know he would have admired my action over Khe Sanh, liked the guys who were with me, and understood why the Marine Corps had to get rid of us afterward—why I didn't finish my tour either.

This is how it happened.

1

Mickey

Seated in the darkened cabin of the Boeing 707, I brushed crumbs from my stateside utilities and reminded Bill the odds were against us.

Long legs folded against the seat back, he slouched even lower in his seat. "Doesn't matter, R.T.," he said, a *Sports Illustrated* covering his freckled face. "We'll get the same squadron. I feel it."

"What else do you feel?" I said, grinning.

"I feel hungry."

If I hadn't known Bill since flight school, I would have found that hard to believe—he'd just eaten his in-flight meal and half of mine. Shaking my head, I pulled *The Bridges at Toko-ri* from the seat pocket in front of me. "Okay, Carnack, if you know we're going to the same squadron then tell me where, which base?" I looked toward the front of the airplane, toward the other two Marine Huey pilots on our flight. "Marble Mountain? Walt and Rod say that's the place to be."

"It is if you're lookin' for ass-kissin' career opportunities like Walt." Bill adjusted the magazine and folded his arms over his thick chest. "Too many generals and colonels for us."

"So, we're not going to Marble?"

"No. Goin' to Quang Tri. Together." He sighed. "Wake me for breakfast, will ya?"

"Sure." I opened the book to my napkin bookmark.

Minutes later, after reading two pages and remembering none of it, I replaced the napkin and closed the book. It was two o'clock in the morning, June 16, 1969. The cabin was dark and still, and beside me, the magazine propped on Bill's chest rose and fell in a steady rhythm. Isolated in the hazy beam of the miniature spotlight above me, I closed my eyes—thinking.

It didn't matter to me. I didn't care where I was assigned—Marble Mountain, Quang Tri, or some other place. Quang Tri was near the DMZ—more flight time, no generals, fewer Walt Dupponts. An assignment there would have been fine with me, if it was a good squadron. That was all I cared about. I just wanted a good squadron and hoped Bill was in it. A jock like him didn't need me to take care of him, but I had promised his wife Laura I would.

Hours later, after a landing, a roll call, and a bumpy truck ride in the dark, I sat on my bags and watched a creeping gray sky light our surroundings—a wooden watch tower and a chain-link fence topped with barbed wire. We were on the inside looking out, dozens of tired Marines strewn along a concrete slab with a tin roof.

I stood, walked to the fence, and hung my fingers on the rusty links.

Far below, an orange sun bulged from the placid South China Sea and lit a flat city veiled in a smoky haze and pressed against a huge crescent-shaped bay—Da Nang. At the eastern tip of the bay, extending into the sea, the ground rose sharply to form Monkey Mountain. On the coast to the south, beyond Da Nang, steep rocks like out-of-place Arizona buttes jutted from the sand dunes—the Marble Mountains. I'd read about these places. Now I was looking at them. It didn't seem real.

From the west side of the city, and with a sound like distant thunder, two F-4 Phantoms, twin afterburners glowing white hot, climbed south, away from the huge concrete airfield, and arched inland toward the dark mountains. Over the water off the northern end of the runway, flying over tiny fishing nets and small black boats, a four-engine transport plane, dwarfed by the bay, turned onto final approach to the airfield.

Up close, with light from the climbing sun, the hamlet beside us took on size and dimension—a slum of cardboard and tin-roofed huts built astride dry rice paddies littered with plastic bags, styrene cups, and C-ration wrappers. On a paddy dike across a field, a small brown-skinned boy in baggy black pajamas appeared asleep on the back of a slow-moving water buffalo. Ahead of them, the fields abutted a ragged hibiscus hedge, the dead sections stark and bare. The water buffalo and boy disappeared through a gap in the hedge and into a grove of banana trees, and I returned to my bags.

By mid-morning, wing headquarters had decided all four of its new Huey pilots were needed at Phu Bai.

After protests from Walt and Rod and a satisfied "Told you so" from Bill, we retrieved our bags and walked toward a truck bound for Da Nang airfield. That's when the memory surfaced—the hands of my instructor at Ellyson Field. Rough as stucco and ribbed with pink tendons, the hands were scarred from burns suffered when his CH-46 was shot down at Hue during the Tet Offensive. He had been based at Phu Bai.

I turned to Bill. "Phu Bai?"

"North," he said, chewing the last bite of a Snickers he'd liberated from my briefcase. "Near the beach."

Phu Bai Marine Air Base, built on the north side of a Vietnamese civilian airport with one east-west runway, was flat, sandy, and even hotter than Da Nang. A main road of dirt and gravel, quiet with an occasional jeep or six-by to churn the dust, entered the base off the west end of the airfield, then curved to parallel the runway and split the base in half. We arrived from the civilian side of the field on that main road, bouncing on our bags in the back of a six-by with no top and no sides, perspiring, and coated in a layer of fine powdered dust.

Three hours later, check-in procedures at the air group headquarters and Walt's rejected appeal for a transfer to Marble Mountain behind us, we walked a mile down the road to the last sandbagged shack on the right, HML-467, the local Huey squadron. A four-foot square sign in front of the large shack said our new commanding officer would be "Lt. Col. Donald C. 'Mickey' Houser."

A tall, collegiate-looking corporal in a green, sweat-ringed T-shirt introduced us: "Four new lieutenants for you, sir!"

Inside the dim office, a muffled voice replied, "Thank you ah…Straderman. Come in, gentlemen, be—" A ringing telephone cut him off.

We filed into the office and stood at attention in front of a gray metal desk. A copy of *Baseball News* lay open on the desk top. Seated in a swivel chair, wearing a battered navy-blue baseball cap and a green flightsuit, Lieutenant Colonel Houser held a 1950-style phone to his ear.

I glanced at Bill. Marines don't wear covers or caps indoors.

"Who?" the colonel said, his weathered face wrinkling. "Where? No, sorry, can't place you, Major, but ah…what can I do for you." He shook his head. "Well, no, not really…well, we're in good shape right now, ah…wait a minute, just a minute."

He cupped the mouthpiece and nodded to us. "At ease."

I took a deep breath and relaxed my shoulders. Beside me, Bill hung his head, whistled softly to himself, and found a nail in the plywood floor that needed attention. He tapped on it with the heel of his boot. Rod snickered. From the other end of our line, Walt leaned forward and shot Bill a look. I elbowed Bill and he stopped.

To our left, a fly buzzed and bounced against the rusty screens of a window. In the far corner, a framed and signed eight by ten photograph of Mickey Mantle hung from a nail. Below the photo, on top of a pine ammo box, an oscillating fan hummed and whirled toward the colonel and the Marine Corps and American flags behind him. In the other corner, above a galvanized pail of baseballs and two fungo bats, a weathered, well-oiled fielder's glove hung from another nail. The office smelled like a locker room in a pine forest.

The colonel had leaned back, crossed his long legs on the desk top, and pushed the cap to the back of his head. "Quantico...yes, Station Squadron, SOES, yes, ah...Louise, that's right, DeMayo, his daughter, yes, he's fine, the congressman is fine—eighth term. Well thank you, thank you, but as I was saying, Major, I ah...oh?"

The colonel's eyes brightened. "Yeah, that's right, I wore number seven...yes, center field." He laughed. "They've called me 'Mickey' ever since. Well thank you, thank you, but again, Major ah...Angus, yes, again Major Angus, we don't need...

"Oh, you did? Yeah, of course." He turned and looked at Mickey Mantle's picture. "Yeah, good times, saw 'em every time they played the Senators—hell, I still wear the cap he gave me in '55. That's right, great...great guy. Oh, no, no, thank you, but I ah...well I hit a few, but ah...well, thank you, but, Major—"

He listened a few seconds, nodded, pulled his feet off his desk, and turned to lean his forearms on the desk top. "Well, I guess so, but—" He scratched at his hairline. "Well, no, I don't guess I'd object to that, but...no, couldn't hurt I guess, well...sure. Okay, Major ah...Angus, yes, good day to you."

The colonel placed the receiver on the phone, shook his head and stared blankly at the desk top. "Angus," he muttered, "never heard of him." He shook his head again, straightened, snugged the cap down to his eyebrows, and stood to his full height—six-five, at least.

"Well, let's see ah...where were we, gentlemen. Oh yeah! Welcome aboard, glad to have you, I'm Lieutenant Colonel ah...Lieutenant Colonel Houser." He turned to me and tried to bend over the desk to shake my hand. We were too far apart.

At the risk of moving without permission, I swallowed hard, took a half step forward, and extended my hand across the desk. "Good afternoon, sir. I'm Lieutenant Ross Teemer." I received a firm but bony handshake and slipped back to my position.

Bill followed, smiling, just giving his name.

Rod Wysowski—small, brown wavy hair—gave his name and mentioned how much he admired the way the colonel had decorated the office.

Walt Duppont—taller, blond, country-club nose and chin—gave his name, concurred with Rod's appraisal of the decor, and mentioned how much he, Walt, looked forward to serving the colonel.

The colonel nodded to each of them, paused, raised his eyebrows, and looked around the room as if trying to figure out what they were talking about.

He sat at his desk again and held out his hand. "Relax, men, at ease, let me tell you about 'Hardball.'" He smiled. "That's our call sign, Hardball."

He leaned back in his swivel chair. "Men, this squadron is as good as it gets. We're winning this damn war, and we're winning it because of squadrons like this one—ball bustin' squadrons, aggressive, take-the-fight-to-the-enemy squadrons like this one—Hardball."

He popped erect and snatched the cap off his head. "See this cap, see this logo?" He touched his finger to the Yankee logo and outlined the N and the Y. "This ah...logo stands for excellence and tradition—Yankee tradition." He tapped the name tag over his left breast pocket. "See this? Well, in the world of combat helicopters, these letters and numbers stand for excellence and tradition too—HML-467, 'Hardball,' a tradition of ah...excellence in combat and the finest Huey gunship squadron in the Corps!"

He slapped the cap over his silver-gray flattop and snugged it to his eyebrows. "You lucky young men aren't going to have to stare at the ground and kick rocks when your kids ask what you did in the war to defeat communism and save the people of South Vietnam. You're with the best!"

We smiled.

The colonel nodded. "Now. By regulation, you'll have ah...six more days to get adjusted to the heat and humidity before you can fly. Use that time to get settled into your quarters, draw equipment, and finish your processing. In ah...four days you'll have an opportunity to participate in the Friday Evening Parade. You'll love it. The troops love it." He nodded his head firmly. "Good for morale."

The colonel looked at his watch and Bill and I glanced at each other. Participate in the what?

The colonel clasped his hands. "Now, before we break for happy hour, here's the best part: after a few weeks of combat experience, you'll be flying a secret mission, the highest priority mission of the war—Thunder Clap." He winked. "What do you think of that?"

I looked at the desk. What was I supposed to think of that?

"Outstanding, sir!" Walt said.

The rest of us nodded.

The chair squeaked as the colonel pulled his shoulders back. "Damn right. Any questions?"

"No, sir!" we said in unison.

"Very well." The colonel slammed his wrinkled hands on the desk and stood tall. "Now...before you're dismissed, I'd like to know just what kind of young men the Marine Corps is sending me these days."

He cleared his throat, studied each of us with yellowed gray eyes, then leaned forward and asked, "Can any of you guys play baseball?"

2

Angus

On our fifth day at Phu Bai, a Friday, I stood with Bill and others under a bright late-afternoon sun in front of a steel and sand revetment wall, a wall that radiated heat like a convection oven.

Across the flight line from us, standing in the shade of the squadron building, Lieutenant Colonel Mickey Houser, in faded utilities and his baseball cap, talked with a muscular major I'd never seen before. The major wore new camouflage utilities.

I flexed my knees as the colonel returned the salute of the major and marched to the reviewing platform of wooden shipping pallets in front of us.

In front of the pallets, an overweight captain, spit-shined and starched, looked over his shoulder, received a nod from the colonel, and screamed, "AT-TENN...HUT!" The pop of boot leather echoed off the revetment walls as the colonel took his place on the platform.

"REPORT!" barked the captain.

The Oriental lieutenant in front of our six-man officer's platoon took a quick breath and brought his hand to a salute. "Officer platoon, all present or accounted for, sir!"

The captain returned his salute and looked at the next platoon—five men, barely a fire team. The acting platoon leader, a gunnery sergeant, held a salute and boomed, "Staff platoon, all present or accounted for, sir!" Then the next platoon, eight men: "Shop platoon, all present or accounted for, sir!" Then the last platoon, nine men: "Maintenance platoon, all present or accounted for, sir!"

The captain returned the last salute, and commanded, "PRE-SENT, ARMS!"

As one, every Marine in the formation snapped to a salute and Bill, standing rigidly beside me, whispered out of the corner of his mouth, "Who's that?"

"Who?" I answered.

"The loud captain in the starched cammies."

"Orndorff."

Having done an about-face, the captain brought his hand to a salute and barked at Lieutenant Colonel Houser, "SIR, THE PARADE IS FORMED!"

"TAKE YOUR POST, SIR!" replied the colonel, returning the captain's salute.

"Is he a pilot?"

"Who?"

"Ordfuck."

My fists tightened. "It's *Orn-dorff*, asshole. Can't you see he's wearing wings?" Marines don't talk when at attention. Bill knew that.

"But does he fly?"

"OR-DERRR, ARMS!" Our right arms fell in unison.

"Ross. Does the starched one fly, man? Does he cheat death?"

"How the hell do I know?" I muttered.

"Well, you read. Have you seen him on the flight schedule?"

For some reason, Bill had decided back in flight school he didn't have to read the schedule. I would always be there to tell him when he was supposed to fly.

"No."

"PERSONS TO BE DECORATED OR PROMOTED, CEN-TER, MARCH!"

Immediately, the two Marines who had stood at attention to the left of the platform marched forward, did a right flank, then halted two paces in front of the colonel. The first one, a lieutenant, muttered, "Right, face." They turned to face the colonel.

"Who's the lieutenant?"

"Brunnengarber."

"Who-garber?"

Damn. "You remember. The guy we heard about in flight school who gave up carrier qualification so he could get to helicopters faster."

"Ohhh, yeah. Lieutenant Dumb Shit."

The colonel stepped off the platform, exchanged salutes with the two men, and positioned himself in front of the lieutenant.

The captain read from a clipboard at his post on the platform: "The President of the United States takes pleasure in presenting the Distinguished Flying Cross to First Lieutenant Myron A. Brunnengarber, United States Marine Corps, for service as set forth in the following citation."

"Myron?" Bill asked.

I grinned. Thank you, Mom, for not naming me Myron.

"...as co-pilot aboard an armed UH-1E (Huey) helicopter, and in spite of rapidly deteriorating weather conditions in mountainous terrain, and dangerously low fuel supply, and darkness of night, and heavy volume of enemy fire, and severe damage to his helicopter caused by enemy fire, he was undaunted and diligently monitored his instruments and equipment, and provided a continuous flow of vital information, and delivered exceptionally accurate machine gun fire against a superior hostile force." The captain finished by reading that Myron's actions were, "in keeping with the highest traditions of the Marine Corps and the United States Naval Service."

"How 'bout that?" Bill whispered. "That fuckin' Myron is one heroic sombitch!"

I nodded.

"He's still a dumb-shit for giving up carrier quals."

The colonel pinned the DFC medal on Brunnengarber's camouflage utilities, shook his hand, returned his salute, and side-stepped to face a corporal with an Errol Flynn mustache.

The captain turned the page on his clipboard and read, "The Department of the Navy is pleased to present the certificate of completion of Jungle Environmental Survival Training at the U.S. Naval Air Station, Cubi Point, Philippines, to Corporal Billy M. Earley, USMC."

While a salvo of distant artillery boomed behind us, the colonel presented Earley his certificate, shook his hand, returned his salute, and stepped back onto the platform.

Brunnengarber mumbled the commands and he and Earley marched to their original position.

"Now what?" Bill whispered.

"Announcements."

The colonel swelled. "PA-RAAADE...REST!" Thirty left boots hit the ground as one and thirty pairs of hands slapped together behind thirty strong backs. Bill grinned.

The major, the one the colonel had stood with earlier, stepped forward from the shadows. He was broad, with hair curling around the neckband of a green T-shirt under his new utilities. He marched onto the platform and halted at parade rest to the colonel's left rear, gold wings shining over his breast pocket.

"Jesus Christ!" Bill whispered. "Who's the hairy fireplug with wings?"

I shook my head.

The colonel glanced at the major and looked at the formation. "Officers, Staff Non-commissioned Officers, and ah...Marines of HML-467. First, I would like to thank you for another week of outstanding service to your squadron, your Corps, and ah...your country. HML-467 compiled more hours of combat flight time last month than any Marine squadron in Vietnam. We are on schedule, this month, to accomplish that again. And, in spite of some combat damage to two of our aircraft during the first part of this week, maintenance and ah...aircraft availability have been outstanding. Keep up the march."

I'd heard talk at chow about the damage the colonel referred to. A co-pilot had suffered a concussion—just grounded for a few days and released—and Carl Tess, the lieutenant in front of me, had a broken arm with bandages. He wore a green sling around his neck.

"New business." The colonel cleared his throat. "We are very fortunate to have aboard our squadron this afternoon a major with a distinguished career in aviation, including fighter aircraft, and who, after the appropriate orientation period, will be assuming the position of ah...executive officer of this squadron. I've had the pleasure of serving with this officer in the past, and I can assure you that he is an outstanding professional who will add to the 'can do' reputation of ah...HML-467."

Tess had mumbled and Bill had uttered a four-letter oath when the colonel mentioned "fighter aircraft." We hadn't heard anything good about former fixed-wing guys who had converted to helicopters—especially majors, and especially fighter pilots. As my Huey instructor at Camp Pendleton used to say, "Will Rogers never met a fighter pilot."

The colonel glanced at the major again and smiled. "At this time, I would like to introduce to you your future Executive Officer, Major Richard P. 'Bull' Angus. Please step forward, Major ah...Angus. I'm sure the men would like to hear a few words from you."

Bill leaned his head toward me and whispered, "Hey, Ross."

"Be quiet, Bill."

"Do we call the new major 'Major Angus' or 'Major Bull?'"

"Call him 'Major Bullshit' for all I care. Just be quiet."

"Roger. Major Bullshit it is."

Major Angus stepped forward. He was, as Bill described, 5'9" to 5'10" of hairy fireplug—thighs and trunk as wide as his shoulders. He approached the front of the platform with his arms held by his sides, the elbows bent, the thick hair matted with sweat and the muscles bulging under the rolled-up sleeves of his utilities. Head held back and cocked to the right, his face was rough: broken nose, scar under the chin—the kind of face that might belong to a prizefighter or a former street kid who got his ass kicked a lot. The tension I felt in my gut told me I'd met this guy, or his type, before, a long time ago. I couldn't remember where or when, but as I stood there in the sun watching him, I was sure it hadn't been a positive experience.

The major stopped at the edge of the platform, looked down on us for a few seconds, and screamed, "SQUADRON, AH-TENN, HUT!"

Surprised, we snapped our eyes straight ahead and lurched to attention.

Glancing at the platform, I caught the major's shaded eyes, barely visible behind eyelids pressed into narrow slits, traversing over us. No one moved or breathed—not even Bill. Finally, the major cocked his head back another notch and screamed, "AT-EASE!"

Bill and I scuffed our left boots to a more relaxed stance and let out a breath. His frown matched mine.

"Gentlemen!" The major's voice was loud, too loud, out-of-place loud—even for the Marine Corps. "Your reputation precedes you! When I arrived on Okinawa this week for processing to Vietnam, I asked anyone I could find, wearing wings or otherwise, 'Which is the best, most aggressive, most outstanding Huey gunship squadron in the 1st Marine Air Wing?' The answers I received were uniformly brief and precise: HML-467. Everywhere I went, everyone I asked: HML-467, HML-467."

I glanced down the line to my left at the Staff NCO platoon and the two thin platoons of enlisted men beyond them. As with our officer's platoon, they consisted mostly of desk types, new guys, and the walking wounded. By and large, they were quiet and attentive.

"So, just to be sure, I called ahead to Wing Headquarters at Da Nang. I've got a buddy there. I said 'Joe, which is the best Huey gunship squadron in the Wing?' You know what he said?" The major smiled. A few self-conscious chuckles dribbled from the ranks to my left. "H-M-L-4-6-7! That's what he said!" A few more smiles and chuckles joined the others, but the Staff NCOs weren't chuckling or smiling. Neither was Tess, the guy with the sling.

The major turned and smiled at the colonel. The colonel, standing tall under Mickey Mantle's baseball cap, smiled and nodded proudly. The major returned his narrowed eyes to us.

"But!" he screamed, looking down on us again. "My friend Joe added this comment: 'Bull, HML-467 is a great squadron, and it has an outstanding Commanding Officer and Sergeant Major, but, Bull, listen to me, you should consider HML-567 here at Marble Mountain. We're five minutes by jeep from downtown Da Nang, we have ice cream, hot showers, and flushing shitters. HML-467 is at Phu Bai. And Phu Bai sucks!'" A roar of laughter rose from the troops, including some of the Staff NCOs.

Behind us, two CH-46s taxied off the runway and west toward their revetments, and for a few minutes, the combined clatter of their rotor blades caused the major to pause.

"What do you think?" Bill whispered.

"I'm not buyin' it."

"Well…me neither."

A long, saber-shaped dust cloud had just touched the far end of our formation when the major raised his head again. "Well, I'm here! And you know what?" He put his hands on his hips and looked first to his rear at the squadron headquarters building, a faded plywood structure with rusty screens, then to his left at the maintenance tent with the rotten canvas hanging in shreds from its steel erector-set frame. "Joe was right—this place sucks!"

The troops exploded with laughter, back-slapping, and foot-stomping. Even Rod Wysowski got involved—laughing, clapping his hands. He elbowed Bill and whispered over the laughter, "This guy is okay." Bill grinned, then glanced at me.

"Now!" the major screamed. "The last time I was in this God-forsaken part of the world was 1965. I was driving an F-8 fighter. *I'm* a fighter. I joined the Marine Corps to fight! Not to bore holes in the sky, not to train to fight, not to wait to fight, but to fight! We didn't do shit in the F-8s. The MIGs wouldn't fight us, and there were damn few landing zones large enough for us to land those beasts, crawl over the side, and kick their asses right through their straw hats like we wanted to.

"So!" The major leaned over the edge of the platform, his fists clenched, his elbows bent, his acne-scarred neck stretched forward. "This time in the barrel I said, 'I want helicopters. I want helicopters with guns. I want to be with a bunch of ass-kickin' fighters like me who'll bring glory to our Corps and peace to this fucked-up country!'"

He paused, looked from left to right at each platoon, straightened himself, and held both hands toward the formation. "Well now. They trained me in Huey gunships, and they sent me to 'Nam. I arrived here, in lovely Phu Bai, this morning. I've had a chance to look around a bit now. I've met some of you fine Marines. I've eaten in your fly-infested dining facility, taken a dump in one of your more malodorous 4-holers, and I think I can say…I think I can *already* say, without reservation, to our Commanding Officer, Colonel Houser…" The major paused, did an about-face, snapped to attention, brought his hand up to a salute, fixed his eyes on the colonel, and finished by barking the rhythmic, Marine cadence from boot camp, "I like it here, I love it here, I've found myself a home here, sir!"

With a roar from the men of HML-467, the colonel, showing more teeth than a Pepsodent ad, returned the salute, stepped forward, stumbled over a warped board in the platform, and shook the major's hand. The men, including most Staff NCOs, continued to shout and pump their fists in the air, grinning at their new executive officer. Even Bill—now joining Rod, Walt, and the wrinkled warrant officer next to Walt—nodded his head and smiled. Besides myself, only the Oriental lieutenant out front, and Tess, the bandaged lieutenant, remained silent.

For my part, I'd never heard of a stiff-winger, particularly a fighter jock, who volunteered to give up his suck-and-blow job for a helicopter. Something wasn't right. Besides, it was a Teemer family tradition to applaud acts, not boasts.

I turned a disapproving look to Bill.

He shrugged his shoulders and whispered, "Ah, loosen up, R.T. He's here to kick ass, man. You gotta like *that*."

"SQUADRON! AH-TENN, HUT!" The captain, out front again, watched the squadron pop to attention, did an about-face, brought his hand to a salute, and reported to the colonel, "SIR, THE COMMAND IS PREPARED FOR REVIEW!"

The colonel, now in the center of the platform with the major to his left, returned the salute and, over the rumble of a Marine CH-53 departing the airfield, barked, "PASS IN REVIEW!"

The captain finished his salute, did an about-face, and barked, "PASS IN REVIEW!" then "SQUADRON, RIIIIGHT-FACE!" Our heels rotated and popped together, changing the formation to a column of platoons.

As the Oriental lieutenant snapped into place in front of me, a scratchy recording of "Semper Fidelis," the traditional pass-in-review march by John Philip Sousa, erupted through the rusty screens of the squadron building and swelled over us: brass horns, deep bass, and drums. My body meshed with the music, my blood pulsed on the down beat, and my feet pumped rhythmically, irresistibly inside my boots.

The Oriental lieutenant's head bobbed. "FOR-WARD…MARCH!"

The seven of us stepped off, each left foot hitting the steel matting on the down beat. Behind us I could hear the other platoon leaders order their platoons forward. We were moving—not much to look at, but it felt good anyhow.

Behind me I could feel Bill smiling, visualize the spring in his step, hear the stomp of his boot with mine and the others, and I knew it was worth it. All the Mickey Mouse bullshit, the standing around, the waiting, the sweating at attention was worth it. We were marching, marching in step to "Semper Fidelis," and in the company of Marines. The tingle up and down my sweat-soaked back, and the catch in my throat, were there, as always.

Without enough room to turn us around on the flight line, the Oriental lieutenant marched us a couple of platoon lengths, ordered a column right, a quick column left, and snaked us behind one of the long narrow revetment walls and through the empty revetment itself. The next platoon did the same.

Inside the revetment, the music dampened and I was surprised to hear the Oriental lieutenant and Tess whistle a tune, a happy tune. It was a marching song, something from my childhood, something with the same beat as "Semper Fidelis." By the time we reached the end of the revetment, Bill whistled along with them.

Two column lefts later, back on the flight line, on the same line as before but in the opposite direction, we headed straight for a head-on collision with the last platoon. That's when I heard the singing and saw the smiles on the faces of the young Marines closing on us. As we merged, they got louder, singing the same tune all of us now whistled, singing to the beat of "Semper Fidelis." The words were familiar. I thought of kids in turtleneck sweaters while the PFCs and lance corporals got louder still, and closer, grinning at the impending collision, enjoying their marching song. I thought of big ears—mouse ears, and laughed as the corporal in front of the maintenance platoon ordered a column right at the last second and missed us, the men behind him singing, "M-I-C, K-E-Y, H-O-U-S-E, Mic-key House…"

Mickey "House." Mickey. I grinned as we marched on and the troops snaked behind the wall, singing their song, enjoying being Marines, enjoying the absurdity of an evening parade in a combat zone. Beside me, Tess whistled loudly, a fresh bounce to his step.

Now, as we approached the pallet platform, the whistling died away. It was back to "Semper Fidelis," which, as we were taught over and over in training, in Latin means "Always faithful"—to our mission, to our country, and especially to our Corps.

In my peripheral vision, the colors, the same flags I had seen in the colonel's office the day we joined the squadron, fluttered and popped for the first time from their position behind the reviewing stand. The red-white-and-blue, the scarlet-and-gold, shimmered from the radiance of the low sun in the west.

It was a confusing picture, skewed by my angle. The flashing colors were those of Belleau Wood, Iwo Jima, and the Chosin Reservoir. But standing in front of those glorious images, growing larger as we got closer, were a gangly lieutenant colonel wearing Mickey Mantle's baseball cap, and a battered, hairy major known as "Bull."

"EYEEES…RIGHT!"

The Oriental lieutenant brought his hand to a salute, and Tess, on my left, snapped his head to the right toward the platform. Because I was on the end of our two-man rank, I kept my eyes straight ahead, but blinked as a gust of wind, light dust and sand swept over us.

Bull Angus.

Now passing the platform, marching within fifteen feet of the major, I felt it—a tension, a charge of electricity through the dust. My gut twisted.

"REA-DY, FRONT!"

The Oriental lieutenant finished his salute, Tess snapped his head and eyes to the front, and the blaring music of John Philip Sousa faded behind us.

After thirty yards, the Oriental lieutenant halted us. Over the clatter of a CH-46 taxiing out of a revetment behind him, he did an about-face and dismissed us by shouting, "In a military manner, STRAGGLE!" In unison, we took one step backward with our left foot, did an about-face, and scattered.

I looked for Tess. I'd remembered Tess speaking of a new major before the parade. Maybe Tess knew something. Maybe he had some scoop on this guy Angus.

Bill grabbed me by the arm. "How 'bout it, Ross? Food, man. The fly farm. You and me."

"In a minute, Cat. I want to talk to Tess first."

Bill wouldn't let go. "Did I tell you the special tonight is rice and beans with fruit cocktail?"

I shook my head and looked for a hole in the group of men straggling back toward the shredded hangar. On the other side of the group, Tess and the Oriental lieutenant headed toward the gap between our squadron building and another building just like it.

"Come on, Ross. Mickey's big hand is on twelve and his little hand is on five—chow time. How 'bout it?"

The plea in his voice plus the mention of the word "Mickey" stopped me. I removed his hand from my sleeve as I watched the two lieutenants disappear between the tin-roofed buildings. I turned to Bill. His freckled grin had "fun" written all over it—lots of teeth, lots of wrinkles around his eyes. What the hell. Those guys would end up at chow sooner or later anyhow. "Okay, asshole. Let's go eat."

"Great idea, R.T. Why didn't I think of that? You may remember this is one of those 'all-you-can-eat' establishments. Nobody leaves Sergeant Rappo's mess hungry. No sir. He's Italian you know. The man knows some shit about cooking."

While Bill rambled on about our impending meal, we slid between the neighboring squadron's buildings and turned left on the sandy dirt road that led toward the main area of our base and the mess hall. Suddenly, I realized he already knew the mess sergeant's name. I grinned and tried to push him off the road. He didn't miss a beat.

"Rappo says he'll be doing a pineapple upside-down cake tomorrow night. That's got to be good."

"Got to?" I said.

"Oh, yeah man! Got to!" He slapped me on the shoulder and the blow, like being hit by a playful bear, threw a puff of dust off my utilities and knocked me into the deep ruts on the side of the road. He yelled after me, "Get up here, man! We're never gonna get there if you keep playin' around!"

I tightroped the ridge of a rut, hopped back onto the road, and caught up with him.

Bill grabbed my arm and pushed me, playfully, trying to throw me off stride. I pushed him back, he finally let go, and we walked by a white communications trailer in silence.

After a minute, Bill turned, frowning. "What's eatin' you, Ross?"

"What do you mean?"

"You know what I mean."

"I don't. What?"

"You're walkin' along with your head hangin', your feet shufflin'. What's up? I mean, we just had a nice parade on a beautiful summer afternoon, in the company of the finest people in the world, and you act like we've just been to a funeral. What's the problem?"

"Nothing. I was just thinking."

"That again! Damn, Ross. You think too much, man."

"Yeah, I know. But I need to talk to Tess."

"About what? His broken arm? Hell, he was shot down, man—he crashed. People who crash break arms. No mystery there."

"Not just that. A bunch of stuff."

"Like where to take your laundry? Or what return address to use on your mail? Shit, Ross, lighten up, man. You're gonna die of ulcers before the gooks can get a decent shot at you."

Bill smiled again and threw a half-hearted headlock on me. We stumbled over each other's dusty boots, laughing, and for the moment, I relaxed. It was hard to think, or worry, with a clown like that draped around my neck.

"Don't think, huh?" I asked, pushing his arm away.

"That's it."

"Just enjoy?"

"That's right, 'Lieutenant Sweat-the-small-shit.' Don't think, don't worry, just enjoy."

"Words to live by?"

"Certainly. As a matter of fact, they're on the Catlett family coat-of-arms: Non-semper thinkis, Non-semper worryis, Semper enjoyis."

"Your family speaks Latin?"

"Man, we speak Latin, eat Latin, and sleep with Latins. Get in step, maggot!" Bill had slipped into his "drill instructor" mode and now marched beside me with his face in my left ear. "Your left, your left…your *other* left, maggot!"

I got in step, smiled at Bill's pained expression and loud voice…and slowed as a memory opened like a parachute in my mind. Wallace.

Unaware of my sudden insight, Bill pumped a finger at the ground and yelled even louder, "Left…left."

I stutter-stepped, fell in step again, and resumed the march at his pace, not ready to discuss the memory, not eager for more harassment or good-natured lecturing.

Seconds later, distracted by a departing OV-1 Mohawk, Bill quit calling cadence and I relaxed to my thoughts again…to the connection. Wallace and Angus.

Wallace Vanderwick, attorney at law—my stepfather.

I was eleven when Wallace had my sister and me sit before him on the couch. With my mother standing to the side, smiling, admiring the man who would replace my father, Wallace told us of all the nice things he'd heard about us. He told us of how successful he was and how he couldn't wait to take us places and buy us things and for us to be a family. Bullshit.

Wallace. Angus.

Angus' speech to the squadron, his praise of its reputation, his fighter pilot talk, even his enthusiasm for joining us—hell, that was a Wallace speech; those were the words of a man who would take, not give; that was bullshit.

I splattered a dirt clod, squashed another, and stared hard at the dusty horizon. I didn't know why Angus was at Phu Bai or why he'd asked for our squadron, but I was dead certain of one thing. If Angus was there to mess with my Marine Corps the way Wallace had messed with my family, this was going to be a very, very long war—for both of us.

3

Going Down

I didn't hear the door open at the front of our hootch, or see the flashlight approaching my space, or hear the footsteps.

"Morning guns," the voice said, blinding me with light.

I rolled toward the wall and covered my eyes. "Can't be," I slurred, "I haven't been here seven days yet."

"I don't give a shit how long you've been here, Teemer, I'm just the friendly messenger. You're flying. Got a 0530 brief, co-pilot for Major Hardy, wing on Colonel Houser."

Half an hour later—shaved, fed, and alone—I jogged away from the mess hall and out of the lights of the main complex. On the dark road to the squadron, already sweating under my flightsuit, I dodged potholes dimly lit by a hazy half moon and felt the tension squeezing me, tightening around my thumping chest. I wasn't ready for this; I didn't have maps, frequency cards, or a weapon. And I was flying with a major.

At least I wasn't with Mickey. With a grunt, I leaped a gravel-lined pothole and thought back to the guy with the flashlight, the SDO—how he had laughed, how he had stopped and stuck his head back into my space and whispered, "Hardy's okay, but Mickey will get you killed!"

"Right," I whispered between breaths. "Mickey will get you killed." I pounded past another pothole.

In the distance, the flight-equipment shack appeared brightly lit and snug against the squadron building. I blew out a breath, forced it, shaking my hands as I ran. At least I could get the flight gear I needed.

A few minutes later, breathing hard and leaning on a chest-high counter, I learned my helmet wasn't ready—still kitchen-appliance white, still without a communications pig-tail and amplifier. I spray-painted the helmet while the sergeant behind the counter located the missing pieces and had me sign for a survival vest, bullet bouncer, and .38 revolver.

Exactly at 0530, clammy, and smelling like a paint shop, I slid onto the pine bench across from Major Hardy and beside the recently decorated Myron Brunnengarber. Myron, known as "B-12," was a former enlisted Marine who still had the haircut of a drill instructor. He was scheduled to fly as the colonel's co-pilot.

The major sipped from his coffee mug and read from a briefing checklist lying on the picnic table between us. B-12 took notes with a pencil from the sleeve pocket of his flightsuit. I did the same and wondered about the colonel, our section leader, the man who should be giving the brief.

As if they didn't expect the colonel to show, the major continued briefing and B-12 continued to take notes while other crews, on other missions, filled the tables behind us.

Twenty minutes later, while Major Hardy discussed the emergency procedure of the day—lost communication—the colonel entered the front of the ready room and stepped to the ODO counter. Looking past the lieutenant standing behind the counter, he examined a plastic board attached to the plywood wall. Written in grease pencil on the board were the aircraft assignments, weather, and duty runway information.

The colonel shook his head. "That bird won't do. Get me number ah…7."

The room quieted. Major Hardy twisted to look over his shoulder.

The lieutenant, the ODO, took a cigarette from his thin lips, looked at the board, and turned to the colonel. "I'm sorry, sir, but number 7 is down for a hundred-hour inspection. Maintenance has assigned you number 10."

Pushing his Mickey Mantle baseball cap to the back of his head, the colonel placed his kneeboard on the counter and leaned forward. "I don't want number 10, Lieutenant. Seven's my bird. I want number ah…7."

The lieutenant, his mustache curled down over his upper lip like so many undernourished spider legs, looked at the board again. "Honest, sir," he said. "I can't. Number 7 will be down all day."

The colonel straightened to his full, Ichabod-like height. "And your name is ah…?"

"J.P. Padgett, sir."

"Yes…Paddock. Well, Lieutenant ah…Paddock, in the Marine Corps, we don't use the word, 'can't.' Get me number 7."

J.P. nodded. "Yes, sir."

Head down, the colonel pulled a pencil from the tube on his kneeboard and J.P., looking at Major Hardy with pleading eyes, gestured with his hands.

The major made a dialing motion and pointed at the end of the counter.

J.P. nodded and reached for the green phone to maintenance. "I'm getting number 7 for you now, sir."

Writing on his kneeboard, the colonel grunted.

Behind me, benches scraped the floor and the other pilots, burdened with survival gear, map cases, helmet bags, weapons, and with flashlights in hand, rose and struggled through the screened door to the dark flight line.

By the time we followed them, a simmering orange sun had already crested the palm and banana trees to the east and the taxiways throbbed with departing Huey gunships. Our crew—a crew chief and gunner—waited by our fully armed Huey. My butterflies took flight.

The rest of the morning, I sat in a daze, befuddled by voices on two radios and the intercom, lost in procedures I didn't understand and confused by geographic locations I didn't know. Operating below the DMZ, I was at least able to comprehend our mission—cover for two CH-46s on resupply missions for the Marines on the ground, the "grunts."

By 1110, I'd made a list of frequencies and call signs on my kneeboard, located and marked a few fire bases on my map, and had a better feel for where we were and where we'd been. Then DASC, the voice on the radio who assigned missions, released us; we could go home or stay and look for something to do. The colonel, call sign "Hardball 6," flying a Huey with a freshly painted number 7 over a faint number 10, decided to stay. Minutes later, "Lima 1-4," a radio operator on the ground, had a target for us.

I leaned out of the left seat, blunt-tipped pencil in hand. Under my shoulder straps, a thick green plate of armor—a "bullet bouncer"—pressed against the bulging vest of survival gear worn around my ribs. Vibrating to the beat of the blades, with sweat saturating my clothing and slicking the ear cups of my helmet, I searched the jungle for movement.

Flying at our right front, two o'clock low, Hardball 6 turned right as Lima 1-4 described a bunker complex occupied by the North Vietnamese Army and discovered by one of Lima Company's patrols. While the company got organized for an assault, we were to keep the enemy in their holes, "soften them up." I checked my map to confirm we were over the right grid coordinates—we were—and looked through the hazy blue sky to the west, to Hill 208.

According to Major Hardy, we'd lost a bird at the base of 208 a few days before. I couldn't see any sign of it.

A mike keyed and I heard the major on the ICS, our intercom. "Rockets. Both sides."

"Yes, sir." Although we hadn't fired at anything that morning, we'd prepared to do so several times. I no longer fumbled with the switches located on a panel between the pilot seats and behind my right hand.

"When I pull off, you cover us with the TAT."

"Yes, sir."

Two M-60 machine guns, called the "TAT-101," protruded from a traversing turret under the Huey's chin. The TAT-101 flexible gunsight hung from a hook at my right-front. Electrically controlled, the gunsight aimed and fired the guns in the turret; the guns pointed where the sight pointed. At least it was supposed to work that way. We didn't have those things in training so I'd never actually seen them work. I removed the gunsight from its hook and armed the guns as per the major's instructions earlier in the day.

A few minutes later, after the colonel had fired and pulled away from the target, we dove at the earth and jungle trees he left smoking below us—the NVA still invisible to me, still silent. My hands tensed on the TAT sight grips. The ground rushed at us. Then I twitched as two rockets burst out of our pods, one on each side, the left one showering me with grains of fiery rocket propellant as it streaked under my open window.

Gritting my teeth against the needles of pain and berating myself for forgetting a basic rule learned in training, I threw the window up with my free hand and beat at the sparks burning through my "flame retardant" nomex flightsuit.

The major, ignoring my flailing arm and gloved hand, fired another two pair of rockets—one pair after the other—then pulled out at 500 feet and 120 knots, banking hard to the right. I swiped at a burning pain on my knee, threw the switches from rockets to guns, and while the Huey groaned and struggled to climb in the hot thin air and my body shuddered with the beat of the blades, I flinched from the sudden fire of the door gunner behind me, put my lighted bulls-eye on the trees below, and pulled the triggers.

A pounding burst of fire recoiled against the chin turret and the Huey jerked right, pitched down, and threw me violently left against my straps, swinging the blazing TAT guns toward the Marines on the ground. Sucking a breath, I released the triggers and let the gunsight swing away in one hand, the turret silent now, my chest thumping against my survival vest and my eyes wide and searching the cockpit. Did I throw the wrong switch? Did I fire the gun wrong? I sat erect, looking for a cause, an explanation. I'd heard nothing!

The major righted himself, his left hand on the collective control stick by his knee, right hand forcing the cyclic control stick between his legs into his left thigh—feet pumping.

Nothing made sense, no sounds, no feels, just sudden turmoil—the Huey jerking to the right as if trying to turn and fly backwards, then settling into an unsteady yaw to the right. I'd have heard something if we'd been hit. Wouldn't I?

Whatever the cause, the major countered it, and now the crew chief on the right side opened fire, joining the gunner, doubling the noise, making it sound and smell as though I were trapped in a 55-gallon drum with a string of exploding firecrackers. I squinted, wished I'd worn ear plugs, and watched the Huey's nose nudge toward center as the major reduced power. The gunner on the left stopped firing. On ICS: "Came from behind us, Major."

"Copy."

We slowed past 90 knots and climbed through 700 feet. I put the TAT away and safed the switches. As my heart rate settled, I looked around the cockpit again and took a deep breath. It finally made sense—tail rotor failure. I hadn't caused it, and we could still fly. My shoulders relaxed, the crew chief stopped firing, and the major, his eyes on the horizon, pulled up on the collective, adding power, carefully. The yaw increased a degree.

Damn! I pounded my knee. Mayday call. Co-pilot's job. Should have thought of that sooner.

Before I could move, someone keyed his mike and took the frequency away from me. "Lead's in hot." The colonel.

I twisted right, looking for the colonel's Huey. Above and to our right rear, it leveled off, pointing at the target that was now well behind us. His call was to let us know he was shooting again so we'd be out of the way and ready to cover him.

I looked at the major, questioning. He had briefed us to look out for each other, stay in visual contact, teamwork. Couldn't the colonel tell we were in trouble?

His eyes shaded behind his helmet's sun visor, the major glanced over his shoulder and keyed his mike. "Hardball 6, this is 6-Dash-Two, over."

The colonel's Huey nosed over for another dive at the target, a dive without cover from us, something that wasn't done according to the major.

The major tried again: "Hardball 6, this is Dash Two, we're at your two o'clock, off cold with a tail rotor failure from enemy fire, level 800 feet, heading for Dong Ha. How copy, over." The FM and UHF radios hissed.

The major glanced at his radio transmit select switch. The switch, correctly set for the UHF, an aircraft-to-aircraft radio, was not the problem.

I looked to the horizon. Eight to ten miles of dry, sparsely vegetated, NVA-controlled hills and abandoned rice paddies stretched before us. Somewhere in the dust cloud in the distance—close, but not close enough to get excited about—lay the small airstrip at Dong Ha, the first safe place to land.

The major took his finger off the switch on the cyclic stick and stepped on his floor switch. "Hardball 6, Hardball 6, how copy, over?" More hissing.

I looked behind and through the right side of the cabin to follow the colonel's gun run. Our crew chief, a short but sturdy corporal in a greasy flightsuit and scarred flight helmet, stood on the skid, suspended from the cabin deck by his nylon "monkey strap." He faced the tail, his body pressed to his door-mounted M-60 machine gun by the 80-knot wind stream. Against the blue sky in the distance beyond him, two rockets smoked for the ground from the colonel's Huey.

"Ross, you give 'em a try. Maybe it's my transmitter." Then, as if he knew what the crew chief was doing by the shift in the weight in the cabin, the major added, "Droopy. What do you see back there?"

I reached to my right, snapped my transmit select switch from ICS to UHF, and pressed my lip mike closer to my lips—mentally rehearsing what I was going to say and acutely aware that nobody wanted to hear some new guy co-pilot embarrass the squadron by saying something stupid over the radio.

I stepped on the floor switch and flinched as a roaring-wind sound suddenly leaped into my earphones and a faint screaming voice inside the roar said, "The blades are spinning, sir...a gnat's ass out of track...other 'an that, I can't see shit." Abruptly, the roar and the pressure in my ears stopped.

I looked at the major, my face tight with pain.

"Thanks, Droop," he said, grinning. "Now get buckled up and secure all your tools and weapons." He nodded at me. "Go ahead, Ross. Try 'em again."

I stomped the floor switch. "Hardball 6, 6-Dash-Two, over." Quiet hissing. "Six, this is Dash Two on uniform, over." That sounded pretty salty. "Uniform" was slang for UHF. I'd heard Major Hardy say that earlier in the day. More swishing and hissing.

"Try 'em on fox."

"Yes, sir." I leaned into my straps and forced a straight face, feeling really involved, really helping out. Now he wanted me to use the "fox mike," or FM radio, the one normally used to talk to the grunts.

"Hardball 6, this is 6-Dash-Two, over."

"Ross. You're still on UHF."

Shit! Fists clenched, I snapped my transmit select switch from UHF to FM, blurted, "Hardball-6-this-is-Dash-Two-on-fox-mike-over," and pounded my knee. Too fast.

The radio jumped to life. "Dash Two, this is 6, go ahead." It was B-12's voice. At least somebody was at home back there.

"Six. Dash Two has a tail rotor failure. We're at your two o'clock, about a mile, level 800 feet. Heading for—" I looked at the major and mouthed, Dong Ha? He nodded. "—Dong Ha, over."

The radio hissed back. Then the grunts called the colonel on FM and B-12 replied. Why did he answer them and not me? Then on UHF, the colonel called, "Off cold," telling us he was clear of the target and it was okay for us to make our next gun run. Was he even listening? Then the grunts called on FM to advise the colonel both of us had taken fire on our last pass. Then somebody named "Streetcar HST" called somebody else I didn't catch, then nothing—nobody answering anybody—hissing, then the grunts called again asking, "Copy that, sir?" More hissing, then B-12 called the grunts to say his "dash two" had taken some hits and we were going to RTB, return to base. I let out a breath. At least B-12 knew we'd been hit.

The grunts rodgered B-12 and said they would take it from here; they were in the assault.

Shaking my head, I turned.

On the edge of his seat, shoulder straps extended, Major Hardy looked at the ground.

I leaned forward and tried to see what he was seeing—bomb-cratered hills, low jungle, and abandoned rice paddies along a stream. I cocked my ear and listened to the blades beating, the transmission whining, the radios swishing in and out, and paused, not breathing. There was something else. A whistling noise. An extra vibration.

The major sat back, held the controls with his finger tips, and looked out his window directly below us. "Ross, switch me to guard and lock your harness."

"Yes, sir."

I leaned out of my seat and hesitated, remembering guard was a powerful channel for emergencies only, so powerful that in training I was led to believe if I ever switched to guard without it being an honest-to-God emergency, it would make me sterile. But this was for real. I twisted the channel select knob to "G," and sat back to lock my harness.

The major, still looking out his window, keyed his mike. "Mayday, May—"

I caught my breath as the Huey snapped right and down again, throwing me forward and left even more violently than before and jerking my hand off the harness-locking handle at my side while in the windscreen before me, the rotating ground appeared where the horizon used to be. I tried to sit erect again, the engine noise falling off now, unwinding, blades popping overhead. My body lifted lightly in my seat, negative G. I spun my head to the major and saw the collective pushed to the floor, the cyclic stick pressed against his thigh with no effect, and thought, what, what?

My body settled again, now able to get back against my seat, actually pushed there when the major pulled on the collective after getting us into an autorotation—a power-off glide or fall with only the air rushing up through the blades to keep them spinning. Descending rapidly, the Huey turning in a right-hand spiral, I groped for and found the harness lock.

Con Thien, a desolate island of destruction on the horizon, rotated by. The dust cloud of Dong Ha swung past us again. Wind whipped by my ear. Pressed left by centrifugal force I struggled to get away from the armored-seat panel, had to slide it back, both hands on its leading edge, couldn't exit with it there. Trees, I could pick out trees! With a final effort I threw my weight to the right and pulled. The panel slid back.

More trees. A clearing. Position report! Leaning against the force pressing me back, I groped for the transmit switch, grabbed it, switched, and searched the instrument panel for information, calling: "Mayday. Hardball 6-Dash-Two on guard…going down…Quang Tri 3-0-0 at—" Shit!

I threw myself back in my seat. Major Hardy pulled the collective to his armpit. The big blades took a last desperate bite into the air and the turning fuselage stopped, leaving us hanging above a bare patch of dirt like a yo-yo on a string. A red-orange dust cloud, kicked up by the rotor wash, engulfed us—leaves, twigs, and trash whipped by. And out my window, a figure, a running figure in khaki. I blinked and it was gone.

The Huey wallowed and turned slowly again as the blades, disconnected from the drive of the engine, lost their momentum and mushed around overhead so slowly I could count each one. I didn't. I braced against my seat and slammed my eyes shut as we settled into the dirt cloud and bounced, bounced again, and slid sideways to a crescendo of exploding pops and lurched to a stop against something I couldn't see.

I felt the sudden stillness, noticed a roar in my ears, and checked my body. Can I wiggle my toes? Yes. Do I feel wet, as in bleeding? No. Pain? Yes, but mild—left shoulder. With a sigh, I opened my eyes, reached for my shoulder, then heaved forward in the dust cloud—coughing, spitting. Hunched over in my straps, the roar in my ears suddenly died, unwinding in pitch and volume. The coughing probably cleared them.

Through the dust, the major took his hand away from the fuel control switch, turned the battery off, and gestured at me with his thumb. My head sagged; it was the Huey's turbine engine making the roaring sound, a sound I'd never heard without the noise of the blades with it. Nothing wrong with my ears.

The major coughed, the dust settled around us, and I turned to my door but couldn't move it—blocked by limbs. Then I remembered the images, fuzzy, framed by my window. Was that cardboard trash I saw? In the jungle? And had I seen a man or a bush?

I slumped back in my seat, shoulder tingling. I'd have to go the other way. Using my right hand to release the three-point buckle at my waist, I pulled myself out of the seat and over the pedestal panel toward the cabin, uphill, fine dirt falling from my lap.

Breathing hard, I reached the cabin deck, stepped toward the crew chief's doorway, and got my head snapped back. Grimacing, cussing softly, I squeezed the pigtail connection on my helmet. The coiled black comm cord sprang away, spanking the overhead above my seat, and I stepped toward the doorway again, then stiffened with the sound of scraping metal. Reaching to unfasten the kneeboard hanging around my ankle, I wondered if I'd ever been that stupid in my life. I stuffed the kneeboard into the calf pocket of my flightsuit.

On his side of the cockpit, the major pulled the emergency jettison handle on his cockpit door and kicked it free. It fell to the dirt and rattled like an empty hubcap.

I'd seen enough to know the major was okay, but as I half-stepped and half-hopped to the flattened grass beside the skid, I wasn't so sure about Droopy and our gunner, a cocky kid with greasy black hair and bright white teeth.

The cabin was empty.

4

Fire Fight

As the dust cloud drifted away, I jerked my helmet off and turned to face Major Hardy.

He stood by the cockpit and tossed his gloves on top of his helmet and bullet bouncer—both lying in his armored seat. His survival vest, two gray zippered pockets the size of manila folders, hung under each arm by adjustable shoulder straps.

"You okay?" he asked.

"Yes, sir." A piece of cardboard lay on the ground behind the major and I wondered if he had seen what I'd seen, or thought I'd seen—the man in khaki.

"Where's Droopy?"

I hesitated as he removed a heavy .45 pistol from the holster on his hip. He pulled the slide back, examined the round that sprang from the magazine, then let the slide go—feeding the round into the chamber with a clunk. He released the safety and looked up at me through thick eyebrows.

"Droopy? I don't know, sir. He wasn't in the cabin."

"How 'bout Scapelli?"

"No, sir. No sign of either of 'em." So the kid's name was Scapelli. That fit—dark hair, dark eyes. I dropped my helmet to the ground and reached for the flap on my bullet bouncer. "Major, did you see—"

A metallic ping split the air, followed immediately by the heavy ca-clunk of a machine gun bolt flying home, and we dropped to the ground like two dusty sacks of feed grain—both facing north toward the sound, only one of us with the good sense to have a weapon drawn.

"Come on."

"Yes, sir." I felt a lump swell in my throat, drew my new .38, and crawled after him, looking for the man in khaki and struggling to keep up.

But I couldn't keep up and the major was five yards ahead before I realized why. I still wore my bullet bouncer, and in a pocket on the front of it was a survival radio I was using as a plow blade. I pounded the ground with my fist, flipped onto my back, and yanked the flap on top of the pocket.

Shit! The damn thing was Velcro and, in the stillness of our dusty little hilltop, it separated with a rip that was deafening. I could hear the major pause, feel him look at me, and crawl on.

Holding my breath, I slid the radio from its pocket. The bullet bouncer itself was in a vest-type garment fastened to my body with lots of Velcro, so I decided it would have to stay—no more noise. Holding the radio in my free hand, I rolled onto my armor again, and crawled after the major.

Fifteen yards away from the Huey, where the ground began a gradual descent, I pulled abreast of him and raised my head. Ten yards ahead of us, maybe one-third of the way to the bushes, a man-made hole penetrated the ground. Protruding from the hole was the back of a dusty red head with only a hint of a neck—Droopy. I grinned sheepishly. Droopy held a cocked M-60 to his shoulder.

I nodded to the major and we crawled forward, covering the remaining ten yards and spilling into the dusty hole together.

Seated to Droopy's left, panting, eyes closed, his back resting against the forward wall, the major could hardly whisper. "What, Droop…what ya got?"

On Droopy's right, beside his flight helmet, I sat gasping for air. And my throat was killing me. Running my tongue over dried lips, I remembered a flask of water I had in my survival vest, but it was under my bullet bouncer—the one with all the Velcro. I dropped my hand and waited to hear Droopy's answer, waited to hear him say it was okay, he didn't see anything, and I could risk some noise.

Droopy knelt on a faded cardboard C-ration carton. He looked north from behind his M-60 and answered in a whisper, "Just before we hit, three gooks hauled ass down this trail in front of us—two new guys in piss green—one salty guy in khaki."

Damn. With a sigh, I got on one knee, turned, and raised myself to the lip of the hole.

"Weapons?" The major asked, still leaning against the wall.

"The new guys had AKs. All I saw was web gear on the other, but Major…the ground around this hole is lousy with sandal tracks; there must be more of 'em."

"Yeah, I saw that. You think they've seen us?"

"Don't think so—too busy running away when I saw 'em…but maybe."

"Okay. Stay on the trail."

Droopy nodded. "Yes, sir."

The major rested his chin on his chest and set the .45 in the bend of his waist. Sweat spidered down his dusty cheeks. Breathing regularly now, he pulled the zipper back on his survival vest, and looked up. "Where's Scapelli?"

"Don't know." Droopy stared at the trail. "Sorry, sir. I saw those gooks just before we hit. After that, all I could think about was gettin' out of the bird and gettin' my gun on this trail. I guess I shoulda...shoulda watched him or something."

Now holding a thick, palm-sized survival radio, the major pushed himself to a more erect position. "You did just fine, Droop. We'll find him."

While listening to their conversation, I had eased higher. I was also thinking about Scapelli. The colonel and B-12 were going to be overhead any second. Hell, that dust cloud we kicked up could have been seen for miles. So the kid was out there somewhere and we needed to find him. If he was hurt, we needed to get him ready to be moved.

Squinting against a blinding sun, I looked around. Located on the edge of the flat crown of a low hill, our hole was dug on the terrain feature known as a "military crest" and faced north. There were similar holes curving right and left. Behind us, the bare crown of the hill was the size of a baseball infield and edged with trampled grass. The Huey had hit near the eastern edge of the dirt, then spun and dribbled its way west and into the thick bush at the southern edge.

Turning to face the Huey, I backed against the forward wall and shook my head. Bent or broken at every joint, it lay nose up and listing to its left. The two rotor blades were cracked and bent—one hanging from the rotor head by a single bolt. Half the nose and the left fuselage, as far back as the rocket pod, were covered in thick bush as tall as the Huey itself. There was no way I could have gotten out of my cockpit door, even with a good arm. In fact, I was having trouble understanding how any of us had gotten out at all.

Shading my eyes, I searched for Scapelli, but because of the gentle crown of the hill, didn't see him or anything below the line of the Huey's cabin floor. I tried listening for him by putting my hands by my ears, but that didn't help either. Nothing. No sounds at all.

As the major extended the radio's antenna, I turned and looked along the line of Droopy's gun.

Just down the slope and to our left, a well-worn trail led through the grass and into the head-tall bush that surrounded us. Judging by the size of our hole, its commanding view of the trail, and the piles of expended brass and ammo links scattered around its lip, it had once been a U.S. Marine M-60 position. If we were going to end up in a fire-fight, Droopy had chosen the right hole.

But I didn't think it would come to that. Now that Major Hardy had his breath back and a feel for the situation, I expected to see him get the colonel on the radio and get us out of here. I—

Wait a minute. I stared at the ground. No sounds at all. No Scapelli, no animals, no birds and…no helicopters. Where was the colonel? Where was the whop-whop sound of our wingman—the man who should have been right on our fanny?

I raised my head to the sky and looked west, where we'd been hit, then south, then east, then north. The white-hot sun glared at me. I lowered my head and a drop of sweat splattered onto my bullet bouncer.

Maybe he's gone for help. Maybe he's just over the hill trying not to give our position away, waiting for our radio call. He's got to be here somewhere. Marines don't leave their wingman. I searched the sky again, listening, listening hard, then sighed a long muffled sigh.

On the other side of Droopy, the major adjusted his radio.

Okay. Maybe there was a good explanation for the colonel's no-show. I was just a lieutenant, right? I didn't have the big picture and everything. The major had known the cocking sound had come from Droopy, so maybe he knew everything was cool with the colonel too. Still…I wanted to know.

I leaned around Droopy. "Major. Shouldn't the colonel be overhead by now?"

Droopy shifted, glancing at the major. Dirt trickled onto the flattened ration carton.

Major Hardy raised his head, the crease between his eyebrows deepening, the eyes steady. "Alright," he whispered, "you two listen up. I've switched to beeper. That'll let anyone in our area know we need help. The colonel can't be far, so he or someone else will be here in a minute. Meanwhile, we've got things to do."

Major Hardy pointed at me. "Ross, I want you to go back to the bird." I nodded, not believing what I was hearing. "Look around for Scapelli, then get all the smoke grenades, frag grenades, weapons, and ammunition you can carry, and get your butt back here."

"Yes, sir."

Bad plan, I thought, but then, in a bizarre way, it kinda made sense. The major had the radio and was the most experienced radio operator. Droopy had the gun and was the most experienced gunner. I had the bullet bouncer.

"One more thing." He pointed at Droopy. "As you probably remember, Droop, this hill was the site of some pretty heavy contact a month or so ago. It's important ground. The gooks have been here in numbers before, and are probably still here in numbers now." Droopy nodded.

Great. Armor on my front—bullets from my back. I examined my vest to see if there was any way I could turn it around on my body without making any noise. Maybe I could cut the straps with my knife, or—

"Questions, Ross?"

"No, sir."

"Okay. Now, Droop, presumably, they were still running down the trail when you found this hole. They don't know exactly where we are yet. But when Lieutenant Teemer hops out, it'll be obvious, and we may come under fire. Don't fire until you know we've been spotted or to protect the lieutenant."

While the major continued to whisper instructions to Droopy, I considered my route to the Huey. And the hill. We were off the crown, on the down slope, on the "military crest." That meant to get to the other side, I would have to go slightly uphill first. Until I could finally get the curve of hill between me and the NVA, I was going to be a sitting duck for someone below us shooting up. Crazy.

I puffed my cheeks, let out a breath, and checked my .38 one more time. All six chambers had a ball round, not those fancy signal flare rounds.

The major turned. "Ross, when—" Droopy's hand dropped onto his shoulder and he froze. I froze. I think my heart stopped.

"Listen."

In the bottom of the hole, the major and I stared at each other—not breathing, not moving, not even blinking. Droopy must have heard something but all I could hear was the dirt trickling onto the cardboard in front of his knees.

After several seconds, Droopy relaxed his grip and gave the major's flightsuit a tug upward. The major and I rose toward the lip of the hole.

Looking down the trail, my heart and lungs started up again. No sounds. Maybe ol' Droop was getting jumpy, maybe hearing rabbits or birds in the underbrush. Then I heard it: the crunch of dried leaves. Damn. Not a rabbit. Not on the trail either.

More crunches off to our right.

"Go, Ross. Now!"

"Sir?"

"Go, go, go!" The major reached around Droopy and tugged on the sleeve of my flightsuit. I sprang from the hole.

Teeth clenched, boots digging, arms flailing, I stretched for the Huey, straining against the weight bouncing under my chin, wincing with every footfall on the packed dirt, and thinking: too loud, man, you're making too much noise, you sound like a Clydesdale!

Tough. I kept pounding, raising my knees high, while ahead, the Huey appeared in full sight, bobbing up and down. I pumped harder, liftin' those knees, then blinked as I imagined something on my back.

Gunsights!

I zigged left, then flinched as gunfire exploded behind me and bullets cracked the air by my right ear and I ran faster, harder, cheeks bouncing.

He's gonna shoot again, he's adjusting. Do something!

I cut to the right and more rounds split the air and the ground erupted on my left, splattering me with dirt, stinging my legs. I accelerated, eyes bulging, amazed I could go faster, amazed someone was really trying to kill me.

Move!

I darted left, tucking my head as more rounds tore past my ear and a gutteral boom-boom-boom split the air behind me, and sucking a hysterical breath I screamed, "God, they've got an M-60 on me!"

That's Droopy, you dumb ass!

The M-60 ripped off another burst and I felt stupid and slow and exposed and I thought, sprint! My legs wouldn't sprint so I just ran, sucking air, makin' it hurt, the damn bullet bouncer like an anchor on my chest but the Huey getting closer, bouncing up and down in my vision, blurred by sweat.

Finally, exhausted—head back, butt muscles on fire, the M-60 booming behind me—I threw my feet out and collapsed into a slide behind the skids and under the wrinkled fuselage, safe in a streak of dust, flat on my back.

Eyes closed, gasping, I had to get rid of that bullet bouncer—suffocating under that thing, couldn't even swallow. I ripped the flaps loose and pushed it over my head with a grunt. It thumped to the ground behind me.

Too exhausted to roll off the back part of the vest, I lay with my arms flopped out to my sides, struggling for air, my mind flashing images and thoughts and replaying the scenes from seconds before. How do the grunts put up with this shit?

Then, throat burning, chest heaving, I suddenly froze. My hand. Wet.

Not good, Teemer.

Shut up! Couldn't be that bad. Just blood, just a nick, and I could handle that; I had gauze, a tourniquet, sulfur—all in my vest, so I could fix it; I could bandage myself, stop the bleeding. I could do that.

Holding my breath, I eased my head over and stared down my right arm. The hand was there, intact, still holding my .38, and lying in a puddle of jet fuel.

Closing my eyes, I sighed a chest-collapsing sigh, then rolled away and settled under the crumpled tailboom.

Watching the bush ahead, the .38 on my stomach, I removed both gloves, unzipped the pouch of my vest, and reached for the water bottle. Quiet. The last gunfire was from Droopy's gun, so he must have scared them off. I tried to remember how many had shot at me. It sounded like two. Maybe three.

A crunch in the bushes. My fingers locked around the bottle. Another crunch—from the tall bush just to the left of where my legs pointed. Scapelli? My hand slipped from the bottle and snaked to the .38.

More slow, cautious crunches in the bush—coming closer.

I carefully, painstakingly, rotated so I faced south toward the sound and stretched my feet toward the major and Droopy. I wanted to call out. It probably was Scapelli. But what if it wasn't? I moved again, crawfishing my way around the part of the tailboom touching the ground, glancing behind me. Couldn't see Droopy or the major because of the crown of the hill. More crunches. I stared ahead, squeezing the .38's grip.

In front of me, a limb moved. I licked my dry lips and cocked the hammer. More movement.

Bursting over the tops of the trees to my left, the high-pitched whine of twin turboprops filled my ears, followed by a flash of green and an immediate lowering of pitch and volume as a Marine OV-10, armed with rocket pods and a 20mm cannon pod, flashed overhead and banked sharply right.

Halle-damn-lujah, we were saved!

A burst of AK fire from behind me ricocheted off the Huey's rotormast and I jerked my head into my shoulders. Damn it! An M-60 fired—Droopy. Another AK fired from behind me and more to the right. More M-60 fire. Sudden quiet.

Rapid footsteps and whipping branches from the bush, this time parallel to the Huey, heading west. More footsteps. Now there were two of 'em, moving together and in the same direction, away from my hiding place. I let out a breath and swallowed thickly, flinching from the pain.

Behind me, the OV-10 was a faint drone in the hot sky, a lonesome drone. Couldn't tell if it was still flying away or coming back. I looked, but couldn't see it.

An AK fired from the other side of the hill and the footsteps continued west, growing faint.

Up on elbows, I belly-crawled south toward the bush. After a few yards of trampled grass, now facing tall weeds and a line of thick green leaves and limbs, I stopped.

"Scapelli!" I whispered...and waited. I turned my head more to the right, toward where the bush curved to meet the Huey. "Scapelli!" Nothing. I crawled east away from the Huey, paused, listened, and whispered again, angrily, "Scapelli!"

Two AKs opened up from over the hill. A stream of stray bullets whined above my head. The M-60 boomed back.

Blinking away the sweat, I crawled farther east. No trail, no signs—just glossy leaves and twisted limbs. Shaking my head, I pushed up on locked arms and hissed again, forcing it: "Scapelli!"

A burst of AK fire cracked overhead. With a grunt, I dropped to the ground and squeezed the .38's grip, listening for Droopy's response. But he didn't respond. Another burst of AK fire. Still no response. Rising on my hands, I strained my ears, begging for his gun to fire, for moans, anything. Nothing. My chest squeezed. If Droopy was hit, they'd need me *now*!

I leaped to my feet. "Scapelli!"

Silence. Nothing moved. My head twitched and my eyes flicked left and right. I could see the whole clearing!

You crazy?

Dropping flat on my chest, I pounded the ground and my .38 exploded, kicking my palm, sending a spasmodic jerk through my body and the bullet ricocheting through the limbs. God, that was stupid! I stared at the smoking pistol, shaking it, then forcing a deep breath, I exhaled slowly, quietly. While the blood pounding in my ears slowed, I decided if Scapelli hadn't shown himself or answered by now, he was dead, captured, or—

Gunfire—two AKs at the far end of the clearing, Droopy's flank. The M-60 finally responded.

Suddenly the ground from the center of the clearing to the western end jumped six feet into the air as a grinding rumble of machine-gun fire erupted from the eastern sky. Instant dust cloud. The OV-10 flashed overhead in a climbing turn and I ran for the Huey's cabin, cursing myself between quick breaths.

Struggling through the brittle limbs around the left rocket pod, I fell onto the cabin floor. The odor of jet fuel was everywhere. Do AKs fire tracer rounds—the kind that start fires? Didn't matter.

Crawling, I found three frag grenades and two smoke grenades in a steel ammo box strapped under the troopseat. I dropped those down the front of my flightsuit where they were trapped by the web belt around my waist. No M-16s. Scapelli's M-60 was in the doorway, but it had been forced down beyond its stop by a large limb, pinned against the gun-mount—useless. I salvaged a belt of M-60 ammo from it, wrapped it around my neck twice, and crawled across the cabin floor toward Droopy and the major.

The back of Droopy's head protruded from the far left corner of the hole, motionless. I slumped in relief as his red hair shook and flames shot from his gun, aimed to his left. Couldn't see the major. I cocked a foot under me and perched on the edge of the deck, staring ahead, a long way ahead.

The area in front of Droopy suddenly erupted in dust, limbs, and leaves and the roar of the cannon on the diving OV-10 washed over me. I sucked a breath. Thirty-yard wind sprint.

I hit the ground and was immediately blown off stride by a Huey making a power-off landing—sliding across the ground and lurching to a stop in front of me. Back in stride, I burst through a cloud of dust, leaped past the green-clad gunner by the door, and into the cabin.

Skidding across the cabin deck, I jerked to a stop and collapsed onto the troopseat—next to an M-16. I sat, gripping the edge of the canvas seat, panting, looking left and right. The gunner I'd just passed sat with his back to me, hands on his M-60, neck stretched, looking behind us. Another gunner, on my right, yelled something, waving his arm. I spun the M-60 ammo from my neck and watched the door, the noise so loud I wanted to scream. I waited, leaning forward trying to see through the dust to Droopy's hole, the seconds ticking by.

Where were they? Clenching my teeth, I grabbed the M-16 on the seat, leaped out of the cabin into a cloud of dust, and ran smack into Droopy.

"Get in!" he yelled over the screaming engine and churning blades, pushing me.

"The major!" I yelled back.

"Get in!" he yelled again, shoving me into the cabin. He dropped to one knee and fired toward the hole, past the distant and vague form of the major running at us, his pistol drawn.

I crouched in the doorway as the ground splattered around the major's feet and he went down, tumbled, but bounced up on one leg and continued toward us—half running, half hobbling, still holding the pistol. I ran toward him.

"Get in!" he yelled, as I tried to put his arm over my shoulder.

"Let me help." I yelled back.

He shoved me toward the Huey. "Get in, god-damn-it!"

I turned and ran the few yards back to the Huey, my eyes squinting through the dust and rotor wash. The gunner on that side, and Droopy, continued to fire past my legs toward the hole.

I dove for the cabin deck and slid against the troopseat. Droopy rolled against me. The major rolled over both of us and the Huey lifted, then dropped and slammed onto the hill. Shards of plexiglass rained on us. A ricocheting round smacked into a troopseat post by my head.

We lifted a second time. The Huey staggered as more rounds plunked into the airframe and one smashed against the right-seat pilot's armored seat. He flinched and threw up his arm in a belated defense as the left-seat pilot kept the Huey flying, both pilots still erect, and…wearing Army helmets!

I lay there, my eyes blinking in disbelief, my fists pressed against my ears, door guns firing. The Huey tilted forward, accelerated through the dust cloud, and climbed to the left.

Major Hardy pulled himself onto the troopseat and grabbed the left-side gunner by his sleeve. Over the transmission, engine, and rotor noise—plus the M-60 fire—my aching ears couldn't hear what the major yelled, but as we continued in a sharp left bank, the gunner poured hundreds of ball and tracer rounds into our wrecked Huey. The major nodded his approval.

The resulting explosion engulfed the crumpled gunship in a boiling cloud of smut-black smoke with a churning, fire-ball center. The fire ball, burning bright red and orange, rose with the cloud of smoke, flickered, and faded to a swirling mass of gray and black. As I watched, transfixed by the explosion, the pilot snapped us level, dove for the relative safety of the treetops, and both gunners stopped firing.

I rolled onto my back, sweat-soaked, gasping, fists still clenched. Droopy was on his back beside me, his heels to his buttocks. His chest ratcheted up and down and his baggy eyes stared at the overhead. On the troopseat, Major Hardy sat with his elbows on his knees and his face in his dirty hands while the air stream rippled his flightsuit.

The Army gunner tossed a plastic canteen onto the deck by my arm. It landed with a thud. He was a skinny kid who looked lost inside his flight helmet. I returned his thumbs-up, pulled the canteen to me, and unscrewed the cap.

The water was warm. I grimaced as I swallowed and thought of lying under the tailboom, craving water, listening for Scapelli…Scapelli, the Marine we'd left behind. I screwed the cap on the canteen. That was wrong. We had to do something.

I looked at Droopy but he stared at the overhead. I knew he could see me watching him, but he wouldn't look at me.

Behind him, the gunner sat in the gunner's well, facing out, hands on his gun. A coiled comm cord looped from his Army helmet to the overhead and bounced in the air to the beat of the Huey.

I heard voices and pushed off the deck to sit.

On the end of the troopseat, Major Hardy put his arm around the gunner and pulled him close, close enough to yell into his helmeted ear, "UHF: 3-0-8 point 5!"

I sat erect and Droopy popped to a sitting position beside me, eyes alert, glancing at me then at the major, then making a fist as the major yelled again, "Fox mike is 28-5!"—our other squadron frequency.

The gunner's lips spoke into his mike while in the cockpit, a gloved hand dropped to the radio panel.

"Kiwi!" the major yelled, "LZ Kiwi!"

5

LZ Kiwi

Minutes after our rescue, the dusty city of Dong Ha slid by on our left, and Major Hardy, eyes squeezed against the air stream, pointed ahead and gestured down. The gunner next to him nodded, spoke into his lip mike, and we descended in a left turn.

Five hundred feet below us, separated from an area of tents and plywood huts by a dirt road, a large square of steel matting, half the size of a football field, appeared in a dry and barren clearing. On the edge of the matting, two Marine Huey gunships, both heavy with rocket pods and guns, sat at idle RPM. Another Marine Huey, this one without guns—a slick—hovered across the matting toward the gunships. In the center of the matting, painted in white, was the word "Kiwi."

I sat erect in the troopseat and pointed for Droopy's benefit. Stretching his neck, Droopy looked around me and smiled for the first time since our rescue. All three Hueys had black, claw-hammer symbols painted on their vertical stabilizers—our guys, "Hammers" from HML-467.

A minute later, on the ground in the center of the matting, Major Hardy pulled Droopy and me into a huddle by the right skid. Over the noise, he pointed to a shelter on the north side of the LZ and yelled something about us waiting there.

Droopy, like a tired and dirty little league catcher talking to his coach, stood in front of the major and yelled, "I wanta go!"

The major shook his head. "Too much weight!" he yelled. "Now shove off!"

I pointed at my chest and mouthed, me too? He put his hand on my shoulder and held up one finger with his other hand as if to say, wait a minute, and turned to the Army pilot.

Droopy trudged toward the shelter with his M-60 balanced on his shoulder and I waited—my palms pressed against my ears. It was only then I realized I'd left my helmet by the crash site.

The major took a piece of paper from the pilot, shook his gloved hand, pounded him on the shoulder, and turned to me. "Keep this for me," he yelled. "I'll be right back." He turned and half-jogged and half-limped toward the waiting Marine Huey slick. I stuffed the folded paper into the breast pocket of my flightsuit and followed Droopy.

The shelter, a tin roof supported by four steel posts, provided shade for two pine benches. As it was midday, both benches were still in the shade. I sat next to Droopy on the bench facing east just as the Army Huey lifted to a hover, turned on the spot, and departed. As it turned, I saw the white screaming eagle of the 101st Airborne painted on its nose with the word "Nightmares" painted above it in red.

Immediately behind the Army Huey, one Marine gunship, then the other, slid across the matting on the tips of their skids and struggled into the air. The slick, with Major Hardy, one crewman, and a big box in the cabin silhouetted against the dusty sky, followed. In a loose formation, the three Marine Hueys turned and climbed toward our crash site.

I watched them for several minutes, listening as they grew smaller, their "whop-whop" sounds overlapping each other and fading like an out-of-sync percussion section of a parade band.

When they were specks on the horizon, I turned to Droopy. "Think they'll find him?"

"I don't know, sir." Droopy had his elbows on his knees and his cheeks in his hands. The M-60 rested against the bench.

"Suppose he's alive?" I asked, slipping out of my survival vest and dropping it to the sandy ground at my feet.

"Maybe."

"Any idea what happened to him?"

"No, sir." He readjusted his cheeks on his hands and stared at several simmering rows of green GP tents. A sign on the road read "3rd Marines."

I slouched against the back of the bench, crossed my arms, and wondered if Droopy had been close to Scapelli. If so, he was probably pissed at me, the "fucking new guy" lieutenant, for not finding him.

I leaned forward. "Look, Droop, for what it's worth, I thought you did a hell of a job back there, and I'm sorry I wasn't more help. I really did try to find Scapelli."

He looked away. "I know you did, Lieutenant. Hell, I heard you scream his name all the way from the other side of the hill. At the time, I thought it was a stupid thing to do, but...well, I kinda admired you for doin' it, you know?"

"You...you thought I was stupid, huh?"

Droopy turned and looked at me, his eyes widening when he saw the disappointment on my face. "Shit no, Lieutenant, I don't think you're stupid."

"You just think I act stupid?"

"No, sir. I…I just said—"

I dropped the frown, laughed, back-handed him on the shoulder, and we smiled together. "Just kidding, Droop. Hell, it probably was stupid. I sure thought so at the time. Anyhow…thanks for covering my ass, man. You did good."

He dropped his head and nodded, the smile fading. "You did alright too, Lieutenant…but I sure could have used those grenades you went after."

"Grenades? Hey." I unzipped the front of my flightsuit. "You want grenades? I happen to have a very nice selection here in all the latest colors and frag patterns. Help yourself."

Droopy chuckled softly and shook his head. "No thanks." He unzipped the sleeve pocket of his flightsuit and took out his cigarettes and lighter. That's when I noticed he was trembling. I didn't know what to do then. I didn't want to embarrass him by mentioning it, but I felt compelled to say or do something.

"Where are we, Droop? What is LZ Kiwi?"

He snapped the lid shut on the lighter, took a long drag, and exhaled forcefully—pushing the smoke as far away as possible, slumping with his arms on his thighs and his head hung over his hands. The smoke from the cigarette curled into his dirty face and around his grit-lined neck. I waited, but he didn't respond or even indicate he'd heard me.

I decided to let it go.

He took another drag, blew the smoke at his dusty boots, and paused, watching the smoke spread and drift away. Finally, he cleared his throat and spoke, but the scream of grinding transmissions in low gear covered his words.

I looked up, beyond Droopy, to where a pair of open-bed six-by trucks rolled on the dirt road north of us. They rumbled past, trailing a billowing cloud of dirt and grit. The cloud hung in the thick air, drifted east toward the tents, and away from our shelter.

"Say again, Droop?"

"Nothin'."

"You asked me something, didn't you?"

"I was just wonderin'." He took another quick drag. "I was just wonderin' if uh…if you were, you know…superstitious. Are you?"

I hesitated. This was one of those times when, as an officer, I felt I was expected to say something profound or sagacious, something to clarify the situation for the young Marine looking to me for answers. I couldn't think of anything profound or sagacious. I pulled on the zipper on my flightsuit, raising it a few inches, and said, "Yeah. About some things, I guess." He didn't say anything. "You know, like in sports—baseball. I guess I'm superstitious about crossing bats. Stuff like that."

He stared at his boots again.

I had decided that was the stupidest answer I'd ever given in my life when he raised his head and looked toward the tents. "That's twice for me in one week, Lieutenant. Twice. I was shot down with Lieutenant Tess a few days ago, Monday I think."

Tess, the guy with his arm in a sling. I hadn't seen him at chow the day before, so I hadn't talked to him about Angus or the crash. "You were with Tess?"

"Yes, sir. Hill 208." We sat quietly for a few seconds. "Bad luck comes in threes, don't it, sir?"

"Well..." I turned to face him, my left arm on the back of the bench. "Sometimes. But I think good luck comes in threes too. Were you hurt last Monday?"

"No, sir. Not a scratch."

"Was anybody? Besides Tess, I mean."

"No, sir. Just the lieutenant."

"Were you hit today?"

He held his arms in the air and looked at himself. "Nothin'."

"Well, shit, Droop. It looks to me like, rather than being bad luck, you're a friggin' four-leaf-clover. In two crashes, with the potential for eight dead Marines—including yourself twice—we've got two slightly injured, counting the major who was limping but wasn't showing any blood, and one missing. And the injured are going to get a Purple Heart without loss of limb or function. That's good luck—damn good luck!"

"Really?"

"You bet!"

"But what about Vegas?"

"Vegas?"

"Yes, sir...I mean Scapelli."

"You call Scapelli 'Vegas?'"

"Yes, sir. It's 'cause of a liberty we had there one time from Camp Pen. It's a long story, sir."

I smiled. "I'll bet."

He took another drag on his cigarette and flicked the ash between his boots.

I leaned against the backrest and crossed my arms. "Well, let's see, Droop. What kind of guy is Vegas?"

"What do you mean, sir?"

"Well, is he the kind of guy that's always doing stupid stuff—maybe gets into trouble a lot? Or...is he smart—the kinda guy that breezes through life untouched by the disasters that seem to happen to everybody else?"

"Shit, Lieutenant, he's both."

"Both?"

"Yes, sir. He's always in trouble, but he always skates, you know?"

"The guy who falls in a bucket of shit, but comes out smelling like a rose?"

"Yes, sir. That's him."

"Sounds like he's a survivor then."

"Oh, yes, sir. He's a survivor alright. That's what's so strange about us being here and him being back there. Usually, like in Vegas, it's the other way around."

I leaned forward, pulled my leg onto the bench, and sat facing him. "Come on, Droop, tell me—I don't think we're going anywhere for a while. What happened in Vegas?"

He looked askance at me, carefully, studiously. Finally, he looked at his boots again and said, "Well, it was just a typical liberty, you know? At least until we got the hookers—I guess that's when things kinda went downhill. Up to then we were just drinkin' and gamblin' and havin' a good time—Vegas was teaching Frenchy and me how to play craps."

"Frenchy?"

"Corporal Boudette—he's with HML-667 at Quang Tri. Anyhow, Frenchy and I were doing okay at the table, about two hundred dollars ahead I guess, when Vegas decided it was time for our next lesson—hookers. So we cashed in and went to the phones to call for some girls. Well, with our winnings and everything, we decided to go all out. We got rooms and ordered champagne—lots of champagne.

"We each had separate suites, Frenchy and I side by side, and Vegas across the hall. We all started over at Frenchy's.

Anyhow, the girls got the room numbers all fucked up so we'd already finished two bottles of champagne before they finally found us. Frenchy was pissed they were so late—he's not a patient guy—especially when he's drunk and horny."

"He was already drunk?"

"Yes, sir. Remember we'd been drinkin' at the tables too." He watched me nod knowingly then continued. "So…so the girls came in, had a drink, then Frenchy started taking his clothes off. Then his girl started fussin' at him, 'No, not until you've bathed!' That pissed him off even more so he started gettin' into it with this girl—who was no light-weight, sir—a good six foot of woman. Well, the fussin' led to screamin', then to throwin' things—she threw a champagne glass at him, he threw a lamp at her—you know.

"They were wrestling on the floor and my girl and I were sitting on the top of the sofa cheering them on when the security guys showed up. Vegas and his girl slipped out during the throwin' part I guess. I just remember there was only Frenchy and me when security got there.

"Those guys were real assholes, Lieutenant. They didn't want to hear our side of the story, they just started trying to pin Frenchy to the deck. Well, hell, I couldn't let them do that, so I jumped in. Meanwhile the six-footer and my girl, who was a doll, I mean she was gorgeous, well they beat-feet into the next room, the one I'd gotten. So…shit, in our condition, we were no match for those two thugs. We ended up in the tank with a few lumps on our heads."

"So where was Scapelli?"

"Well, while the two security guys were beating on us—we put up a good fight, sir—they didn't take us down easy. Anyhow, Vegas came across from his room and got the two girls out of my room and over to his. The girls were running from those guys too—something about that hotel not being on their turf."

"Then what?"

"Then the security guys turned us over to the cops, who took us to the slammer for the night."

"And Scapelli?"

"He got laid by all three girls, won over five hundred dollars at the blackjack table, then brought the girls and a limousine over to bail us out around 0700."

"Better late than never," I said, smiling.

"It might as well have been never. The MPs had already come and taken us back to Pendleton. Anyhow, we got back and all of us got busted to PFC."

"Even Scapelli?"

"Yes, sir. The first sergeant told the skipper Vegas'd left us to be taken by the enemy and needed to learn that Marines don't…" his voice lowered, "leave Marines."

We stared at the ground a minute. I got that feeling again and turned to look at him. "Well…we didn't have a choice, Droop. Not a decent choice anyhow. Besides, the major's gone back for him—he hasn't really been left yet."

"I know."

"And he's a survivor, right?"

"Yes, sir." His head was back in his hands now, the cigarette crushed into the coarse sand under his boot.

From the road, another Marine six-by, this one coated in powdered dirt and pulling a green water-tank-on-wheels known as a water-buffalo, turned toward us. It rumbled, clanked, and squealed to a stop behind our bench. Drifting behind the truck, a dust cloud enveloped our shelter.

Through the yellowish fog, I saw a man hop from the cab to the ground, walk to the back, and unhitch the water-buffalo. For the first time, I noticed an existing water-buffalo beside the new one. As the dust cloud drifted east, the man appeared as a muscular black Marine in a faded green T-shirt. With unhurried, fluid motions, he walked back to the cab, repositioned the truck, and hitched it to the old water-buffalo. Seconds later, the truck circled our shelter and rumbled to the dirt road, the tailgate chains clanging against the steel tailgate with every bump.

"Come on, Droop. I'll buy you a drink." He didn't answer, but stood and followed me to the water-buffalo. "And, listen…whether we find Scapelli or not, you're not a jinx, or bad luck, or any of that crap. You're good and I'll fly with you anytime. Okay?"

He stopped by the wheels on the water-buffalo and looked up, head cocked, eyes puzzled.

"Okay?" I asked, smiling.

"Yes, sir. Okay." He grinned sheepishly and stepped to the faucet my outstretched hand indicated was his.

He let the water pool in the palm of his hand, took a drink, bathed his face and neck, then took another long drink. After he finished, I did the same.

Wet-faced, I unzipped my flightsuit, and dried my face and neck on my T-shirt.

"Lieutenant?"

"Yeah," I said, from behind the shirt.

"Remember when you asked the major about where the colonel was?"

I pulled the T-shirt off my face. "Yeah?"

"Well, I was wondering the same thing. I've been in this squadron eight months, sir, and I've never seen one bird leave another. Do you know what happened to him?"

"Shit, Droop, I'm not even sure I know what happened to us. I was hoping you could tell me where he went."

We walked to the shelter. Overhead, two CH-46s flew northwest, both with bulging cargo-nets suspended under their bellies. I wondered if I knew any of the pilots.

Droopy stopped at the first support post, leaned against it, and folded his arms across his chest. The sun fell on his legs and the top of the bench where we had sat earlier. I sat on the opposite bench. Droopy scuffed the ground. "I don't have any idea where he went. By the way, you're new aren't you, sir?"

"I'm about as new as they get."

"I thought so."

"Hey, Droop, give me a break here. I wasn't that screwed up, was I?"

"Oh, no sir. I didn't mean it that way. I just don't remember seeing you before. And I noticed Major Hardy had to tell you all the radio frequencies."

"True enough. But I've written them down. I'll have them memorized next time." I ran my fingers through my short hair. "Speaking of radios, where did the OV-10 come from? Did the major find him on the survival radio?"

Droopy sat on the bench next to my grenades. He faced me now, leaning forward with his arms on his thighs and his fingers intertwined. "He tried to call Mickey first, I mean Hardball 6, Colonel Houser. He didn't answer, but 'Mustang Duke,' the OV-10, came up and asked if we needed assistance. He was coming back from a mission. Only had about ten minutes on station and guns remaining."

"Where's he from? Quang Tri? VMO-8?"

"Yes, sir. I don't know who he is, but I've been on missions he was on before. He's good."

"His timing is good, that's for sure. How about the Army Huey? How did he get in the act?"

"He heard your call on guard while he was going into Cam Lo to drop off some passengers. I guess he monitored the major talking to Duke and heard Duke tell us the Direct Air Support Center—actually they're in a bunker just down the road from us—you remember us talking to Dong Ha DASC during the morning for mission assignments?"

"Yeah, I know who they are. I didn't know they were right next to us though."

"They're about a hundred yards down the road. Anyhow, they said they didn't have any 46s or other Marine assets available for us for at least forty-five minutes. No Air Force Jolly Green either. We were taking fire from two different positions by then, so the major decided to take anything he could get."

"Enter the Army Huey from Cam Lo."

"Yes, sir. The Army guys called Duke and said they could be there in five minutes."

"Those guys did a hell of a job."

"I think they were both warrants. Those guys don't give a shit—they're crazy."

"They may be crazy, but they're the kind of crazy I want in my war. You don't think we could have held out for forty-five more minutes, do you?"

"No, sir, but I think I would have rather died there than have to be saved by the Army."

"Really? Why?"

"I don't know. The Army just seems to always be taking credit for what Marines have done. I just don't like 'em."

"Can you give me an example?"

"Of what?"

"When the Army has taken credit for what Marines have done." I actually knew a couple of occasions in military history when that had happened, at least military history as taught by the Marine Corps, but I wanted to see what knowledge was behind Droopy's obviously heartfelt convictions.

"Well,...how 'bout World War Two!"

His sharp tone and the flush on his cheeks told me to let that dog lie. "You're right, Droop. McArthur took a lot of credit for stuff the Marines did."

"Damn straight he did!" Droopy sat erect now, his hands slid back to his thighs.

I stood and stretched, squeezing my shoulder blades together, and stepped out from under the shelter to check the sky to the west. Empty blue.

Stepping back into the shade of the shelter, I leaned against the support post next to where I'd been sitting and folded my arms across my chest. "Droop, what were our birds doing here at Kiwi? Couldn't DASC have sent them to get us?"

Droopy's shoulders had relaxed. He reached for another cigarette. "That was the sniffer package." His voice wasn't even yet but at least the red cheeks had faded to pink.

The sniffer. Now it made sense. I'd never seen one, but I knew it was one of the mission capabilities of the Huey. The scoop under the chin-bubble picks up air that is analyzed by the box in the cabin. All this is done while flying low over the trees. Supposedly, the crewman sitting behind the box can tell you when you're over people hidden in the jungle just by the urine readings. The gunships are there as an escort, for protection.

With the metallic snap of the zippo lid and a puff of smoke, Droopy replaced the pack of Marlboros and silver lighter in his sleeve pocket, stood in front of the bench, and turned to face westward. "I guess DASC didn't send the sniffer because they were still sniffin'. They must've just finished when we got here."

I thought Droopy might have stood because he heard something, so I looked to the west. I heard a helicopter, but it wasn't the heavy whop-whop of a Huey and it wasn't in sight.

"Well, if the Army Huey heard my call, why didn't the sniffer package?" I suddenly remembered why. "Probably because we were so low, huh?"

"Probably," Droopy said, still looking to the west. "If our guys had heard you, they'd have dropped everything and come running—I guarantee it. Except for Mickey and a couple of others, we've got a load-hackin' squadron. We take no shit from noooo-body."

I grinned, but made sure he didn't see me.

"Lieutenant, I guarantee you the gooners who shot us up are catching hell right now. They're learning an important lesson, one their Uncle-fucking-asshole Ho didn't get around to teaching them: fuck with Hardball and you get hammered."

I grinned again, imagining a cartoon image of a Huey gunship flying low over our crash site. Donald Duck and his three nephews were leaning out the Huey's windows and cabin with huge hammers, pounding the gooners like they were armed ants at a picnic. It was great. Then I remembered what he'd said about Mickey "and a couple of others." Besides the colonel, who else did I need to look out for in this squadron?

I stepped from the shelter again and looked west, shading my eyes. Still no helicopters in sight. I checked my watch. 1235. I figured they'd been gone about twenty minutes. Time enough to get it done—if Scapelli was there.

As I stepped back into the shade, Droopy turned around and sat by his M-60. The sun was full on his back now. I couldn't believe he just sat there and let his dark-green flightsuit soak up the sun. But he didn't seem to notice, or if he noticed, he didn't seem to mind.

I sat on the shaded bench. "Still, Droop, the colonel couldn't have gotten very far. Surely he heard my call."

"I don't know, sir. That colonel is one fucked-up heavy. He hasn't been here long and I've only flown with him once, but once was enough."

I sensed our conversation had moved to the officer/enlisted boundary, and as a fellow officer, I should defend the colonel. But…hell with it. Based on what I'd seen so far, there wasn't much to defend and besides, one day I'd be flying with the guy and I needed to know all I could for my own survival. I leaned forward and asked, "How fucked-up is he?"

Droopy glanced at me and stood. He crushed his cigarette in the sand and turned toward the water-buffalo. "He got us lost, that's all. 'Scuse me, Lieutenant, I think I'll get another drink."

Watching him walk away, I thought I heard, or maybe felt, a heavy-bass whop-whop sound from the northwest.

I stepped to the edge of the shade. The sound grew louder. I walked into the sun, shading my eyes with both hands. Louder still. Multiple whop-whops. Definitely.

"Droop!"

"I hear 'em."

"Where?"

"Can't see 'em yet." Droopy stood by the water-buffalo, his hands shading his eyes, his thirst apparently forgotten. "There's at least two of 'em though…by the sound. No…probably three, yeah, must be three. Hueys—definitely Hueys."

I unzipped the sleeve pocket of my flightsuit, grabbed my sunglasses, and with my eyes still on the horizon, slipped them on. The hazy sun blinded me. The whop-whops grew louder. I yanked the glasses off my head. No lenses! The crash—my arm and shoulder against the armored seat. I stuffed them back into the pocket and shaded my eyes.

"There!" Droopy shouted.

I followed Droopy's extended arm and found the three Hueys higher than I had expected, at least two miles away, the slick lower than the gunships. "I see 'em!"

All three descended, then green smoke streamed from a rocket pod on each of the gunships.

"They got him!" Droopy yelled, nearly leaping out of his flightsuit, throwing his fist in the air.

"How do you know?"

"Green smoke—mission accomplished!"

They continued their descent, passed south of the LZ, then turned and approached east to west in trail.

Even before the slick passed us for the near corner of the LZ, we could see the three figures in the cabin. The crewman and Major Hardy sat erect against the aft bulkhead, smiling. The one sitting on the edge of the deck with his flightsuit half unzipped, his feet dangling over the side, his fingers making the peace sign as he glided by, was obviously PFC "Vegas" Scapelli—dark hair, dark eyes, and a lot of pearly white teeth.

Droopy stepped toward the edge of the matting, his arms crossed, a dimpled grin from ear to ear. As the slick landed, I stopped beside him, fighting the rotor wash and shielding my eyes from the blowing sand. I shouted in his ear, "How ya feelin', Corporal 'Lucky?'"

"I feel great!" he said, smiling, his eyes glued to his friend, his arm shielding his forehead. "Really great!"

Seconds later, as the slick pilot cut the throttle to idle, Droopy looked at the matting, then raised his head to look me in the eye. "Just between us, Lieutenant, I'll tell you this much about the colonel: basically, he's as fucked-up as Major Hardy is squared-away. And Lieutenant, they don't come any more squared-away than Major Hardy—you'll see."

We retrieved our gear and returned to the Huey. There I watched the little red-headed crew chief with the big heart and the Marine-green pride greet his friend Scapelli by tossing his M-60 at him. Scapelli caught the gun against his chest, slid it behind the green box, and tackled Droopy as he stepped into the cabin. They wrestled like puppies as Major Hardy watched and laughed.

Major Hardy. I paused beside the Huey, watching him enjoy Droopy and Scapelli. Was he really the exception as Droopy suggested? Surely not.

I stepped into the cabin, past the tussling, grinning friends on the edge of the deck, over the legs of the smiling crewman, and sat against the bulkhead. The major, beside me, smiled and handed me a surprise—my helmet, the fresh green paint peeled and blackened on one side. We laughed and shook hands and his grip felt strong and comfortable.

The Huey lifted to a hover.

Slipping the helmet onto my head, I felt the noise dampen and leaned against the vibrating bulkhead, breathing deeply, imagining what Major Hardy would say to Lieutenant Colonel "Mickey" Houser when we got back. Man…was I going to enjoy that.

6

And the Colonel?

On our way from LZ Kiwi to Phu Bai, in the Huey thereafter known among the lieutenants in the squadron as the "Jolly Green Sniffer," the major's laughter and smiles and verbal jabs at Scapelli for having all manner of twigs and leaves stuck in his flightsuit gradually gave way to an erect posture and silence. Now, as we turned and hovered into the revetment, he glared at the ready room with cool, steady eyes—a glare that reminded me of Marshal Matt Dillon getting ready to enter the Long Branch for the men who had horse-whipped Chester.

Watching us taxi in a swirl of dust and sand, his eyes shaded by aviator sunglasses, First Lieutenant Myron Brunnengarber, B-12, stood in the ready room doorway and toyed with the dog tags hanging from his neck.

Once in the revetment and even before First Lieutenant Franklin Ono, the sniffer pilot and "Oriental lieutenant" from the parade the day before, could touch the skids to the ground, the major scooted to the edge of the cabin. He stepped onto the steel matting with the Huey.

Straddling the skid, rotor wash whipping his flightsuit, the major yanked his survival vest off the deck and threw it over his shoulder. Droopy, Scapelli, and I hopped to the matting beside him.

As Ono cut the throttle to idle, the major turned for the ready room. B-12, his head lowered to avoid the spinning blades, his dog tags bouncing off a T-shirt exposed by a half-unzipped flightsuit, jogged toward the major and yelled over the noise of the blades and the screaming turbine, "You okay, sir?"

"We'll talk inside!" Major Hardy said, brushing past him, limping, his left boot tucked under his arm, the left sock matted with brownish-red blood.

B-12 pulled up beside us, shaking our hands and hanging onto Droopy while he pounded him on the back and yelled, "Damn, I'm glad you're okay, Droop!"

Droopy struggled out of his grasp yelling, "I'm okay, I'm okay!" then tossed his M-60 onto his shoulder and tramped after the major. Scapelli hurried to catch up with them. I followed, slinging my survival vest over my shoulder. B-12 fell in beside me.

By the time the screened door had slammed shut behind us, the major had stopped at the last table and dumped his boot, survival vest, and pistol belt at his feet. He stepped between the bench and the table, facing back toward where we'd entered, and sat with his kneeboard in front of him.

I dumped my vest and helmet on the floor, sat on the bench opposite the major, and piled my rolled pistol belt and .38 on the table between us.

An oscillating fan with blue plastic blades hummed from a shelf along the outside wall beside our table. The fan blew hot air over me and rotated toward the middle of the room. Scapelli sat in a chair at the end of the table and lit a cigarette. Droopy collapsed on the end of the major's bench, propped his elbows on the table, and placed his sweaty cheeks in his hands. With a sigh, he closed his eyes.

The dim twenty-by-forty ready room, lit by two light bulbs spaced along an electrical cord stapled to the ceiling, smelled of vinyl fabric, stale tobacco, and for some reason, pork-and-beans. We were its only occupants except for the operations duty officer, First Lieutenant J.P. Padgett.

I heard J.P.'s stool scrape and turned to find him standing behind the counter consulting a clipboard. His tanned face glistened and he wore a green T-shirt instead of his camouflage utility shirt. He took the half-finished cigarette from his thin lips, looked up from the clipboard, and called across the room, "Flight time and aircraft status, please, Major."

Massaging his eyes with the palms of his hands, the major responded, "Five point two, and the bird is a hard down, as in, 'Take it off the damn board.'"

The smile left J.P.'s face. "Uh...will it be recovered, sir?"

The major put his hands on the table. "Negative. It will remain on permanent static display in grid 1-1-6-3. Where's the colonel?"

"He's not here, sir. He...he left to hit baseballs down at the end of the flight line. I think he's found some new guy to go with him."

I rested my forehead on the table behind my pistol belt and grinned at the thought of Walt Duppont out in the hot sun shagging fly balls for the colonel. On our first day, back in the colonel's office, when the colonel had asked if any of us could play baseball, Bill had said, "Colonel, Lieutenant Duppont played ball at the Academy. He tells us he's pretty good too!" Walt had tried to correct him, but it was too late. The smiling colonel dismissed us immediately and began describing to Walt when and where they would practice.

"Ross," the major said, tapping the table, "you okay?"

I snapped my head up. "Yes, sir. I...I was just resting my head."

He grunted and looked at B-12. "Well, Myron, did you or the colonel do an after-action report?"

"No, sir." B-12 had sat beside me, bringing with him a half-finished C-ration can of beans-and-franks and a plastic spoon. He pushed the can aside. "The colonel just got the flight time from me, signed the yellow-sheet, and went into his office—to change, I guess, 'cause the next time I saw him he had a bat and glove and was in PT gear. I don't think he knew you were down, sir."

The major leaned over the table, his bushy eyebrows arched. "He didn't know? Did you know?"

B-12 straightened. "Yes, sir. I mean, no, sir. Not then. I copied your call that you were going to Dong Ha with a tail rotor problem. I thought the colonel would follow you, but he told me to tell DASC we were RTB and had me switch freqs."

"You didn't hear Ross on guard?"

"Guard? No, sir. You know how the colonel is, sir. He doesn't fly with the receiver selector on guard, just T&R."

With controlled, measured force, the major pulled a yellow pencil from the wire spring on the top of his kneeboard. He hesitated, then gripped the pencil in a white-knuckled fist, pounded his fist on the table, and glared at B-12. "Did you know we ended up in a fire-fight on some barren hill in no-man's land? Alone!"

B-12 swallowed. "No, sir. I mean, yes, sir, but not until I got back and had J.P. start checking on you."

The major shot a glare at Lieutenant Padgett. "J.P.?"

Cigarette hanging from his lips, J.P. had been leaning on the counter, watching B-12 dance to the major's questions. At the sound of his name, he bolted upright and ashes fell to his skinny arm. He swiped at the ashes, yanked the cigarette out of his mouth, and said, "Uh, yes, sir! That's how we both found out. I called DASC on the land-line and they told me."

"And the colonel?"

"The colonel?" J.P.'s eyes widened. "Uh…the colonel." He glanced at B-12 and back to the major. "The colonel never said anything about it, sir. He never asked, and uh…by the time B-12 and I got an answer from DASC, he was gone. We didn't actually hear from DASC until just before Ono brought you in. You know how they are, sir."

Neck extended, jaw muscles rippling, the major stared at J.P., then at B-12, then at the door. Then drawing back, he lowered his head and pressed pencil to paper, his finger tips white. "Call sickbay," he said. "Tell 'em the four of us will be over there in an hour for physicals. And bring me the after-action reports. Now."

"Yes, sir." J.P., a folder in his hand, crunched his way across the sandy plywood floor. "I've got them right here, sir."

The major tapped the table. "Put 'em here. Ross, help Myron with the mission report form. We'll do the after-action report later—together. Droopy, Scapelli, get started on yours."

"Aye, sir" and "Yes, sir" were said on top of each other as Scapelli and Droopy took two forms from the pile and moved to the next table. I slid down the bench toward B-12.

The six pilots with the sniffer package jostled through the doorway.

B-12 looked up. With the noise of scraping benches, falling gear, and loud voices increasing all around the room, he glanced at the major, leaned toward me, grinned and whispered, "So, Ross…how'd you like morning guns?"

"Interesting," I said, holding back what I really wanted to say—that it would have been better with a wingman.

He snickered. "Well that was nothing. You were lucky. If you'd been on Thunder Clap, your ass would have been grass."

B-12 leaned away and I stared at the table. Since the colonel had mentioned it on our first day, I'd heard a lot about Thunder Clap—at chow and in the hootches, usually with an "I-know-something-you-don't-know" smirk. It was a secret mission into Laos in support of the Army Special Forces and the CIA and officially denied by the United States government. I'd be flying it after a hundred hours or so of experience on other missions. And I'd be flying it with everybody, including "Mickey and a couple of others," as Droopy had described them.

I rested my elbow on the table and my forehead in my hand. So what? When the time came to fly Thunder Clap, I'd be ready. My luck would hold. I dropped my hand and watched B-12 finish the form.

7

Echo Off the Walls

I didn't recall Droopy's question about superstition until after our post-crash physicals, until after supper, and after I'd returned to our dim hootch—Quonset Hut 8. At the last cubicle on the right, I set my pistol belt in a folding chair, collapsed on the edge of my rack, and stared at the rack across the aisle—Bill's rack, the "dead man's rack."

Loyd Whitlock, the Bell Helicopter technical representative assigned to our squadron, had told Bill and me about the dead man's rack on our first day at Phu Bai. He'd handed us a beer from his TV-size refrigerator and told us to call him "Granny." Then he suggested we might want to move. "One med-evaced, two killed in action, in just over a year. Now nobody wants to be in it or near it," he said. "No shit. Ask anybody."

Bill knew it was open season on new guys, so he'd played along, sipping his beer, pretending to be scared, and asking about other available spaces. It wasn't until he noticed the little man with the pot belly and balding head was serious, that he turned to me and asked what I thought.

"Up to you," I'd said. "It's your rack."

At the time, there were only two other empty spaces available. One was in a hut crawling with majors and captains. The other was next to Walt Duppont.

"Fuck it," Bill'd said. "That's superstitious bullshit. I'm stayin' right here."

I closed my eyes and rubbed my temples. It *was* superstitious bullshit. We were both going to be okay.

I stripped down to a towel and flip-flops and slapped toward the hum and rattle of the air conditioner.

On my way through the musty wool blanket that served as a curtain in the doorway between the back of the hut and the common area in front, Granny, head down, burst through the outside door chuckling to himself.

"Ross!" he blurted, stopping short. "Check it out, man—up at the head. Those two buddies of yours are a trip." He laughed, wrinkling his tanned and freckled bald scalp, and glanced at my attire. "Oh, good—you're going up there anyhow. Check it out, man. It's unreal."

"What's unreal?" I asked, smiling with him, stepping around him for the door.

"I can't tell you—don't want to spoil it. Hell, I couldn't do it justice." He stepped backward to the curtain then reversed himself and stepped toward me. "Shit! Come on, I'll go back up there with you—I gotta see that again—no wait!" He spun around toward the curtain and held up a finger. "Let me get my camera—just a second."

I waited by the front door and he reappeared with a 35mm Pentax around his neck. He chuckled and shook his head. "Those guys are a trip, Ross. Come on. You won't believe this."

"Who?" I asked, holding the door for him.

"Catlett and Wysowski."

I should have known.

We weaved around the sandbag wall, turned right onto the sidewalk, and walked toward the last pink light of the evening.

"What'd they do?" I asked.

"Oh, hell, I don't want to spoil it for you. Let's just say they've had a little contest."

"Any damage? Bill's contests usually lead to damage—usually to someone else's property."

Granny chuckled and stroked his chin. "No…no damage—not yet anyhow." He laughed again, a deep belly laugh that shook his whole body.

We looped left, around a row of quonset huts, and turned right onto another sidewalk. Ahead on the left, perpendicular to the sidewalk, stood the quonset-hut head. On the right, a raised water tank. The tank, a rubber-walled, open-top arrangement that provided water pressure for the facilities, was perched on a twelve-foot platform supported by braced telephone poles. Leaning against the braces were two lieutenants in old-style khaki flightsuits, each with a beer and a cigarette in his hand—one talking, one smiling.

As we approached, the closest lieutenant, noticing the Pentax riding on Granny's chest, pointed with his beer can toward the screened door of the head and asked, "How 'bout some eight by ten glossies for my two-year-old, Granny? He could use some visual aids."

Granny chuckled. "You got it, Hip."

Loud arguing voices from the interior of the head, followed by a chorus of laughter, stopped us at the screened door. Under a rusty conical light fixture, Granny turned to Hip and asked, "What's going on now?"

"I don't know. I thought it was over."

Granny reached for the door. "Those guys are unreal. Maybe Rod rallied."

As Hip and the other lieutenant stepped onto the sidewalk and followed Granny and me through the door, I recognized Bill's voice. "Shit!" he shouted. Another roar of laughter rocked the hut.

Inside, under bright light bulbs in the ceiling and through thick air reeking of human excrement and crumbling urinal cakes, we sloshed across a wet concrete floor and past dripping showerheads. At the far end, ten or more guys in various stages of undress gathered around the last two porcelain commodes along the right wall. Carl Tess, his green arm-sling matching his boxer shorts and T-shirt, stood in front, and as I could have guessed, Bill, wearing only a pair of PT shorts, dog tags, and flip-flops, stood in the center.

Granny and I climbed onto adjoining commodes.

"That doesn't count, asshole!" Bill pumped a finger at the commode in front of Rod Wysowski.

"Fuckin'-A it counts!" Rod answered, his hands on his bare hips.

I whispered to Granny, "Why is he naked?"

"It doesn't fuckin' count, goddamn it! You owe me a case of beer!"

"As I recall," Granny whispered, "when they got started, Rod said Wysowski men compete like 'fuckin' Greek Olympians,' and when 'fuckin' Greek Olympians compete, they fuckin' compete in the fuckin' nude!'" Granny glanced at Rod. "Probably just a psych job."

"I don't owe you shit! I won!" Rod turned to the crowd and gestured with his hands. "Didn't I?"

At the sight of Rod's sunburned face, delicately balanced on a hairless and flat-chested nude body, pleading with them for their support, the crowd burst into laughter and fell into each other. Rod looked into their faces in disbelief. "Well, goddamn it? Did I have the biggest shit or what?"

"*You are* the biggest shit, but you didn't shit the biggest shit, Shit-face! *I* shit the biggest shit." Bill turned to the crowd and leaned forward. "Right?"

"People!"

A huge muscular guy wearing flip-flops and a pair of faded-red PT shorts walked from the screened door and elbowed his way through the crowd.

"Blue Dog!" Tess shouted. The crowd immediately fell away, muttering, "Blue Dog, Blue Dog rules."

Blue Dog—sloped head, wrestler's neck, narrow-set eyes—stepped between Bill and Rod, turned, and in the manner of a high priest presiding over a pagan sacrifice, held his hands high. The room hushed.

"People, people, be still now...be calmed. Blue Dog is among you." He lowered his arms, crossed them on his massive bare chest, and someone in the crowd shouted, "Speak to us, Blue Dog!"

Bill noticed me balanced on my commode behind the crowd. He caught my eye, shrugged his shoulders, turned his hands in the direction of Blue Dog and mouthed, who the fuck is this guy?

I shrugged.

Blue Dog raised his hand. "Blue Dog will speak, but first he will seek counsel." He turned to Tess. "What say ye, 'One-armed Huey Driver,' what dissension among my people has disturbed the Blue Dog's evening respite?"

From the back row, a lieutenant in a utility cover snickered at the reference to Tess, and Blue Dog shot him a squinted glare. The offender lowered his eyes.

"Blue Dog, ruler of all that flushes and washes, master of those that fart and crap and piss in the name of blessed relief, potentate of all that breathes and flies in the space and among the karma that is and that will ever be shitty, I, Tess-of-one-arm, apologize in the name of these transgressors—for they are fucking-new-guys and know not the error of their ways."

"Are they of your people, Tess-of-one-arm?"

"Affirmative, your shittiness. They are FNG Huey drivers and drive under the sign of the hammer."

"And have you observed them in this dispute?"

"Indeed I have, your impotence."

Another snicker from the crowd. Another sharp scowl from Blue Dog. He looked at Tess again. "And what say ye about this dispute?"

From beside Blue Dog, Rod leaned backward, looked around Blue Dog's back at Bill, and mouthed, who the fuck is this guy? Bill shrugged.

"I say this dispute is the result of improper and inadequate delineation of contest rules and will require the wisdom of Blue Dog before a fair and proper settlement will be accorded."

"Does it involve the passing of gaseous or solid or liquid body waste on these premises?"

"Indeed it does, your Four-Holiness."

"Then Blue Dog will pass judgement, as he passes judgement on all who pass, and on all that they pass. Amen."

"Amen." The crowd mumbled in unison.

Blue Dog turned to face the commodes. He reached out with his long arms and huge hands and gathered Rod and Bill to his sides. "FNG Hammers...these are Blue Dog's commandments: I will hear from you one at a time. You will state your case before me as you would make a UHF transmission—brief and to-the-point. You will not break in on another's transmission. You will not raise thy voice during thy transmission. You will accept Blue Dog's decision as a signal Charlie and RTB without further transmissions."

Blue Dog looked at Rod. "Pale One with face-that-burns, how copy Blue Dog's commandments?"

"Who the fuck are you?" Rod asked.

Tess reached out and poked Rod on his shoulder. "Just answer the fucking question."

Behind me, Granny made a sound like a leaking air hose and I had to grab him to keep him from falling off his commode and knocking me off mine.

Rod looked at Bill. Bill nodded.

"Okay, Mr. Blue Dog," Rod said, "I copy."

"And you, Loud-of-mouth, what say ye to Blue Dog's commandments?"

"I copy."

"Very well."

As several men in flightsuits entered the head and pressed against the crowd—stretching their necks and pointing at the commodes—Blue Dog dropped his arms and turned to face Rod. "Pale One, what say ye about the rules of this contest?"

Rod rolled his eyes. "Look, Mr. Blue Dog, this asshole behind you bet me a case of beer that he could out-shit me. That's all there was to it—except that he didn't, and I won."

"Bullshit!" Bill yelled, peering around Blue Dog's shoulder, stabbing a finger at Rod.

A gasp rose from the crowd. Blue Dog stiffened and rotated to face Bill.

"Shit," Tess muttered, shaking his head and stepping forward.

Blue Dog pushed Tess away with his right hand and grabbed Bill with his left. Bill flinched, but too late.

"Loud One," Blue Dog sighed. "You have just violated Blue Dog's third commandment, and in so doing, come very close to violating Blue Dog's *fifth* commandment." The crowd murmured. Blue Dog hung his head.

Tess stepped forward again saying, "Come on, Blue Dog, he didn't know about the fifth!" but Blue Dog stiff-armed him in the chest and grabbed a handful of arm sling and T-shirt. He probably took a few chest hairs too because Tess' face spasmed, his eyes slammed shut, and he squealed, "He's just a fuckin-new-guy, Blue Dog. Please, not the fifth!"

Blue Dog released him with a push. "Back off, Tess-of-one-arm. Blue Dog said FNG Loud One came *close* to the fifth!" Blue Dog sighed again and closed his eyes. "Fortunately for the Loud One, Blue Dog took negative fire today, did not have to fly with any field grade officers, and found cold beer in the reefer upon his RTB. Blue Dog has mercy in his heart."

I leaned backward to Granny and whispered, "The fifth?"

With one hand on the curved ceiling above him and the other on my shoulder, Granny whispered, "Thou shalt not piss off the Blue Dog."

Blue Dog expelled a deep breath, released his grip, and looked down on Bill while Bill shook his arm and stared at the large white hand print on his bicep.

"Loud One. Because you are an FNG, and because you drive under the sign of the hammer—and let it be known that blessed are those who fly under the protection of the hammer, for they shall be saved—I, Blue Dog, High Priest of Piss, Sultan of Shit, and Father of Feces, forgive thee. Transgress not again and thou shall rest quietly in the shithouse of the Blue Dog forever. Amen."

The crowd mumbled, "Amen," and sighed a collective sigh.

"Now, Loud One, what say ye in this matter?"

Bill glanced at Rod, and Tess—who gave him a wide-eyed "Don't-fuck-it-up" look—and cleared his throat. "Blue Dog. I am Cat's Ass, FNG Huey Driver."

"Negative!" Blue Dog screamed, "You are *Loud One*, FNG Huey Driver!"

Bill stiffened, glanced again at Tess—who shook his head and showed tendons where his neck used to be—and continued, "Blue Dog. I, '*Loud One*,' report the following: My fellow FNG and I have been in this land for six days. During a chance meeting in this facility of yours, we learned that for those six days we have shared a common ailment—constipation."

Blue Dog sighed and nodded. "I know of the ailment of which ye speak—though it has been many moons since I have experienced it myself."

"Yeah. Well, Rod, the 'Pale One,' and I felt the urge to move during this chance meeting, a result of the previous evening's fare of beans and rice, I'm sure, and I bet him a case of beer that my shit would be bigger than his shit. It was, and I won." Bill looked around Blue Dog's shoulder and pointed at Rod. "But this little Polish-Fart-Bag here won't admit it."

Rod leaned to his side and opened his mouth, but Tess held up a hand and Rod relaxed to a naked at-ease position.

I stepped quietly from my commode, tired, my knees shaky. Granny joined me, chuckling, patting me on the shoulder. We'd lost sight of Rod but we could still see Bill's head and a lot of Blue Dog.

"Tess-of-one-arm!"

"Yes, Blue Dog."

"Did you witness both of these shits?"

"Indeed I did, Blue Dog."

"And was one shit larger than the other shit?"

"Indeed it was, Blue Dog. But not by much."

"Which one, say ye, had the largest shit?"

"After both contestants got up from their respective commodes, I noted that FNG Loud One had out-shit the Pale One by a marble-size dingleberry." The crowd mumbled their approval and Granny sprayed spittle all over the back of my neck while making more air hose noises.

We climbed back onto our commodes in time to see Rod raise his hand and open his mouth to speak. Tess caught him by the arm, cut him off with a hard look, and added, "But then the Pale One remarked that he wasn't finished and sat back down." Rod looked up at Blue Dog and nodded. Tess continued, "He, in fact, wasn't finished and managed one more small turd."

Blue Dog studied Tess for a second, and asked, "And did that belated turd make a difference?"

Silence. All eyes looked at Tess. A drop of water fell from a showerhead and landed with a ping behind me. Tess cleared his throat. "That last turd," he said, "did bring the Pale One's total shit to a quantity larger than the Loud One's total shit."

The crowd, now numbering over fifteen, erupted into cheers and a smiling Rod Wysowski threw his closed fists over his head and danced the Ali-shuffle, his uncircumcised member flailing to the rhythm of his dance.

Convulsing in laughter, Granny put the top of his head between my shoulder blades, leaned into me for support, and beat on my shoulder with his fist.

I just shook my head. I'd known for a long time those two guys were full of shit.

As the cheers and noise died down, Bill opened his mouth and held out his hand, but Blue Dog turned away and raised his hands and eyes to the ceiling. Bill's hand dropped to his side.

Observing their leader's posture, the crowd hushed.

With his eyes closed and his face, arms, and extra-large body fully extended toward the heavens, Blue Dog turned to face the corner of the hut behind and to the left of the crowd, and spoke, "My winged brothers, Blue Dog has heard the arguments in this case and will now seek divine guidance from the spirits in the vastness of space for his decision. Join with me. Join up tightly my fling-wing brothers. Match thy RPM with mine as I evoke the powers of our guiding star, the planet Your-anus."

Blue Dog, his eyes still closed, began a one syllable, vibrating hum that sounded like "Ommmmmm." The crowd, some hesitant at first, turned, emulated Blue Dog's extended posture, and joined their voices to his. Granny poked me in the back as he stepped from his commode, then he faced the corner and raised his arms. I joined him.

As Blue Dog led us and we inhaled deeply, exhaled slowly, and joined our voices in the "Ommmm" hum, the hut seemed to lighten. The entire room seemed to lift and float. Amazing. The power we possessed as a united, vibrating body was tremendous.

After three deep breaths and three vibrating ommmms, Blue Dog lowered his arms and eyes and faced the crowd. "Turn to me, my winged brothers, and hear my decision."

The now sedate crowd, scuffing their boots and flip-flops on the concrete, turned slowly to face Blue Dog. I eased onto my commode and braced myself against the curved ceiling. As Granny used me for support to remount his, Bill and Rod stood mellow and motionless, facing Blue Dog.

"FNG Pale One and FNG Loud One. Blue Dog has taken note of your fierce competitiveness and your outstanding performance." Blue Dog paused, glancing into the two commodes behind him. "It was a worthy contest—well played, and you both have brought credit to Blue Dog's domain. However. We are Marines, and we know that it's not how you play the game, but how you kick their ass and take their name. Amen."

"Amen," the crowd said.

"So," Blue Dog continued, "there will be but one victor in this contest." He turned to face Rod. "Pale One, you shit the biggest shit, but as in chess, you removed your ass from the commode signaling the completion of your move at a time when your shit was not the biggest shit. That was a shitty mistake." He turned to face Bill. Placing his catcher's-mitt-sized hand on Bill's shoulder, he added, "Therefore I, Blue Dog, pronounce Loud One the winner of this contest. Amen."

"Amen," the crowd said, and parted as Blue Dog glided toward the exit saying, "Go now. RTB in peace and may thy turns remain in the green forever."

As the crowd gathered around the commodes and discussed the contestants' efforts, Rod padded over to retrieve his shorts from a chrome hook on the wall and Bill and Granny and I gathered in the center of the room.

"Who the fuck is that guy, Granny?" Bill asked.

Granny smiled, checking the focus on his camera. "Why, that's the 'Priest of Piss, the Sultan of Shit, and the Father of Feces.'"

"No shit, Granny, who is he?"

Granny looked up as the screened door slammed shut. "That, my friend, is First Lieutenant Hamilton Bortz, one of the H-34 drivers from HMM-669. Their tribe lives on the other side of this head. They call themselves the 'Dog People,' claim this head and the water tower as their own, and are the last of their breed."

"Last of the 34 drivers?" I asked.

"Affirmative. All the old, single-reciprocating-engine UH-34Ds, called 'Dogs,' except theirs, have been replaced by the twin-turbine CH-46. Those guys are history."

Bill scoffed. "Shit. Are they all that fuckin' big?"

"No," Granny chuckled, "not hardly—well, most of the crowd in here were Dog People—they're just like the rest of us only a little more troublesome—even worse than the 'Frog People,' the 46 drivers. With the exception of Blue Dog, I'd advise you to stay away from 'em."

Bill scoffed again. "'Frog People,' 'Dog People.' Shit, man, is this a Marine Air Group or a fucking zoo?"

"As in any war involving Marines, Bill, sometimes it's hard to tell."

Rod squeaked up to us in his flip-flops and shorts and pointed toward the door. "Who the—"

"Hold it, guys," Granny held up his hand. "Let me get some pictures. I'll tell you more over a cold beer at my place." He grinned. "Rod's buyin'."

As Granny squished toward the scene of the competition and took the Pentax from around his neck, Bill grabbed me by the arm. "Ross, listen up, man. I got scheduled today. No shit. It was great!"

"Really?"

"No lie, Ross." Rod spit into a drain in the floor. "That's all the asshole's been talking about."

"No shit, man—a piss-ant, write-in slick mission, but it was great. The duty-driver got me up at six-fucking-thirty. Flew with the guy that lives between you and Granny—the guy we could never find—Shockley. Get this: They call him 'Shit-Hot Shockley.'" He laughed. "Damn, it was great!"

"Tell him about the 'subway' and the 'key-hole.' Wait 'til you hear this, Ross."

"Yeah, the subway. Damn, Ross, you won't believe this. We took the subway around Hue City. Shockley—"

Granny squished back into our group saying, "Okay, Marines, let's roll."

We turned toward the door.

"—so, anyhow, just after we depart Phu Bai, we get to the edge of Hue City and Shockley—"

I suddenly remembered why I'd come to the head in the first place and stopped. "Hold it, Cat. Let me get a quick shower—meet you guys back at the hootch."

Bill turned and followed me toward the showers. "Okay. But hurry up, man. I gotta tell you this story."

"Well, I wanna hear it, but tell me while I shower, okay? It's been a long day—I've got a story of my own."

"Yeah? Where the hell you been anyhow? Find the base library or something?"

"Hey, Cat!" Granny stood in the doorway. "Cold beer?"

"Yeah, comin'!"

Bill looked at me and backed toward the door. "Hurry up, man. We went north too—almost to the DMZ—there's some serious shit goin' on up there—hairy shit!"

I turned on the water and stuck my hand in to test the temperature. "Yeah, I know."

"What?" Bill hollered from the doorway.

"Nothin'!" I shouted. "See you at the hootch."

"Roger!"

I hung my towel on a hook and stepped in front of the tepid stream, lowering my head as the water splattered off my scalp and shoulders. At my feet, the red dirt of the crash site and the powdered gray dust from LZ Kiwi fell away and swirled in a vortex around the algae-covered drain. I relaxed my arms and shoulders, feeling the water flowing around my ears and down my cheeks, and I chuckled softly inside my cool liquid cocoon. Bill didn't even know I'd flown today. One of these days I was going to have to teach that boy how to read a flight schedule.

And he had a war story already—complete with a swashbuckling character and colorful places: "Shit-hot" Shockley, the "subway," the "keyhole."

I grinned and opened my eyes. The water pouring off my cheeks converged to a forced stream off my chin, shooting in an arc toward the wall. As I had since childhood, I pretended the solid stream of water was machine gun fire and lowering my chin, I "walked" the water around the front of my flip-flops, outlining my toes. Then I stopped, thinking of Droopy, how he'd held back the NVA while I'd looked for Scapelli, and Major Hardy, how he'd gotten a round in the heel of his boot that knocked him into the dirt, and how he'd bounced up and kept going, and how the Army guys had risked their lives for us, for total strangers, and how Scapelli, "Vegas," back from the dead, had flashed us a peace sign from the Jolly Green Sniffer. And it seemed so…unreal.

Then through the stream, I noticed my feet. They were tanned and washed and comfortable in my flip-flops. Then my legs and thighs. They were healthy and strong and…scratched. There were scratches—scratches and bruises all around my right shin and calf—parallel streaks of scratches as if made by a wire, a wire spring attached to a kneeboard, a kneeboard that was in a pocket on my calf and bouncing and slamming into my leg as I ran, ran hard, ran scared. Now beneath the sheets of water splattering and rushing over my body, my heart pounded, my lungs pumped, and I smelled…jet fuel. Jet fuel! My God, it *was* real. I didn't get those scratches at a base library.

I snapped my head out of the stream of water, took a deep breath, and smelled again the dank, humid mixture of human waste, cigarette smoke, and urinal cakes. I let out a long, chest-collapsing sigh, a sigh that became a moan and echoed off the moldy shower walls. Hearing it, I self-consciously looked out, left and right, to make sure I was alone. I was.

I stepped under the shower again. The water pounded off my back. I put my hands to my face, pulled them toward my ears and down, squeezing the water out of my eyebrows and scraping it off my cheeks and mouth and chin. I let my hands fall away and looked at my chest. Rising and falling more slowly now, it was whole and safe and clean. Then my arms. They were whole and they were safe and they were clean. I sighed again, a soft, easy sigh, and raised my hands, palms and fingers, and I saw they were also whole and they were also safe and they were…trembling.

8

Helpless

In towel and flip-flops, calmed and soothed by twenty minutes of pounding shower spray, I weaved behind a sandbag wall to the unlighted entrance to Hut 8 and stopped. A monotone voice drifted through a crack of light around the air conditioner. I heard my name. I opened the door and the voice ceased.

Inside, around the card table, Bill, Granny, and Major Hardy sat staring at me, casting shadows from the bare bulb in the ceiling. Bill, slack-jawed, gaped across the table.

"Evening, Major," I said, crossing the room toward the back. I didn't know what I'd interrupted, but if they had been talking about me, then so what? I was too tired to worry about it.

Or so I thought. By the time I stepped into my space, I really was worried about it—or at least thinking about it, wondering what they were saying, sensing deja vu, and that, finally, led me to a similar scene, a similar entrance, a similar response—years before. I told myself it was mental fatigue and to forget it, stop it.

I sat at my ammo-box desk and rubbed my eyes. The childhood scene reappeared. Not now, I said. Go away. Too late, the memory was already in focus—my parents, sitting at the kitchen table in the middle of the afternoon, staring at me as I held the kitchen door, my little sister running past me yelling, "Hi Mom, hi Dad."

Without taking her eyes off me, my mother answered, "Hi Hon," then pushed away from the table and followed my sister to the refrigerator. My father, in khakis—short-sleeve shirt with captain's bars, ribbons, and wings—told me to take a seat.

I set my books on the counter, glanced at my frayed sneakers—no mud—and wondered what I'd done. At the table, my father stared into a cocktail glass and repeatedly flicked ashes from his cigarette. Maybe it was the BB gun. The day before, our old-maid neighbor had yelled at me for shooting her pine cones. Her pine cones! As if I could really hurt the pine cone crop with a BB gun.

I stepped to the table, pulled my mother's chair closer, and sat, watching my father's eyes. From past experience with his disciplinary technique, I knew this was the discussion phase. I'd have a chance to explain my side of the story, then when found guilty anyhow, we'd go to the bedroom and he'd whip me with a leather belt. During the discussion and the whipping I was expected to be a good Marine and take it like a man. If I didn't, if I whined or cried during the discussion or the whipping, he'd hit me harder.

Placing my arms on a place mat, I decided it wasn't the neighbor, it was Mary Elizabeth McCall. She had chased me all over the playground during recess that day, then fell in a mud puddle, screamed like a stuck pig, and told the teacher I'd pushed her. That must have been it. I thought the teacher saw my side of the story, but maybe she didn't and called my parents. I was sure that was it. Mary Elizabeth, the colonel's daughter, the brat.

But that wasn't it.

My father smiled, reached over, and slapped me on the shoulder. "How'd it go today, Tiger?"

Smiling, breathing easier, I said, "Fine" and watched him take another drag on his cigarette. He blew the smoke at the high ceiling, flicked the ashes, and requested another Scotch and water.

As ice cubes clinked into a glass behind me, he told me he'd gotten orders to Korea. He said while he was gone, I was to be the man-of-the-house and to take good care of my mother and sister. That was it. Five days later, March 28th, 1953, he left. I never saw him again.

"Ross." Major Hardy stood at the opening to my space.

I popped out of my chair, grabbed the seat back, and pulled the chair out of my way. "Yes, sir."

"I'd like to talk with you a minute."

"Yes, sir…here?"

He smiled. "Yeah. If that's okay. Only have a minute."

"Yes, sir."

He stepped across the aisle, picked up Bill's chair, and returned to sit beside my locker. I turned my chair to face him and sat, the wet towel still around my waist.

Still in his flightsuit, the major rocked back in his chair and crossed his leg. The flip-flop he wore on his injured foot hung in the air, clinging to his toes by black rubber straps. His heel, bandaged with a square gauze pad and surgical tape, was swollen and purple.

He folded his arms. "We had quite a day today, Ross. I didn't get a chance to talk with you about it in the ready room or at sickbay. I just wanted to make sure you're okay."

"Yes sir, I'm fine."

"Well, that's good. Sometimes you don't feel the bumps and bruises until later though. Does that arm hurt?" He looked at my left shoulder. I'd forgotten about it, but as I pulled the arm into view, I could see it was already black and blue around my smallpox vaccination.

"No, sir. I remember it hurt at the time—well, it went numb actually—when we hit. But it's fine now—just a bruise."

"Well, I'm glad it's okay. Listen…Ross." He rocked forward onto the front legs, put both feet on the floor, and leaned forward, resting his forearms on his thighs. "I've got to leave first thing in the morning—orders to Iwakuni, Japan—permanent orders. There are a couple of things I'd like to go over with you before I go."

"Yes, sir."

"The first thing is that piece of paper I gave you back at LZ Kiwi. Do you still have it?"

"Yes, sir. It's in there, in my flightsuit." I pointed at the gray wall locker beside him. "Do you want it?"

"Yes, but not right this minute. I'll get it on the way out. That paper has the names, unit, and address of those Army guys who saved our butts. They really hung it out for us today, Ross. They didn't have to do that—not their job. Anyhow, I'm going to write them up for a Silver Star. In my absence, I'd like you to see that it goes through our channels here, then on to their unit. Okay?"

"Yes, sir, glad to do it. The OV-10 guy too?"

The major smiled and shook his head. "Ol' 'Mustang Duke.' Yeah, Duke did a good job. But he's supposed to do a good job—like us, he gets paid to take care of Marines. Don't worry, I'll send him a bottle of Scotch and a picture of me smiling. Duke's a former H-34 driver—that picture will mean more to him than a medal."

"Yes, sir."

Up front, the air conditioner kicked on again and the bare bulbs in the ceiling flickered. The major shifted in his seat.

"Ross, the last thing: before I was presented with these orders tonight, I was looking forward to flying with you again and finishing what I started today. Obviously, I can't do that now. And unfortunately, there's a lot to being a good gunship pilot we didn't get to—in fact, most of it." He glanced at his hands. "But…on the other hand, we covered the basics, and I think I saw enough today to know you're going to be a good one. And we need good ones, Ross. We need tigers and we need team players."

"Yes, sir." I sat straighter.

"Lieutenant Tess—you know him? Tall. Arm in a sling."

"Yes, sir."

"Well, he's writing the schedule tonight. I told him to schedule you with Jim Teach tomorrow, Lieutenant Teach. Teach is good—good Marine, good pilot. Listen to him. He can finish where I left off." He sat erect. "Understand?"

"Yes, sir." I'd met Teach. He lived in our hootch, just across from Granny. Quiet guy.

"Well, that's it then. Listen to Teach." He smiled as he stood and slid his chair across to Bill's space.

I stood and met him in the aisle.

"Okay, Ross," he said, offering me his hand. "Help me get those Army pukes decorated, learn how to be a good gunship pilot, and ah…take care of yourself too, okay?"

"Yes, sir," I said, shaking his hand, hesitating. "Major, I ah…"

"Yes?"

"Ah…nothing, sir. I'll get the paper for you."

I opened my locker with a clang and pulled the paper from my flightsuit pocket. He took it, stuffed it in his breast pocket, and walked toward the door. I followed.

Before he reached the curtain, I straightened. "Sir?"

He stopped and turned. "Yes?"

"May I ask you a question about today?"

He crossed his arms over his chest, the faintest of smiles on his cheeks. "Sure. Go ahead."

"Well, sir…it's about the colonel. Why wasn't he there when we needed him? I mean, you wouldn't have left him."

He glanced toward the front, nodded, and extended his hand toward the back of the hut.

At my locker again, he turned and faced me, his hand massaging his neck, his eyes wrinkling at the corners. A smile spread across his tanned face. "Ross…you're beginning to remind me of another lieutenant I knew once—used to see him in the mirror a lot." He dropped his hand. "Listen, you're right—he should have been there, but I don't know why he wasn't. I suspect it has more to do with his background in fixed-wing or his rank than anything else. I just don't know. But even if I did know, it wouldn't matter. The only thing that matters is that the Marine Corps, in all its wisdom, has made him the CO of a combat Huey gunship squadron—our squadron. Now we can complain about that or press on and do the best we can with it. I recommend you press on."

"Yes, sir." I looked at the floor, disappointed there wasn't a logical explanation for the colonel's behavior—something I'd overlooked, a teaching point, a lesson to be learned. And I had put the major on the spot. Didn't want that. I raised my head. "Major, what happened to us—the bird I mean, the Huey? I know it was a tail rotor problem, but..."

"Yeah, the Huey." His eyes brightened. "You know, that gooner nailed us pretty good—damn good shootin'. Well, he must have hit the tail, and I guess at first we just lost pitch control on the tail rotor—maybe the sprocket chain was hit—not good, but we could have stayed in the air long enough to get to Dong Ha and make a slide-on landing. That's pretty basic stuff you probably practiced at Pendleton or New River."

I nodded. "Yes, sir. Pendleton."

"Yeah. But the last part—" He smiled, the creases in his cheeks deepening. "—the 'Whirling Dervish' part. Your manual doesn't cover that very well, but it's called 'loss of tail rotor components.' In other words, our tail rotor blades and the tail rotor gearbox flew off—bad news, loss of weight aft, center of gravity shift, couldn't fly so had to get into an autorotation. I'm willing to bet you didn't practice that—autos without a tail rotor."

"No, sir," I said, matching his smile.

"Well, that's what happened. Got to go."

He stepped toward the front, but pulled up. "Ross, if you get me talking flying, neither of us will get any sleep tonight. But listen, before I go, I want to pass this on to you: a lot of flying, particularly helicopter flying, is done with your sense of touch and hearing. If you learn to feel and listen to what the bird is trying to tell you, as well as read your instruments, you can anticipate its behavior. As long as you're thinking ahead of the aircraft, anticipating its next move, and controlling it before it starts controlling you, you'll be okay. Today that bird told me it was losing its tail rotor. It vibrated my feet, it whistled in the air, it said, 'Pick out a landing site, Hardy. Lock your harness and get ready to chop the throttle. I'm losing my tail feathers.'"

I nodded, feeling stupid. I had heard all that, felt all that, but it said nothing to me except, "problem." The major looked into my face and slapped me on the shoulder. "It'll come, Ross. In fact, it's already coming. I bet you know what a one-to-one vertical beat feels like and what it means."

"Yes, sir. It seems like every Huey I've ever flown has a blade out of track."

"Well, there it is. The bird is telling you a blade's out of track. And RPM. I'll bet you can already tell when your rotor RPM is in the green just by the sound—you don't have to read the rotor tach to know."

"Yes, sir."

"It takes hours in the bird, Ross, that's all. And while all helicopters have some sounds and feels in common, like rotor RPM, each type also has its own little nuances and personal characteristics. Listen for 'em. Feel for 'em. It'll come."

"Yes, sir."

"Now, let me get out of here." He started for the front, talking as we walked. "But I'll be in touch. And don't forget I'm counting on you to help me decorate those crazy warrant officers. And listen to Teach." He stopped at the curtains and offered me his hand again. "You're part of a great squadron now, Ross. A squadron with a load-hackin' reputation I'm very proud of—a reputation earned with the sweat and blood and sacrifice of some great guys. I'm counting on you to take care of it for me. Will you do that?"

"Yes, sir. I will."

"Thanks." The major released my hand, split the curtains, and was gone.

Minutes later, after I'd returned to my space and changed my wet towel for a pair of green boxer-shorts, I felt a tight, burning pain in my gut—a knotting pain, like my insides were one of those thick rubberbands on a balsawood airplane that would make bigger and bigger knots the more I turned the plastic propeller.

Massaging my stomach with both hands, I walked to Granny's refrigerator and reached for a beer—bottom shelf, right rear corner—my corner, according to Granny. Bill had the left rear corner and as usual, it was empty.

From the front of the hut, cards shuffled and men laughed: Bill...Granny... Rod, and someone else, someone I didn't know...maybe Shockley. I'd have the back of the hootch to myself for awhile.

At my desk, I tried to drown the stomachache with a long cold drink. I figured it was indigestion, too much macaroni and cheese at supper. Another swallow helped, but not much.

Placing the beer in front of me, I massaged my stomach, smelled the pinesap oozing from the knots in the ammo-box desk, and without warning, more memories surfaced—the tough part, the part I'd usually been able to suppress. Too tired to fight it, the pine smell carried me back: hot July day, black Ford, two officers in Alpha uniforms. They stopped in front of our house.

From my rope swing under a pine tree in the side yard, I saw them get out, wipe their faces with white handkerchiefs, and walk across the sandy yard to our house.

Even at eight years old I had a sense of why they were there. Maybe it was the Alpha uniform, the khaki blouse on top of a long-sleeve shirt and tie. My father had always hated that uniform. Or the way they never looked up or didn't talk on their way to the door. I didn't know. I just knew eight-year-olds weren't stupid, especially when they were the acting man-of-the-house.

I dug my bare heels into the sand, hopped out of the swing, and ran for the front door.

Turning the corner of the house, I saw my mother through the open front window. She hurried to answer their knock—a dish towel in her hands, a blue-checkered apron tied around her waist. She had no idea who was behind that door, but I did, and they were going to have to go through me to get to her.

In one leap, I cleared the side of our concrete stoop and was between the overdressed, perspiring men and my mother as she opened the door. I knew one of them, a Captain somebody. He was a friend of my father's and lived down the street. He caught me by the arm and patted me on my back as I slid to a stop.

My mother gasped and put both hands and the dish towel to her mouth as soon as she saw who it was and how they were dressed. I stood in front of her, facing the captain who had caught me, patted me, and said, "Hi, Ross," as if nothing were wrong.

They were very polite and didn't stay long and I made sure they didn't get near my mother. I stood by her chair while the two men seated across from her explained why I didn't have a father anymore, not even a body to bury—lost at sea on a night mission in an F9F Panther jet.

When they got to that part, my mother tried to send me to her room to check on my sister. But I said no. My sister was fine. She was taking a nap. Sometimes the man-of-the-house has to be firm. So, I didn't budge from her side while they explained that was all they knew so far and she kept her arm around my waist and squeezed me over and over.

The rest of that day was a blur of women bringing food. Most of them tried at first to treat me like an eight-year-old, but they learned.

Two weeks later, my mother was in the hospital and I had lost a brother, a miscarriage. She was sick, seriously sick, and I almost lost her too. I had been the man-of-the-house for four months and I'd already lost a brother and was doing a lousy job of taking care of my mother. That's when I first remember having stomach pains. Havelock, 1953.

I rubbed my eyes. The memory stayed. I rubbed again, but kept seeing my mother holding the dish towel to her face, the terror in her eyes. And I remembered how helpless I felt when she was in the hospital and they wouldn't let me see her, or let me be with her, or let me take care of her like I'd promised my father I would. My stomach burned and twisted as I massaged it with one hand and my forehead with the other. I pushed at the memories, pushed at the pain, pushed and pressed and rubbed.

Minutes later, maybe seconds, body heavy, I took another drink, folded my arms on the desk, and rested my head.

What happened next is fuzzy. Somebody shook me. And there was Bill's voice. The lights were out except the tensor reading light on my desk. I had my head on my arms and the half-finished beer in my hand. I raised my head and through squinted eyes, recognized Bill. He took the can out of my hand and helped me to my feet.

"Is it time to go?" I mumbled.

"Go where?" Bill asked, turning me toward my rack as I stood.

"Fly."

"No. It's one o'clock—time for all us steely-eyed combat pilots to be in the rack." He pulled back my poncho liner and top sheet as I rolled onto the thin mattress, the springs squeaking in protest.

A voice at my feet, maybe it was Granny, said, "You're not scheduled until this afternoon, Ross—afternoon guns."

I rolled over to the wall, away from the light, and pulled the covers to my shoulders, sinking into a dark warm cave. On a parting breath, I said, "Teach?"

"Negative," the voice said. "Major Pyhr."

9

Loves to Kill

At 1000 the next morning, the musty hootch, lit by sunlight filtering through opaque fiberglass panels in the ceiling, was still and quiet. Already shaved and in my flightsuit, I stood by the card table, massaged my sore shoulder, and again questioned the flight schedule. Signed by Carl Tess and co-signed by Major Lewis, the operations officer, it said I was with Major Pyhr, not Teach: 1100 brief, 1200 take-off, mission 55—afternoon guns.

At the top of the schedule, Bill's name was with Ono's: 0530 brief, 0630 takeoff, mission 55—morning guns. Grinning, I picked up the schedule and walked toward the back, toward the sound of Bill's heavy breathing.

"Hey, Cat." I pulled the folding chair to his rack, sat, and bounced his shoulder. "Cat!" Moving an empty beer can off my tape player, I switched to rewind. It reversed itself, groaning and rattling and slowly picking up speed and I shook his shoulder again, hard. His jowls rolled; his mouth fell open; he passed some gas.

"Cat! Reveille, man. Fall out for PT."

I switched to play, heard the chorus to "Bernadette," and knew I'd gone too far. I reversed for a couple of seconds and turned the volume to max. I snapped the switch to play again and bingo, the Four Tops were right on cue. "Shake Me, Wake Me" blasted from the little Panasonic.

The Cat-man stirred.

I shook his shoulder and shouted over the Four Tops, "Cat. Wake up, man—you've got a 0530 brief."

His eyes squeezed shut, his hands drew the pillow over his head, and he muttered, "What's that god-awful noise?"

"The Four—" I turned the recorder to stop. "—The Four Tops, one of my—your favorites. Good, huh?"

He shifted to his side, facing me, head still covered by the pillow and voice still muffled. "Yeah. Those guys are great. Fuckin' loud though. What time is it?"

"It's 1005."

"And I've got a 0530 brief?" He raised the pillow and peered at me with one bloodshot eye.

"Yeah, 0530." I popped the flight schedule with my finger. "You have morning guns with Ono."

"Oh. Well, shit. I guess I missed it."

"Yeah. I guess so."

I stood, pulled the chair out of his way, and Bill sat on the edge of his rack. He rubbed his eyes. "I guess this means I missed chow too, huh?" he said, slipping his feet into his flip-flops.

"That's right, Sherlock. You missed chow, you missed your brief, you missed your flight. So far, you've had one of those 'all wrong' days." I leaned against his wall locker and crossed my arms.

"Well, where the fuck were you?"

"I was asleep. I didn't have a 0530 brief. You're gonna have to learn to read the schedule, Cat."

He nodded, the face and eyes fading to blank. I knew the look. He was thinking. Easing to his feet, his boxer shorts skewed to one side, he pushed me away from his open locker and pulled his arms back in a long, luxurious stretch.

Dropping his arms, the freckled grin, the fun-fun look, returned. "Well, fuck it, R.T. What are they gonna do—shave my head, make me a Marine helicopter pilot, and send me to 'Nam? Don't worry about it, man, you're forgiven." He plucked a towel off the locker door. "I'll clean up, then we'll scrounge something to eat from my buddy Rappo."

I shook my head. I was forgiven.

We walked toward the front. "I've got to go, Cat—1100 brief and I need to get some stuff at Flight Equipment first. See you at the ready room. And listen, you're not gonna believe the flight I had yesterday. Gotta tell you about it."

"Flight Equipment?" Bill split the curtains and led me through the front and out the door. "Oh, yeah—your flight. I heard about that—Major Hardy told us. Left some shit behind, huh? Did I tell you about flying with Shockley? It was great, man. Sierra hotel—shiiiit hot!"

We turned right at the sidewalk, squinting against the bright sunlight. "Yeah, well I'll listen to your story if you'll listen to mine. But later. I don't want to be late—don't want them to shave my head and make me a Marine helicopter pilot and send me to 'Nam like they're gonna do to you."

Bill laughed. “You’re taking this shit too serious, Ross. I’m tellin’ ya—you’re gonna get ulcers.” He pushed me toward the main road and turned left. “See ya later.”

I stopped as a couple of guys in greasy flightsuits, probably 46 drivers, walked between me and my view of Bill. I swapped nods with them as they went by, but I didn’t know them and they didn’t appear to know me. When I looked back toward Bill he was already turning behind the end quonset hut. I started to yell after him, something like, just taking care of you is giving me ulcers! The rest is a piece of cake! But, suddenly he was gone and I didn’t yell anything.

Fifteen minutes later, I left the dirt road and crossed to our sandbagged squadron building. U-shaped, with the tips of the U pointing toward the road and enclosing a sand yard the size of a typical two-car garage, the rusty-roofed building looked cooked by the hot sun and abandoned. Even the huge plywood sign with the big black claw-hammer logo was missing.

Up the steps and inside the screened door, sweating, breathing hard from slogging through the soft sand, I removed my cover and heard the cool sounds of rustling paper and whirling fan blades. I turned left to the S-1 office—the big room in the corner of the U—and stopped at Straderman’s desk. The air from the fan on his desk swung over me, and I raised my arms, feeling the sun’s fire leave my flightsuit.

Straderman looked up from his typewriter and rocked back on the rear legs of his chair. He locked his long fingers behind his head and changed his expression just enough to indicate he knew who I was. “Lieutenant Teemer. Just the man I need to see. Is Lieutenant Catlett with you, sir?”

“Nope. Just me. What’s up?” I put my arms down as the fan swung toward the corporal.

“Captain Orndorff would like to see you, sir—you and Lieutenant Catlett.”

“Together?”

“Together or individually—doesn’t matter.”

I sat in the metal chair by his desk and slid into a slouch. “Can it wait?—I’ve got a brief in a minute.”

Straderman wore his jungle utility shirt and trousers, the shirt collar soaked with sweat. “I was just told to tell you to see the captain, sir. I don’t know if it’s urgent or not.” He dropped onto all four chair legs and put his sweaty arms on the desk beside his typewriter. A pile of official-looking forms, weighted with a hand grenade, lay by his hand. “You couldn’t see him right this minute anyhow.” He turned and nodded to my left, toward the two offices in the wing of the building. “He’s with the XO.”

“In that case,” I said, as I stood and raised my arms to the passing stream of air, “tell him I came by to see him, had to go fly, and will try him again later.” I smiled and added, “How ’bout that?”

"Whatever you say, Lieutenant."

Without expression, Straderman turned to the typewriter and pounded the keys. The fan swung toward him, rustling the pile of papers, and I walked away, wondering if the hand grenade was live or inert.

Down the hall, at the other corner of the U, I entered the ready room and stopped, listening to the worker-bee drone of the fans. Through the rusty screens across the room to my left, the flight line was a white-hot blur. I was alone. Even the ODO's stool was vacant. It was 1050.

Stepping to the counter, I examined the aircraft status board on the wall. Sixteen of the twenty aircraft had an "up" arrow by their number. Two of the remaining four were up for maintenance test flights. Only twelve birds were scheduled.

As the blue-bladed fans—one on the shelf by the screened wall and the other on the floor behind the Ops counter—stirred the hot air around me, I picked up a worn clipboard. The day's flight schedule was clipped on top—already dog-eared and defaced with multiple pencil corrections. My name was scratched through. So was Bill's.

"Hey, Teemer." From the short hall off the ready room—the other leg of the U—Carl Tess, a coffee mug in hand, walked toward me. He wiped his mouth on his sling, stepped around the end of the counter, and side-stepped past the fan on the floor. "Hey, all those with an 1100 brief, step across this line—not so fast, Lieutenant Teemer."

I smiled and held out my hand. "Hi. Ross Teemer. Glad I finally get to meet you."

He slid onto the stool and set his ceramic mug by the clipboard. "Yeah? Carl Tess." He shook my hand and asked with a puzzled look, "Why?"

"Well, I don't know. You've been around. I thought I might learn some stuff from you."

"Yeah. Well, I've been around alright. I've been around so much I'm fuckin' dizzy."

I leaned against the counter. "How's the arm?"

He sipped his coffee, then held his arm and sling at chest level. "Well, hell…I guess it's okay—itches like a son-of-a-bitch, though." He lowered his arm. "I bet you think you're flying today."

"Not anymore. I see I've been scratched."

"Yeah, all you FNGs have been scratched—can't fly until tomorrow—after your seven days are up."

"How come? I flew yesterday."

"Yeah, and got your ass shot off too. I heard about that. So did the new XO and he's pissed."

"Pissed at me? I didn't ask to fly early."

"He's pissed at everybody: you, me, Major Lewis, and especially Major Hardy." He lowered his voice and leaned forward, bracing his forearms on the counter. "You might have noticed he's not around anymore—Major Hardy."

"The XO did that? Angus?"

He glanced over his shoulder toward the hall to the CO, XO, and S-1 offices, toward the sound of the pounding typewriter keys. "Yeah, he did that; but don't ask me how. I just know things have really changed around here."

"Because of Angus?"

"Hell yeah, because of Angus. Two days ago Major Hardy was the XO; he was in charge. The grunts needed missions flown; we had the birds up; we had the pilots, so we flew the missions. If we had to bend a few rules to do it, then so be it; the grunts needed us, so we were there—Hardy rules."

"Angus has different rules?"

"Oh, yeah—very different." He glanced over his shoulder again and stuck a pencil under his cast. Working the pencil back and forth, he leaned closer. "As he told me and Major Lewis last night—after calling us over to his hootch at *midnight*—'The fucking grunts don't tell us what we'll do or won't do—we tell them!'"

He sat erect again, extracted the pencil, and tapped it on the edge of the clipboard. "We scratched a gun mission down south today 'cause Angus said you guys couldn't fly yet—had to move those co-pilots up to guns north to replace you. That hasn't happened, scratching a mission I mean, since Operation Dewey Canyon, back in February. Had a lot of combat damage back then, lot of birds down, some people lost. But since then, since Major Hardy got here—and come to think of it, that was around February as well—turning down missions has not been our style. We don't say no to the grunts."

I shifted to my right side so I could watch the hallway to S-1. Behind me, I could hear the faint clatter of CH-46 rotor blades. "Carl, I talked to Major Hardy last night, late. He seemed, well, almost emotional—about leaving I guess. I would think he would be glad to get out of here."

"Yeah, I talked to him too; he came by here while I was writing the schedule. Hardy's a funny guy. He's all business when he's flying or taking care of squadron affairs. But when it comes to the squadron as a being, or to the individuals in the squadron, the people, he can get pretty touchy." He paused, grinning. "I saw him drag a visiting fighter-puke out of the club by his shirt-collar one night—just because of something 'unflattering' the guy said about helicopter pilots."

"The guy was bad-mouthing helicopter pilots in a helicopter pilot's club? What a dumb-shit!"

"Yeah, can you believe it? Anyhow, Hardy just dragged him out and threw him toward the hootches and said don't come back."

"Did he? Come back, I mean?"

"Shit, no. The guy he was visiting, a major in the H-53 squadron—he was a major too—did I tell you that? Anyhow, they left and didn't come back."

He paused for a second and leaned forward again, resting his forearms on the counter. "Hardy was great—really cared about the mission and about his people. He cared what happened to you too. Well, hell, he cared about all of us. But he really wanted you on that schedule today, and he wanted you with Teach—nobody else."

"Can I fly with Teach tomorrow? I can fly tomorrow, right?"

"Oh, yeah," he said, with a smirk. "You can fly, but under Angus rules."

"What does that mean?"

"That means, and I quote the major: 'All first flights by new guys will be flown with field grade officers only.'"

"Well, I've already had my first flight, and it was with a field grade officer—Major Hardy."

"Doesn't count."

"Why not?"

"That was B.A.—before Angus. All you guys are to get a fresh start and learn under the guiding hand of 'The Bull,' a major with exactly 68 hours of helicopter time. Or one of our other gifted field grade officers: Mickey, Sweet Lou, or maybe Pyhr, 'Funeral Pyhr,' we call him." He shook his head. "No doubt so you new guys can reap the benefit of their extensive knowledge of Huey gunship operations."

"You don't sound too convinced."

"I'm not. I've been around, remember?"

"Are they all as bad as the colonel?"

"In some ways, the colonel is in a class by himself. But basically they're all typical fixed-wing guys who got sent to helicopters. They didn't want it, don't like it, and can't wait to get away from it. Except Major Pyhr."

"He likes helicopters?"

"No, he likes war; actually, he *loves* war—he loves the killing part. Helicopters can get you closer to the killing, so, in a way, I guess he does like helicopters." He frowned, looked at his clipboard, and shook his head. "He's crazy."

"And I was supposed to fly with him today?"

"Yep. The first Angus rule came down yesterday—first flights with field grade. That's why I couldn't schedule you with Teach. It wasn't until we had all the mission requests from the grunts filled, and Major Lewis had approved the schedule I wrote, that the shit hit the fan and we got the second Angus rule: Stick to our regulations and don't let the grunts tell us what to do."

A screened door slammed and Tess straightened. In the hallway to the S-1 area, several pairs of heavy boots crunched toward us. It was 1110.

A skinny major of average height, wearing a baggy flightsuit, led three other pilots into the ready room. With thinning brown hair and a nose too large for his face—and without acknowledging our presence—the major, trailing smoke from a cigarette wedged between his fingers, weaved between tables and benches to the screened wall. After extracting a flight bag, bullet bouncer, and survival vest from a curtained cubbyhole under the shelf with the blue-bladed fan, he returned to the front of the room and dropped his gear at the foot of the counter. The name stenciled in black on the red vinyl curtain to the cubbyhole was "Maj. Pyhr."

I walked to the back and sat alone as the others extracted their gear and stepped to the front beside the major. I recognized Teach and Henstrom, a guy I'd met earlier, but didn't know the third guy. According to the schedule, his name was Gamez, another lieutenant. No one spoke. Only Teach gave me a nod of recognition.

Tess stood by his stool and withdrew a second clipboard from a shelf under the counter. He cleared his throat. "Major, you have aircraft 15, third revetment in the second row. Teach, you have aircraft 8, fifth revetment in the second row. Weather on call, Major." An aircraft droned overhead and the fans hummed, but still, none of the pilots spoke.

The major, with smoke curling past his face from the cigarette now stuck in the corner of his mouth, wrote on his kneeboard. A second later, with a sucking sound, he pulled the cigarette out and blew the smoke down the front of his flightsuit. The cigarette again between his lips, he made a gun out of his right hand, and simulated a shot at Tess.

"Yes, sir." Tess looked at his clipboard. "The weather in the local area is clear, ceiling unlimited, visibility three to five miles in haze. Winds light and variable. Altimeter 2-9-9-5. Runway niner is the active. No weather in the forecast. Target area weather is three to 5,000 scattered, five miles vis, winds 2-9-0 at five to ten. Altimeter 2-9-9-4. Forecast is for 5,000 broken, possible thunderstorms." He paused and looked at the major.

Major Pyhr took another drag on his cigarette and shot at Tess again.

"Yes, sir. Intelligence report remains the same as yesterday. The 3rd Marines are still running search-and-destroy operations southwest of Con Thien." He glanced at me. "We lost a bird in the 1-1-6-3 grid yesterday due to ground fire. They were supporting Lima 1-4 at the time." He moved his eyes from face to face as he added, "Be advised, there's at least one gook out there with his shit in one bag, a real dinger, a shooter."

The major raised his finger.

"Yes, sir?"

"Freq?" the major asked, in a high-pitched voice.

Tess cocked his head. "For Lima 1-4?"

Pyhr nodded.

"I don't know, sir. Ah…maybe Ross, Lieutenant Teemer, remembers." Tess stretched his neck in my direction and the four pilots, including the one named "Funeral Pyhr," turned to look at me.

My heart jumped into my throat. "I—" I started to say, I don't remember, but a figure came to mind. "—I believe it was 3-9 point 2-5."

They wrote the radio frequency on their kneeboards and I let out a breath, amazed at myself for remembering and grateful to Major Hardy. He had explained to me early the day before, after B-12 had told us to switch to "Jack Benny plus two-bits," that B-12 meant 39, Jack Benny's perennial age, plus .25, or a quarter—two bits.

Up front, everyone except Major Pyhr returned to Tess. The major, his right eye closed to a thin slit against the smoke swirling up from his cigarette, stared at me a few seconds, then finally turned around.

Tess put the clipboard on the counter. "Mutters Ridge is still hot. The 4th Marines have been in contact in that area for several days. A 46 took some hits going into LZ Mack yesterday afternoon, and an active .50 cal. was reported north of the Rockpile the day before yesterday. That's it."

Major Pyhr took one more drag on his cigarette, dropped the butt in an open C-ration can on the counter and reached behind him for his cover. He stared at me a second, gathered his survival vest, bullet bouncer, and flight bag, and left through the screened door to the flight line. Without a word, the others followed.

The door slammed behind them and I stood. I strolled toward the front, watching them through the rusty screens, and Tess joined me at the door. In the midday sun, the four pilots, loaded with flight gear, weapons, and map cases, humped across the sweltering steel flight line.

After several seconds, I whistled softly. "That guy is weird."

"Yes, he is. That guy is very, very weird."

"What happened to the standard NATOPS briefing, the ol' checklist routine?"

"Doesn't believe in it. He briefs at chow before he gets here. It usually goes something like this: 'I'm Hardball 1-9, you're Hardball 1-9 Dash Two. Turn at 1145 (or whatever). Ground check on squadron common FM and UHF. Stay off the radios, cover my ass, and stay out of my way.' That's it." He shook his head, still following the progress of the four pilots as they turned into the second row of revetments.

"Likes to kill, huh?"

"*Loves* to kill. Loves the war. War and killing in the name of God and country have brought new meaning to his life. Makes you proud to wear the uniform, doesn't it?" He turned and walked toward the counter.

I watched the last guy, Henstrom, disappear behind a revetment wall, and followed Tess.

He mounted his stool and picked up the C-ration can Major Pyhr had used as an ashtray.

I slid my arms onto the counter.

"I'd offer you some sliced peaches, but, unless you like yours with cigarette butts, I'm afraid I'm fresh out."

I smiled and shook my head. "Thanks anyhow."

He turned sideways, bent over, and I heard a dull thump as the soiled can of peaches dropped into a trash can on the floor under the counter. Raising his head as he pushed the trash can away, he asked, "You know why he wanted Lima 1-4's frequency, don't you?"

"Just for general reference, I guess—in case DASC sends them to work for 'em."

He tried to get at another itch with his pencil. "Nope. He wants that gook—the one that shot you down. I guarantee you that's the first place he'll go this afternoon—no matter what DASC says."

"You can't be serious. He'll disregard the mission he's assigned and go do his own thing?"

"I guarantee it. See, Ross, my naive-little-FNG-friend, this war is for the major's personal entertainment—it's not about defeating communism or defending the freedom-loving people of South Vietnam or any of that other propaganda bullshit. It's entertainment—more fun than Disney Land—*cheap* entertainment. I mean, shit, the taxpayers are paying him to have all this fun. He absolutely loves it."

"Damn." I looked toward the flight line. "As James Michener said in *The Bridges at Toko-ri*, 'Where do we get such men?'"

Tess stopped scratching. He stared at me, the eyes squeezed hard. "You're quoting James Michener? Shit, Ross. I can tell already, you're not going to fit in around here. Whatever you do, don't let any of these field grade officers know you're literate."

"No?"

"No! Trust me. If they even think you're smarter than they are, you'll end up like Borenmann."

All I knew about Borenmann was he lived in our hootch between Tess and Teach and I'd never seen him. "Well, okay, I won't." I paused. "That's the only quote I know anyhow."

He wrote something on the clipboard and looked at me. "I'm only trying to help, Ross. Life can get pretty fucked-up around here. And the fucked-up war is only a side fuck-up. Know what I mean?"

Before I could answer, a screened door slammed. Tess and I looked toward the S-1 area where a single pair of boots crunched down the hallway in our direction. The relaxed, steady pace was familiar.

Bill swept into the room. "R.T.! You asshole! Missed your flight, huh?"

"No, Cat. I know you'll be disappointed to hear this, but I was on time for my flight. Didn't matter though because Lieutenant Tess-of-one-arm scratched me."

"Yeah? What say, Tess?" Bill elbowed me aside and leaned against the counter. "Why are you fuckin' with my buddy Ross?"

Tess looked across the counter at Bill and laughed—probably remembering the scene in the head the night before. "You're scratched too, Catlett. Get out of here."

Bill noticed Tess didn't say anything he wanted to hear so he ignored him. "How'd you break that arm anyhow? Slip on some soap in the shower or something?"

Tess opened his mouth, but Bill turned his head, elbowed me, and asked, "Can we go now?"

I glanced at Tess and said, "Sure." It was 1145. Outside I heard a turbine engine's sudden low whine, and another, as if answering the call of the first, joined in. "Where we going?"

"Chow."

"You shittin' me? You just ate."

"That was an hour ago, and it was just a snack." Bill backed toward the hall. "Can we bring you anything from the chow hall, 'Tess-of-one-arm.' Say ptomaine-poisoning—something to remember us by?"

"No thanks, Catlett. Your absence will be enough."

"Well, good. Let's do it, R.T."

I followed Bill toward the front door, but kept my eyes on Tess. "I'll be back later—sure you don't want anything?"

"No thanks. Well, maybe a couple of oranges."

From the hallway, I answered, "You got it," and turned in time to see Bill stiffen and slow.

Captain Orndorff, his soft arms crossed over a starched utility shirt, a gargoyle frown on his pudgy face, leaned against the screened door and glared at us.

10

Trust Me, Sir

As soon as Captain Orndorff opened his mouth, Bill's neck reddened.

"Lieutenant Catlett. You and your buddy Teemer are holding up the program. Sign here." The starched captain pushed a government form under Bill's nose and tapped his finger at the bottom.

"What's it for?" Bill asked, his hand on the screened door.

"Allotment for savings bonds, Lieutenant. You two are keeping the squadron from being 100% enrolled."

Bill and I looked at each other. We'd been down this road before—in flight school and Camp Pendleton. Both of us knew Series E bonds were a bad investment—especially Bill—he was the one with a degree in finance.

"This squadron doesn't have room for stragglers, Lieutenant." He tapped the form again. "Sign it."

I grimaced. Without ceremony and in one clumsy step, the captain had just crossed the line; nobody accused Bill of not pulling his weight.

Bill took his hand off the door and leaned toward the captain. "Sid," he said, his voice strained. "I'm late for chow. I don't make financial decisions on an empty stomach. I'll be back in an hour and we can discuss it then."

Orndorff's oval face flushed. "Lieutenant Catlett…you will call me 'Captain Orndorff' and you will address me as 'Sir!'"

"Listen." Bill said, leaning closer, chin first. "We're going to go eat now. We'll be back. Later."

The captain—about my size, four inches shorter than Bill's six-two—stood firm, his arms crossed, the allotment form crumpled in his fist. "Lieutenant, I'll decide when we talk about this, and I didn't hear your last remark end in 'Sir.'"

His neck and freckled face florid, Bill glanced at me as if to ask, can I kill him?

I shook my head, thankful the two Hueys taxiing out of their revetments were making lots of noise.

Bill pressed further into the captain's face. "Look, Sidney," he hissed. "There's something you need to know—something you need to understand. You see…you're just another first-tour company-grade officer like me. You're not a 'Yes, sir,' you're not a 'No, sir,' you're just a 'Fucking-Sidney-Orndorff'—that's it. Got it?"

The captain's face went white. "Cat-lett!" he stammered, his hands trembling, "you…you and Teemer will report back to me this afternoon! At that time, you will reconsider your participation in this program, or I'll have you both in front of the CO and you can tell *him* you don't want to participate. Do…do you read me?"

"Sure, Sid," Bill answered with a tight smile, holding his head erect. "We'll see you after chow."

I followed Bill out the door and jogged with him to the mess hall, waiting for him to say something, waiting for him to explain why he was pushing the envelope with Orndorff. He ran with his eyes straight ahead and never said a word.

By the time the two of us, all dusty and sweaty, walked through the mess hall's screened double doors, the officers' section was closed. The enlisted wing, a warehouse-size room with exposed steel rafters and a concrete floor, was still open. Sergeant Rappo, wearing a stained butcher's apron over a white T-shirt and trousers, stood between the serving line and the double doors to the kitchen. He nodded as we stepped into line behind another squadron's flight crews who were also getting a late meal. In the corner, a huge, steel-caged floor fan blew at our backs, cooling me, drying me, and giving me a sense it was propelling the short line forward.

As I reached the pile of aluminum trays and cylinders of utensils, I recognized Scapelli and marveled at a system that would bring a man back from the dead to give him mess duty. In a sweat-soaked T-shirt, utility pants, and utility cover, he spooned cabbage onto outstretched trays, flashed his white teeth through wide smiles, and chatted with each man in line.

He recognized me across the steaming pan of cabbage and served me with a spoon the size of a small shovel. "Hey, Lieutenant, how's it hangin', sir?"

"Doin' good, Scapelli. Good to see you again."

He laughed and held the edge of my tray while he added a second helping. "Yeah, it's good for us to be seein' anybody again, right, sir?" He looked at Bill and reached for his tray. "I remember you. You're Lieutenant Catlett, aren't you, sir?"

"Yeah, how'd you know?"

"I work in the S-2 shop, Intelligence. I remember when you came in and signed for your maps and shit." He looked at me and poked his spoon in Bill's direction. "The lieutenant asked for a city map of Hue. Can you believe it, sir? Like he was going into town for the evening—dinner and a movie perhaps." Scapelli laughed and waved the spoon around. "A city map!" He nodded to Bill and slid the spoon into the pan. "We got a big charge out of that one, Lieutenant. You made our day, sir."

Bill accepted his large serving of cabbage, looked at me, and shrugged. "Well, hell. We might get a chance to go into Hue one day—it could happen."

"Yeah," I said, "and a fresh new Texaco street map would really come in handy too. I agree, Cat. Don't pay any attention to this guy, he'll laugh at anything."

Scapelli laughed and waved us down the line with his spoon.

Once seated in the center row of pine benches and tables with clear plastic tablecloths, I saw Straderman stroll out of the kitchen. He pointed a teasing finger at Scapelli, picked up a tray, and started down the line.

Reminded of the scene at the screened door, I asked Bill between bites of meat loaf why he had made such a big deal out of it.

"For crying out loud," he said. "He's only been a captain for two months. Besides, he's first-tour, just like you and me."

"How do you know?"

"Shockley told me. I got the scoop on this guy, R.T." Bill slurped a pear half into his mouth.

"Well?" I asked, taking a bite of stale bread.

"Well, he's a zero. You remember the story we heard back in flight school about the guy who shot himself in the foot playing 'quick-draw' at the rock-quarry?"

"That's him? Orndorff?"

"That's him. Shot the pinky toe off his right foot. That kept him in Pensacola and out of Vietnam for another six months. And that's not all."

I cut another piece of meat. "He had the toe bronzed and he wears it around his neck."

Bill looked at me in disgust, a load of cabbage halfway to his mouth and dripping cabbage juice all over the bread on the edge of his plate. "No, asshole. Do you want to hear this story or what?"

I smiled and nodded, chewing my meat loaf.

Bill shoveled the cabbage into his mouth, chewed twice, and swallowed. "So he gets to New River for transition to the Huey, finishes that, but instead of orders overseas, he gets assigned as a 'gopher' on some air group staff—another six-month delay."

I took a drink of the warm Kool-aid known as "bug-juice," swatted a fly away from my cabbage, and noticed Straderman had sat at a table in front of us. "So, then he gets to 'Nam, right?"

"Yeah, but get this: the night his plane landed at Da Nang, the out-of-town gooners decided they had too many rockets in their inventory so they fired a few at the lights of the big city. Sidney is asleep in the back of a six-by waiting for a ride to Freedom Hill when the first one lands in a ditch below his feet." Bill stabbed his fork into my last piece of meat, popped it in his mouth, and mumbled, "Guess-wha-appened?"

I watched my meal slide behind his bobbing Adam's apple and wiped my mouth with my paper napkin. "It killed him and now he's back from the dead as an administrative officer—to haunt us."

"Not exactly. Oh, he's here to haunt us alright—he's alive, he's a captain, and he's in our squadron; but now he's missing...*both* pinky toes!" Bill threw his head back and laughed so hard even Straderman turned around. "Is that a hoot, or what—*both* of 'em!"

I laughed with him. Even the guys at the tables around us laughed. They had no idea what was so funny, but Bill laughing and pounding on the table so hard the silverware jumped off his tray was enough to draw them in.

"Wait," Bill said, trying to catch his breath. "There's more." He coughed into his fist, cleared his throat, and grimaced as he swallowed whatever it was he had coughed up. "Okay...now get this: he gets out of the hospital at Da Nang and finally shows up here at the squadron. Well, on his first flight, hell, the *first mission* of his first flight, they have an engine failure and autorotate into a bamboo thicket near the Rockpile."

"Another toe lost?"

"No-no. No, the asshole still has..." He looked at the ceiling as if to do some difficult mathematical calculations. "oh...*eight* toes!" He bent over again, laughing, pushing his tray away so he could pound his head on the table.

I pushed him on the shoulder. "So he didn't lose another toe?"

Bill sat up, tears running down his cheeks. "No, not this time." He wiped his mouth and eyes on his sleeve. "This time...this time a sliver of bamboo comes up through the cockpit and takes off his left pinky *finger*! Can you believe that?" He threw his head back, put his face in his hands and laughed again, muffling it with his hands, then screamed, "Shockley calls him the 'Incredible Shrinking Man.' Ahhhhhhh God, I love it!"

His laugh turned into a coughing spasm, but he recovered quickly, cleared his throat, and said, "By that time, the guy's been in Vietnam eight days and has two Purple Hearts without ever completing a combat mission. Enviable record, wouldn't you say?"

I shook my head. "Then there was another recovery period, right?"

"Yep, and it continues to this day. The finger is healed, but Sidney has decided he was not meant to be a combat pilot."

"He doesn't fly?"

"Oh, he flies alright. He still gets his flight pay from the taxpayers just like you and me, but the difference is he doesn't earn it—local bounce pattern only—five hours a month. Actually Shockley doesn't think he flies even that much. He thinks the five hours is mostly pencil time."

"Well, with two Purple Hearts he could be gone anyhow, right?"

"Nope. Need three. He wouldn't go home even with three though—needs this combat tour for his career. He's a lifer."

I stabbed my fork at a stray shred of cabbage and shook my head. "How come the CO puts up with this? Don't we need every pilot we've got?"

"Yeah, we do, but Shockley says the guy is a bureaucratic masterpiece. He's made himself indispensable to the CO—does everything for him. Runs his parades, does all his paper work, even kisses his ass to keep it shiny. Mickey can't afford to make him fly—too much to do on the ground."

Bill looked at his plate, over to his plastic glass, and finally at my glass. "Tell you what, Ross, I'll get us some more mystery-meat if you'll get the bug-juice."

I stood, holding my glass, knowing full well what he was up to. Stepping over the bench, I snatched the glass from his outstretched hand. "I'll get your bug-juice, asshole. Hold the mystery meat."

"Ah. You don't want any? Well, hell, I'll pass too then. Hey, as long as you're up, get me some of that butterscotch pudding, will ya?"

I walked to the chow line and called to Scapelli as he carried the last of the pudding to the kitchen. He returned the tray to the counter for me and I scraped the edges. "So what's the story, Scapelli, how'd you end up on mess duty?"

He leaned against the counter, pushed the soiled utility cover to the back of his head, and shoved his hands into his pockets. "Actually, sir, I was supposed to start yesterday. But I thought I'd be clever, get myself on the flight schedule and have an excuse to delay it—the old 'duty calls,' or 'needs of the Corps' ploy."

"Almost delayed it forever, huh?"

"Yes, sir, I—" He snapped his head toward Sergeant Rappo as Rappo burst through the double doors from the kitchen. Yanking his hands out of his pockets, Scapelli snapped his head back to me. "Say, Lieutenant. There's more of that in the kitchen—some cake to go with it too. Want some, sir?"

"Yeah, but—"

"No problem, sir. I'll bring it out to ya."

Before I could say anything, he had snatched the tray out from under my spoon and marched toward the kitchen. Pausing in front of Rappo, he shrugged, nodded in my direction, and continued through the doorway. Rappo looked at me, stared behind me for a second toward Bill, then without changing expression, disappeared into the kitchen.

I returned to the table with a bowl and a half of pudding.

"Is this it?" Bill asked. "Where's the bug-juice?"

"Hold your horses, cabbage-breath. You can feed on this while I'm getting it."

The bug-juice dispensers, both nearly empty, rested on a table in the corner of the room. I tilted them on their front edge and slowly filled two glasses.

When I returned, Scapelli, Bill, and Straderman all sat together around the table, laughing and slurping the pudding. The last of the other mess-hall patrons had finished and filed out the rear screened door. A bowl of pudding and a piece of white cake were at my place on the table.

Scapelli pointed at Straderman as I slid onto the slick pine bench. "Lieutenant, you know Corporal Straderman, don't you, sir? He's a buddy of mine." Tall, thin, serious Straderman looked at me and did something I'd never seen him do before—smile.

"Of course. How you doin', Corporal Straderman?"

"Fine, sir." Straderman returned my nod. "Lieutenant Catlett tells us you two didn't get along too well with our Captain Orndorff."

I turned to Bill. He had that "I'm guilty, but I don't give-a-shit" look on his face; it's the same as the freckled fun-fun look but with more pronounced dimples.

"Cat?"

"What? I just told 'em about him whining to us about the bonds, that's all."

Scapelli leaned forward. "Yeah, and the lieutenant backin' him down too. That was great, sir. Then what happened?"

Bill glanced at me. "Oh, nothing. We have an appointment with him this afternoon to *rediscuss* the issue."

"There's an easy solution to the problem, you know, sir." Straderman, sipping a cup of coffee, had a conspiratorial gleam in his eye.

"Yeah?" Bill asked, grinning.

"Yes, sir." Straderman turned to me. "I heard what you did for Scapelli, Lieutenant—trying to find him and all." He laughed, "Even though you almost killed him in the process, I think I can return the favor."

"Whoa!" Bill threw up his hands. "What's this about almost killing Scapelli? Major Hardy never mentioned that in his glowing description of your heroic actions under fire."

"What heroic actions?" I said. "I didn't do anything heroic, nor did I nearly kill Scapelli. I don't think."

Scapelli laughed, laid his forearms on the table, and leaned toward me. "Ah, Lieutenant, do you remember firing a shot from your .38?"

Uh-oh. I wrinkled my brow. "I'm afraid I do. How close was it?"

Scapelli laughed and elbowed Straderman. "It was close enough, sir."

"Shit, I'm sorry, really. The damn thing went off when I dropped to the ground—shouldn't have had my finger on the trigger I guess. I never saw you. Were you close?"

"I was in the bushes about twenty yards away."

Bill held out his arm and said, "Wait a minute. I still don't understand how you got away from the rest of 'em in the first place."

"Yeah, I haven't heard that part of it either," Straderman said.

Scapelli pulled the cover down to his eyebrows and flicked a crumb off the table top. "Well, as long as we're in the 'true confessions' phase of this heroic story, I'll tell ya. But it can't leave this table 'cause I failed to mention it on the after-action report."

Everyone said, "Sure, no problem," and Bill crossed his fingers on his lap.

"Okay. We're spinning out of the sky, right? We bounce and I'm holding on to the quick-release on my lap-belt so I can unbuckle and haul-ass away from the bird when it stops." Scapelli paused and looked at each of us to make sure we were tuned in.

"Well, the second bounce must have yanked me sideways and jerked my hand with the quick-release handle in it 'cause the next thing I knew, I was airborne. I curled up in a ball and went through some bushes before hitting the ground. That kinda knocked the wind out of me—dazed me or whatever. Just before I passed out, I remember hearing people running through the bushes in front of me and thinking they didn't sound familiar—definitely not ours. Then things went black.

"When I came to, I was soaked with sweat and everything was quiet. I started crawling in the direction I was facing, but after a few yards, realized I was going downhill and probably away from the bird. When I turned around I heard the shit hit the fan from where you guys must have been."

He wiped the table with his hand. "I tell you, Lieutenant. I never heard anything prettier than that M-60. That meant at least one of you guys was alive and I wasn't by myself. Man, that was a relief."

I nodded.

"Anyhow, I got all excited but somebody moved in the bushes around me again, so I hunkered down. Every time the M-60 fired a burst I'd use the noise as cover—I'd throw some more leaves over me. Then one of'em got so close I couldn't even do that. Those little fuckers stink, you know that?"

He looked at each of us in turn and we nodded as though we knew exactly what he was talking about.

"Did you see the OV-10?" I asked. "Or the Huey?"

"Never saw the OV—bushes too thick. Heard him though. I think that's when the gooks took off."

"Scapelli!" Sergeant Rappo stood at the counter with his hands on his hips and a cigarette hanging out of the corner of his mouth. Behind him, two Marines in T-shirts mopped the floor.

"Uh-oh. Be right back." Scapelli threw his legs over the bench and marched toward the sergeant.

Bill hopped up. "Maybe I can help."

Straderman and I watched as the sergeant launched into a furious, one-sided conversation with the PFC.

Joining them before Scapelli had a chance to respond, Bill flashed his smile, held his arms out to his sides and spoke to the sergeant. Rappo folded his arms across his soiled chest.

Bill pointed at me and Rappo cocked his head to one side, looking right at me. I nodded and smiled and wondered who I was supposed to be this time. In the past Bill had gotten himself out of jams by describing me as everything from a general's aide to the son of the Venezuelan ambassador. My high school Spanish almost didn't survive that one.

Rappo's arms fell to his sides. He raised his right hand with all five stubby fingers extended, and I read his lips as he said, "Five minutes."

Bill waved Scapelli back toward our table and said, "Thanks, Sergeant," over his shoulder.

Scapelli slid onto the bench beside Straderman and asked, "No shit, Lieutenant, you up for the Medal of Honor?"

I looked at Bill as he slid in beside me. "*Medal of Honor*?"

Bill's eyes darted toward the kitchen where Rappo had paused in the doorway to watch us. "Play along, R.T., you're a fucking hero. Smile heroically. Say heroic things."

I looked at Scapelli and Straderman. "No. No Medal Of Honor. My friend here has an imagination almost as large as his ego." I nodded at Scapelli. "Now, back to the part where I almost killed you."

Scapelli smiled and lightly thumped the table with his fist. "Yeah, the good part." He leaned closer. "So after the gooks moved away from me, I thought I heard someone calling. It could've been a gooner trick, so I laid low another minute or so. Then, wham-o, I heard you scream my name. I knew that had to be you 'cause I would've recognized Droopy's voice or the major's. Well, I had eased into a push-up position to look for you when I heard a shot and a limb splintered over my head. I dropped flat to the ground and got all confused again. I never saw you, but the shot came from the direction of the scream, so I thought maybe you saw me and thought I was a gook. I didn't know what to do then. I was afraid to call out 'cause of the gooks in the area—I still can't believe you called out like that."

"Yeah, well I have a hard time believing that myself. I was getting a little desperate, I guess."

"Well, I finally decided I'd crawl closer so I could call out without yelling." He laughed. "I would have made a white flag, but I wasn't wearing anything white!"

I looked down at my bowl and scraped some pudding onto my spoon. "I'm afraid I'd given up on you by then."

"It's okay, Lieutenant. I should've had the balls to holler back at you after the shot. Worked out okay anyhow, sir."

I looked up. "Yeah, I guess it did, but still...how come you didn't get on the Huey when it landed?"

Scapelli shook his head. "I didn't know what was happening. I couldn't see shit through those bushes. By the time I'd crawled close enough to see some daylight, all hell had broken loose and rounds were flying everywhere. I heard the Huey, and was crawling toward the sound as fast as I could, but didn't see it until it was lifting." He put his elbows on the table and rested his cheeks in his hands. "Man, that was a bummer. I hit rock bottom then."

Bill stared at his glass and turned it around and around with his fingers. Straderman had his forearms on the table and turned a spoon in his hands. Neither touched their cake.

I had a sudden thought. "Damn, you must have been pretty near our Huey when it blew!"

His head popped up out of his hands. "Oh, yeah. That nearly did me in too. The rounds from that gunner were hitting all around me, so I spun on my belly and took off back into the bushes. I was setting a new land speed record for the belly-crawl when that hummer blew—singed my butt."

"Scapelli!"

"Oh, shit. Time's up." He threw his legs over the bench and sprang toward the kitchen. "Later, sir."

The three of us watched Scapelli jog past the critical eye of Sergeant Rappo and through the kitchen door.

Bill took a sip of bug-juice and shook his head. "I still haven't heard how he was found. The major just said they went back in the sniffer bird and got him."

Straderman put his spoon down, looked at Bill and smiled. "I can tell you what he told us, sir. I don't know if you should believe it though."

"Hey, we're FNGs—we'll believe anything."

Straderman scooted closer to the table and leaned on his forearms. "Well, according to Vegas, it went something like this: He crawled back down the hill until he came to a trail. He figures it was the trail the gooners had been on when he first heard them running. He followed it until he came to a small clearing under some tall bush—tall enough to stand under. There he found four sets of packs and equipment by an extinguished cooking fire."

Straderman paused, took another sip of coffee, and added, "This is the part where he usually says, 'This is no shit…there I was…'"

"Uh-oh," Bill said, "bullshit alert."

"Anyhow, he says he hid in the bushes with his K-bar fighting knife, and when they came back to get their gear he slit their throats. They conveniently came back one at a time."

Bill punched me in the shoulder. "Well, hell. I believe that! You believe that don't you, R.T.?"

I swallowed my last spoonful of pudding. "If you believe it, Cat, I believe it, 'cause if he was shittin' us, you'd see right through it. Can't shit a shitter, right?"

"That's a fact." He turned to Straderman. "Then what?"

Straderman stood and straddled the bench as he gathered the glasses and dishes onto the tray Scapelli had left on the table. "Well—" He paused as we stood and placed our dishes on the tray. "—he said he was drinking water from their canteens when he heard the sniffer package. He waited until one of the guns made a low pass, then he ran into a clearing waving his T-shirt. Rinkes, the gunner in the low gunship, recognized him, and the rest, as they say, sir, is history."

"You really believe that?" Bill asked.

Straderman slid the tray to the end of the table, stepped over the bench, and walked around to the tray. "Yes, sir." He chuckled. "Well, some of it anyhow. He had to have gotten that NVA canteen he brought back in his flightsuit from somewhere."

"No shit. A canteen, huh? Here, let me get that." Bill grabbed the tray from Straderman. "Tell Lieutenant Teemer what you meant by helping him with Orndorff. I'll take this to the kitchen—need to talk to Rappo anyhow." He leaned to me and in a coarse whisper added, "Get the gouge from this guy, R.T. It's bad enough we've got to fight this chicken-shit war—we shouldn't have to finance it as well."

Bill turned and smiled at Straderman while he held the tray with one hand and popped his aviator sunglasses over his eyes with the other. In the role of the Hollywood busboy, he balanced the tray over his shoulder with one hand and took off for the kitchen, exaggerating an erect posture and long stride. Straderman and I walked toward the side door by the bug-juice dispensers.

"He's trying to get you guys to start an allotment for savings bonds, right sir?"

"Yeah. Vehemently trying."

"Well, if we're 100% enrolled in the program, it makes the captain look good to the CO, the CO look good to the group CO, the group CO look good to the wing CO, etc. Then it works back down and finally, the captain gets an 'attaboy' on his fitness report."

"Who's looking out for the individual Marine, the guy who's losing money on his savings?"

"I don't know. Nobody I guess. Major Angus is worse than Captain Orndorff, so he's no help. Major Hardy had the right approach, but he's gone. He kinda held the captain in check when he was here."

"Hardy didn't push bonds?"

"Not unless the Marine didn't have any savings program at all. Even then he only encouraged it. He didn't jam it down his throat."

We were through the screened door. I let it shut behind me and drew my cover from my calf pocket.

"Lieutenant?" Straderman put his utility cover on his head and reached for the sunglasses stuck in his breast pocket.

"Yeah?"

"Just go ahead and sign those papers this afternoon. Then come back to see me in a few days. Tell me to cancel your allotment when you come back and I'll take care of it."

"Okay, but won't the captain have to sign that too?"

"Someone will have to sign it, but I'll make sure it's not the captain or Major Angus." He smiled. "Trust me, sir." I returned his salute and watched him trudge through the sand toward the main road to the squadron building.

A minute later, I walked toward the kitchen looking for two oranges. If Tess was writing the schedule for the next day, and I was going to have to fly with a field grade, I wanted to make sure it wasn't that weirdo Major Pyhr. Oranges weren't much of a bribe, but they were all I had.

11

Funeral Pyhr

An hour before dawn the next morning, in flightsuit and pistol belt and still wondering how I'd gotten scheduled with Pyhr, I stepped from our hootch into the heavy night air and stopped. I heard footsteps. The outline of a man appeared—baggy clothes, walking briskly, his small shoulders drooped and his head and neck protruding forward like a vulture in a utility cover. Like Rod Wysowski. I squatted against a sandbag wall.

"Morning, asshole," I said, rising from the shadows.

"Shit!" Rod leaped off the sidewalk, landed in a judo stance, and lunged for my throat. "Goddamn it, Teemer! You scared the shit out of me!"

Laughing, I fought off his hands. "Easy, Rodney. I was just saying good morning."

"Well, don't say good morning to me ever again, damn it. Especially after last night. Shit!"

He pushed me down the sidewalk and we walked toward the main road, adjusting our covers, his breathing still rapid.

"So what happened last night? Why you so touchy?"

"Shockley stories. At the club. Where the hell were you?"

"I was in the hootch. Reading, I guess. What'd I miss?"

We turned onto the darkened road and a jeep full of men in flightsuits bounced past us toward the mess hall.

"Shockley told us about the night a bunch of Viet Cong sappers got through the wire here. Blew up a bunch of birds an' shit. Including a hootch."

"Anybody hurt?"

"Nope. Not in the hootch anyhow. Shockley said it was a hootch for medical officers and chaplains. All of 'em were on shopping trips to Hong Kong or Bangkok at the time, so the VC got a big bang, but no kills."

I stepped to the side of the road as another jeep rolled by. "When did all this happen?"

"'67 I think he said. Most of the damage was on the flight line." Rod kicked a rock and laughed. "You remember how our flight instructors would talk about that Alpha model 46, how the ass end would fall off in flight and kill everybody? Well, Shockley said after the attack, the 46 guys awarded the VC sappers the Marine Corps Life-Saving Medal for destroying eight of their birds. They hated that piece of shit."

"The 'Flying Claymore,'" I said.

"Yeah, a fucking anti-personnel mine with rotor blades." Rod laughed again. "And get this. When they were policing up the bodies, they found one of the base barbers among the VC."

"Really?"

"No shit. Nguyen-the-barber, second chair on the right."

"Damn. I just got a haircut yesterday—second chair on the right—and the guy's name tag said 'Nguyen' something."

"Hell, Ross, half the gooks in this country are named 'Nguyen.'" In the dim light from the street light behind us, I could see his cheeks drawn up in a look of disgust. "Couldn't be the same guy anyhow. He was waxed, remember?"

I heard footsteps and turned. B-12 and Henstrom, the crew that would fly wingman for the major and me, followed behind us.

At the sidewalk to the officers' wing of the mess hall, Rod and I slowed, waiting for them to join us. The florescent light shining through the screens of the mess hall lit their faces.

Inside, after side-stepping down the serving line, B-12 picked out a table in the corner. Henstrom and I followed while Rod, scheduled as Major Lewis' co-pilot, sat at a table with their wingman, Teach and Gamez.

A few minutes later—over the conversations, shuffling feet, and clinking dishes in the room—I asked my silent table mates, "Where is he?"

B-12 looked toward the door and swallowed a piece of toast. "Any minute now."

I slipped my fork into my last hunk of scrambled eggs. Henstrom, blond head lowered, pushed his remaining eggs around with his toast.

"Myron?" I asked.

"Yeah," he said, without looking at me.

"Any advice on flying with Pyhr?"

"Yeah." He reached for his cup of coffee. "Don't fuck up."

I watched him a second to see if he would smile. He didn't. The screened door squeaked and I looked up in time to see Major Pyhr and Major Lewis enter.

Over the heads of a roomful of bustling men in flightsuits, I watched Pyhr go straight to the coffee urns. Major Lewis, or "Sweet Lou" as Tess called him, picked up a tray, greeted the Vietnamese waitress, and started down the serving line.

With a hand full of toast and an over-filled cup of black coffee, Major Pyhr sat next to B-12 and across the table from Henstrom and me. He dropped the toast on the checkered tablecloth, took a slurp of his coffee, and reached to the calf pocket of his flightsuit.

My chest tightened. He was going for his kneeboard, and I didn't have mine. B-12 reached into his breast pocket. Henstrom his. I remembered yesterday's flight schedule. The three of us withdrew folded paper from our breast pockets and ballpoint pens from our sleeve pockets at the same time, like it was rehearsed.

Pyhr curled his lip and nodded his approval. He laid the kneeboard on the table, stabbed a pencil into the small spring on top, and reached into his sleeve pocket.

The Zippo lid snapped shut, and Pyhr withdrew the filtered cigarette from his mouth with a sucking sound. His black eyes, deep-set and shrouded by drooping eyelids, never left my own. He blew the smoke into his coffee cup and tapped the writing on his kneeboard. A cigarette ash splattered onto the page.

"Lieutenant Teemer," he said, in a high-pitched whine, his eyes pressing me.

"Yes, sir."

"Didn't I hear you say yesterday…that you were shot down in the 1-1-6-3 grid?"

Somehow that didn't sound right, but my training made me hesitate to say "no" to a major. Besides, I really wasn't sure why it didn't sound right. As the major continued to stare at me and I realized I had to say something, I answered, "Yes, sir. We did go down in the 1-1-6-3 grid."

He eased toward me and suddenly his eyes narrowed, his huge nostrils flared, and spittle sprayed into my face. "Then why the fuck didn't I find Lima 1-4 and the 'Dead-Eye Gooner' there yesterday, *Lieutenant*?"

My chest tightened another notch. "I—I guess 'cause Lima 1-4 was operating in the 0-8-6-5 grid, sir. That's where we were hit. We made it a few clicks towards Dong Ha, the 1-1-6-3 grid, before the tail rotor came off and we went down."

He leaned even closer, sliding on his forearms. The twisting plume of smoke rising from the cigarette between his yellow-stained fingers disintegrated. "Then, *Lieutenant*, why didn't you goddamn tell me that yesterday? Huh?!"

I flinched, feeling the spray on my face, my eyes widening at his stupidity, amazed that one officer would speak to another officer like that, amazed that he would assume some sinister plot against him by me, someone who didn't even know him. I glanced at the paper in front of me, the heat building on the back of my neck. Henstrom and B-12 shifted in their seats. Even the conversation at the table behind us stopped.

"I'm sorry, sir. When I was asked where the bird went down, I answered as accurately as I could. I'm sorry I didn't anticipate you wanted to know where we were hit."

"Sorry is right, *Lieutenant*. You were goddamn sorry. And because you were so goddamn sorry, I spent my valuable time and the taxpayers' valuable dollars searching the 1-1-6-3 for gooks and a grunt unit that were miles away!"

My hand squeezed around my fork and my mouth opened, but the major slid back to an erect posture and turned to B-12.

"Since when are you a HAC, Brunnengarber?"

B-12 cleared his throat. "Yesterday, sir. Check ride with Lieutenant Ono."

"Think you can cover my ass today?"

"Yes, sir."

"You better." The major pulled his kneeboard closer. "What's your number?" He pulled the pencil from the spring across its top.

"Hardball 2-5, sir."

"Okay 2-5, I'm 1-9, so today you're '1-9 Dash Two.' We're goin' early—turn at 0600. Ground check on 42.5 fox and 268.5 UHF. After that, stay off the radios. Can you do that?"

"Yes, sir."

The major crushed his cigarette into the remaining piece of toast, put his hands on the table, and stood. "Okay, Marines. Let's go get some gooks."

The turn up, taxi for refuel, taxi for takeoff, and departure were a nightmarish reversal from my flight with Major Hardy. No checklists. No crew-coordination with me or the crew in the cabin. Pyhr's only words were curt commands to change radio frequencies. I had them memorized.

Forty-five minutes after take-off, and following a low-level flight up Highway One that left at least one Vietnamese couple cowering in an algae-covered ditch—their market bundles abandoned on the road—we crossed the Hieu Giang River into Leatherneck Square and made a beeline for the 0-8-6-5 grid. Dong Ha DASC, the Direct Air Support Center and controlling agency for missions and aircraft in the area, was not consulted. As far as they knew, the gunships they needed to run mission 55 had not yet arrived.

Without a word from Pyhr, I withdrew the Cam Lo, 1:50,000, map sheet from my packet, and folded it with the 0-8-6-5 grid square in the center. I turned it slowly to the right until it was oriented to the northwest heading we were on, and picked out terrain features ahead of us and found them on the map.

We had cruise-climbed to 1500 feet and leveled off at 90 knots when I found the valley I needed. The valley floor, vibrant green and thick with jungle trees, concealed a high-speed trail. Thanks to bomb craters accumulated over the years, I could pick out an outline of the trail already, but finding the trail intersection I needed and the target Major Hardy and I had shot at was going to be more difficult. I re-adjusted my map to our heading and looked for two streams.

Now only a click away from where I expected to find the trail intersection, the ICS keyed and I tensed.

"Well, *Lieutenant*?"

"We're almost there, sir. The trail below us, on the heading we're on now, is the main trail."

"Gimme 39.25."

"Roger." I switched the fox-mike, or FM radio, to 39.25, and heard him call B-12 on the UHF radio at the same time.

"Balls 1-9 Dash Two, this is 1-9. Go Jack Benny plus two-bits."

Over the tone in my headset—the FM radio adjusting itself to the new frequency—I heard B-12 respond to the major's command by keying his UHF transmission switch two times, or "two-clicks," confirming he had heard the command and was complying. B-12 was indeed staying off the radios.

A second later, the tone in my headset stopped and I heard B-12 check-in with, "Two's up."

The major switched to FM. "Lima 1-4, Hardball 1-9, over."

Off to our right, two small streams converged to form a larger stream that ran due north into the DMZ. I knew our target had been due south of that stream junction, so we were over the trail intersection but couldn't see it. If I were flying, I would have banked to the left, then reversed to the right to put the intersection, identified only by a unique pattern of concentrated bomb craters, in the center of a right-hand orbit.

"We should be right over it, sir."

"*Should be*?"

"Yes, sir." I wanted him to fly to the side of the spot we were over, so I could pick out the burned area made by Major Hardy's white phosphorus, or "willie pete," rockets. But how could I do that without sounding like I was telling him what to do?

"Lima 1-4, Balls 1-9, over." He looked out his window to the ground, and turned right. The radios hissed.

"Lima 1-4, Hardball 1-9! Answer the phone, goddamn it!"

I stretched my neck, looking around him, looking for the landmark I needed. I pointed. "Three o'clock, sir—a scorched spot beside a clump of bomb craters. The grunts had us shooting there, but the gooner that nailed us was about 100 meters southwest."

Pyhr yanked the Huey harder to the right, leveled off without completing the circle, and dove northwest, straight for a southern turn in the DMZ.

I had no idea what he was up to, but all my training and all my instincts were telling me it was wrong. If we were going to make runs on the target area, I was taught to roll in from over the friendlies, and pull off over the friendlies *after* finding out where the friendlies were. Three days ago all the friendlies were south and east. We were heading northwest. I was taught to keep the sun behind me when possible. The sun was barely up to the east. If we were going to come back to the target, we were going to be flying into the sun, not with the sun to our backs. I looked at my map. The large river I could see in the valley ahead was the Ben Hai.

Approaching the edge of the DMZ, flying at 110 knots and in a 1000-feet-per-minute rate of descent, we passed through 800 feet and the major yanked us right again.

"Put me over that scorched spot!"

"Yes, sir."

I leaned out of my armored seat to look around him, straining to pick up the bomb craters or something that would lead me back to the target area. All I saw was a problem: a boot-shaped ridgeline between us and the valley floor.

He continued the turn and descent, 115 knots, the aircraft shuddering from a genetic one-to-one vertical beat. We passed 500 feet on our radar altimeter, the one reading actual height above the ground. Now 300 feet.

I glanced at my map, guessing where the target would be based on our heading and the shape of the ground below us, and pointed as I realized the brush-covered high ground, the top of the foot of the boot-shaped ridge, would be directly in our path to the target. "One o'clock, sir."

Pyhr snapped us wings-level, raised the nose slightly to break our rate of descent, then jerked some pitch on the collective to keep up the air speed.

I sensed a problem. A red light flashed and a warning beep went off in my headset—low rotor RPM. Pyhr's head jerked up and down from the horizon to the instrument panel, his eyes wide. Too much pitch, you asshole! He reduced collective and the RPM needle climbed, returning to the green arc. The horn and light went off. We were now off course.

"One o'clock, sir."

He jerked us ten degrees right.

Passing through 100 feet on the radar altimeter, we darted into the blackness of the shadows from the boot-shaped ridgeline. The tallest part of the ridge, the leg part of the boot, was to our left—a steep slope of grass, ferns, and gray rock that was crowned with tall, top-heavy jungle trees. 110 knots. Deep in shadows, we flew toward the top of the foot.

"A heading parallel to the treeline to our left will take us right to it, sir. Just on the other side of this ridge."

"Make me hot. Rockets."

"Yes, sir." I set up the switches.

As the ground rose before us, he hugged the tree line to our left and the radar altimeter continued to fall. Thirty feet. I couldn't decide if he just didn't want to pull the nose up and acknowledge he'd gotten us in a crack or whether he really believed the ground would run out of altitude before we did. I caught myself on the edge of my seat, extended in my straps, and forced myself to sit back and lock my harness. Twenty feet.

Trees flashed by—huge trees, the trunks beside me, limbs above. I wanted to look, but I couldn't take my eyes away from the spot on the hill, the spot where we were going to hit. It was either that or climb, and with the jungle canopy hanging over us, that wasn't such a hot idea either. I gripped the armored panels at my hips. Ten feet.

The green hill came fast, then faster. He pulled pitch, but it was too little too late. I braced. We hit. Our skids and underbelly slashed through the thick bushes with the sound of a speeding car leaving an asphalt road onto gravel. At the same time, we shot from the shadows and my eyes were slam-dunked by the brilliant white light on our bug-smeared, scratched, and weathered windscreen.

I sucked in my breath and squinted at the vertical speed indicator. It jumped as I was pressed into my seat. He had pulled a lot of pitch and we were climbing. Break right, asshole, now!

Cracks, like gunshots, split the air by my left ear. The Huey jumped. Thumps in the back. The low-RPM warning horn blasted from my earphones again and I twisted my head, away from the blinding light filtering through my eyelids, then cracked my eyes to find us skimming the top of a lush-green jungle in a slight left turn, bathed in brilliant white sunlight, the warning horn suddenly silent but with a scream—an adrenaline rush—swelling inside me. I squeezed it back.

"Goddamn it! God-damn, fuck!"

With sunlight sparkling on the spittle spraying from his mouth, his teeth bared, the major screamed at the world, and I looked away, turning to the engine instruments, to the gauges. All were good. The Huey had slowed but held altitude in spite of a more pronounced vertical beat. I checked over my shoulder.

Leaves and twigs swirled around the cabin. The gunner, half hidden under a pile of leaf-laden tree branches, was slumped and limp. The crew chief, Corporal Earley, the guy with the Errol Flynn mustache, crouched on the deck in front of the gunner and pulled branches off his head.

"Where's that fuckin' scorched spot?"

I turned and stiffened. Pyhr stared at me. Hate poured from his eyes and spittle hung from his mouth and lip mike.

"Two o'clock, sir." I pointed to our right. "If you'll turn back toward those bomb craters, we'll pick it up."

He jerked away, yanking the Huey to the right, and I was left looking at the back of his scratched and scarred helmet.

"I've got it, goddamn it. One o'clock."

The shortest distance between where we were and the last known location of the Dead-Eye Gooner was to go straight to a point 100 meters southwest of the scorched spot, flying with the sun lighting our windshield. That's what he did.

I glanced over my shoulder again and Earley, standing over the gunner, gave me an "okay" sign.

I looked ahead, tightened my chin strap another notch as Major Pyhr tried to get more air speed out of the crippled Huey. Didn't work. Every time he got it over 80 knots, the violent vertical beat ripped the controls out of his hands.

Pyhr didn't notice. We dropped to bush-top level at 70 knots, found the scorched spot, and flew over the Dead-Eye Gooner's last known location—three times. If Pyhr wanted Mr. Dead-Eye to expose his location by shooting us down, it seemed like a foolproof plan to me.

But it wasn't. By 0735 we were low on fuel and had to give it up. Pyhr, cursing God, the gooner, and me, turned us toward Vandegrift Combat Base, "Vandy."

On our way to Vandy, eight miles to our southwest, Pyhr checked in with DASC, explaining we were delayed en route with radio problems. Without further questioning, they assigned us to escort two CH-46s on resupply missions out of the Vandy LSA, the "Logistical Support Area."

Vandy LSA said the 46s were resupplying some of the more secure zones without us and we were cleared to refuel.

Approaching the Rockpile and the valley that led south to Vandy and the fuel pits, I wondered how many exhausted and thirsty Marines in unsecured zones were still without food, water, and maybe even ammo because we had tried to get ourselves shot at. And how effective were we going to be in protecting these 46s in a bird that bounced through the air like a car with square wheels would bounce down a street? How were we going to put rounds or rockets on target when the target was a bouncing blur?

I sighed, helmet pounding my head, and stared at the grass-covered valley before us. In four months, maybe even three, I'd be a HAC. It would be different then. I would be able to take care of those grunts and 46 pilots like Marine aviators are supposed to, like Major Hardy did, like he asked me to do. The frog drivers and the grunts, the guys with the dirtiest, most dangerous jobs in the Marine Corps, wouldn't have to wonder where I was. I would be there when they needed me.

To my right, Funeral Pyhr, his lip mike pulled down to his chin, a burning cigarette bobbing from his lips, flew on.

12

Sun Dog's Cherry

Adam Henstrom, his blond hair still wet from the shower, stopped me on my way into the head and said Tess was looking for me. Above us, from inside the water tank, Bill and a few others hollered at each other and occasionally a ball would splat against the rubber wall. Henstrom didn't know why Tess wanted to see me, so I thanked him and told him I'd find Tess after my shower. We parted as a loud, sharp splat brought a howl from Bill and hysterical laughter from the others. Bill screamed, "Didn't hurt. Go Hip, go!"

Inside the head, water sprayed off B-12 and Tom Gamez and over the concrete lip of the open-walled entrance to the shower area. I hung my towel on the nearest side wall and B-12, over the sound of rushing water, yelled, "There he is: the latest survivor of The Funeral Pyhr Thrill Show!"

When I stepped to the shower beside him, he held a bar of soap to my face, and asked, "Tell us, Lieutenant, what was it like out there today?"

I turned on the cool water, nodded to Gamez, and pointed at the soap. "Are we live, or is this to be broadcast later?"

B-12 turned to face an imaginary camera and held the soap to his mouth. "This is Dan Lather reporting *live* from a combat shower in a fiercely contested head very close to the DMZ. I'm here with the Marines. That's right. I'm just as brave, courageous, and bold as these guys, only I'm much smarter and more important. I'm a reporter."

"What's on your mind, Dan?" I asked.

"Fame. No, uh…let's see…oh, yeah. I asked about your mission today, Lieutenant. What was your body count?" B-12 stuck the soap in my face as Gamez—tall, on the gaunt side of thin, his brown hair a uniform stubble—stood on the other side and grinned through the fine mist.

I lathered my hands. "We started out with four bodies and, in spite of the efforts of our leader, we returned with four bodies."

"No, no, Lieutenant. How many did you *kill*?"

"He didn't kill any of us, this time." I let the stream hit my back and soaped my arms and shoulders.

"No, no, Lieutenant. How many of the *enemy* did you kill?"

"None of us killed him either, although we wanted to."

"No, no, no. Well…never mind. If you didn't kill anyone, you obviously don't have a body count. And if you don't have a body count, you're not worth the time of an important reporter like me." With his knuckles, B-12 made a rat-tat-tat noise on a water pipe while he faced the camera again. "This is your man on the scene, America. I'm Dan Lather, under heavy fire, with the Marines. Good night."

Gamez held his fist to his mouth. "This is Trusty Walter in New York. We know you're full of shit, Dan, but thank you anyhow for that report."

The three of us chuckled together as B-12 turned off his shower and sloshed toward his towel on the wall. "No shit, Teemer. What'd you think of Pyhr?"

I straightened, placed my soap in a tray, and stepped under the water. "I think he's nuts."

"You and everybody else," Gamez said, turning off his shower.

B-12 toweled his hair. "I thought you guys had bought it for sure when you hit those trees."

"Trees?" Gamez gave a short laugh. "You guys hit trees?"

"Yep." I turned off my water and sloshed to the wall.

"I don't suppose Pyhr told you what he was trying to prove flying that low," B-12 said.

"He didn't say shit."

"That figures." B-12 leaned against the edge of the side wall, his arms crossed over a bulldog chest. "My guess is he was trying to draw out that dead-eye gooner. Trolling."

Gamez joined us. "Was anybody hurt?"

"Yeah, the door gunner. Right, Teemer?"

"Yeah, but nothing serious." I dried my shoulders and arms. "He took some lumps from the limbs that flew in the cabin, but otherwise, he was okay."

B-12 saw Gamez's mouth fall open. "No shit, Tom. I joined up as close as I dared afterward—didn't want that crazy fucking Pyhr to see me. Saw Earley standing over some limbs trying to give the gunner a drink." He jerked his head back and laughed. "Henstrom and I were crackin' up. That damn Huey dribbled Earley around the cabin like he was a fucking basketball; that poor son-of-a-bitch was gettin' water everywhere but in the guy's mouth." He laughed again and turned toward the screened door. "Anyhow, I'm glad Pyhr didn't kill you. That would've been a hell of a note on my first HAC hop. See ya."

The door slammed and Gamez stepped beside me. Behind him the floor drain gurgled. He put his hands on the towel on his hips and asked, "Was the gunner really okay?"

"Yeah," I said. I laughed at the memory of those two guys in the cabin and wrapped the towel around my waist. "You ever flown with Corporal Earley?"

"Yeah, I think. The guy with the pencil line mustache?"

"Yeah."

"Yeah, I've flown with him."

I smiled. "Well, later in the flight, after we'd refueled and run a few resupply missions, I looked over my shoulder to check on him and the gunner. There on the ends of the troopseat, next to the M-60s, were two bushes with feet."

"What?"

"No lie. Those clowns had taken the leaves—they were huge leaves too, the length and width of, oh…a loaf of bread I guess. Anyhow, they had these leaves stuck into the pockets of their flightsuits, and their waist tabs, and boots, and even under the visors of their flight helmets. They were a riot. Camouflaged, just like the NVA—as if to say, 'They'll never see us now!'"

Gamez laughed, shaking his head.

Behind us, the screened door creaked. Rod Wysowski, in flightsuit and boots, was halfway into the head when a partially deflated volleyball plopped behind him, and a deep voice yelled, "Point!" Rod turned in the doorway as Bill answered, "*One* point! Nine-four, you." Another voice hollered, "Little help out there!"

Rod propped the door open with his foot, picked up the ball, and underhanded it in the air toward the top of the water tower. It fell with a splash, and the third voice yelled, "Gracias."

Rod walked in and saw us standing together by the shower area. "Hey, you guys. Got some news. Don't go away." He headed toward the urinals. "And Teemer, Tess is lookin' for you."

"I know. What for?"

"Didn't say. Wait a minute. Got to drain the dragon."

Gamez chuckled. "I've got some tweezers if you need any help finding it."

"Very funny, *Tex*."

I turned to Gamez. "Tex?"

"I made the mistake of telling him I was from Texas." He dismissed Rod with a wave of his hand and glanced toward the door. "So, other than the tree thing, quiet day up north, huh?"

I snapped the lid shut on my soap dish. "Yeah. It's a good thing too. Our bird was in bad shape. Hey Tom…is Pyhr always that lucky?"

"Yep." He glanced at the door. "The guy is a fuck-up looking for a place to happen and yet he always skates—not a scratch, not a court-martial, nothing."

I shook my head.

"Doesn't apply to his co-pilots or wingmen though. Ask Akerman or Tess."

"Wait a minute. Tess was flying wing on Pyhr when he was shot down?"

"That's a roger."

"And Akerman?"

"Took one through the calf muscle about two months ago. He's okay now."

"While flying with Pyhr?"

"Rog-o."

"Wow."

"Yeah, flying with him is like hanging a sign around your neck with a big bulls-eye on it."

Rod walked up with a strained look on his face and his hand in the lower zippered part of his flightsuit. "Almost didn't get that monster back in there. Damn, it's heavy."

"What's on your mind, Rodney?" I said.

Rod extracted his hand and zipped his flightsuit. "You see the list of Hardball numbers?"

"No."

"Well, it's out. We're officially Hardball pilots now—the shit hottest of the shit hotty. Major Lewis finished updating it when we got in this afternoon—*after* I smooth-talked him into doing it during our flight." Rod looked up at the ceiling. "The poor slob was putty in my hands."

I avoided Rod's eyes and looked at his breast pocket. "Okay, Mr. Smooth, let's see it."

Rod grinned. "Shit, I don't have it with me. It's back at the hootch."

"Well, what's my number?"

He laughed. "I don't know your number, asshole. Your number doesn't mean shit to me. *My* number is forty, four-dash-zero, 4-0. Good one, huh?"

"Well, it's got a zero in it. That's appropriate. How about Bill and Walt?"

"Walt is I-don't-know-either, twenty something. Bill is thirteen, 1-3."

Through the screened door, I heard Bill yell, "Ten-seven! Big rally, biiiiig rally!"

I frowned. "You sure?"

Rod had picked a bugger out of his nose and wiped it on his rolled-up sleeve. "Sure of what?"

"That Bill is thirteen."

"Hell yeah, I'm sure. So what?" Without giving me a chance to answer, he looked up at Gamez. "Hey, how 'bout that flight today, huh? Shit-hot or what?"

"Yeah, guns south is a good mission." He thumped a thick dark stain on Rod's flightsuit. "I see you enjoyed the ice cream at Marble Mountain."

Rod looked at his chest and laughed. "Yeah, I liked it so much I decided to wear it home. Ice cream! Can you believe that, Ross? Whoopee-aiy-ay, give me guns south, any day!" He backhanded me on the arm and headed toward the door. "See you guys at chow."

Tom and I followed, relaxed and slow.

"Ross. You and Catlett been friends long?" He stopped in the sunlight streaming through the window over the sink.

"Yeah. Since flight school. Why?"

"'Cause I think he's crazy, that's why—staying in that rack and all. I'd be moving."

"Well, he's not moving. He thinks the dead man's rack routine is superstitious bunk."

"It's not. The history of that rack is real." He crossed his thin arms, his deep-set eyes soft. "He's pushin' it, Ross. Now he's 'Hardball Thirteen,' you know?"

"Yeah, I know. But he's pretty stubborn. I don't think he'll move."

He looked away. "Did you know Pete Clemence?"

"No. Don't think so."

"He was in HML-567, the Huey squadron at Marble Mountain. Fraternity brother of mine at Texas. Our wives are good friends. Anyhow, we went to OCS together, then flight school, then New River, then here. He was killed two weeks ago."

"Oh. Sorry."

"Yeah. Well, anyhow, he always wore number thirteen—high school sports, intramural sports, whatever. Flaunted it. Even had it painted on the back of his flight helmet."

"Humm."

"And the day he was killed...he was in aircraft number thirteen."

"Damn."

He nodded. "Well, Pete was a great guy, lot of fun, but...he was kinda cavalier about the risks we take, you know? So, anyhow, I'd just suggest you keep your buddy Catlett from pushing his luck. With Thunder Clap and all the other shit we have to fly, why roll the dice more than we have to, you know?"

Outside the door, a loud splat rang against the tank wall, the deep voice yelled, "Game!" and Bill yelled, "Damn!" and someone slapped the water.

Tom smiled. "Sounds like Blue Dog is still undefeated. Catlett must have given him a good game though."

The screened door went dark with shadow, then flew open. Walt Duppont, wearing his white Naval Academy bathrobe, entered drying the side of his face with a green towel. Water dripped from his hair. "What the fuck is going on out there?"

He stomped around us as Tom sauntered backward toward the door. "It's called 'Pit Polo.' Two guys on a side and you play by invitation only—Blue Dog's game with Blue Dog's rules." He pushed the door open and nodded. "Later, Ross."

I nodded back. "See ya, Tom."

"Hey, Teemer." Walt was at the first urinal, relieving himself through the overlap of his bathrobe.

I looked out the door for Bill. "What?"

"Understand you tore up your bird today."

I sighed. "I didn't tear up anything."

He laughed and the familiar smirk appeared. "Right."

I glanced away and shook my head. "How'd your flight with Colonel Houser go?"

"What flight?" Head down, Walt worked his urine stream around the edges of the urinal. "I was scratched by Angus. He took it."

"Major Angus?"

Walt shook himself, backed away from the urinal, and walked toward the showers. "Major 'Bull' Angus to you, Lieutenant. Our esteemed executive officer."

I leaned against a sink. "But he's only been in country for four days."

"So?"

"So he's the one insisting all new guys go the full seven days before their first flight."

"Shit, Ross. You amaze me sometimes." He hung his bathrobe on a hook and took a plastic soap dish out of its pocket. "Angus is a major, the XO. He makes the rules, so he breaks the rules. That's life."

I faked a smile. "Of course. So how are you and Mickey Mantle getting along?"

Walt placed his soap dish under the showerhead and turned on the water. Facing the wall, he adjusted the spray against his chest, turned his head to the side, and said over the noise, "You can't be too friendly with the guy who writes your fitness report, Teemer. You'll learn."

I watched his head disappear in a sheet of spray and brought my hand to my chin, considering his teaching point: kiss up. Or, as I'd heard Walt say before, "Humor the bastards." Might work. Probably wouldn't. The Marine Corps of Colonel Chesty Puller, Major Joe Foss, and Gunnery Sergeant Daniel Daly probably wouldn't reward ass-kissing over performance. Captain K.D. Teemer wouldn't. He used to tell me, "Let your work speak for you." So to hell with Walt. He could do it his way, and I'd do it mine. We'd see. I pushed off the sink and walked away.

Outside the screened door, I found Bill, Blue Dog, and two other guys I recognized as Dog People standing on the sidewalk. Bill had his arms extended out to his sides. The rest of them, all in red PT shorts, all soaking wet, and all standing in puddles of water, were in front of Bill studying his chest.

"Does it hurt?" asked the one I knew as Hippy Dog.

"Shit, no."

"Well it's a good lick," said the guy I didn't know, a short chunky guy covered in thick black body hair.

"It will heal," said Blue Dog.

"Of course it will heal. Shit. This thing will be gone by morning." Bill put his arms down. "It's nothin'."

"What's goin' on, Cat?" I said, approaching the group.

Bill grabbed my arm and pulled me into his circle of wet friends. "Hey, R.T. Check out my chest, man." He threw his arms out to his sides again and swelled his muscled chest. "How 'bout, 'The Mark of the Blue Dog,' huh?"

I stood in front of him, holding my head back. Dead center on Bill's chest, right between his nipples, and glowing against his light, freckled skin, was a circular red spot the size of a volleyball, probably a slightly deflated volleyball. The spot throbbed.

"Good hit," I said.

"Yeah, but I stopped that sucker—no point, no score." Bill dropped his arms. "Here, Ross. Meet Hip, Blue, and Harry."

I shook hands with Hip, then Blue, then the short chunky guy and asked, "Harry?"

He answered, "Yeah, as in 'Hairy Dog.'"

Blue Dog reached out and placed his huge hand on Bill's shoulder. "We have to go now. But before we take our leave, let me speak for my people by saying you played well. You brought honor to our pit." He pointed at Bill's chest. "The wound you bear glows red with the passion you displayed in the competition. It is a proud wound that, like the rising sun, warms the hearts of those who struggled with you." He turned and looked at Hairy Dog on his right, then Hippy Dog on his left. "My brothers. Henceforth you will know this one as 'Sun Dog.' We will drink beer and tell lies in his honor and to glorify his name. He is one of them, but he also is one of us. He is welcome in our lodges. Amen."

Hip and Hairy muttered, "Amen."

"We go now." Blue Dog and party, leaving a trail of wet footprints, turned and disappeared around the corner.

Bill punched me on the shoulder. "How 'bout that shit, huh? I'm a fucking Dog Person!"

"I'm happy for you, Sun Dog."

Bill grabbed my arm and turned me toward the sidewalk to our hootch. "Let's go eat, man. That ceremony made me hungry."

"Yeah, I was kinda moved by it myself. Let me stop in here a minute so I can take a dump."

I paused by the door to the head, but Bill yanked me away.

"Get outta here, R.T. You're just fucking jealous."

He tried to grab my towel, but I knocked his hand away and we walked on, turning left to pass in front of Colonel Houser and Major Angus' hut, then around it to the right toward Hut 8.

"You think I'm jealous because I don't have a 'dog name?'"

"Yeah, 'cause you're not a honorary Dog Person, like me."

"Yeah. I guess it'd be nice to have a bunch of 34 drivers telling lies about me and drinking beer to my name. In their lodges of course."

"Damn straight it would. Can't have too many friends, you know."

"More words to live by?"

"That's-a-right."

"I suppose that's on the Catlett family coat-of-arms too?"

"Certainly is, just under the two mailed fists shaking hands. 'Makis Manyis Friendis.'"

"Amenis?"

"Not 'Amenis,' asshole! You makin' fun of my family coat-of-arms?"

"Negativis."

"Well, you better not." Bill paused as two guys in camouflage utilities walked by. "Did you fly today, R.T.?"

"Affirmativis."

"Hey!"

"Okay, okay. Yes I did. Major Pyhr, morning guns north. Logged 5.8 hours of combat flight time, which should put me exactly nine hours ahead of you."

"How many missions?"

"Five more combat missions which gives me ten. That's halfway to my first Air Medal and exactly nine ahead of you."

"You're trying to piss me off, aren't you?"

"Of course not."

"You're still jealous of my name, aren't you?"

"Shit, no."

"Yes you are." Bill scratched his chin. "I tell you what. I'll give you an honorary-honorary Dog Person name. How 'bout that?"

"I'm not jealous of your name, Sun Dog."

"See there? You're jealous. You used my Dog Person name again. You wouldn't have done that if you weren't jealous."

"Forget it, Cat."

"No. We're friends, so if I've got an honorary Dog Person name, then you should have an honorary Dog Person name. Course, it won't be as significant as mine; you didn't bring honor to their pit and all."

"That's right, so no name. I didn't earn it."

"No. You get a name, damn it. I've got to nip this jealousy thing in the bud. You will be…'Small-Shit Dog.' Like it?"

"Oh yeah. Beautiful."

"Good. After chow we can drink beer to your name and you can tell me lies about your flight today."

We had scuffed to a stop at the door to our hootch. I reached for the door handle. "Good idea. I think I'll start with the one about us flying through a tree."

Inside, Carl Tess and Franklin Ono sat at the card table gasping for breath, tears streaming down their cheeks.

Bill spoke over my shoulder. "Hey, 'O-Shit,' what's happenin'?"

The lieutenant, in flightsuit and boots, ignored the misuse of his name and pulled a cushioned metal chair away from the table. "Have a seat, you guys." He looked at Tess and grinned.

Tess, dressed only in a green T-shirt and boxer shorts, shook his head, and said, "God help us."

Bill leaped around me, grabbed the empty chair, and sat with a squish. Water ran off the seat and pooled at the base of the legs. He pointed across the table. "Grab a chair, R.T. I saved one over there for you."

I slapped him on the back of his head, spraying water across the table, and walked around Ono, squeezing between his chair and the recently inoperative window air conditioner. On the other side, I crouched under the curve of the quonset hut's roof, pulled out the chair, and sat.

Tess and Ono looked at Bill, the little puddles he had created, the red fireball glowing on his chest, and grinned at each other.

Bill crossed his arms. "Well?"

"Tell 'em, Carl," Ono said. He turned to Bill. "You know Mickey and Major Angus flew together today, right?"

"I don't know." Bill looked at me. "Is that right, R.T.?"

"Yeah, that's right," I said, nodding my head.

"Yeah," Bill said, looking at Ono, "we knew that."

Ono looked at Tess and arched his thin eyebrows.

"Anyhow!" Tess leaned forward. His slingless arm-cast clunked onto the table.

Bill held up his hand. "Wait a minute. Is this going to take long? I mean, it's already chow time."

"No."

"Good."

Tess drew his arms closer to his body. "May I continue now?"

"Sure, man. Let's hear it. I'm ready."

"Okay. I was in the ready room."

"Excuse me." Bill put his hands on his knees. "Would anyone like a beer?"

Tess banged his cast on the table and hissed between his teeth, "Catlett..."

"Okay, okay," Bill said, raising his hands. "Sorry. Go ahead. Cleared to speak."

Tess turned to me. "What is it with this guy?"

"Just ignore him. I do. You had the duty again, right? ODO?"

Tess eased back into his chair. "Yeah, ODO. Until this friggin' arm heals, I'm your permanent operations duty officer." He glanced at Bill—who remained quiet—and sighed, "Okay. First of all, I didn't schedule Angus with Mickey. Angus did that himself, late last night in Major Lewis' hootch." He pointed at me. "And by the way, I've been lookin' for you. I didn't want to schedule you with Pyhr either. Pyhr ordered me to. Sorry."

I nodded.

"Anyhow, I knew as soon as Mickey and the Bull left the ready room this morning we had an adventure on our hands: no NATOPS crew brief, no weather or intelligence, just your basic 'kick-the-tire-and-light-the-fire' attitude." He shifted in his chair. "The blind leading the blind."

I scooted closer to the table.

"They were the last launch of the morning, so after they left the ready room for the flight line, I went back to the Ops office for a cup of coffee. When I got back to the ODO counter a few minutes later, I heard the igniters pop and the engine turn, and about the time I realized the sound wasn't right, Sergeant Whipple started hollerin'.

"I put my coffee down, went to the screened door, and saw the engine turning and smoking and *hemorrhaging*. The aft blade was still tied to the friggin' tailboom! Anyhow, Sergeant Whipple ran over and tried to get it untied, and I ran out the door and tried to get the colonel's attention—waving my arms, running my hand across my throat in the 'cut' sign. Nothing. They just sat there, helmets on, eyes down."

Ono lowered his head and chuckled. "I'm sorry. I'm getting ahead here. This next part is beautiful."

Tess smiled and coughed into his hand.

Bill grinned and winked at me.

"Anyhow, Whipple got the tie-down loose about the time I got in front of the cockpit. The blades whipped into motion, rocking the Huey and making a whacking sound every time the blade with the tie-down rope on it passed the vertical stabilizer and tail rotor." He looked at the ceiling. "God, the sound was unreal; the tail was being beat to shit. And the damn Huey rockin' and hoppin' on the pad; I'm tellin' ya, it looked like pieces could be flying any minute, so I did a Road-Runner 'beep-beep' and hauled ass!"

We laughed, Ono's eyes disappearing.

Tess took a deep breath. "Anyhow I jumped behind a revetment wall, and amid the whacking and rocking and hopping, watched 'Bull' Angus prepare to abandon ship." He laughed, caught himself, then continued, the pitch of his voice getting higher. "His straps went flying, his kneeboard went flying, his cockpit door flew open; man, he was all assholes and elbows, couldn't get out of that piece-of-shit helicopter fast enough; it was coming apart on him and he was scrambling for his life!"

Ono gasped for breath, and held up his hand. "That's when I finally got curious about all the commotion. I ran out of the line shack just in time to see Angus go over the side. The Bull was hysterical, scared out of his ever-lovin'-mind! God, I wish you guys could have seen it!"

Tess held his cast to his stomach. "Yeah, he tripped over the collective trying to get out the door and fell flat on his face. He knew he was dead for sure then 'cause the damn Huey was hoppin' in his direction, coming to get him, wouldn't let him get away. Screamin', he took off on all fours—like a clumsy bear in a survival vest—stumbling, rolling, back on all fours, finally to his feet and running for his life!" Tess shook his head and leaned back in his chair, laughing and holding his stomach.

By now, tears poured down our cheeks and I had stitches in my sides, delicious stitches, camaraderie stitches; for the moment at least, I forgot we were laughing at men I'd have to fly with one day.

In a minute we had exhausted ourselves; all of us slouched in our chairs, arms limp at our sides, taking sporadic breaths.

Bill sat straight, rocked back on the legs of his chair, and wiped the tears from his face with his shoulders. "Did Mickey finally figure it out?"

"Oh, yeah," Tess said, "but not on his own. After Whipple released the blade, he ran to the cockpit and got him to cut the engine." Tess closed one eye. "Then there was this sickening wind-down: Whack . whack . . whack...whack. I winced every time that rope cracked the tail. Man, what a mess."

"Did they burn it up?" Bill asked.

"Oh, yeah," Ono said. "A hard down. Engine change."

"Cost us a mission too," Tess said. "Had to take a bird off a later launch and give it to Mickey—so he could try again. The 3rd Marines didn't get the VR they needed."

I gestured with my hand. "I can't believe they missed that on the preflight. Hell, step one is 'untie the blades,' right?"

Tess shook his head. "Shit, Ross, the colonel's not going to do a preflight. Even if he knew how, I'm sure it never occurred to him. He's the fucking colonel for Christ's sake." He grabbed his cast and twisted it back and forth. "And Angus? Shit, he's a fighter pilot, remember? And the XO. He's above that menial shit. Lieutenants and enlisted men do preflights!"

Tess' tanned face flushed dark and he spit out his words. "Shit, neither of 'em did a preflight!" He pounded his good fist on the table, shifted his eyes to Ono, and threw his arms out at him. "It's only a piece-of-shit helicopter, right? It's not like it's a *real* aircraft!"

Ono pushed his chair back and stood. "Calm down, Carl. Gettin' bent out of shape won't help." He turned for the door.

Tess screamed after him, "Fuck'em, 'O!' Fuck them and the F-8s and A-4s they rode in on!" He bent his head and wiped his mouth on the sleeve of his T-shirt.

"Yeah, but you're too short to let it get to you now. Cool it." Ono opened the door. "I've got to go. Your friendly, neighborhood maintenance-test pilot has got to go back to work." He chuckled and pointed at Bill. "See ya, Cat-shit."

Bill turned, but before he could respond, Tess called after Ono, "I'll be down there after while."

The door slammed shut.

Tess stood, twisting and pulling on his cast. "Fucking assholes!" He turned to Bill. "You can go feed now, 'Cat-puke.' And get a belly full too 'cause you're gonna need it tomorrow." He stepped toward the back, but before he disappeared behind the curtains, he turned to Bill and forced a wrinkled smile. "I think it's time you lost your cherry, Marine. Pyhr style."

After the curtains fell together, Bill scooted his chair to the table and leaned forward on his forearms. "What the hell does that mean?"

I rubbed my eyes with my fingers. "It means you're in deep do-do, Cat. You're flying with Major Pyhr tomorrow."

Bill lowered his head and looked down at the table. "Pyhr. I think Shockley told me about him." He raised his head again and looked me in the eyes. "He's that suicidal fucker, right?"

"Yep."

"Yeah, thought so." Bill put his hands on the table and stood. "Well, shit. That's his problem. Can we go eat now?"

13

Dangerous Grass

When I woke up the next morning, Bill was gone. It was 0500. I lay awake in the dark, surprised to hear rain pounding on our tin roof and wondered if I'd told him everything I could about Pyhr. I decided I had.

I woke up again at 0630. The ceiling lights were on. Light rain fell on the roof. Lying with my hands behind my head, I watched drops of water run down the curved ceiling and drip onto the corner of my rack. And I heard footsteps.

"Hey, Ross." Jim Teach stopped by my wall locker.

"Yeah."

"Breakfast?"

"Sure. Ah…"

Jim saw me glance at his shaving kit. "Just got up. Be about twenty minutes."

"Sure." I threw my covers back. "I'm right behind you."

Twenty minutes later, Jim and I sloshed through dark puddles on the main road. The rain had slacked to a light sprinkle and some gray appeared in the low clouds ahead. Beyond the mess hall, on the other side of the shadowy hangars and squadron buildings, multiple sets of rotor blades beat the wet air.

Jim hadn't said much but that didn't surprise me. I'd been around him enough to know he was a better listener than a talker. He did ask me if I was doing okay, if I needed anything, and we laughed together when I said, "Yeah, can I have your fan?" He said no, no fan, but he would loan me a set of camouflage utilities—supply was still out. I accepted even though I knew they would be a size too large. We walked most of the way in silence.

The mess hall was hazy from cigarette smoke and crowded. The Huey, 34, 46, and H-53 pilots on the first launch of the day had gone, but there were others like us in flightsuits who had later launches, and there were the ground types in their camouflage utilities on their way to a variety of desk jobs. I didn't know anyone, but I recognized the assistant S-1 officer from our squadron, Warrant Officer Henry Glazener, the old guy in the thick black-rimmed glasses. That reminded me I needed to go see Straderman about the bonds.

Across the table from me, head down, occasionally looking away, Jim ate his eggs and toast without comment. I poked at my hash-browns, wondered why they were always raw in the center, and thought of how much Jim reminded me of my first high-school football coach; he even walked like him—smooth, athletic, confident. Didn't talk like him though. Coach Day was a motor mouth.

After he had finished his breakfast, Jim wiped his mustache and mouth with his napkin. He pushed his plate a few inches forward, leaned toward me, and rested his arms on the table. "Ross, one of these days we're gonna get hash-browns cooked all the way through. It's gonna happen. Only a matter of time."

I smiled and looked at his plate. A hash-brown pattie lay alone and abandoned, its crispy perimeter shredded as though nibbled by a rat. It looked a lot like the one in my plate.

"I can count on that, huh?"

He stuffed his crumpled napkin under his plate and smiled like Coach Day: eyes bright, mouth crinkled at the corners, positive. "Yep. Time's on our side." He sipped his coffee, then set the mug on the table, his finger still hooked in the handle. "Ross, I ah…I'd like to go over a few things with you this morning, if possible. You need to go anywhere, you got time?"

"No. Plenty of time. I was hoping we'd get a chance to talk."

"Okay. That's good. I ah…well," he grinned. "If you can handle one more 'this is a no shit' war story, I'll start by telling you about my first flight in this squadron. Can you handle it?"

"Sure." I grinned with him and wiped my mouth.

"Okay. It ah…" He glanced at a group of guys in flightsuits leaving the table next to us. "It was a gun mission and we were Dash Two and the guy I was flying with was a hot-shot lieutenant. We were just south of the DMZ, near Con Thien. You've been up there by now, right?"

"Oh, yeah."

Jim grinned again. "Yeah, that's right—the 'exploding tree incident.' Shockley told me about that. Anyhow, the leader asked for our fuel state, then said we'd go back to Vandy to refuel. My HAC, the hot-shot, didn't want to go. He wanted to make one more gun-run. But he didn't say that to the leader, he just did it. So, pulling off the target, without a wingman covering us, we got stitched good—chin bubble shot out and a round through the HAC's foot. I took the controls and flew direct to Dong Ha. Lost the number one hydraulic system on the way. Anyhow, did a slide-on landing at Dong Ha, got the HAC med-evaced, and haven't seen him since."

Jim took another sip of coffee. "That...well, that was the kind of stuff that went on before Major Hardy got here. Until then it had been a collection of field grade officers doing their own thing and lieutenants following their example. Don't get me wrong now—it wasn't a bad squadron; the hammer was a symbol the frogs and dogs respected...but the squadron was slack. Major Hardy changed that in thirty days."

Jim looked at the table. I thought maybe he was waiting on me to say something, but he cleared his throat and looked up again. "It ah...it wasn't easy. Some even fought it. But Hardy stuck with it. He set the example, then identified a few key players—people he felt really wanted to learn and would spread the word to others—and trained them the Hardy way. It worked. He made it happen."

Several officers slid past me toward the door.

"Tess and Ono were two of the first. Then he taught me, and later B-12. After a while, at least one of us was getting to every new guy that came on board. Things like flight discipline, mutual support, and priorities like mission first, take care of your wingman—stuff like that; that started to take hold—at least among the company grade, and really, for a while, even Major Lewis. Anyhow, right now, unlike before, most of us know what the other guy is going to do even before he does it. Casualties are down—ours and the transports we cover—and our missions are up. We're gettin' it done, Ross, and we're gettin' it done right."

Jim took a breath and coughed to the side. "Okay, you with me so far?"

"Well, yeah. I guess so."

"Well, not having seen the squadron the way it was before, I imagine it's hard for you to appreciate the way it is now. Anyhow, Major Hardy's system worked—his procedures and tactics and all that stuff made us a much better squadron. But that's not all. That's not even the best part. Hardy also gave us the intangible, the invaluable intangible: attitude.

"After Hardy took over, that black claw hammer on our tail came to symbolize the fastest guns in the territory. We're good and we know it. And the guys we're here to protect know it too—they love to see us coming, they ask for us first, they know we'll hang it out for 'em. I like that, Ross. I'd hate to see that change."

He straightened and took another sip of coffee. "Anyhow, now that Hardy's gone, what's bothering me is, I'm afraid this squadron could go right back to where it was before Hardy got here...or worse. Tess, Ono, B-12 and I talked about that last night. Talked about it a long time." He stroked his mustache. "We don't want that. We care about this squadron as much as Hardy did. For us it's like playing on a really tight football team—everybody hitting together, running the same plays, going on the same count. None of us want to go back to flying with a bunch of loners and hot dogs." He paused, watching me. "So, that's why

I wanted to talk with you…we need you with us." He paused again. "What do you think?"

I looked at the table, to my napkin, and recalled Major Hardy seated by my wall locker, his flip-flop dangling in the air, his heel bandaged and swollen.

"Jim…I don't think you were there, but Major Hardy came to see me the night before he left. We talked over some stuff. He talked about you. He also said something about me taking good care of the squadron for him. I got the part about you teaching me stuff, but I couldn't figure how a co-pilot, the ultimate new guy, a know-nothing lieutenant, was going to be able to take care of an entire squadron." I shook my head. "I guess this is what he meant—a group thing."

"That's right. You can't do it by yourself. I can't do it by myself. But together: you, me, Ono, Tess, B-12, we can teach others; we can keep this thing going."

"Well, it sounds fine to me. I mean, I'll learn, and when I'm a HAC, I'll try to be as good as Hardy. But to do more than that…I don't know if that's my place."

"Well I do." Jim watched me a second. "I know what you're thinking."

"What?"

"That the Marine Corps teaches leadership should come from above. That the CO and XO should lead by example. That it's their job to set the high standards, 'in keeping with the highest traditions of the United States Naval Service,' etcetera."

"Something like that. They have the experience, or at least they are supposed to have the experience. Anyhow, they have the mandate; they get paid to do that."

"Well, you've seen the new XO and the CO. Have you observed them leading us toward higher standards?"

"No. But what about the NATOPS officer or the Ops officer? Isn't some of this their responsibility?"

"Major Lewis is Ops. He likes to blend in, not take the lead. He'll follow the loudest barking dog. Who do you think that will be with Hardy gone?"

"Angus."

"Right—Angus, the F-8 pilot with sixty something hours of helo time. I heard about that little speech he made at the parade last Friday, and the episode with Mickey yesterday, and the new rule that new guys have to fly with field grade first, and that we're turning down missions now. I don't think Angus is the next Ben Hardy."

"No, I guess not. How 'bout Captain Cain? Is he any good? He's NATOPS, right?"

"He's okay, but he's not here to rock the boat. He's here to get a good fitness report from his reporting senior—Mickey."

Jim stroked his mustache. "Look, Ross, all Major Hardy asked us to do is learn to do it right, then take a little extra time to teach others. He picked you just like he did the rest of us. In effect, he gave us a second collateral duty. It's not official now that he's gone, but the need is still there."

"But why me? Did he say?"

"No. He just said you were a tiger, and a good Marine."

I rubbed my forehead. "A tiger, huh?"

"Yep."

Jim glanced at my plate, finished his coffee, and leaned toward me. "You don't have to decide now, Ross. We can just talk about our flight this afternoon, about tactics...learn some stuff. The extra part, the part where you teach someone else, you won't have to do that for a while anyhow. Plenty of time. So, how 'bout it? You ready to go talk Huey guns?"

Looking across the table at me, his block jaws set, the alert eyes radiating confidence—the whole scene reminded me of the afternoon Coach Day asked me to go out for quarterback. I wasn't sure what I was getting into that time either. But he asked, I did it, and everything worked out fine.

"It's okay, Jim. Count me in."

The corners of his mouth crinkled. "Great. Let's go."

We stood and walked toward the screened door, Jim relaxed, flowing between the chairs and tables. He held the squeaking door open behind him and I caught it on my way out.

It had stopped raining. A thin layer of low, fast-moving clouds slipped overhead. I figured the hot sun would be back within hours.

We spent the rest of the morning talking gunship tactics, techniques, and responsibilities, and everything Jim said connected with what I'd been taught from Basic School through transition training at Pendleton. It made sense. It was right.

Before I knew it, it was time for the formal briefing with B-12 and Duppont, our wingman.

An hour later, we were airborne. The sun was out, the sky was clear and clean, and I was switching radios with an extra snap.

By 1330 we were over Highway 9 at 1500 feet, heading west out of Dong Ha. Dong Ha DASC had given us artillery clearances, called "Sav-a-planes," and assigned us to the 9th Marines for resupply out of Vandegrift Combat Base. We were to work with "Cattle Prod 2-0-1 and 2-0-1 Dash-Two," two 46s from Quang Tri. DASC also had said Hardball 1-9 was still on that mission from the morning and we were to replace him. Jim took the assignment without comment and told me to switch the FM radio to 42.5, Vandy LSA's frequency. He called B-12 on the UHF.

"4-3 Dash Two, 4-3, go Vandy LSA, over."

"Switching."

The tone in the FM radio hummed in my ears…and stopped as the radio locked on the new frequency. Silence. We waited. I looked at Jim.

"New guy," he said.

Walt Duppont. I looked over my left shoulder. Fifty yards behind us, to the side and slightly above, B-12's Huey rose and fell on the afternoon air currents. Walt had his head down. The hissing in my helmet changed and B-12 called, "Two's up."

Jim answered with two clicks and pointed to the ground ahead. Alongside Highway 9, an area like a great silver lake shimmered in the afternoon sun.

"Cam Lo?"

"Yeah. Otherwise known as 'Silver City.'" Jim's hand fell to the throttle grip on the collective. "Those are tin roofs that make it shimmer like that. All the people Secretary of Defense McNamara displaced from the area to our right, Leatherneck Square, were moved there…few years ago. Hauled 'em out of their homes, off their farms, and away from centuries of buried ancestors, and built that nice ghetto for 'em." He glanced at the instrument panel. "All so he could bulldoze a strip south of the DMZ from the beach, across the piedmont, and through 5000-foot mountains to the border with Laos. Gonna put in a lot of gee-whiz electronic stuff that would keep the bad guys from crossing into our territory—as if they couldn't get in through Laos. Any PFC could have told him it wouldn't work. It didn't, so never finished it. Harvard man."

Jim glanced over his shoulder. "How's the wingman, Hutch?"

The crew chief, Sergeant Hutchins, stopped scratching the stubble on his pointed chin and reached for his mike button. "He's lookin' good, sir. Five o'clock."

We flew on in silence, westward over the highway, past Cam Lo, past Camp Carroll to our left, then where Highway 9 and the Cam Lo River squeezed together south of Dong Ha mountain, Jim lowered the collective and stabilized us in a 500-feet-per-minute descent. 100 knots.

"So your buddy, Catlett, is with Pyhr today, huh?"

"Yep."

He glanced at the eight-day clock in the corner of the instrument panel. "Well, either the 9th Marines have gotten into some trouble, or Pyhr was out screwin' around this morning. Usually the morning pre-planned resupply missions would have been completed long before now. We'll know soon enough."

"Two, 4-3, go Vandy tower."

"Switching."

I made the switch, leaned back in my seat, and locked my harness. The sky to the west was clear and dotted with bright white cumulus clouds. No Hueys in sight.

After another delay, B-12 checked in with, "Two's up."

Elliott Combat Base, a sprawling complex of sandbagged gun positions, bunkers, and dirt roads, appeared on the edge of a valley to our left. North of Elliott—across a stream that joined the Cam Lo River—an isolated shaft of dark, moss-and-fern-covered limestone known as "The Rockpile" jutted 700 feet out of the valley grass. In the valley floor, the tail of the Cam Lo snaked north then west below Mutters Ridge, a battle-scarred and defoliated ridgeline overlooking the DMZ.

Jim called Vandy tower, got us cleared for a straight-in to the fuel pits, and turned left over the guns of Elliott. Still descending, we followed the highway south toward Vandy.

"I know DASC said these guns were cold right now, but sometimes DASC doesn't get the word. It's best to fly directly over them. Just in case." He nodded toward the ground. "For some reason, this whole complex is called the Rockpile. Real Rockpile is north."

Ahead, a convoy of trucks and jeeps, like a segmented, mechanical snake, stretched south on the highway. Jim's smile widened as he dropped to 50 feet and we sped beside the dust-covered vehicles.

"Look at this, Ross."

Stretching my neck, I looked out Jim's window at the dusty stream of Marines. Standing in the back of their trucks, swaying on their feet as the trucks hit pothole after pothole, they waved their rifles at us or made hammers with their fists and pounded on their rifle stocks or their neighbor's helmet. Mouths open, heads back, they yelled something I couldn't hear—apparently, something warrior-like.

I glanced into our cabin. Sergeant Hutchins grinned at them from behind his gun and returned the pounding hammer sign by thumping his fist on the feed tray of his M-60.

"Those grunts are too much, Ross. They'll get so screwed up they'll drive you crazy sometimes, but hell, they'll make you proud too."

The lead jeep slid by and Jim returned his gaze to the horizon. We skimmed the highway now, gradually crossing it from left to right. Ahead and closing fast, a gap in the low hills opened into the valley containing Vandy.

"Hutch. You still got him back there?"

"Yes, sir. Five o'clock, going to trail."

"Okay. Landing check, Ross."

We squirted through the gap in the grass-covered hills.

Inside the valley, Jim reported on final and requested Dash Two be cleared to the LSA. That was approved and Jim's hand dropped to his select switch. "Two, 4-3 on fox, pick up some dream sheets for us and we'll meet you back at the pits, copy?"

"Two, copy."

Off to my left, a steel parking lot lay soaking up the afternoon sun. Painted with grid lines like a bingo card—numbers down the side, letters across the top—it was dotted with netted piles of crates, boxes, or water cans, or a mixture of all three. Each pile lay in a separate grid ready for pickup by a transport helicopter.

The dream sheet, published daily, listed each pile, or load, by line number, telling us which unit in the field would get the load, where that unit was located by grid coordinates, what FM radio frequency they were on, and their call sign. It was known as a dream sheet because you were dreaming if you thought all the units would be where the sheet said they were, and on the published frequency.

Jim brought us to a hover on the runway, eased the Huey around 180 degrees, and as he air-taxied sideways to the pit area, he keyed his mike. "Vandy LSA, Hardball 4-3."

"4-3, Vandy LSA, go ahead, sir."

"Roger, Vandy, 4-3, ah…anything left to run on your dream sheet?"

"That's affirmative, sir. We got a late start, and ah…we've got troops in contact."

I looked at Jim. Troops in contact? As in fire-fight? Is that where Bill is?

Jim glanced at me, expressionless, and asked over the radio, "What's first, Vandy?"

Before the LSA responded, my eardrums were blasted by a loud squeal, a squeal I'd learn to associate with the radios of a CH-46. Cattle Prod 2-0-1 called Vandy tower on UHF.

Jim pointed at me, held up one finger, then reached over to his mixer switches and flicked off the UHF. I nodded and listened as the 46s requested and received clearance to the LSA.

Seconds later, on the ground in the fuel pits at idle RPM, Jim and I threw our cockpit doors open. I felt a hot breeze across my sweaty face and smelled the engine's exhaust, a smell like burned kerosene. The gunner and crew chief jumped out and walked toward the Marine standing by the closest fuel nozzle.

Jim turned. "The LSA said Pyhr and the resupply birds haven't been able to run line five on the dream sheet yet—got a shoot'em-up going." He pointed at my map case behind the center console. "Get the one-to-fifty out for the Khe Sanh area. I'll betcha that's where they're at." He made a notation on his kneeboard. "Pyhr is working with the unit in contact. We're supposed to run line ten with Cattle Prod 2-0-1 first. That'll finish the routine stuff. Then we can help Pyhr with line five."

I nodded, said, "Okay," and pulled the map case into my lap.

We wouldn't know what running line 10 involved until B-12 joined us with our copy of the dream sheet, but I figured it must be important if they were sending us there first instead of to help Bill. Or else the contact wasn't that heavy. Or else that was the way it was done no matter what. Or—

A gust of wind with the sound of pounding rotor blades hit us and I reached out to catch my door. To the side, the T-shirted Marine who operated the fuel pits ducked his head, held his utility cover down, and disappeared in a dust storm. B-12 landed behind us and slid into position for the second nozzle.

As we refueled, I held the door with my foot and found the map I was looking for. I folded it to put the Khe Sanh area in the center. On my two previous flights, I'd never been west of Vandy, so I took a minute to look over the landing zones I had marked from a map in the ready room and tried to get a feel for how they fit in with the mountain peaks, ridgelines, river systems, and roads I could easily pick out from the air.

The feeling I got, however, wasn't what I expected. The more I studied the map sheet, the more uncomfortable I became. The place was eerie. Either from television news, or from listening to my instructor's war stories, or maybe from my talks with Jim, I felt as though I knew that place, as though I had been there before, as though the Khe Sanh area had a personal feel to it well beyond its historical significance. I moved my finger west to the Laotian border—it was close—then back to the plateau with the airport runway symbol at Khe Sanh. I felt it again, a tension in my skin. I pulled my finger away.

B-12's gunner appeared. Jim took the dream sheet from him, looked at it, then handed it to me. "Line 10 is a load for Fire Base Cates. I recognize the grid coordinates. Piece of cake."

I heard a scrape and a tap on the side of our Huey and turned. Our gunner—short, heavy, with small black-rimmed glasses and a mustache even scrawnier than J.P. Padgett's—pulled the brass fuel nozzle to his chest and dragged it and the attached hose to the steel rack. In front of a half-buried fuel bladder, the Marine waited for him with a clipboard.

I found Cates and confirmed the grid coordinates on the dream sheet at line 10 matched its location. It was just north of Highway 9, about halfway between Vandy and Khe Sanh.

Clipping the dream sheet to my kneeboard, I noted line five was "Kilo 1-4," on 35.5, at the 883382 grid, and circled that area on my map.

Jim rolled the throttle on and the Huey lurched to life.

"Line five is two miles southeast of Khe Sanh, Jim."

"That figures. Is it Kilo or Delta?"

"Kilo."

"Those guys—hell, that whole battalion—they've always got a fight goin' somewhere. We'll bang out this line 10, then go join the party."

A minute later, B-12 called, "Two's up."

Jim answered, then looked to his right, across the valley toward the LSA, and called Cattle Prod 2-0-1. The CH-46 was obscured by a low hill and a build-up of huts and hard-back tents between us. When he didn't get an answer after three tries, he shook his head. "Line-of-sight radios. If you can't see 'em, you can't hear 'em. We'll try 'em again when we're airborne."

With clearance from the tower and a verbal "okay" from the crew, Jim lifted the Huey a few inches off the ground and nudged it forward, scraping the packed clay and gravel with the tips of the skids. Now with a full bag of fuel, four crew members, eight guns, 4000 rounds of linked ammo, fourteen rockets, spare gun barrels, tools, grenades, personal gear, and various personal weapons of choice, the Huey was well over its designed takeoff weight—a "fact of life to accomplish the mission," as Major Hardy had said—and it was struggling. Beating the air against the ground and swirling the dust around us, the Huey bounced onto the runway, into the waves of heat rising from the steel matting, and slid into takeoff position, facing south.

B-12 coaxed his Huey along the same route and in the same manner. Jim explained what B-12 was doing, how he nursed the power, and pedals, and used his ground cushion to keep moving forward, how he avoided catching the ammo links that hung under the TAT mounted under the Huey's nose. "Next to getting lost," Jim said, "the ultimate disgrace is to break your ammo links."

B-12 squatted into position at our four o'clock.

"Well, he made it. Let's roll."

I nodded, looked down the short, makeshift runway, and checked the ragged windsock on the hill. No wind.

Jim visually swapped thumbs up with B-12, eased the collective up until the Huey lifted inches off the matting, and nudged the cyclic stick ahead a fraction of an inch. We mushed forward on the edge of our ground cushion, accelerating but falling. The tips of the skids bounced, flew, then fell and scraped, the rotor RPM dropping to 6400, the screaming engine unable to keep the big blades at a constant RPM with the pitch, or power, Jim had set with the collective. So Jim took off a sliver of power to get them back, and now, still sliding on the tips of the skids, the RPM crept up to 6575, and once more Jim nudged the cyclic stick and squeezed on more power with collective. The tips flew again and our forward speed increased another couple of knots, and again the RPM dropped and once more we skipped along on the tips, scraping steel on steel.

Ahead, the runway ended abruptly and we were over halfway there, closing fast. Beyond its boundary, razor wire, strung and stacked across our path, waited in a grassy field. Meanwhile, the steel matting flashed under the chin bubble at my feet, the tips bounced, and I couldn't see how we could avoid breaking the ammo links or at least catching a skid shoe. Squeezing my map, I scanned the engine instruments and Jim tried one more time to regain the RPM we needed by sacrificing some power.

The sacrifice worked again; the turns came back to 6575. But this time, with a net gain of five knots, and as the skids skipped off the matting, Jim squeezed the collective back up, pressed his left thumb to the fuel-governor toggle switch just above the throttle grip, and nudged the right pedal forward—a trick I'd forgotten about, but had seen in flight school. The Huey cocked to the right, shuddered, groaned, and staggered into the hot humid air with a positive rate of climb. Below us, rusting in the sun, the indolent razor-wire drifted by, harmless, gaping up at me as if in disappointment.

In one coordinated motion, Jim brought the Huey back to balanced flight with pedal, started a gentle left turn with the cyclic, reduced pitch and power with the collective, and to prevent engine damage, beeped the governor back down with his thumb. The RPM stabilized again at 6575.

"A little hotter today than I thought," he said, grinning. "Use 6600 for takeoff. Do as I say, not as I do."

"Right, Coach," I said, grinning with him, knowing as well as he did that 6600 wouldn't have made the difference.

Jim returned his scan to the horizon, shook his head, and made a wide turn that gave me a chance to look over my left shoulder and watch B-12 slip, slide, skip, and sweet-talk his Huey into the air. Once past the razor wire, he hugged the ground in a left turn inside our own, built up some air speed, then cyclic-climbed to our altitude of 500 feet.

Jim called Cattle Prod 2-0-1 on the FM radio and together they decided to use our squadron UHF frequency, or "squadron common," and to meet at line 10.

I heard Jim key his mike again. Anticipating a call to Vandy Tower and a switch-call to B-12, I reached for the channel select knob on the radio.

"Ross."

"Yeah." I pulled my hand back.

Jim looked to the west and continued a left turn around the LSA. "Hope you took good notes back there. The next landing and takeoff are yours."

"Okay." And even though I had to slip that word past a lump in my throat, I meant it. I was ready.

"But, Ross. Don't plan on using the grass area. That's mined."

14

Make Me Hot

En route to Fire Support Base Cates, climbing through 1500 feet, I rested my map on my knee and recalled a promise I'd made only two weeks before. Travis Air Force Base, California. Our flight, a Continental Airlines Boeing 707 on government contract, had been called for boarding, and I had just left the newsstand with a *Los Angeles Times*. Ahead, Bill grabbed his San Diego State gym bag in one hand, a *Sports Illustrated* in the other, kissed his wife Laura, and with adventure in his step, walked toward the line forming at the glass doors.

Laura watched him go, eyes flooded, a tissue squeezed in her hand.

I reached for my briefcase on the bench beside her and hesitated, trying to think of something to say, something to make her feel better. Already, the crowd of uniformed men with short haircuts filled in behind Bill. I put the paper under my arm and decided to just get tough and go. I stepped by her and touched her shoulder.

"It'll be fine, Laura. He'll be okay."

"Oh, Ross," she said, turning and throwing her arms around my neck. "Please take care of him for me."

"I will. You know I will."

"Oh, I know, I know." She squeezed me hard and stood on her toes to rest her head on my shoulder, sobbing, sniffling, patting me on my back as I patted hers. "And, and take care of yourself too, okay? Promise?"

"I promise."

Laura squeezed my neck again, lingered a second, then she kissed me on the cheek, eased down off her toes, and wiped the lipstick away with her soggy tissue. Still toe to toe, she hugged me once more, stepped back, held her head erect, and sniffled, "I'm okay. Go ahead. He might get on the wrong plane if you're not with him."

We laughed, looked into each other's eyes for a second, blinked, and I walked away.

It wasn't much of a promise, considering it was given to a woman in tears. And it wasn't like I didn't think Bill could take care of himself; hell, from my experience the guy was indestructible—rolling his Corvette after happy hour on the day he soloed, the crash in a T-28 after a bird strike. Both incidents had been only good bar stories to Bill—a couple of stitches here, a lump there—no big deal. But to me it said trouble; could he be that lucky forever? He really was tough as nails, and I was confident that whatever happened, he would always walk away, but still, he worried me...and I'd made a promise.

"Found Cates yet?"

"Ah...yeah." I pointed southwest. "That-a-way."

Jim laughed. "Roger."

Flying south above Highway 9—now just a dirt and gravel road—we passed over Ca Lu, a bare spot of sandbags and razor wire on the Quang Tri River. There we turned with the highway to the west, southwest, and followed it as it tightroped its way between the Quang Tri River on the left and the steep mountains on the right. Map in hand, I visually matched the peaks and valleys and streams in front of us with the lines of brown and green and blue on the map, following our progress and gaping at the scenery.

From our altitude of 2500 feet the view was spectacular: deep river valley below, lush, sparkling mountains on our right; it was the Pali of Oahu, Hawaii, on a mammoth scale—waterfalls everywhere. And unlike the scarred, pock-faced land of Dong Ha or Leatherneck Square or even the stripped and ripped hills of the Mutters Ridge area, this was virgin jungle, triple canopy, *National Geographic* stuff. I whistled softly at every new waterfall discovered sparkling in the sunlight beside us.

Ahead, the shimmering blue river made a wide fishhook to the south and almost completely encircled a 700-foot, stripped and leveled peak I identified as Fire Base Shepherd. Directly across the river and three clicks, or 3000 meters, to the north was another stripped and flattened peak. This one was over 2200 feet tall, towered over the river valley, and was our destination, Fire Base Cates.

I looked at Jim. "Cates? Two o'clock?"

"That's a roger. What'd they give us for Cates?"

"32 point 2-5."

"Hardball 4-3 Dash Two, this is 4-3, go working fox, over."

I made the switch as B-12 answered with two clicks on our squadron UHF frequency. He checked in five seconds later on fox. Duppont was getting faster.

We climbed to 3000 feet, and when abreast of Shepherd, made a climbing right turn. Below and to our right, Cates, a bare hilltop bristling with 105mm howitzers, bathed in sunlight, and wreathed in shadows cast by a tiara of thick white cumulus clouds drifting above, looked lazy and quiet. We slipped in under the clouds, flying in their shadows, using the limited air space between them and the ground.

"Hotel 1-4, Hardball 4-3, over." Quiet hissing.

"Hotel 1-4, Hardball 4-3, over."

"Ross, you've got to keep in mind these radio operators don't know when we're coming. It's not like they sit in the hot sun all day with a PRC-25 radio stuck in their ear just waiting for us to show up. Gotta be patient with 'em. The guy down there could be on the edge of the LZ takin' a whiz."

The hissing in the radio broke and an out-of-breath voice answered, "Hardball 4-3. This is Hotel 1-4. Ah…over. Sir."

Jim smiled, looked down to his right, and circled the base. "Think we got a new guy here, Ross, maybe a trainee. Gonna need even more patience."

"Roger, Hotel. 4-3 is a flight of two Huey guns west of your LZ at this time. Are we in sight? Over."

"Hardball 4-3, this is Hotel 1-4. You are in sight, sir. You are at my twelve o'clock. Over."

Jim smiled again. "Roger, 1-4. Give me a clock direction to you, as if you were sitting in my seat, over."

A long pause.

"Hardball 4-3, this is Hotel 1-4. Sir, did you say you wanted a clock direction? Over?"

"That's affirmative, 1-4."

We had circled to the east and back into the sunlight.

"Hardball 4-3, this is Hotel 1-4. You are at my twelve o'clock. Over."

Jim dipped his head, the pig-tail cord sliding across his camouflage helmet. "Okay, 1-4. Let's pretend you are me and you are sitting in my seat. Roger?"

"Hardball 4-3, this is Hotel 1-4. Roger, sir. Over."

"Okay. You are in my seat. Now. Where is your unit in a clock direction from where you are sitting in *my* seat? Over."

Another pause. "Hardball 4-3, this is Hotel 1-4. I'm in your seat, sir?"

"Roger, 1-4. *Pretend* that you are in my seat, and remember the nose of the aircraft is always pointing to twelve o'clock, then tell me where your unit is located."

Another pause, and I felt an urgency, a desire to put words in the Marine's mouth. I could still remember how I felt on my first mission with Major Hardy. Even though I knew what to do and how to do it, the radios were intimidating.

Finally the hissing stopped again and the voice came back strong. "Hardball 4-3, this is Hotel 1-4. My unit is at your three o'clock, over."

I heard pounding like a cattle stampede and turned to see Sergeant Hutchins and the heavyset gunner stomping their flight boots on the cabin deck and clapping their gloved hands.

Jim smiled again. "Roger, 1-4. We've got you at our three o'clock. We'd like a zone brief when you're ready and stand by for a couple of 46s with some resupply for you, over."

The zone brief that followed was excruciating and appeared to be read from a text, but it made sense and was complete. Jim made some notes on his kneeboard, and asked 1-4 to stand by with a smoke grenade.

"Everybody's got to start somewhere, Ross. In two weeks this guy will be the saltiest DJ on the radio. And we can say we knew him when."

We had made a couple of complete circles by then and were now back on the north side of the LZ.

"We've got 46s at two o'clock, sir. And Dash-Two is lookin' good at seven o'clock."

"Roger that."

The 46s came in around 5000 feet, weaving between the white clouds, the lead aircraft trailing a full cargo net from a thirty-foot pendant under its belly. Jim made sure they had us in sight, confirmed the location of Cates with them, and relayed the zone brief after the lead aircraft said he was ready to copy.

"The lead transport pilot is in charge, Ross. In the interest of time and efficiency, we run the show, but he always has the last word."

Seconds later, Cattle Prod 2-0-1 called on the UHF and requested smoke. Jim relayed the request to Hotel 1-4 on the FM radio and a thin stream of yellow smoke appeared on the top of the bulldozed peak.

"Smoke away, sir."

I smiled, relieved he didn't say, yellow smoke away. If the NVA were listening, and as many radios as they had captured over the years, it was reasonable to assume they were, they could throw the color announced and sucker the 46 into a trap. My fellow-new-guy had done it right.

A yellow, funnel-shaped cloud grew along the ground as the westerly breeze carried it toward Vandy.

The obnoxious squeal leaped into my ears again and 2-0-1 identified yellow smoke and called, "In left."

The "in left" call let Jim know the 46 intended to make a left-hand spiral. Knowing that, Jim could set up his covering pattern accordingly. Major Hardy had told me that a left-hand spiral also usually meant the co-pilot was making the approach.

I reached for the TAT gunsight.

"You want this one?" Jim asked. "I'll talk you through it."

I looked at him. Not even Major Hardy had suggested that. "You mean I take it?"

"Yeah. And soon too 'cause he's already starting his approach."

I looked up. At 5000 feet over Cates, the twin-rotored helicopter was in a left-hand descending turn—small and dark green against the white clouds. "Okay. I got it."

"You got it, Marine."

Jim watched me take the controls, let go, and held his hands out in the standardized, "I'm off the controls," pose.

"Okay, Ross, hold what you got, continue the right-hand turn while I get the circuit breakers and the switches. I'll have you set up for rockets." Jim turned to the panel between us and lowered his head. In a few seconds he called, "Okay, you're on standby. I'll tell you when you need to be hot."

The 46 grew larger. It passed above us southwest of the peak, flying in the opposite direction, counterclockwise, turning to the east, nose down and inside our turn.

"Okay, Ross. Start descending at a rate and air speed that will put us at 1000 feet above the ground, say 3200 to 3300 indicated, and right on that frog's butt as he rolls onto final. Remember he's gonna be landing into the wind, so that means we've got to be heading west at the same time he is." Jim looked up at the 46. "You guys got the zone brief, Hutch?"

"Yes, sir."

Now we were on the west side of the LZ and the 46 was on the south side…and falling like a runaway elevator. I'd figured I'd level off at 3300 feet indicated, but it looked like I was going to be late to my perch position if I did that. I needed the descent to keep up the air speed. Either that or take a short-cut right over the LZ. It really depended on what the 46 did. If he went one more spiral, I'd have enough time to get over there.

"He's gonna throw out the speed brakes here, Ross. Better hustle butt over there."

Sure enough, out the right-side cabin doorway of our Huey I could see the 46 cock his nose and begin to break his descent. No more spirals.

I sucked the collective up until the RPM dropped, turned hard right, lowered the nose, and pointed it toward the east side of the mountain. The air speed climbed to 110 knots and the altimeter slowly unwound past 3200 feet.

"Okay, got to boogie, got to hustle. Again, you want to be on the perch, ideally 1000 feet AGL, or about 3200 indicated for this one, at 65 knots, and lined up with the frog as he gets onto short final—that's when he's most likely to take fire and you need to be in position to suppress it."

We sailed by the north side of the LZ at 115 knots and 500 feet above the ground, still descending, still bouncing in our seats from the beat of the blades. The turns had dropped to 6500 and the EGT was at red line. I stole a glance to our right and was shocked to see the 46 at my altitude and pointed in my direction, but…not yet on final.

I had a chance, but everything depended on what that co-pilot in the 46 did. He was carrying an external so I knew he couldn't come in hot; he may have dropped like a rock, but he was going to have to make that rock descend like a feather before this was over.

And despite what Jim had said about taking fire, I knew he wouldn't have let me do this if he had thought this was going to be a hot LZ. Plus the co-pilot was flying the 46, another sign taking fire was highly unlikely. Besides, as steep as the mountain was, as soon as I passed over the edge of the peak, the radar-altimeter needle started climbing and I was quickly back to a fairly safe 1000 feet above the jungle, even though still only a few hundred feet above the peak itself.

I picked up the 46 again, then he disappeared behind Sergeant Hutchins and his M-60, both silhouetted against the sky in the cabin doorway. The 46 had his nose cocked high, still in a left turn but the fuselage was rolling out to the right.

"Show time, Ross." Jim's hands were fists, vibrating on his thighs. His voice was steady, but he kept looking at the instruments, and back to the 46, and back to the instruments.

Trust me, I wanted to tell him. I'm going to pull this out of the fire somehow.

After a two-count, my brain said this was it. I eased the cyclic stick back into my lap and caught the jump in the rotor RPM with a little more up collective. The shuddering Huey broke its rate of descent, stretched its stubby nose out to the sky, and clawed its way up toward the gray base of a huge white cloud, altimeter climbing, air speed dropping.

Slowing past 75 knots and climbing above 2900 feet, I nudged the cyclic to the right, eased in right pedal, and the Huey responded, gliding into a climbing wing-over turn. I kept the turn coming with cyclic and pedal, reduced the collective to 20 pounds of torque as the peak came into sight, and rolled us back to wings level on a heading of 2-7-0, due west, and dropped the nose. We were at 65 knots, 3200 feet and the 46 was wings-level coming over the eastern edge of the LZ.

Jim keyed his mike, exhaling as he talked. "Your switches are set, big guy. Get your sight down, set your torque, and make your run—in this case to the northern side of the LZ as he will probably wave-off left if he has to, or depart left when he's ready. What's your Hardball number?"

Sweat pooling in my eyebrows, I tried to get ball, torque, RPM, heading, dive angle, and target line-up all under control plus reach for the hinged gunsight above my windscreen *and* give myself an adequate chewing-out for forgetting it. "What?"

"Your Hardball number. What is it?"

"Ah…3-3. I'm 3-3."

Jim keyed his mike on UHF. "Hardball 3-3 is in."

Hearing my call sign for the first time on the radio I wanted to scream, "Hey, man, did you hear that? That's me!" But the thrill was fleeting; I had my hands full, and besides, that wouldn't be cool. If nothing else, I'd learned that in Marine aviation, you've got to be cool. Cool is everything.

"Okay, 3-3, give me a pull-out at 2400 feet, zip by the frog to show him our colors, then climb back to 3200 in a left-hand pull. Make it easier on you next time."

I answered with two clicks and we roared by on the 46's right side, eye level with him as he held his load suspended a few feet above the steel matting of the LZ. On the edge of the matting, barely visible in a cloud of dust, a man in utilities, wearing black-rimmed goggles and a green bandanna over his nose, braced against the dirt storm and patiently directed the 46 over the spot where he wanted the load released.

Jim called, "Hardball 3-3's off, left pull," and I climbed out, counting my blessings, admiring the clear air and the brilliant white clouds, and feeling a rush of blood and the thrill of success. Damn, what a great day to be alive.

Below, the 46 pickled his load on the matting and Jim talked me through covering his departure. Meanwhile, above us, like Tail-end Charlie during a game of crack the whip, B-12 zig-zagged at 3400 feet, maneuvering to cover us or the 46 if either of us needed him.

My beginner's luck didn't hold on the 46's departure, but Jim let me handle the second aircraft anyhow, fine-tuning my technique and understanding of how to anticipate the 46's needs and actions. Then he reiterated what we'd discussed that morning. "Going into a hot LZ is a hairy business," he said. "Our mission is to protect the guys who have to do that by firing at those firing at them, or by drawing fire away from them—even if it means flying between them and the guys shooting at them, taking their hits. Do whatever you have to do."

Major Hardy had said pretty much the same thing except he had added, "Frogs don't get shot down on our watch!"

Both had made it sound like our mission was the same as the "Torpedo" on Coach Day's kick-off squad.

By 1430 line 10 was complete and Jim took the controls.

"Ya done good, Ross. We may survive that next landing and takeoff after all." He reached for his select switch. "Got to say goodby to our Hotel buddy. Hotel 1-4, Hardball 4-3 over."

"Hardball 4-3, this is Hotel 1-4, go ahead, sir."

"Hotel 1-4, 4-3. Nice job. Look forward to working with you again."

"Thank you, sir. Next time bring cold beer."

Jim spun his head toward me, laughing. "Damn. This guy is getting saltier by the minute." And back to FM: "We'll do our best, Hotel. 4-3, out."

The 46s climbed between the clouds, heading east for Vandy and the LSA, and Jim turned us southwest and leveled off at 3000 feet. "Well, switch me to line 5 on fox, give me a heading over there, and I'll see if Funeral Pyhr is up their freq."

Oh, yeah. Line 5. Bill. "Ah…2-2-5 for now."

Jim turned to 2-2-5, switched B-12, got a check-in, and made the call. The hissing in the radios swished in and out.

"We may not be close enough. I'll try later."

The Quang Tri River, with Highway 9 hugging its northern bank, hooked around Shepherd to the south and was joined by the Rao Quan River. At that junction, the Quang Tri became the Da Krong and Highway 9 turned west. After climbing several hundred feet, the highway leveled off on a finger of land called LZ Hawk, an abandoned landing zone. Beyond Hawk, the highway climbed another 800 feet in a mile and a half to the Khe Sanh plateau.

Line 5, or Kilo Company, was two and a half clicks south, southwest of Hawk.

"Direct Hawk, Jim."

"Copy."

Shepherd and the hook in the Quang Tri passed off to our left. Still hadn't seen or heard anything from Pyhr's flight. Nothing on either radio. Even Jim was silent.

South of Hawk, Kilo's location was on one of a series of knobs on an irregular east-west ridgeline three clicks southeast of the Khe Sanh plateau. Approaching it from the northeast, it looked like any other tall mountainous ridgeline, only darker, more steeped in shadows. I looked to the horizon where the shadows were cast from a solid wall of towering cumulus clouds on the west side of the plateau.

Dark and sinister, the clouds leaned toward us, groping upward and outward like something evil. Below them, a curtain of fog, rain, and mist. In the middle, a thin shelf of protruding gray clouds spread eastward and, as we flew on, over the top of us, covering us like a damp shroud.

Now in semi-darkness, we flew over Hawk, itself trapped under a blanket of shadows. The temperature dropped. I pushed up my cockpit window. Still the radios were silent.

"Pick up the highway, Jim."

Two clicks.

"Where the highway bends, hang a left and go due south."

Jim nodded and reached for the UHF radio. "Cattle Prod common. 289.2?"

I moved the map off my kneeboard and flipped to the frequency card clipped under the scratch pad. I was still running my thumb down the list looking for HMM-169 when I heard the tone change in my headset. Jim didn't switch B-12.

"Hardball 1-9, Hardball 4-3 on uniform." No answer. Jim looked at me. "That right? 289.2?"

I had my finger on it. "Yeah. 289.2."

"Okay." He looked to the horizon. "Hardball 1-9, 4-3. You up this freq?" The radios hissed.

Jim lowered his head and reached for the radio again. The tone in my headset changed and locked onto channel six, our squadron common.

I shivered, a chill from the sweat under my survival vest and bullet bouncer, and thought about the guys in the back, Sergeant Hutchins and the gunner with the wimpy mustache. They must be freezing. Jim turned and pushed up his window.

We were over the bend in the highway now. Jim turned left to 1-8-0.

"Kilo, Kilo, this is Hardball 4-3, over." More hissing.

Back to my left, Shepherd and the river valley we had passed were patterned with sunlight and light shadows, warm, inviting. Back to the right—sinister darkness. Ahead was a two-tiered mountainous ridgeline soaked in cold shadows.

We passed over a small burned-out village. Ahead, a trail, like a bony finger, pointed up the slope. Thirty meters away from the village, the trail slipped under the jungle canopy and disappeared.

"Kilo, Kilo, Hardball 4-3, over."

The ground below us leveled off for a few meters, then it began the final climb to the crest.

"They should be on top of the ridge, Jim." I pointed with a gloved finger. "Twelve o'clock."

He answered with two clicks and stared ahead of us, holding 3000 feet and 90 knots.

"Dash Two, 4-3 on fox. How copy?"

"Loud and clear, 4-3."

I looked left, above and behind us. B-12 was at our eight o'clock, his rotor blades scraping the bottom of the cloud layer and throwing wisps of condensation.

"You hear anything from Kilo?" Jim asked.

"Negative."

Two clicks.

We crested the ridge, the radar altimeter indicating there was 1500 feet between us and the high ground below.

"Kilo, Kilo, Hardball 4-3, over."

The hissing went dead and in a hushed tone, a deep southern voice answered, "Hardball 4-3, Kilo."

Jim turned right. "Kilo, this is 4-3. We're a flight of two Huey guns in a right-hand turn. Do you have us in sight? Over."

"That's a negative, 4-3. Hear ya, but can't see ya, over."

"Roger, Kilo. Do we sound close? Over."

"Wait two mikes, 4-3."

"Roger."

I looked over at Jim. "What's up?"

"He wants us to wait a couple of minutes. Maybe they're on the move and he can't see us for the jungle canopy." Jim shrugged his shoulders. "Who knows."

We circled right, swinging the Huey's nose by the dark wall of clouds and rain to the west. On our next southerly swing, Kilo spoke again. "4-3, this is Kilo."

"Go ahead, Kilo."

"Interrogative. You workin' with Hardball 1-9? Over."

"Kilo, this is 4-3. We're here to replace 1-9. We're gonna run your resupply for you, over."

"Roger, 4-3. Wait one."

"Roger."

"Now what?" I said.

"We wait one, I guess."

While we waited, orbiting the ridgeline at 3000 feet, I looked into the cabin. Hutchins sat on the troopseat, facing outboard, his legs drawn up on the seat in front of him. He rested his arms on his knees and for the first time, I noticed he sat on a bullet bouncer. The gunner faced forward, his elbows on his knees, his camouflage helmet in his hands, a soiled chin-strap dangling by his Adam's apple. The windstream whipped his sleeves and legs.

The gunner looked up at me a second, expressionless, then dropped his left arm and turned his head to look out toward B-12. That was his job. When the wingman was on the gunner's side he was supposed to keep an eye on him.

"Hardball 4-3...Kilo." The Marine with the deep southern voice breathed hard.

"Go ahead, Kilo."

"Hardball 1-9 said...1-9 said he would refuel and come back. Have you talked with him? Over."

I stretched my shoulders and sighed.

"Negative, Kilo. We were assigned by DASC to replace 1-9 and run your resupply."

"We're moving, 4-3. Haven't called...for resupply yet. Later, over."

"Roger, Kilo. Copy, later." Jim glanced at me, shrugged, and looked at the ground. "Interrogative, Kilo. We heard you were in contact. Need our guns?"

"Wait one."

The Huey's nose swung around to the west, and once again I felt the pull, the attraction, and looked up. This time I found the Khe Sanh plateau buried in fog and rain and low clouds and hidden from me. The high ground south of the plateau and southwest of us, the Fire Base Tenaru area, was visible, but indistinct, just dark lumps on the earth. Still, I couldn't pull my eyes away. Then the sky flashed, lighting the interior of a monstrous cloud that climbed tens of thousands of feet into the sky above us. I blinked and sat back into my seat. Jim, looking down and behind us, needed to know about that.

Before I could speak, the deep voice in the jungle returned. "Hardball 4-3, Kilo."

"Go, Kilo."

"Affirmative…on the guns, 4-3. My six wants you to recon by fire…grid 8-8-2…3-7-0, over."

"Roger, Kilo," Jim looked at me. "Copy grid 8-8-2-3-7-0," and on ICS asked, "Got it?"

A quick glance at the map told me the grid they wanted fired on was one click south of where the dream sheet had them located. I nodded, held the map up, and tapped the location with my finger. "High ground. Click south."

"Kilo, can you observe our fire?"

"Negative."

"Any friendlies in that area?"

"Negative."

"I'll need a fix on your location. Can you talk me over you?"

"Wait one."

Jim smiled and looked at me. "Well, at least they've got something for us to do."

"4-3, Kilo."

"Yeah, Kilo, go ahead."

"My six says…we don't need to observe. Just spray that area…over."

"Kilo, 4-3, copy that. Just tell me where you are on the compass from that grid, over."

"North."

"Copy, north."

"Jim, did you see that lightning back there?"

Jim had rolled out heading east and had us over the ridgeline where Kilo was supposed to be located. "No, I didn't. Heading our way?"

"Yeah. And bringing friends."

"Okay." Jim looked to his right. "Can you vector me to a perch position?"

"Roger. Turn right at this next draw. Go due south."

Jim answered with two clicks and descended. I figured if he wasn't worried, I shouldn't be either. I shifted in my seat and adjusted my bullet bouncer. Shouldn't be, but was.

Jim turned right at the draw, and right again where I had him lined up with the target.

"Give me rockets on the right side. I'll fire one willie pete on the first pass. Then I'll ask 'em to confirm the target. These guys are good, but don't always have their grids right—don't want to hit any friendlies."

I nodded, remembering how difficult land navigation had been at The Basic School. Much easier when you're above looking down. I set up the switches.

Jim raised the nose to kill off another ten knots of air speed. At 2700 feet indicated, he relaxed his pull on the cyclic and let the Huey fall into a dive. "Make me hot," he said, and on UHF, "Two, 4-3 is in hot for a mark. Stay high and dry, over."

"Negative, 4-3! Wave-off!" The high-pitched voice was on UHF and didn't belong to B-12. "This is Hardball 1-9. Go around, 4-3. *Go around*!"

Jim raised the nose and pulled the collective. The Huey shuddered and stabilized in an 80-knot climb.

"4-3 off cold." And on ICS, "Make me cold, Ross."

"Good! Now stay high and dry! That's an order!"

I switched everything off and searched for Pyhr to the north and east. Didn't see him.

"Kilo, Kilo, this is Hardball 1-9, over."

"This is Kilo. Go ahead, 1-9."

"Roger, Kilo. Balls 1-9 is inbound from the northeast. You back in contact with those gooks yet?"

"Negative, 1-9. Still looking."

Jim climbed straight ahead, due west. A light spray of rain dotted our windshield and a gust of wind tossed the Huey upward. In the gloom ahead, the inside of another mammoth cloud lit up, closer than the last one.

"Looks like a storm," Jim said.

No shit.

"Kilo, you still where we left you?"

"Negative, 1-9. Moved south. You taking over for 4-3?"

"Affirmative."

"Roger. Can you hit the 8-8-2…3-7-0 grid for us?"

"Are the gooks there?"

"Maybe."

"Roger. Stand by."

Jim turned to the right, over the original ridgeline, and leveled off at 3000 feet, his fingers drumming the throttle grip on the collective.

"How's he doin', Hutch?"

"Okay, Lieutenant. Five o'clock."

"Jim, you got Pyhr in sight yet?"

"Yeah, low level, just now crossing the ridge under us. One o'clock."

I leaned forward and stretched my neck. Should have known he wouldn't be at a safe altitude. Couldn't see him.

We were really moving now. Strong gusts of wind kicked us forward, to the east.

"Do you see Ono?" I asked.

"I see Pyhr's wingman. He's in trail, way out of position." Jim turned toward me. "You didn't see it, did you?"

"What?"

"The schedule change this morning. Ono was scratched by Angus." He looked down and to the right. "That's the Bull himself down there. Here. Take a look."

Jim rolled right for a second and back to wings level—long enough for me to see what I hoped I wouldn't see.

A thousand feet below us, flying above the shadow-soaked hills and into a gusting headwind, was the white-striped rotor disk of Pyhr's Huey. A couple of hundred meters behind him, another white-striped rotor disk followed in trail—Angus.

"You don't fly over the same ground as the guy in front of you," Jim had said that morning. "The first guy wakes them up, then they're ready for the second guy when he comes by. Or else the rounds intended for the first guy hit the second guy. But most important: you can't cover the leader from back there. Don't do it."

I slumped back into my seat, shaking my head, and blinked at another flash of lightning. Rain pelted our windscreen. Turbulence tossed us up and down. And Jim, anticipating the winds would blow us east, turned right to orbit the area between the target and the ridgeline.

"There he goes, Ross. Right over the damn target."

I stretched forward and followed Jim's gaze to our two o'clock. Pyhr headed southwest, flying straight over the area he was supposed to be shooting at.

"What the hell is he doing?" I asked.

"Heck if I know. Maybe he doesn't know he's there; it's hard to navigate that low. Or maybe he's trollin'."

"Kilo, this is Balls 1-9, over."

Before Kilo could answer, the shadows below Pyhr's Huey erupted with twinkling yellow lights, clumps of them, some spitting green fireballs that sprang skyward passing in front of, behind, and beside the little black-green Huey. As I sucked in my breath and squeezed my mike switch to shout a warning, Pyhr's Huey snap-rolled to the right and dived for the shadows. The green tracers followed, rear and left side—Bill's side. Angus, too far behind and way out of position, pitched his nose into the dark sky and banked right, away from the threat and any opportunity to help his leader.

The tracers continued to track Pyhr. His initial dive left him with another split-second decision: climb up the slope of the ridge or run along the side of it.

Either way he was still in their sights. I wanted to scream at him: Right! Right turn! Take the wind! But someone screamed at me.

"Make me hot! We're in!"

Standing on the right pedal—the collective pulled into his armpit—Jim put two Gs on the Huey and took us from a ground speed of 120 knots to near zero in seconds. The Huey shook and shuddered and slammed to a stop in the sky. Below us, Pyhr banked hard right.

I threw the switches. "You're hot rockets, both sides."

"Hardball 4-3's in hot." Jim leveled off and dropped the nose. The air speed jumped to 70 knots. Rain swept the windscreen.

"Got your six, 4-3." B-12 calling.

Pyhr skimmed the jungle canopy as tracers ricocheted off the trees on the ridge beside him and arched into the darkness. His door gun blasted back, lighting the wet-green fuselage of the Huey with its muzzle flashes.

Jim's thumb twitched on the firing button and our Huey staggered as two rockets leaped from the pods and screamed for the ground, showering us with sparks; he hadn't waited for the optimal sight-picture, he just let 'em fly. His thumb twitched again and two more rockets flew after the others, then two more. Even before the first two hit, I could tell they were going to be long, but the second and third pair were dead on target, smoking right toward the muzzle flashes. Then the Huey jumped, dropped, and we lost sight of everything: ground, Pyhr, ridgeline, and horizon, blinded by the rain and dark clouds, thrown into our straps, unable to do anything but hang on tight—couldn't even talk.

"Altitu—, airspee—. Call—." Jim pulled collective.

"Clear behin—, Lieutenan—!"

Jim banked right, twisting his neck to look behind him, bouncing in his seat. "Stay on the —ges."

"Twenty-three hundre— descend—. Hundred —ots," I stammered, my bullet bouncer pounding my chest. I had just gotten the switches off. "You're —old."

The thin clouds melted before us and the tailwinds threw us back into the dusky and less violent sky. Jim and I both exhaled as he keyed his mike. "Where are they, Hutch? Got 'em?"

"Negative."

"Two, 4-3, you got us?"

"Negative…affirmative. We're one o'clock, 2700."

"1-9 Dash Two, this is Balls 1-9, where are ya?" Pyhr. I stretched left, then right. There he was, squirting out from under the clouds, along the ridge, without the tracers in pursuit.

"Two is northeast, over the ridge." Angus.

"Hold at 2000. I'm coming."

"You okay, 1-9?"

"Yeah. Got one bleeding."

I looked at Jim. One bleeding?

Jim shook his head, the mouth pulled tight under his mustache.

"You're in sight, Two. I'm three o'clock low. Tally?" Pyhr.

"Ah...affirmative 1-9, you're in sight." Angus.

"Okay. Pick up my six. I know where those bastards are now. They're dead meat."

"They're socked-in, 1-9. Take a look."

Behind us, the target area had disappeared in driving rain, low clouds, and darkness.

"We'll wait 'em out then, goddamn it. This rain'll pass."

My face flushed with heat. Who's bleeding, you asshole?

"4-3 Dash Two, 4-3, fuel state?" Jim.

"Five-fifty, 4-3." B-12.

"Roger. Break. Hardball 1-9, Hardball 4-3, over."

"What?"

"4-3 and flight will be going back for refuel, over."

"So?"

"You want us to tell DASC anything?"

"Yeah, tell 'em to go fuck themselves."

"Wilco."

Jim had turned us to the northeast, toward Vandy, and B-12 had joined up at our four o'clock.

Jim keyed the ICS and read my mind. "I don't think it's Bill." He glanced at me. "Pyhr couldn't find his butt with both hands; he needs a co-pilot to keep him from getting lost. I don't think he'd hang around if he had a wounded co-pilot. Besides, now that we're leaving, I'll bet he'll RTB anyhow."

Below and behind us, Pyhr's Huey crested the ridgeline.

"Why? Looks to me like the prick's gonna stay."

"Because the competition's leaving. See, he wants all the gooks to himself. So, if we leave, we won't get his kills, and he can leave too." Jim shrugged. "I could be wrong."

"Kilo, Kilo, Balls 1-9."

The radios hissed, then, "Balls 1-9, Kilo."

"Roger, Kilo, Balls 1-9 has one WIA, gonna have to RTB."

"Roger that, 1-9. Interrogative. We heard some fire. Did you hit the 8-8-2, 3-7-0? Over."

"Roger. We found'em. Be advised, that hill is lousy with gooks, over."

"Thanks, 1-9. Kilo, out."

We flew to Vandy in silence. Jim gave me the controls as we passed over Fire Base Shepherd. I don't know what he was thinking on the way back, but my thoughts were divided. Part of the time I thought of fallout. We'd saved Pyhr's ass and done Angus' job. Neither of them struck me as mature enough to thank us for that. The rest of the time I thought of Bill.

We were in the fuel pits at Vandy when Pyhr's Huey landed up on the hillside at Delta Med.

Pyhr's crew chief and gunner stepped out, one helping the other walk. I couldn't tell who it was, but by the way he limped, he was gonna be okay. They had landed facing south and we were parked facing north, so our left sides faced each other and I could clearly see the Cat's Ass. As the dust cleared around him, Bill saw me. He pointed his thumb to his cabin like a hitch-hiker and made a "OK" sign.

I pointed at Bill and asked with a thumbs-up sign, are *you* okay? The hot dog actually pointed back at me, laughed, beat his chest, and made a muscle. It was a piece of cake, he said. The Cat's Ass is indestructible, and you, R.T., are sweatin' the small shit too much. I smiled back and shot him the bird.

We took off a few minutes later; the LSA had another resupply for us, a new line number, an "on call" mission. With an afternoon breeze providing ten knots of headwind, the takeoff was no problem.

Just before dusk, we were sent to Kilo Company again; they had humped back to the east and set up on the ridgeline for the night. We covered Cattle Prod while they delivered chow, water, and ammo. Smooth mission. No fire.

While we were there, Khe Sanh remained a mystery, concealed by long shadows from the west, shadows from a towering table-topped mountain in Laos. Jim identified the mountain as Co Roc. "Bad place," he said. "You'll see more of it on Thunder Clap."

By the time we got back to the hootch that night, it was eight o'clock. A corner of my bed was still wet from the leak in the roof that morning. Across from me, Bill's gear was dumped on the floor.

I walked over and took Laura's picture off the ammo box by Bill's rack. I touched my thumb to the crack in the glass across her hairline, a careless crack that made it look like her blonde hair had black roots. She smiled up at me, a camera glint in her blue eyes. I wanted to tell her stuff. I wanted her to know that it was okay, that I wasn't the only one looking out for her husband, that he was alive and well tonight thanks to a guy named Jim Teach. You'd like him, I wanted to tell her. We'll introduce him to you one day.

I set the picture back in its place and added aloud, "Send cookies."

15

Missing Messages

Less than a week after Major "Bull" Angus was introduced to us at the Friday Evening Parade, and the day after I saw him cut and run when his leader took fire south of LZ Hawk, I had my first personal encounter with him. Bill was with me.

We were both in the S-2, or intelligence shop, when Straderman appeared in the doorway and said the major wanted to see us. I had just been assigned as the assistant S-2 officer. Lieutenant Ken Shockley, the one everyone called "Shit-hot" Shockley, was my boss. Shockley was never around, so PFC Scapelli was showing me where everything was and what my duties were. I wasn't scheduled to fly again until that afternoon. Bill was hanging around because he was the SDO and was killing time before he had to inspect the mess hall.

"He wants to see us right now?" I asked.

"Yes, sir." Straderman wore full camouflage utilities—the shirt collar soaked with sweat—and leaned against the doorjamb with arms crossed. "You should have come to see me, Lieutenant. He and Captain Orndorff have just had a big pow-wow and the major's pissed."

"Damn." I made a fist. "It's that bond thing, right?"

"Yes, sir." He dropped his arms, turned to go, but stopped and pointed a finger at Scapelli who stood behind me at the filing cabinet. "You better get that shirt on, Vegas. He could be back here any minute."

Scapelli glanced at the shirt draped over the chair, nodded, and continued searching the files.

Straderman frowned and walked away.

Sitting on the floor, Bill looked up from a *Playboy* magazine in his lap. "Scapelli. What was that all about?"

The PFC, in a green T-shirt soaked to his navel in sweat, glanced at the doorway. "A decree from Augustus Angus, sir: no more T-shirts in squadron spaces. Full uniform only."

"Oh."

"Even squadron spaces without fans?" I said, looking around at the stifling ten-by-ten windowless room decorated with wall maps and filing cabinets.

"Yes, sir."

Bill tossed the magazine on a pile of others stacked against the wall and stood. "Let's go, R.T."

"Wait a minute. I thought we were gonna fight this."

Bill put his arm around my shoulder and pulled me toward the door. "R.T., my boy, did I ever tell you about my track coach at San Diego State?"

"Is this the guy they hired so you'd take a scholarship there?"

"That's him. My high school coach too. Great guy. Married one of those girls in the Gidget movie, "Gidget Does Hawaii," or something like that."

"Yeah, heard of him. So what?"

Bill dragged me down the hall by my neck and tried to zip my flightsuit up to my Adam's apple. I had to fight him with both hands to keep it down at chest level.

"Well, Coach Peter, movie star's husband and track strategist el supremo, sayeth unto me one day, 'Cat,'—he called me Cat too, you know— 'Cat', he said, 'there comes a time when you must choose your battles. I don't want you in the pole vault this week. Redlands has a gorilla in that event, a foreign student from Tunisia, an Olympian at Rome. I want you in the broad jump instead.'"

Bill stopped us at the entrance to the empty ready room. "So Coach Peter says Pender, our second vaulter—behind me of course—was good enough to beat their second vaulter, whereas I, the future Cat's Ass, the future Leader of Marines, was a good-enough broad jumper to beat their best jumper; our best jumper was down with a case of the clap from an ill-advised trip to Tijuana, you see. Nasty. One of the worst cases I've ever seen."

Straderman, at the end of the hall to our left, sat behind his typewriter, watching us.

"Where is this going, Cat?"

Bill brushed my flightsuit with his hands, grooming me, paying particular attention to my collar and shoulders. "This battle is small shit, R.T. We can't win it, so let's save ourselves for another event." He smiled his freckled, fun-fun smile of large teeth and eyes. "After all, 'allotments non foreveris.'"

"Catlett coat of arms?"

"Rog-o, Daddy-o."

"I don't believe this, Cat."

"Trust the Sun Dog, man. Follow me."

Five minutes later, Straderman escorted us into the major's office where we snapped to attention in front of his desk, eyes straight ahead, Bill on my right. I took a breath. "First Lieutenants Teemer and Catlett reporting as ordered, sir."

Reclined in his swivel chair behind a large metal desk, Major Angus looked up at us. Two brown files lay on the desk in front of him. Toying with a yellow pencil he held between his hands, he left us braced before him and smirked.

"At ease!"

We relaxed to a modified parade rest.

The major held out both hands, the smirk fading to a frown, and nodded toward two folding chairs, one on each side of his desk. "Have a seat, gentlemen."

"Yes, sir."

We pulled the chairs around to the front, and sat. As my parents had taught me not to talk around objects, I made sure not to put the stack of three file trays on the corner of the desk between me and the major. The three trays were labeled "suck," "combust," and "blow."

On the other corner of the desk, exactly between the major and where Bill had positioned his chair, stood a scratched and faded ceramic bull the size of a football. Behind the bull sat a full ashtray containing a still-smoldering filterless cigarette. The painted animal—heavy muscular chest, enraged eyes, defiant head with several yellow and green banderillas hanging from a thick, bloody neck—stared at me as Bill took the extra time he needed to get his chair in just the right position.

Angus, after a few seconds of waiting and watching Bill hop his chair around on the plywood floor, finally squeezed his lips together and sat erect, swiveling his chair to face Bill. When he realized the bull was between them, he smacked the pencil on the desk, placed both hands on the arm rests of the chair, and rolled to one side.

Bill, his head hung over his knees, ignored the warning shot with the pencil and continued to scoot his chair around on the floor, ostensibly to find a position that would avoid two troublesome nails and a crease in the plywood sheets.

"Lieutenant Catlett!"

Bill snapped his head up. "Yes, sir?"

"Take your fucking seat, Lieutenant!"

Bill's eyes darted at me as if to ask, what is this guy's problem? "Yes, sir."

The major stiffened. He glanced at me, back to Bill, and stood, leaning his hairy fists on the desk and pressing his creased camouflage utilities against the drawer, studying us. I looked straight ahead. He smiled, his shoulders relaxed, and he reached for one of the folders.

"Lieutenant Teemer." He held the folder open before him, the one with my name on it. "It says here you are a regular Marine officer, a graduate of The Basic School. Is that correct, Lieutenant?"

"Yes, sir."

"How well did you do at The Basic School, Lieutenant?"

I searched his eyes. "What do you mean, sir?"

He slammed the folder shut and leaned over the desk, wobbling like a threatening pile of bricks. "Are you questioning the clarity of my speech, Lieutenant? My mastery of the fucking English language? Huh?"

"No, sir."

"Then answer the fucking question, Lieutenant!"

"Yes, sir. I did very well at The Basic School, sir."

"Well enough to learn something about military courtesy, Lieutenant?" I opened my mouth to answer, but he cut me off and screamed, "Did you attend that class, Lieutenant?"

"Yes, sir."

Angus stood erect, cocking his large head back and to one side. He looked down his nose at me, his mouth in a satisfied smirk, and glanced at Bill.

Bill returned his glance with an admiring smile.

Angus nodded and looked at me again. "Lieutenant Teemer, Basic School Graduate. As one who did 'very well' at The Basic School, does the phrase 'The CO's Wishes' mean anything to you?" He rocked onto his heels and crossed his arms, his head still held back.

I cleared my throat. "Yes, sir, it does."

"Well, it does. Very good. How about explaining it to us, Lieutenant: to your friend, Catlett, and myself." Angus turned his satisfied eyes to Bill. "You didn't have the pleasure of attending The Basic School, did you, Lieutenant Catlett?"

Bill smiled up at the major. "No, sir. Went from Officer Candidate School to Pensacola. Don't know anything about 'CO's wishes,' sir." The major frowned as Bill continued. "But I do know some stuff about ceramics, sir, and this bull is a fine piece of work." Bill reached for the bull on the desk. "My roommate and I took a course in ceramics at San Diego State—excellent course; the professor was—"

"As you were, Catlett!"

Bill jerked his hand off the bull and sat back, his head erect, his eyes wide and blinking.

Angus took a half-step backward. He huffed, then like a bull who had decided to take one more run at that red cape, he stepped to the edge of the desk and leaned onto his fists. "Okay, Lieutenant Teemer, what does it mean when your CO 'wishes' or 'would like' something?"

"Well, sir," I said, straightening my back against the metal chair, "if my commanding officer were to say to me, 'I would like you to take out an allotment for savings bonds,' well, that would be the same as if he had ordered me, or given me a direct order, to let the Marine Corps take money from my check every month."

He stared at me, his eyes just off the edge of mine. His brow furrowed. Finally he snorted and stood erect, his finger tips on the desk, a smile blooming on his cratered face.

"Lieutenant Teemer...the CO is flying this morning." He paused and let that thought hang in the air long enough for other thoughts, like a chain-of-command diagram, and the definition of the role of the executive officer, to grow off of it. "In his *absence*, Lieutenant, it is my desire, my 'wish' if you choose, that you and your friend, Lieutenant Catlett, *will*, on my command, march your asses out of my office and into the S-1 shop where you *will* immediately sign allotment forms for U.S. savings bonds." The hairy one leaned forward, looked at me, looked at Bill, then whispered, "Do you read me?"

"Yes, sir," we answered in unison.

"Then, dismissed!"

Bill and I stood together. I stiffened at attention while Bill turned and took the time to fumble with an errant chair leg stuck in the crack in the floor. With Angus angrily clearing his throat behind him, Bill released the leg and eased the chair into its original position at the side of the desk. Stepping to the front again, he popped to attention beside me. We did an about-face together and marched from the room.

Under Straderman's guiding hand—and Orndorff's satisfied gaze—we completed the forms and returned to the S-2 shop.

In S-2, Scapelli sat at the desk with a green logbook opened in front of him and a pencil in his hand.

Bill flopped onto the plywood floor and took another *Playboy* off the pile. I walked around the desk and stopped behind Scapelli. "Whatcha got?" I asked.

Scapelli looked at the doorway, pushed the chair back, and stood beside me—the logbook in his hands. "Lieutenant, this is a record of all the classified teletyped messages we get." He nodded at a teletype machine on a typewriter stand against the wall by the desk. "We're the only squadron that has one of these machines. We can receive routine, classified, and top secret. We only have it 'cause of the Thunder Clap mission. Anyhow, I came back over here after I got off mess duty the other night and saw Major Angus here—standing at the file cabinet. I guess he got a key from Mickey."

The logbook page he held before me looked normal, just a list of messages. "So, what are you telling me? Did he do something to the logbook?"

"No, sir. As far as I know, he didn't touch the logbook." He pointed to a check mark in pencil beside the third entry on the page. "I watched him for a long time, sir. Over half an hour. He was going through the files, removing messages." He tapped his finger on the page. "Here. In the last two days, I've gone over every message and checked the ones that are missing." He looked at me. "See for yourself, Lieutenant."

Starting with the third entry on that page, and continuing through the rest of the logbook, there was a check mark on every third or fourth page for a total of a dozen or more. I turned to the cover. "How far does this go back?"

"This is the original book, ah…" He thumbed to the first lined page. "Here. That date-time-group was for October 20th, 1967, about the time the squadron moved in here and got the Thunder Clap mission."

"And you've been through the whole book? From October '67 to today?"

"Didn't have to, sir. We burn everything six months old, so the only ones missing are after January first of this year."

I flipped through a few more pages: no information on what the messages said, just a date-time-group for each and who it was from. I handed the book to him. "Any idea what those messages related to? Or why he would want them?"

"No, sir. But he did come in here the other day and ask me for a map."

Bill looked up from his magazine. "He wanted to go into Hue, right? Wanted a street map."

Scapelli smiled. "Not hardly, Lieutenant. You're still the only one that's ever asked for that."

I nudged Scapelli with my elbow. "What map? What'd he want?"

"He wanted maps of North Vietnam. Not all of it, just the area south of Vinh."

"Did he say why?"

"No, sir. I told him we had maps in the Thunder Clap map cases that included where the north bordered Laos and the DMZ, but that's all."

"What'd he say to that?"

"He said, 'Get the rest.'"

"Did you?"

"No, sir. I found out they're not in the group inventory. Had to order them from wing."

"Does he know that?"

"Don't know. Haven't talked with him since."

I ran my hand through my hair, crossed my arms, and stared at the logbook. Top-secret messages on U.S. military operations being carried around, unsecured, so hootch maids or…*barbers*, or anyone could find them? Why? He could see them anytime right here. "Scapelli, who else has a key to this office and the 'secure message file?'"

"Just Staff Sergeant Morchesski as far as I know."

"And did Major Angus ask you about maps before or after you saw him going through the files?"

"After."

"And you don't know what he wants or how all this fits together?"

"No, sir."

Bill threw his magazine on the pile and stood. "Hey, Sherlock." He poked me on the shoulder and headed for the door. "Let's go eat, man."

I followed him. "I'll be back after chow, Scapelli. You be here?"

"Yes, sir. I'm flying with you this afternoon."

"All right." I pushed Bill into the hallway and stopped. "Hey, can you get copies of those missing messages?"

"I don't think so, sir. But I'll work on it. There might be a way."

"Okay." I turned to go, but had another thought and turned back. "And hey, do you know anything about 'CO's Wishes?'"

"Ah…how do you mean, sir?"

"Like, 'As the acting CO of this S-2 shop, I wish you would put on your shirt.' Seriously, I don't want to lose the most fearless gunner in the squadron 'cause he pissed off the XO."

Scapelli laughed. "Lieutenant, we have an OIC and an NCOIC here. We don't have a CO. There's only one of those in this squadron, and he hasn't said shit to me in weeks."

"Well, keep it handy in case you hear footsteps in the hall, okay?"

"Yes, sir." He smiled. "As you wish, sir."

16

Body Count

The night after our confrontation with Angus, Bill had the duty and searched Angus' office for the missing messages. The next day he told me what he'd done and said he didn't find anything. I told him to forget it—emphatically told him to forget it. Verbally dancing around a field grade officer was one thing. Rifling his office was something else. I said we'd drop the whole thing.

Bill agreed. That's what he wanted to hear anyhow; he was convinced I was making mountains out of molehills again and told me so.

But I couldn't drop it. I asked Scapelli to look at the logbook again and see if there was a pattern to the messages. He was to have that information for me on Friday, our second Friday in Vietnam, a day I was scheduled for morning guns with Major Leslie Lewis and if we returned in time, the evening parade.

I had spoken with Major Lewis, or "Sweet Lou" as Tess called him, before, but hadn't spent any time around him until the morning briefing. Short like Rod Wysowski, but heavier, softer, and balding with close-cut gray hair on the sides, he smiled often, used first names freely, and was easy to like. A straight-stem pipe he found difficult to light completed the picture. Too small to be an aviator, too soft to be a Marine, Major Lewis could have been Elmer Fudd doing Bing Crosby in "On the Road to Phu Bai."

After an uneventful briefing and departure, with Ono and Munzel on our wing, and with the sun sparkling off the Perfume River, we passed over Hue City at 1500 feet and the major let me take the controls. Turning his attention to the ADF, a navigation radio that homes in on low-frequency commercial radio stations and non-directional beacons, he tuned it to Armed Forces Radio. The D.J. was reading a weather report so I flipped my mixer switch off. The major did the same and reached for the pipe in the calf pocket of his flightsuit.

Sergeant Whipple, our crew chief, slipped a wiry gloved hand up to the ADF radio controls and turned up the volume.

"Ross, we got an interesting report yesterday."

"On the squadron, sir?"

"Yes, on some action you were part of, I believe."

"Really?" I didn't know what he was referring to. It could have been the crash with Hardy, or the tree incident with Pyhr, or maybe the mission with Teach south of LZ Hawk. Nothing significant had happened since. I decided it was the Pyhr thing. I'd really expected an accident investigation over that and looked forward to it; Pyhr was a lunatic and the Marine Corps needed to know about it.

"It was from Lima Company, 3rd Battalion, 9th Marines." The major saw me turn my head. "Yeah. They credited Hardball 1-9 with twelve KBA. You were in the area, right?"

I hesitated. Twelve KBA, or Killed By Air, by Pyhr?

"It was on the 24th, in the 8-8-3-7 grid, as I recall. You remember?"

"Yes, sir."

I remembered alright. But I didn't remember Pyhr firing a shot. Unless they did some shooting after we left. But Bill never mentioned any shooting, and they landed at Vandy only five minutes behind us.

"How do they know it was 1-9, sir, or how many were killed? I don't even remember the grunts being there. Or at least not close enough to see what we were doing."

"Well, according to the report, a platoon from Lima Company swept that area at first light on the 25th and found the bodies in fresh graves." The major struck a match. "They said 1-9 hit that grid the afternoon before." He applied the match to the pipe bowl, puffed three times, shook the match to extinguish it, then dropped it into the ashtray under the instrument panel. "Must have gotten a secondary explosion, 'cause Lima reported a huge hole in the ground and fragments of mortar rounds all over the area. You don't remember that?"

"No, sir. The only shooting I saw was Lieutenant Teach putting down six rockets, four of them right down Nguyen's throat. We went IFR in rain before they actually exploded, but that night in the hootch, Lieutenant Catlett told me they were right on the money and the fire they were taking stopped immediately after the rockets hit."

"Catlett? That was Major Pyhr's co-pilot?"

"Yes, sir."

"And they were taking fire?"

"Yes, sir. They were low-leveling over the area when the shooting started—at them. Teach reacted to cover 'em."

The major pulled the pipe from his mouth and exhaled a stream of blue smoke. "You didn't see Major Pyhr shoot?"

"No, sir."

"How 'bout his wingman, Major Angus?"

"No, sir."

"Humph."

Flying past Quang Tri, Major Lewis put his pipe away, took the controls, and called Dong Ha DASC.

DASC assigned us to work with Magpie 3-0-1 and 3-0-1 Dash Two, two 46s from Quang Tri on resupply for the 3rd Marines. We picked up dream sheets at Quang Tri LSA and joined Magpie on their squadron common over the flatlands east of Con Thien.

Our progress down the dream sheet was steady and uneventful until late in the morning when we got to "Mike 1-4," a company-size patrol out of Con Thien and our last scheduled mission of the day. They were on Hill 38, a mound of barren earth between two blue lines, or streams. The hill overlooked a wretched area of bombed-out rice paddies and a decimated village.

While the 46s picked up the load for Mike Company, Major Lewis copied the zone brief, climbed to 3000 feet so we could enjoy the cooler temperatures, and gave me the controls. A few minutes later, as I admired the view of the Ben Hai River and a hazy North Vietnam, the major keyed his mike. "Ross, you've only been here about ten days, right?"

"Yes, sir."

He lit his pipe again, holding a match to the packed tobacco, sucking the flame onto it, and blowing puffs of smoke out the corner of his mouth. "Well…it must have been the day you checked in…or the day after…anyhow, about ten days ago." He paused to shake out the first match, drop it in the ashtray, and light another. "Mike, Lima, and Kilo Companies of the 3rd Battalion, 3rd Marines…kicked the shit out of the 27th NVA Regiment and an NVA sapper battalion…just a few clicks east and southeast of here." He removed the pipe and blew a long stream of smoke toward the instrument panel. "Wiped out half the bastards and scattered the rest. Still finding stragglers." He bobbed his head. "Good fight."

I tried to picture Major Lewis in a good fight and heard Magpie call us on the UHF: "Hardball 1-7, Magpie 3-0-1."

I expected the major to take the controls, but he switched his transmit select switch from ICS to UHF and continued to lounge in his armored seat. "Go ahead, Magpie."

"Roger, we're two minutes out with one external, ah…go ahead and pass the zone brief and have them stand by with smoke, over."

The major puffed on his pipe and passed the brief to Magpie while I continued a left-hand orbit at 3000 feet. I thought we should come down and he should take it, but he showed no signs of doing either. Finally, after he had told Magpie of the secure zone, friendlies north and east at 100 meters, negative fire since they'd been there, recommended east-to-west approach, and smoke on call, he sat straight, turned, nodded to me, and took the controls.

"Hardball, Magpie."

"Go ahead, Magpie." The major descended from 3000 feet at 90 knots and reversed toward a right-hand orbit.

"Roger, ah…wait one, 1-7. Okay. Didn't expect to find you at our altitude. You're in sight, and ah…we'll take that smoke now."

"Roger, 3-0-1." The major switched to FM. "Mike 1-4, this is Hardball 1-7, pop smoke, over."

Seconds later, a green cloud grew from the center of the hard-packed mound below us, and the 46, with the bulging cargo-net hanging under him, dropped out of the sky beside us and inside our orbit.

"3-0-1 is in right."

"Roger that."

At 90 knots, passing 2500 feet, the major had yet to mention how he wanted the armament panel, so I set it up for rockets, both sides, and unhooked my TAT gunsight.

The 46, in a right-hand spiral, did his version of the runaway elevator and was on short final, nose high and pulling pitch, as we coasted through 1800 feet. I leaned into my straps. Neither us nor Ono—who was taking his cue from Lewis like a wingman was supposed to do—was in position and now the 46 was in the pucker zone, low and slow, belly exposed.

"Taking fire, taking fire!" The insistent but under-control voice was on FM.

I grabbed the master-arm switch, looked out the major's window—but couldn't see the LZ—and stared, waiting for an order, holding my TAT sight out of my way.

A curl of blue smoke rose from the major's pipe bowl as he eased his trigger finger around the mike switch. He squeezed. "Mike, this is Hardball 1-7, did you say the 46 is taking fire?"

"Most affirm, sir!"

"Roger." He leveled off at 1500 feet and switched to UHF. "3-0-1, you copy Mike? Says you're taking fire, over."

I looked past the major again and waited for him to kick it over, to dive in, to call for switches hot—to help those guys—and found the 46 escaping above a cloud of dirt, nose low, scrambling into a steady climb—the external load swinging like a pendulum below it.

The major chuckled. “Well, he must have heard one of us; that frog is shittin’ and gettin’!” He nodded. “Good stick though—didn’t pickle the load.”

I squeezed the grip on the TAT and fought back a comment.

“Magpie, Hardball 1-7. Look, ah…if you’ll hold at 3000 or so, we’ll try to get a fix on where that fire came from, over.”

“That would be nice, 1-7. We need a few minutes to count the holes anyhow. Go ahead. Take your sweet time.”

The major smiled and shrugged. “Okay, 3-0-1. Wait one.” He switched to FM. “Mike 1-4, Hardball 1-7.”

“Yes, sir, 1-7, go ahead. You guys aren’t leavin’ us, are you?”

“Negative, Mike. Just tell me where that fire came from.”

“Roger, sir. It sounded like one AK from the gully to our southwest, over.”

“Are we cleared to fire in that gully, Mike?”

“Roger, sir. All our people are on the hill or north or east, over.”

“Roger.” The major flew us into a right-hand racetrack pattern at 1500 feet, turned for a run-in heading of 270 degrees, and called for rockets—switches hot.

I sighed, moved the master-arm switch to arm, and he dropped in at 60 knots.

As the major worked on his target line-up—the ball swinging from side to side in the turn-and-bank indicator—I looked at two gullies southwest of the Marine position. Both were closed on the northern end, draining to the south. The larger was also the closer, 100 meters from the nearest Marines. The smaller gully was 200 meters away. The sniper with the AK was probably in the larger one; it was deeper, led to a stream bed with thick brush—tactical cover and concealment—plus it offered an easier shot at the 46.

The major fired two pairs of rockets at the smaller gully. All hit long. My ear lobes burned.

He called off cold and climbed to 1500 feet and I fired a burst from the TAT, flipped the master-arm off, and turned to watch Sergeant Whipple fire his M-60. No movement in the gully.

In the sky behind Whipple, black smoke puffed from the pods of Ono’s Huey and two willie pete rockets streaked to the ground and burst into brilliant white clouds—both short. A second pair, those with HE—or high explosive—heads hit on the top lip of the small gully, threw dirt and brush high into the air, and covered the gully with a thick cloud of black smoke and brown dust.

“Magpie 3-0-1, Hardball 1-7.” The major still had the pipe in his mouth.

Orbiting above us, the 46 responded, “Go ahead.”

“Roger. I think we’ve taken care of that gook now. You ready to try another approach?”

"Affirmative. But no smoke. Just tell 'em we're inbound. We're leaving three, in right."

"Roger." The major alerted Mike, and the 46 dropped from the sky in a tight right-hand spiral.

This time, as it rolled onto final—nose high in the air, tandem rotors coning upward—the major was in position and diving on the small gully. No fire. Quiet.

Suddenly, close below us, out of coverage from my TAT, streaks of light—tracers—scattered out of the large gully. I pressed against my armored seat as we flew over them, then realized they were ricochets, red M-60 ricochets from the Marines on the hill. Were they taking fire?

I snapped my head to the major.

He pulled off without firing. "Well, Ross, looks like he's gonna be okay this time. That gully was quiet."

Damn! I answered with two clicks and leaned out of my seat to find the 46.

A thousand feet below, nose high in a cloud of dust, the 46's left-side gunner poured .50 caliber fire from an open window to the closer gully—the large gully—while the 46 pilot touched the cargo net to the ground, pickled it, then pitched his aircraft forward and right. A screening cloud of dirt billowed toward the gully. I couldn't see any return fire.

"We're out right."

Behind us, Ono dropped in to cover the 46 and the tracers stopped.

"Hardball 1-7, Magpie 3-0-1 and flight are RTB."

"Copy that, 3-0-1. You okay?"

"Yeah, if you like drafts and leaking hydraulic fluid. Break. Dash Two, go LSA fox."

"Well, nice job, 3-0-1. See you later."

The 46 replied with two clicks.

"Hardball 1-7, Mike."

"Go ahead, Mike."

"Thanks for the water, sir. Tell the 46 we appreciate it."

"Wilco, Mike. Unless you need us, we're RTB, over."

"Wait one."

"Roger." The major turned and smiled. "I guess I should have kept my mouth shut. If we left now, we could be back before they close the chow line."

"Hardball 1-7, Mike."

"Go, Mike."

"Roger, sir. Interrogative. We've got a squad moving toward that draw, sir. Could you put some more fire in there for us?"

The major frowned and shook his head. "Roger, Mike. We cleared at this time? Over."

"Wait one, sir."

The major didn't answer. He took the pipe from his mouth and set it in the ashtray under the instrument panel. "You want this one, Ross?"

My chin dropped. Are you kidding? I cleared my throat. "Yes, sir."

The major nodded toward me.

I hung the TAT gunsight on its hook and took the controls.

"You got it," he said.

"I've got it, sir."

The solid feel of the pedals and the cyclic and the throttle grip on the collective seemed to drain the heat from my neck and ears. I checked the instruments.

"Hardball, 1-7, Mike."

The major keyed his mike. "Go ahead."

"We're in position, sir. Hit that draw when you're ready."

"Roger."

Now I had a problem. I didn't want to fly over that large gully on my way to the small gully if that was where Nguyen was in the first place. Without all that fire from the grunts on the hill and the 46 gunner to distract him, he could nail us good. So now what? The major might take the controls back if I didn't do exactly what he had done. I continued the racetrack pattern at 1500 feet in a right turn.

"Major, did you see the grunts shooting at the other gully, the first one, the larger one?"

The major repacked his pipe. "No. Did it look like they had something in that draw too?"

I grinned and glanced away. "Yes, sir. I think they saw something in that draw as well, and that's where they want us to shoot."

"Well, maybe they do." He put the tobacco pouch in his pocket and straightened, holding a book of matches. "Why don't you give 'em a call. See if that's what they want?"

I looked at him, feeling the guys in back watching me, imagining the disbelief in their eyes. "Really, sir?"

The major struck a match, his chubby cheeks bulging inside his helmet, the stained pipe stem to his lips, "Sure. Give 'em a call."

"Yes, sir." I switched to FM and keyed the mike as I made a base-leg turn. "Mike, this is Hardball 1-7, over."

"Go ahead, Hardball."

"Roger, Mike, ah…do you want us to hit the gully you guys were shooting at, or (Be careful, Ross)…is that what you want? Over."

"Affirmative, sir. It's a large gully east of where you fired before, over."

"Roger."

I eased out a breath. Okay, the perch altitude of 1500 feet I could live with, but I wanted to make one more change. "Major, you mind if I make the run-in more southeast to northwest, ah…still parallel to the friendlies, of course."

The major was on his second match. "Sure, that'll be okay."

He didn't even ask why. Damn, it was my lucky day. "Thank you, sir."

Below, the gully ran southeast to northwest. On our last run, heading due west, the sniper had the protection of the east rim of the draw. Changing to a northwest heading would put him in a miniature box canyon—nowhere to run, nowhere to hide.

I switched to UHF, told Hardball 1-7 Dash Two what I was going to do, and was certain I could hear Ono and Munzel scream at each other, "See, I told you that was Teemer! What the fuck? Over."

I didn't care; they could scream if they wanted to. They didn't know what I knew.

Back on the perch at 1500 feet—gunsight down, 18 pounds of torque—I turned to a northwest heading of 3-3-0 and dropped the nose to a thirty-degree dive. The major flipped the master-arm to arm. I called, "In hot," thinking of what I'd learned on the targets at Yuma, Arizona: consistency was the key to a good gun-run—consistency in dive angle, air speed at release, and sight picture. Plus a centered ball. That's how you got good hits.

The air speed climbed past 75 knots. I kept the ball centered with pedal, lined up the two crossed wires in the gunsight with the black cross on the windscreen and the center of the large gully, and passing 85 knots I fired. The Huey jerked as the two pods absorbed the recoil and the rockets streaked for the ground, trailing sparks for a second, then black smoke.

I stayed with the sight picture. The first pair were going to be long, so I pressed the nose down a notch, got the centered ball, and fired again at 100 knots. I pulled the collective and nose up together then broke to the right in a climbing turn, the Huey shuddering from a one-to-one beat. At the same time, the second pair hit behind the first pair, above the gully, still long.

I recognized what was wrong and calculated a correction. I had won my share of beers on the ranges at Yuma. I could hit the bulls-eye there, and I could hit that draw here but, as Major Lewis reached for his mike switch, I didn't know if I'd get another chance.

"Not bad, Ross. Hell, it's impossible to hit shit in this damn thing." He shifted in his seat.

I grimaced. The words were good but he was moving for the controls.

"I was one dead-eyed son-of-a-bitch in the old AD-1 Skyraider. That was one solid gun-platform." The major reached for the collective, but his hand passed over it to the matchbook lying on the pedestal panel. "But I can't hit shit in this thing."

I climbed back to the perch position, holding my breath, silently begging for one more chance.

He struck a match. "Well, you want another run? We got plenty of rockets left."

I exhaled. "Yes, sir."

The major lit his pipe, blew a stream of smoke at the instrument panel, and said with an exaggerated pose, "Then damn the gooks, Lieutenant Teemer. Full speed ahead!"

I chuckled, said, "Yes, sir," and felt the guys in the back shaking their heads. Didn't matter. They didn't know what I knew: The men in my family were shooters, I was as good as any of them, and the gooner who had just tried to kill Marines on my watch was history.

I leveled off and turned toward the gully, knowing there's more to good shooting than sight-picture and trigger-squeeze; you've got to know the personality of each individual weapon. So as I reached the perch position and raised the nose to bleed off the last ten knots of air speed, I factored in the knowledge I'd gathered on that particular Huey gunship from my first run at the target. If I kept everything else the same: torque, air speed at release, dive angle, altitude at release, centered ball, rear-sight-to-front-sight-to-target alignment, and the wind was the same, then changed one ingredient, a change dictated by the Huey itself, I'd get good hits.

I dropped the nose, confirmed I was over the same spot as before and at 1500 feet—thus insuring the same dive angle—and set 18 pounds of torque. The gully, sparsely vegetated with a dry stream bed snaking down the middle of it, filled my gunsight. I called in hot.

The major moved the switch, the red light on the armament panel illuminated, and the Huey bumped through some rough air. Now at 75 knots, looking for 85—that's where I had fired last time—my eyes darted from gunsight (more right), to air speed, to ball, back to gunsight. Now. My thumb squeezed the red button on the side of the cyclic stick and the Huey spit two rockets toward the ground below, bathing us in sparks and thin black smoke.

They tracked good—on target. That Huey, on that day, shot high and slightly left of the aiming point. So, I had picked out a new aiming point: a clump of bushes low and to the right, short of the draw, and closer to the grunts. Two seconds after I fired the first pair, now with more air speed and closer to the target, I fired again, aiming lower still, knowing that less flight time for the rocket meant less drop. Then, as the first pair exploded on the inside west edge of the draw, I fired again, aiming even lower.

With the metallic thump of the last pair leaving the pods, I pulled pitch, raised the nose, and turned right, the altimeter needle tapping 600 feet before reversing, the Huey bouncing and rattling us in our seats. Meanwhile, ahead and below, the second and third pair dove into the center and east bank of the draw and exploded among the dust and debris of the first.

I called off cold—my heart kicking my survival vest and bullet bouncer—thinking, thank you, Major, thank you! and continued to climb, straining to look over my right shoulder, watching Sergeant Whipple spray the dusty gully, his fire keeping the sniper's head down while we climbed out of range and Ono made the next run. That's when I saw them.

Two figures in dirty uniforms, both with weapons, probably AKs, ran from the billowing dust-cloud at the south end of the gully and sprinted down the stream bed heading southeast, dust trailing off their shoulders and backs. Two rockets from Ono's Huey slammed into the gully behind them. Already committed to a dive angle and run-in heading, Ono could only pull off and key his mike. "Lead, two gooks running southeast along the blue line. You got 'em?"

Whipple turned his gun on the fleeing figures as I looked at the major. He smiled at me, the pipe clenched in his teeth. "You got it, Dead-Eye."

I keyed the mike to answer Ono but was cut out by FM.

"Hardball 1-7, Mike!"

I answered, "Go ahead, Mike." The major waved his hand at me and pointed to the transmit select switch. Shit! Still on UHF. I made the switch and tried again, my hands squeezing the controls. "Go ahead, Mike."

In the background, I heard the major on UHF say, "We got 'em," as Mike jumped back into my earphones, out of breath. "Go high and dry, 1-7...we're on 'em! Go cold!"

"Roger, Mike, 1-7 is off cold." I heard the major call Ono on uniform and tell him to go high and dry.

Whipple ceased fire. Eight hundred feet below us, I got an occasional glimpse of the two NVA soldiers as they ran for their lives, darting in and out of the tall grass and bushes along the stream bed. They were ghosts, must be ghosts; how could anyone have survived those rockets?

Two hundred meters downstream, one of them collapsed. Rising onto his hands and knees, he crawled into the mud and weeds, unarmed, his weapon probably dropped in the chase.

The other one turned away from the stream bed and sprinted up the south bank, his hands clawing at the dirt, an AK slung over his back. The grunts were in position, opposite bank, and fired before the man reached the lip, knocking him to the ground, bouncing him against the bank in a shower of sand, dirt, and lead. A billowing dust-cloud swallowed him whole.

The other rolled onto his back where he was overrun by the Marines and dragged away, a prisoner.

"I'll take it now, Ross. Nice job."

"Thank you, sir."

The major laughed. “Those grunts are something else, aren’t they?”

“How do you mean, sir?”

“Oh, waving us off like that, so they could get credit for the kill.” He chuckled and shook his head. “Body count. It’s all about body count.”

The major checked out with Mike 1-4, then DASC, then flew us to the Marine airfield at Quang Tri to refuel.

In the fuel pits at Quang Tri, Whipple learned from the lance corporal operating our fuel nozzle that Vandy had been hit with 107mm rockets that morning, killing two Marines and wounding more than a dozen. According to the lance corporal, the casualties were from the 9th Marines. Their battalion was at Vandy getting ready to leave Vietnam. The war was ending.

I questioned the major about that on the flight back. He concurred that the withdrawal of Marines had started, but didn’t know about the rockets at Vandy. As he said, smiling, “For up-to-the-minute information, you need to ask the Marines in the fuel pits.”

Five minutes out from Phu Bai, the major got an aircraft status report from Ono, had me switch to the squadron’s FM frequency, and called, “Hardball base, 1-7 is mission complete, five minutes out, both birds are up, over.”

“Roger that, 1-7.” I recognized Tess’ voice. “Tell your TAT operator to see the “five” immediately after shut-down, over.”

Angus wanted to see me?

The major and I looked at each other. His eyes were apologetic, as if he knew why.

“Roger.”

17

Got to Waste Him

Helmet bag and map packet in hand and still wearing my helmet, survival vest, and bullet bouncer, I stepped out of the idling Huey and trotted away. I had already decided Angus wanted to see me because of Bill: Bill'd done something stupid and dragged me into it—something like searching Angus' office.

Turning for the ready room, I jogged past a Huey slick in the next revetment. Duppont, his back to me, sun-bleached hair wet with sweat, pre-flighted the rotorhead. Across the simmering steel matting, Tess stood tall in the doorway of the ready room, squinting against the sun, his casted arm in the air pumping up and down at me, the signal for double-time.

Tess took the bags out of my hands at the door and tossed them onto the nearest table. I looked for Angus, but we were alone. As I took my helmet off, Tess ripped the velcro straps from the front of the bouncer and whispered to me, "The Bull is in a hurry and he's pissed. Good luck."

I slid the helmet into my helmet bag. "What's goin' on? What does he want?"

He lifted the armor off my chest, over my head, dropped it onto the table with a thump, and pushed me toward the hallway to the S-1 office. "No time, just go!"

Scapelli, in a green T-shirt, appeared in the short passageway to the S-2 and S-3 offices. He smiled as I rushed past him. "Got something for you, Lieutenant."

"Be right back," I answered over my shoulder.

I trotted to Straderman's desk and turned left. At the open doorway, I did a right face and stood at attention, breathing hard, sweat streaming down my face.

Angus stood at a clothes rack against the wall to my left, zipping his survival vest, smoke rising from a cigarette between his fingers.

"Lieutenant Teemer reporting as ord—"

"I know who you are, Lieutenant. Come in and stand at ease. I've only got a minute."

"Yes, sir." I took three strides and stood at a loose parade rest in front of his desk. The desk top was cluttered with papers. The ceramic bull stared at my pistol belt.

The major buckled a webbed belt around his thick waist and strode to his desk. A familiar .45 pistol and black leather holster marked with the initials "B.H." hung from the belt. It had looked better on Major Ben Hardy.

Angus took a drag on the cigarette, his eyes searching his desk top. He wedged the filterless butt into the spring on the edge of an ashtray, let the smoke trail from his nostrils, and placed his hand on a pair of typed papers.

"Lieutenant Teemer."

"Yes, sir?"

"Do you remember observing a mission the other day involving myself and Major Pyhr?"

"The one south of LZ Hawk, sir?"

The major eased his head up, his eyes focused on mine. "The 8-8-3-7 grid, Lieutenant. If that's south of Hawk, then yes, that one."

"Yes, sir, I remember observing some of that mission, sir."

The major widened his stance, cocked his head back, and slowly crossed his arms.

I glanced at the desk.

"Do you remember seeing Major Pyhr's aircraft firing on the enemy's position, Lieutenant?"

I hesitated a second and tried to remember such a scene. "Yes, sir. I saw his crew chief firing."

Angus threw his arms down to his side. "The crew chief's M-60 is part of the aircraft, is it not, Lieutenant?"

I swallowed, shifting my eyes to the front. "Yes, sir."

He crossed his arms again and smiled, his teeth small, yellow, crowded. "Lieutenant...these papers..." He picked up the typed sheets and held them at his waist. "These papers describe the action you observed in the 8-8-3-7 grid on 24 June." Holding the smile, he looked up at me. "South of LZ Hawk, if you will."

Placing the papers on the desk, he turned them around, facing me. "Colonel Houser, Major Pyhr, and I have concluded—after receiving a very complimentary after-action report from the 9th Marines—that the action led by Major Pyhr against the enemy on that day is deserving of recognition. Please sign at the bottom of each page...above where your name is typed."

I took a sweaty ballpoint pen from his hand and bent over the papers.

I'd covered the first of three paragraphs, a description of my position in the flight and how I had observed the action but didn't participate in it, when Angus cleared his throat. "I'm in a hurry, Lieutenant Teemer, a flight to Da Nang, squadron business. Sign the paper."

"Yes, sir. Almost finished, sir."

I scanned as fast as I could, amazed at what I read: "Repeated attacks using 2.75 inch rockets, receiving heavy automatic weapons fire, determined and numerically superior enemy force, in spite of damage to his aircraft, taking casualties, deteriorating weather, undaunted, routed the enemy force killing twelve," and finally, "recommend Major Pyhr for the Silver Star."

Angus took another drag on his cigarette and expelled the smoke with a loud sigh. "Finished, Lieutenant?"

I scanned the second page as I answered, "Yes, sir." It appeared to read the same only concluded with, "Major Angus for the Silver Star."

I placed the pen by the papers and stood erect, wondering how I could get into such a mess. "Major, I ah…I didn't see all that stuff, sir."

Angus smashed his cigarette into the ashtray, placed his hands on the desk, and leaned toward me. "You didn't have to see 'all that stuff,' Lieutenant. You saw Major Pyhr's flight attack the enemy!" He grabbed another set of papers and jabbed them at me. "Here is the report from the 9th Marines. They saw the results!" He threw the report on his desk and leaned onto his fists, stretching his ruddy neck toward me. "The rest you'll have to take on the word of *two* field grade officers, Lieutenant Teemer—your superiors. Now, sign those fucking papers!" He slammed his open hand on the pen and slid it across the desk toward me.

I stared at the papers, my arms at my sides, thinking this couldn't be happening. A Marine major asking me to…damn, who would believe that? And why me? Why does this shit happen to me?

Stiffening, I looked straight ahead. "I beg your pardon, sir, but I just can't sign a statement that says I saw something I didn't see. A Silver Star is a very high award."

"Teemer, goddamn it, the wing awards committee will knock it down to a DFC, that's the way the fucking game is played. And your asshole buddy, Catlett, will get a single-mission Air Medal. You want him to get something don't you?"

"Well, yes sir, if he earned it."

"He earned it, goddamn it!" The major stared at me, taking rapid, raspy breaths, then hung his head and glanced at his watch. He looked at the papers on his desk. "Sign, or get the fuck out of here, Lieutenant."

"Aye, sir." I did an about-face and left the room. Behind me, I heard the major yell, "Corporal Straderman!"

I drifted back to the ready room on automatic. I didn't see anyone or anything. Why me? Why did he need a statement from the co-pilot of another flight? How many statements are needed anyhow? Just two, I thought. Wouldn't Teach be the guy?

"How'd it go?" Tess stood beside me.

I sat on the end of a bench, my gear strewn on the table in front of me. I looked up. "Where's Teach?"

Heavy boots marched down the hallway and Tess held up his hand, freezing me. He raised his clipboard and snatched a pencil from his shirt pocket. "Flight time?"

I grabbed the kneeboard from the pocket of my helmet bag. "Five point nine."

"Lieutenant Tess!"

Tess turned. "Yes, sir?"

Without looking at us, Major Angus marched to his cubbyhole and extracted his helmet bag and survival vest. "Straderman will have some papers for me in a minute. See that they get to my aircraft before I depart."

Tess watched him throw the gear over his shoulder before he replied, "Yes, sir."

The screened door slammed shut behind him.

Tess looked at me, smiling.

I frowned. "You were right. He's pissed."

"I think he was born pissed."

The door flew open again as Munzel, a cigarette hanging from his lips, his dirty-blond hair matted and sweaty as always, spilled into the room followed by Major Lewis and Ono.

"Hey, 'Rockets Ross' Teemer!" Munzel threw his gear up next to mine and turned to Tess. "Should have been there, Tess. Teemer here was a one-man blitzkrieg. The major said he had to hold him down he was so pumped—had to sit on him! I mean, Teemer wanted that gook's ass!"

Major Lewis and Ono filed past him, laughing. They threw their gear into their cubbyholes.

"Isn't that right, Major? Tell 'em. Tell 'em about Rocket Ross yelling, 'Make me hot! The som-bitch is mine! Out-the-way Mike 1-4, I'm in hot!'"

Major Lewis tapped his upside-down pipe bowl on the edge of an ashtray, and smiled. "I don't remember it quite that way, Lieutenant Munzel."

"Come on, Major, play along here. He was yelling, 'Kill, kill!' remember?"

The major chuckled, "Oh, you mean the time he put the knife between his teeth."

"Yes, sir, the knife in the teeth. Then when he was out of rockets, he started throwing grenades, and—"

"Hold it, Munzel. Time out." Tess placed his clipboard on the ODO counter. "My man, the fucking-new-guy Teemer, wouldn't yell 'kill, kill' with a knife in his teeth; he's too couth for that. He would have taken the knife out of his mouth first, then yelled, 'kill, kill.' Your story is undiluted, industrial-strength bullshit, Lieutenant." Tess turned to the major. "Of course, your part of the story is the gospel, sir, and will be recorded in the official ODO logbook accordingly."

The major chuckled as he tapped the last of the burnt tobacco into his hand and dropped it into the ashtray. "Thank you, Lieutenant Tess. Now, if you jackals will excuse me, I'll retire to my office." He picked up a B-3 unit of C-rations he'd set on the table earlier, and added, "and enjoy some lunch."

The major slid behind us and Tess dropped a mission report form in front of me.

Munzel slapped me on the shoulder. "Hey, the Bull nearly ran us over coming out the door a minute ago. You talk to him yet? What'd he want? You piss him off?"

I put my pencil to the form, not really certain how to explain what Angus had asked me to do. I shook my head. "I'll tell you later. No big deal."

Tess watched Major Lewis shut his office door at the end of the hallway, then sat across from me and whispered, "You told him to shove it, didn't you?"

Munzel leaned toward Tess. "He did what? He said 'Shove it?' To who? The 'five,' Angus?" He spun his head at me. "You told Angus to shove it? No shit?"

I kept writing, filling in grid coordinates, sweating. I wished I had sat closer to the fan and Tess had kept his mouth shut. "No, I didn't tell anyone to shove it."

Another screened door slammed and two sets of heavy boots crunched down the plywood hallway to the ready room. A playful voice said, "Well, why does it take so fucking long? I mean, shit, all the HAC has to do is fly around behind the leader and say, 'Roger, switching.'"

Jim Teach and Bill walked into the room and slowed, Bill's eyes widening as they found me. "Hey, R.T., what's happenin'?" Then to Ono, and Munzel: "How 'bout it, sports fans? Take any prisoners on 'Early Pistolas?' Huh? Kick some ass? Take some names?"

Munzel pointed at Bill. "As a matter of fact, 'Cat's Asshole'..." and sat on the table, his feet on the bench beside me. "We did take a prisoner, and we did kick exactly one ass."

"No shit?"

Munzel raised his palms and eyes to the plywood ceiling. "If I'm lyin', I'm dyin'."

Bill looked at me. "What, R.T.? One KBA, one POW?"

"Something like that," I said, working on the form.

Bill grabbed me by the sleeve of my flightsuit and bent to my ear. "Well, don't let 'Bull Prick' Angus find out about it. He'll claim he did it and want you to write him up for a Silver Star."

I stared up at Bill, then at Teach leaning against the table behind him, then to Tess across from me.

"You were his third attempt," Tess said, smiling. "You told him to shove it too, didn't you?"

I stood, nodding at Tess, and turned to Bill. "You too?"

"No shit, Kemosabe. Me two. Teach one. You make 'em three."

"Well, I'll be damned."

"I think you'll all be damned," Tess said, standing. "But God bless you anyhow."

Air squished from the end of the table, followed by metal on metal scraping. We turned toward the noise and Ono looked up from his can of pear halves, his thumb working a can opener. "Will someone," he said, "preferably anyone but Munzel, please tell me what the fuck is going on?"

"Lieutenant Teemer?" Scapelli stopped at the entrance to the hallway to S-2 and S-3, and leaned against the wall, his arms crossed.

"Yeah," I said, turning my head. "Be right there."

"I'll tell you what's goin' on," Bill said. But before he could say more, the Huey taxiing toward the ready room stopped just outside the door and made it impossible to be heard without screaming, which Bill did. "That som-bitch Angus is trying to get a sil—" I jabbed him in the stomach, pointed toward the S-3 office, and mouthed, shut up!

As Bill mouthed back, okay, okay, Straderman, a manila envelope clutched in his hand, hurried through the ready room and out the screened door. Through the screens above the cubbyhole shelf, we watched him jog to the Huey's cockpit window, hand the envelope to Major Angus, and jog back. Face flushed and sweaty, he disappeared down the hall to S-1.

The Huey lifted and air-taxied in an unsteady line along the revetments and toward the runway. The dusty rotor wash behind the Huey swelled through the screens and left the ready room in a yellow haze.

Munzel waved his arm in front of his face and coughed. "I'll bet the asshole did that on purpose." He furrowed his brow and ran his tongue around his lips. "Humm...water buffalo dung, a dash of burning shitter, and a touch of jet fuel. I like it. Now, where were we?" He looked at Ono, who sat with his hand over his open can of pears. "Oh yeah. I'd explain this shit to you, Frankie O, but I don't know what the fuck is going on myself. I think I can figure it out though, considering who's involved and—"

"Munzel. Excuse me." I leaned over and handed him the mission report form. "Check this for me, will you? Then turn it in. I'll be in the S-2 office." I turned.

"Sure." Munzel pointed at Ono. "It probably started—"

"Wait up, R.T."

Bill and I walked down the hall and Dewey Munzel continued to explain to Ono what Dewey Munzel didn't know anything about.

Major Lewis' pipe smoke and tobacco smell hung in the hallway as we turned left into S-2 and found Scapelli, a *Playboy* in his lap, sitting on the floor next to the filing cabinet.

I sat at the desk.

Bill stopped and stood over Scapelli. "Hey, Marine. I believe you've got my seat."

Without looking up, Scapelli turned a page. "I'll make you a deal, sir. If you'll let me have your seat, I'll let you read my magazines."

Bill looked at me and held his hand toward the PFC. "Make me a deal? Where is this guy from, New York?"

"No, sir. Jersey."

"Shit, close enough. Okay, Jersey, you've got a deal. Slide over." Bill leaned his back against the plywood wall, slid to a sitting position, and accepted a magazine from Scapelli.

"You know, Scapelli," Bill said, "if you're gonna run a reading room here, you really need to put in a fan for your customers. This place sucks."

"Yes, sir. I'll put that in the budget for next year." Scapelli pointed to a yellow legal pad on the desk. "Lieutenant Teemer, that's the information on those messages you asked for, second page."

I picked up the pad and flipped the top page. The information was in two columns. The first was a date-time-group, the second, the sender of the message, or origin. There were fifteen messages listed, evenly divided among the months with the exception of February. February was crowded.

I looked over the end of the desk. "Hey, Bill."

"Yeah." Bill had his face shielded by the magazine propped on his knees.

"What happened in February?"

"Nothin'. Valentine's Day."

"In the war, asshole. What happened in the war in February?"

"Not now, Ross. Miss November is explaining her idea of the perfect first date. Shit, it took me six months to get Laura to do this—and we were married!"

"Scapelli?"

The PFC lowered his magazine. "Operation Dewey Canyon, sir. 9th Marines kicked ass all the way to Laos."

"Right. Dewey Canyon. Should have asked you in the first place."

"Yes, sir." Scapelli turned a page.

Several of the messages appeared to be from the same source but I couldn't be sure. Message language wasn't like business communication and the class I had on it at The Basic School was long forgotten.

"Come here, Scapelli, you've got to decipher this shit for me."

Scapelli groaned. He set the *Playboy* upside down on the stack beside him, stood, and shuffled to my side.

"Okay, sir, the first set of numbers is the date-time-group, six digits, followed by 'Z,' for Zulu time, or Greenwich Mean Time, then the month and year." (That much I remembered.) "The next column on the same line tells you who it was from."

He moved his index finger to the first line. "Here, the date-time-group, six digits, reads out to be January 10, 1969, at 1008 zulu, or 3-0-8 in the morning local time—we're local plus seven to get zulu. The origin-group, usually 18 to 20 numbers and letters, reads out to be 1st Radio Battalion, 9th Marine Regiment, 3rd Marine Division, Quang Tri, Republic of Vietnam." He stood straight.

I stared at the numbers and letters in the second column of the next line, the next message.

Scapelli bent down again and pointed. "Your guess is as good as mine on this one, sir. It's an Army unit somewhere. Also came in on the tenth. I just file these things."

"Who would know?"

"Staff Sergeant Morchesski would, but he's on R and R."

"How about Lieutenant Shockley?"

"I doubt it, sir. Maybe."

I knew Shockley was flying and wouldn't be back until late, but that was just as well. I didn't really want anyone else in on this yet. I pushed my chair away from the desk. "I'll be right back. You're still keeping this just between us, right?"

"Yes, sir." He nodded at Bill who tapped the back of his head into the wall and moaned, "Oh, you naughty, naughty, girl," and Scapelli added, "Just us three."

I walked up the hall and found Teach by himself in the ready room.

"Jim." I looked around. "Where's Tess?"

Jim sat at the third table. The blue-bladed fan oscillated on the shelf beside him. "Had to take a field grade," he said, looking up from a *Naval Aviation News* magazine. "I'm guarding the fort for him."

"Well, you're the one I wanted to see anyhow." I sat on the bench beside him and set the legal pad in front of us. "Got a minute?"

"Sure."

"Will you humor me and promise not to tell anyone about what I'm going to show you? It could be nothing."

"Sure. You came to the right place too. I'm a specialist on nothing."

I smiled, turned the top sheet over and held my finger to the second group of numbers and letters in the second column. "No shit, now. What does this translate to?"

Jim studied them for a second, then scanned the whole list. "What's this for?"

"It's a list of messages we've received since January 1st."

"Messages about what?"

"I don't know yet. Still trying to figure that out."

"You can't find the actual message?"

"No. Jim, listen, I just need to know who these messages are from."

Jim gave me a sideward look and stroked his mustache.

"Look, Jim. This may be nothing, right? Or it could be something I don't want to drag a good friend into. It involves Angus and it could be trouble."

"Well, I'm already in trouble with Angus. What's goin' on?"

"Really, it could be nothing." I glanced at the hallways and screened door. "It started in S-2. Scapelli saw Angus remove these classified messages from the locked files the other night. He thought it was unusual and told me."

"Angus didn't return them?"

"No. We don't know where they are. Bill even searched his office last night. Nothing."

"Bill searched his office? He's 'Bill the Cat Burglar' now?" We chuckled together. "Ross, you've got to keep a tighter rein on that boy." Jim looked at the yellow paper. "Who else knows about this?"

"Just Bill and me and Scapelli."

"Hmmm. Well, the XO certainly has the right to look at classified messages. But removing them from the files at night and not returning them...I don't know. That seems a little shaky to me."

Jim looked at the column of numbers and letters again. "This second message is from SOG (Special Operations Group), CCN (Command And Control North), Dong Ha. Those are the guys we work for on Thunder Clap—Green Beret teams that go across the border into Laos, super secret." Jim tapped six of the fifteen messages down the line. "These are all from CCN."

"How about the rest?"

"This one and these two in February are from the 9th Marines. This one in February is from the 4th Marines. These in January, February, and April are from 1st Radio Battalion at Dong Ha, and here's a couple from 3rd Recon at Quang Tri."

I looked at him as he ran down the list again. "What do you think? Any pattern?"

"Not anything special. They're all from units in the northern part of I Corps. They're concentrated in February but that's no big deal. The stuff really hit the fan in February. I'm sure there was a lot of message traffic everywhere."

"But they're not the same kind of units, right?"

"No, they're not. CCN is pure recon, across the fence recon. 3rd Recon is pure recon also, but inside the fence. 1st Radio is purely radio intercept. I guess you could say 'radio recon.'" Jim ran his hand through his short hair and asked, "So maybe the rest are recon reports too. You think?"

"Maybe. Do the 9th and 4th Marines have their own recon?"

"No." He shook his head. "That won't work. They rely on division recon, 3rd Recon." Stroking his mustache, he scanned the sheet again. "You know, III MAF has Force Recon…I don't see anything from them, though." He tapped his chin. "But come to think of it, I believe force recon is deep recon, way out there."

I flipped to a clean page and drew a line across the middle of it. Two inches above the line I drew a three-inch circle and tapped the inside of it with my pencil. "Force Recon. Deep, right?"

Jim took the pencil from my hand and circled the area between the first circle and the line, touching both. "CCN." Then he drew another circle below and touching the line. "Regular recon, 3rd Recon."

"So these messages were from units on either side of the border: recon units, and infantry units." I tapped the pencil on the sheet and asked, "So what?"

Jim shrugged. "Beats me. Could be anything. You really need to see those messages."

"I suppose I could make him a deal: You give me the messages. I'll sign your Silver Star write-up."

Jim laughed. "Right. You been hangin' around Scapelli too long."

"Can you believe Angus? I mean…am I just naive, or is what he asked us to do outrageous?"

"Well, maybe both." Jim elbowed me in the shoulder and smiled. "I have a flight-school buddy up at Quang Tri with 'Sea Legs,' the Huey squadron. He told me about a major up there that got a Silver Star for flying into an extinguished parachute flare at night. It knocked a hole in the chin bubble. The major wrote it up as a .50 cal. hit from 'heavy enemy fire.'"

"No kidding."

"That's what he said."

"So, it's common."

"Well, it's not uncommon I guess. But that still doesn't make it right." He shook his head and shrugged. "That's just the way it is."

Jim raised his eyes and looked across me toward the hallway to S-2. "What's that noise?"

I listened a second and snickered. "That's Bill. He's written a song."

"Oh, yeah? Well, what's he saying, or singing? I can't make it out."

"He calls it the 'Hammer Song.'" I cleared my throat. "Goes like this: Now I fly a ham-mer, I hammer gooks in the mor-ning. Hammer gooks in the eve-nin', all over this la-and."

Jim laughed. "Do Peter, Paul, and Mary know about this?"

"No. And I'm sure they'd have a problem with it if they did."

"Got that right."

The screened door down the hall squeaked, and Teach stood. "I hope that's Tess. I need a haircut before the parade."

Jabbing a pencil back and forth inside his cast, Tess stomped into the room. He tossed himself onto the stool behind the ODO counter and buried his face in his hands, mumbling.

Jim and I glanced at each other, stood, and walked toward the front of the room. Jim eased against the counter. "The shit didn't go well, huh?"

I caught a laugh and self-consciously wiped my mouth.

Tess stopped mumbling, opened a gap between his fingers, and cracked his eyes. "He's gone too far this time, Jim. Too far. Way too far. I'm gonna kill him."

"Kill who?" Jim asked. "Nixon?"

"No, asshole. I can't get to Nixon. Angus. The fucking F8 blow-job from hell. The XO from the black lagoon. The bull-prick. Major 'we-tell-the-grunts-what-to-do,' Major instant HAC, instant section leader, Major above-the-rules—" He slammed his good fist on the counter. "—Major 'sign-here-so-I-can-get-a-fucking-Silver Star!'"

"Whoa, hoss. That sentiment is shared by many. You may have to take a number and wait your turn. Nixon would be easier."

Tess looked at his hands, turning them, flexing the fingers, examining them front and back. "No, shit, Jim. I mean it. The bastard has fucked with my Marine Corps and my squadron and my friends for the last time. I've got to waste him. For all of us."

Jim glanced at me. "Okay, Carl. What brought this on? You gettin' cabin fever or something?"

"No. I'm gettin' kill-Angus-fever, and after that stupid-ass parade today, you're gonna have it too."

"Hey, we have a stupid-ass parade every Friday. That's how we know what day of the week it is. So what's one more parade?"

"Shit! It's not the parade, but what I've just learned from the paint shop will be presented at the parade!" Tess leaned forward, injecting the pencil at the wrist, scratching back and forth. "He's gone too far this time, Jim. I can't take any more of this shit." He scratched faster. "You just wait…just wait 'til you see this fucking parade…then you'll know, then you'll know for sure—for no doubt, dead-ass-on for sure; the fucker is killing our squadron—*my* squadron, *your* squadron, *Hardy's* squadron!—and goddamn it, it's…it's . . ."

His scratching slowed. He eased his inflamed eyes to the bare bulb in the ceiling and stared at the dusty light, holding the pencil still, then finally, as if moved by a divine vision, he nodded and a smile spread across his sweaty face.

"It's revolution time, Jimmy Teach," he said, still looking at the light, "revolution time." His chest swelled and he sighed, pulling the pencil from his cast. "Yep...revolution."

18

Revolution

Lieutenant Colonel Houser stood in front of the wooden-pallet reviewing stand, pinned Air Medals on J.P. Padgett and Dewey Munzel, and glanced to the approach end of the runway behind us.

Earlier, before the parade had begun, Henstrom, observing the ten-minute delay, the colonel's anxious manner, and Angus' absence, suggested Angus had flown to Da Nang to request we be the last helicopter squadron out of Vietnam. Maybe the colonel was awaiting Angus' return, waiting and hoping he could tell us wing headquarters had approved his request. It sounded ridiculous, but no more ridiculous than giving a helicopter command to a fixed-wing pilot. It could happen.

Standing in formation directly in front of me, Captain Cain—tall, muscular, faded utility cover shiny with starch—watched the colonel return Munzel's salute. The rest of us watched the ready room where Tess, missing for an hour after abandoning his ODO post, had suddenly reappeared.

Just a shadowy figure behind the screens, Tess approached Straderman, who Orndorff had positioned at the ODO counter by the FM radio in Tess' absence, and gestured Straderman away.

Seconds later, Straderman reappeared behind the screens of the S-1 office.

Back in the ready room, Tess placed what looked like a small suitcase on the shelf above the cubbyholes. Patting the suitcase, he turned and disappeared toward S-3.

Meanwhile, following Padgett and Munzel, Buck Akerman received the Purple Heart for the wound in his calf—the wound Tom Gamez had said had happened with Pyhr. Orndorff read the citation with proper USMC indifference.

The colonel, still dividing his attention between the pocket flaps of the "persons to be decorated" and the approach end of runway 2-7, stepped to the last recipient, Sergeant Whipple, our crew chief from that morning's flight with Major Lewis. Lanky, bony-faced Whipple would receive a Purple Heart and, like Akerman, he had earned it.

According to Shockley, Whipple was hit on a Thunder Clap mission. The bullet, entering between his side and the plate of his bullet bouncer, had followed the curve of the armor all the way around his abdomen, tearing flesh and muscle, then exited without damaging any organs. He still wore a bandage.

Out in front, Captain Orndorff finished reading Sergeant Whipple's citation and the colonel pinned the medal to Whipple's shirt pocket. They exchanged salutes and the colonel resumed his position on the platform in front of Captain Orndorff. Skinny-lipped J.P. Padgett muttered the commands and the four newly decorated Marines marched back to their position of honor beside the pallets.

Next to Orndorff, propped against a sawhorse on the back of the platform, sat what looked to be a large oil painting covered by two olive-drab ponchos. During the "mill around, mill" phase of the formation, Bill had suggested it was a painting of a genuflecting bull kissing Mickey Mouse's ass. Whatever it was, the colonel smiled every time he looked at it. Now it was behind him, and he smiled at us.

The colonel swelled his chest. "PA-RADE, REST!" Thirty-two Marines in four separate platoons stomped the hot steel matting in unison and Bill grinned. In front of me, a wet streak appeared in the middle of Captain Cain's camouflage utilities.

The colonel adjusted his baseball cap, smiled again, and raised his voice above the drone of a departing Mohawk. "Officers, Staff Non-Commissioned Officers, and men of HML-467. I want to congratulate you on another successful week in defense of the wonderful people of South Vietnam. Although our total flight hours have fallen off slightly over the past week, we have again taken the fight to the enemy and won!"

The colonel paused, squinted toward the southeast, then nodded to us. "This week for example, two of our aircraft, one flown by ah...Major Pyhr, and the other by our new, hard-charging executive officer, Major ah...Angus, attacked and destroyed a large enemy bunker complex. In spite of heavy enemy fire and severe weather, they repeatedly attacked the fortified position, killing twelve of the enemy and destroying a large quantity of mortar rounds and other munitions." The colonel pointed a finger and let it drift across our formation. "To those of you involved in that action, my heartiest congratulations. I wish Majors Angus and Pyhr could be here this afternoon so I could congratulate them as well." The hand dropped to his side. "I'm proud to command such people, such leaders, such men of skill and courage. It was a damn fine job in the finest traditions of our Corps."

Once again the colonel paused and looked to the horizon. Standing at ease beside Cain, Ono shook his head so slightly it was probably unconscious. I glanced at the ready room but couldn't see Tess. Bill blew at a fly hovering in his face.

On the platform, the colonel pointed at us again, "So, gentle—" A squeak from the screened door stopped him. He turned. Tess stood in the doorway and held up two fingers, his face slack. The colonel, as though he'd just thrown out a runner at the plate, made a fist, jabbed it in front of his stomach, then caught himself and spun to face the squadron. "Gentlemen! There will be more in a couple of minutes! Ah…AH-TENN-HUT!" We popped to attention. "AT EASE!"

Bill turned his head. "What the fuck, R.T.?"

"Don't know." The unmistakable whop-whop of a Huey approached the field. "Maybe Henstrom was right. Maybe he's waiting on Angus."

A Marine Huey with a black claw hammer on its tail appeared over the tops of the banana and palm trees to the southeast, then turned and made its approach to the taxiway between runway 2-7 and the revetments. A minute later, it settled to an erratic hover over the steel matting and the colonel commanded, "SQUADRON, AH-TENN-HUT!"

I stood, eyes straight ahead, sweat trickling down my cheeks, and listened to the Huey taxi closer and closer to the formation, the scream of the engine and the whop-whop of the blades reverberating off each revetment wall it passed. Then a cloud of dust blew over and the noise suddenly dropped. The Huey was apparently in a revetment, still in a hover.

To my left, Tess watched through the screened door, shoulders slumped.

Behind us and to the side, I listened to the Huey struggle: loud whop-whops, then muted, power on, power off—again and again without resolution. I could picture Angus wrestling with the controls trying to get the confined Huey to obey and settle gently to the skid-size matting in the center of the revetment. It wasn't happening. Meanwhile, Tess neither confirmed nor denied my imagination. He just stood there.

In front of us, the colonel looked over our shoulders and grimaced, his fists clenched by his side. The wrestling match continued, then the engine and rotor noise dropped, unwinding toward idle RPM, and the colonel's face and hands relaxed.

A few seconds later, with the Huey idling in the background, Major Angus appeared in my peripheral vision marching toward the reviewing stand. He still wore his survival vest and pistol belt and carried several manila envelopes. As he approached the platform, he gave the colonel a thumbs-up and saluted him. The colonel returned his salute, waited for him to step onto the platform, and received him with a hearty handshake and a vigorous slap on the back. Behind us, probably with the co-pilot on the controls, the Huey's engine suddenly fell from a scream to a dying moan.

The colonel stepped aside and offered us to the major.

Angus smiled, nodded to the colonel, and stepped to the edge of the platform. He removed the faded green utility cover from his head, wiped his forehead on the sleeve of his flightsuit, and replaced the cover carefully over his matted black hair. Pinned above the bill, a gold oak-leaf insignia glittered in the sun.

Easing to attention, elbows bent, the major scanned the formation. "AT EASE!"

We relaxed.

Beside me, in a falsetto voice, Bill sighed, "My hero."

Captain Cain cocked his head to the left and twisted his mouth. "Shut up!"

Bill turned away. "Yeah, shut up, Henstrom!"

"Marines of HML-467!" The word "seven" echoed off the revetments as Major Angus, still gripping the folders, stepped backward to the side of the draped painting and locked his hands behind his back. "It is my distinct honor and privilege to be back from my flight today in time to make the following presentation."

He lowered his head, then raised it again, higher than before, and cocked to one side. "Men, we are fortunate to have as our Commanding Officer a man of exceptional leadership ability. I'm sure you already know that." He glanced at the colonel, smiling. "Now, I think it only fitting that a squadron with a call sign of 'Hardball' and a Commanding Officer with the skill and athleticism of Colonel Houser…" He put his hand on one of the ponchos. "…be represented by a symbol that is a tribute to both the aggressive, hard-hitting nature of our mission, and the dynamic personality of our commanding officer." The major smiled again and held his hand toward the other poncho. "If you will assist me, sir."

The colonel, smiling, eyes wide and darting from the major to the squadron, stepped to the opposite side of the painting. He placed his hand on its top edge and gripped the poncho.

Angus leaned toward the colonel, whispered a few words, and turned. "Men, starting tonight, our paint shop will work around the clock to paint this powerful new symbol on the tail of every aircraft in the squadron—a symbol that will stand for the best Huey gunship squadron and the best commanding officer any of us have ever had the privilege of serving!" He turned his head to the colonel, smiled, and said, "Now!"

With a flourish, the ponchos flew into the air. The colonel's poncho, released at its zenith, fluttered over his head like a giant green butterfly and settled onto Orndorff's spit-shined boots. The captain only flinched, hardly distracted from his gawk at the red and yellow sign displayed against the sawhorse, the squadron sign, the sign from the front yard of the squadron building.

As one, the formation tilted forward, stretched its collective neck and eyes, and froze. At the bottom of the sign, listed from left to right, were the CO, the XO, and the sergeant major—all the same as before except Major Angus' name was now where Major Hardy's name had been. At the top, also the same as before, was "HML-467" in large letters and numbers. But now, in the middle, where the huge black claw hammer had been, was a large white circle with vertical black pinstripes and a huge black number seven stenciled in its center.

"Jesus fucking Christ," Henstrom whispered. "He's replaced our hammer with a Mickey Mantle bulls-eye. I don't fuckin' believe it." He looked at Bill and me. "And that shit's gonna be on our birds?"

In front of me, Ono turned to Teach and whispered, "Just another reason why."

Cain, the second-tour captain, the career Marine, snapped his head toward Ono, but then, shoulders sagging, returned his gaze to the scene on the platform. Teach answered Ono with a slow head bob.

The colonel, his face still all teeth and wrinkles, followed the presentation with a few remarks expressing his delight, then Orndorff ordered, "PASS-IN-REVIEW" followed by, "RIGHT-FACE," and "Semper Fidelis" blared from the speakers behind the screens. We stepped off toward the shredded canvas hangar in a long limp column.

Because Angus had chosen the first revetment as his parking space—the one we usually marched through—the formation turned right and continued to the second revetment and even further away from the ears of the CO and XO. Here the Mickey song wasn't just whistled, or sung—it was screamed. It was screamed by young voices trembling with emotion, desperate to be heard. Droopy, grease on his cheek, unkempt red hair sticking out from under his utility cover, marched by us in the maintenance platoon singing, "M-I-C, K-E-Y" as loud as he could sing—his fists clenched, his cheeks flushed red as raw meat. Major Lewis, our platoon leader, and Captain Cain, now beside me, said nothing. The rest of us—even Bill—marched in silence.

We finished by passing in front of the ready room. That's when Tess's box was seen on the shelf behind the screens, broken down into separate parts—speakers and turntable. And Tess' hand, from behind the cubbyholes, was seen to grab the arm of the squadron's turntable, and we were all seen to flinch and grimace as "Semper Fidelis" was ripped from the air. And flinch again when Tess' hand activated his own turntable and a wailing, pounding guitar, spiked with drum-shots, blasted the rust off the screens as we passed. Then Tess himself, from behind the cubbyholes, leaped into the air, screamed with the intro, strummed a broom he held, and "duck-walked" the length of the ready room screaming and singing and playing "Revolution" with John, Paul, George, and Ringo.

First Lieutenant Carl Tess, "Tess-of-one-arm," my friend of one week, was flown out of Phu Bai and transferred to Da Nang that same evening.

A KILLING SHADOW

BOOK TWO

19

Hue Subway

After my father was killed in Korea and my mother recovered from the miscarriage and subsequent pneumonia, we moved in with my maternal grandparents in Greenville, South Carolina. Within a year, my mother had finished training as a legal secretary and was working for one of my uncles, her older brother, a local attorney. My uncle's youngest associate, Wallace Vanderwick, a year older than my mother, began seeing her and generally interfering in our lives. At first Wallace ignored me and brushed me off as insignificant. Later, when he realized how much my mother loved me and cared how I was treated, he decided we would be fishing buddies.

I dreaded those fishing trips. I felt certain that anyone who would suddenly befriend another only as a means to an end was basically untrustworthy. My mother had taught me to treat everyone with respect—whether you "need" them or not. "You don't choose your friends based on who can help you the most," she would say. He seemed the classic example of what my mother didn't want me to be, yet she liked him and was convinced I wasn't giving him a chance. So, as much as I dreaded those fishing trips, I went. Time passed. We never caught many fish, and I never learned to like him.

I had that same feeling of dread as I prepared for my first flight with Major Angus and my first Thunder Clap mission. It had been five weeks since I'd been shot down with Major Hardy and just over three weeks after Tess' revolution. My stomach tightened at the thought of combining Angus with Thunder Clap.

Thunder Clap, as a mission, was recognized as the best the squadron had. In the vernacular of Marine aviation, that meant it was the most dangerous and demanding. To qualify for that mission as a co-pilot took 100 hours of gunship experience. For a HAC, it took a flight leader designation, which usually came after 100 hours as a wingman and another 100 hours as a section leader, or roughly six months of combat experience. A flight leader designation meant you were qualified to lead flights larger than two Hueys. Not all section leaders were good enough to get a flight leader designation. Anyone but a field grade had to earn it.

Recently, Dewey Munzel had been Angus' co-pilot the first time Angus flew "the Clap." Afterward, while debriefing a bunch of us in the club, Munzel had described Angus' skill as a gunship pilot as "terrifying." According to him and confirmed by Ono—Bill and I had learned to seek a second opinion on anything Munzel had to say—Angus had ordered Major Lewis to put him on the Thunder Clap schedule. None of us could figure why he was so gung-ho to fly the Clap unless he just wanted more medals. We all agreed it didn't have anything to do with devotion to duty, but I thought it had to be more than just another Silver Star or DFC. Bill, Ono, and the rest didn't agree.

Bill and I had talked about Thunder Clap often and were more than ready to take our turn—even looked forward to it. For us, and for most of the lieutenants in the squadron, it was part of the job, like being on a football team that played a tough schedule. Bill had said it best in one of his one-way conversations with Captain Orndorff. "Sidney," he'd said, leaning from our dining table to Orndorff's, "you wear the uniform, you ride the bus, you warm up on the field, but...you know...you don't contribute for shit, man. You don't get in there, get bloody, and play the fucking game—you're dead weight." As I recall, on that occasion, the captain got up and moved to another table.

Nobody in my childhood experience or my Marine Corps training experience tolerated anyone who didn't pull his own weight—particularly Coach Day. I can still see him in our locker room pointing his finger and yelling, "America wasn't settled and built into the greatest country on earth by people who expected someone else to carry their firewood, hitch their wagon, or block their Indian for them!" Behind his back, we'd laugh about "blocking our Indian," but no one missed the point: Coach Day didn't tolerate stragglers.

No, the mission didn't turn my stomach to knots, it was just part of a job that somebody had to do. But the thought of the mission and Angus together did, and that left me dreading the sunrise.

The sunrise on July 21, 1969, was right on schedule. It swelled out of the South China Sea and penetrated the thin Phu Bai dust as a brilliant yellow ball, fuzzy and hot. And the flight schedule, written by Buck Akerman, Tess' replacement as schedules officer, was executed: Major Pyhr, Thunder Clap flight leader; Wysowski, leader's co-pilot; Major Angus, wingman; Teemer, wingman's co-pilot. The briefing was at breakfast. The takeoff was at first light.

Even before we joined up on Pyhr's wing, I could tell flying with Major Richard P. "Bull" Angus was going to be a lot like fishing with Wallace, my mother's suitor—a guy who treated his bass boat like a toy, and the rules of safe boating as applicable only to other, lesser mortals. Reminiscent of the time Wallace ripped the bottom out of his boat on a submerged stump showing me how fast he could go in shallow water, Angus broke the TAT-101 ammo links as we left the fuel pits for the arming area.

Minutes later, after departing on runway 2-7, Major Pyhr turned right and flew north at 500 feet toward the rice paddies east of Hue. Major Angus, showing me what F-8 pilots were made of, turned sharply inside Pyhr's turn and joined on him in a tight parade position with ten feet of nose-to-tail clearance, one rotor width of rotor separation, and ten feet of step-down. The air was clear and smooth, a perfect day for formation flying, but without briefing it beforehand or announcing his intentions, it was a bad idea. Besides, he had it backwards—helicopters fly in formation with ten feet of step-*up*, not step-down.

Knowing how erratic Pyhr was and that he had no idea we were so close, or that we were under him instead of above him, I kept my eyes darting back and forth from our rotor blades to his and from our blades to his cabin, hoping that Droopy, his crew chief, would turn and see us. He didn't. Then Angus did a cross-*under* to put Pyhr on our right side. As our rotor disk slid below Pyhr's lethal tail rotor, then stopped, then slid again, I gave up on getting Droopy's attention and held my breath waiting for a sudden move by Pyhr that would mesh our blades and ruin our day.

As I waited, Angus finished his cross-under and jerked us into a stepped-down parade position on Pyhr's left side. At the same moment, Pyhr's gunner, a freshly lit cigarette hanging in his lips, his hand still returning the lighter to his breast pocket, happened to turn in our direction. All in one motion, the gunner's eyes locked onto mine and exploded open, the cigarette fell from his gaping mouth, and Pyhr decided to dive for the deck, dragging the gunner with him by his seatbelt.

As they dropped from above us to below us, our rotor disks missing by a few size tens, Angus decided to stay with them and dazzle me with his tail-chase technique, once again unbriefed and unannounced. He jerked us inside Pyhr's ten-degree left bank and dived with him. We were above him now. That made me feel a little better. Then Angus tried to get back under him. At 100 knots, passing through 200 feet, he succeeded.

As terrified as I was, I wasn't about to show it to Angus. I forced myself to remove my hands from the armor on the sides of my seat so he couldn't see my white knuckles, and adjusted the bullet bouncer on my chest. I never took my eyes off Pyhr's buzzing tail rotor blades though; Angus was too busy to check my eyes—staring in fear wouldn't give me away.

If his gunner hadn't signaled us first, Pyhr's next move would have killed us all. I'm sure the gunner did it on Pyhr's command after he told Pyhr where we were.

Angus saw the signal, a push-back motion followed by the palms-up motion meaning, "back and higher," and dropped back just as Pyhr turned hard left. The turn cost him some air speed and dipped his rotor blades into the air space we would have been in had we not backed off, then he steepened his dive and we left the rice paddies for the uncultivated areas lining the banks of the Dai Giang River. Tall palms and banana trees, choked with bamboo, flashed under us.

Pyhr's sharp turn and steep dive had put him right over the muddy water and down between the trees on either bank. Angus had matched his dive and turn—the ball in the turn-needle-indicator rocking back and forth like a marble in an empty bowl—and kept us in trail by three rotor diameters. Still too close. I re-adjusted my bullet bouncer.

The river, its current lazy and relaxed, led us on a watery path through a lush landscape—trees beside us, quilts of brilliant green rice paddies beyond. In minutes, as Angus loosened our position on the leader, I began to breathe easier and enjoy the tranquil scenery, thankful he was forestalling, at least for the moment, his efforts to impress the lieutenant.

Ahead, Pyhr entertained himself by buzzing the occasional Vietnamese boat on the river. These were shallow wooden crafts with from two to six occupants, usually families: the men and women in their black pajamas and conical straw hats, children hatless, father in the back—standing and sculling the craft forward. They were all going in our direction, toward Hue. Pyhr was right on the water, so low his rotor wash was rippling the river's surface.

Angus shook with laughter every time one of the Vietnamese would lose a hat or a basket overboard from one of Pyhr's passes. As they huddled in the bottom of their boats, clinging to their remaining cargo, Angus would fly past and scream out his window, "Have a good day at the market, you fish-head eatin' maggots! We'll fight your fucking war for you!" Yes indeed, Creedence Clearwater Revival would have been proud of us; we were making friends and having a good time on the river.

After five minutes along the waterway, the scenery changed. The bamboo and palms along the banks grew taller and pushed deeper into the rice paddies, sheltering grass huts, an occasional small masonry building with a red-tile roof, and sandy paths. The river darkened from the shadows thrown by even taller trees, smooth-bark trees. The rich brown banks under those trees were higher, steeper, woven with thick black roots, bare of ground vegetation, and occasionally populated with Vietnamese.

The humid air, thick with the smell of burning charcoal from cooking fires and pungent from the stench of decaying foliage and human waste on the water, streamed in our open windows and cabin. I took shallower breaths, raised my sun visor, and lowered my clear visor. Ahead, in the cool shadows at the water's edge, a mother appeared bathing her naked infant next to older children who bathed a water buffalo, their beast of burden. They looked up as we roared by in our beasts of war. I looked ahead for a glimpse of Hue.

Two miles ahead, the white buildings of the city protruded above the green trees and glistened in the early morning sun. Below and ahead of us, low in the shadows, skimming the water, Pyhr approached the Subway.

I'd heard it described enough by Bill to know it when I saw it. Literally a tunnel formed by the towering, curved limbs of huge trees with buttressed trunks, the "Hue Subway" grew around and over the Dai Giang River. Just tall enough and wide enough for one Huey, the tunnel with its river base, tree-trunk walls and arched leaf-laden canopy, turned and twisted its way through the grass-hut suburbs on the east side of Hue. Two miles later, it emptied into the Song Huong, or "Perfume River," and the open streets and buildings of the city proper. Advertised by Bill as an "E" coupon ride better than the Matterhorn at Disneyland, it was upon us.

Ahead, Pyhr's Huey disappeared into the black-green tunnel. I looked at Angus. Would he be the self-sacrificing wingman and stay above the trees, passing up the thrills to serve as a lookout, warning Pyhr of another fool trying the same thing from the other direction? Or would the playground game of follow-the-leader be too strong a challenge? Angus, eyes hidden behind his sunglasses, tensed his grip on the controls, dropped our Huey out of the glaring sun, and flew us into the inky tunnel.

I felt for the harness-locking lever on my seat as my eyes dilated, adjusting to the smoky haze and deep shadows.

A hundred yards ahead, I found the faint outline of Pyhr's Huey. Following the dark river, it banked right and disappeared along the shadowy curved wall of trees. I turned my head to see Angus strain his neck forward. Did he see the turn? We rushed at the wall at 80 knots. Angus squeezed his eyes, deepening the crow's feet at his temple, and as my hands vibrated on my thighs inches from the controls, he jerked left.

No! My right hand shot from my leg and stabbed to the right. That way! He lurched forward in his straps, jerked the controls to the right, and we banked into the turn—flashing our skids at the sickle-shaped trees looming beside and above me. I swallowed, my hands settling near the controls, and found Pyhr ahead of us in time to watch him hit the next turn and bank sharply to the left.

The trees above that turn were thinner and shafts of dusty sunlight streaked diagonally to the water, one shaft hitting Pyhr's Huey like a spotlight as he flashed through it and disappeared.

"Shit!" Angus yelled, jerking on power.

Streaking through the light ourselves, Angus yanked us into the left turn and I held my hand to the side of my helmet, shielding my eyes from the blinding sunbeams, not wanting to miss the boat or the tree or the fisherman's pole we would hit with our rotor blades—not able to steal even a glance at Angus. I could feel him though. He was there, rolling us back into the next shadowy straightaway in spasmodic jerks, and I could hear him, hear him scream at me on the ICS, "Fuck! Where'd he go, where'd he go?"

I looked down the watery tunnel. "Don't see him, sir."

At an uncompetitive 70 knots, losing badly, and with the next turn upon us—a wide, gentle curve to the right with a wide opening through the treetops—Angus cursed, yanked back on the stick, and we shot into the sunlight, alone.

We were also alive and I sighed as inconspicuously as I could. Then I saw Pyhr ahead and below us, passing right to left, still in the subway. We were flying 50 feet above the trees and on the same heading as the river but without the turns. We gained on him. I tried to distract Angus by reaching for my mixer switches, hoping his eyes would follow my hand and overlook the white-striped rotor blades blinking through the canopy below.

"Got him, goddamn it!"

Angus pushed us into a dive, aiming at another opening in the subway roof ahead, an opening Pyhr had yet to reach. I looked left and right searching for any excuse to call him off: another aircraft approaching, an antenna, telephone wires, anything. It was too late. At 90 knots we dived back through the gap in the trees.

Angus was electrified, bouncing in his seat, his pock-marked cheeks pulled into a wide grin and his tiny teeth clenched. He jerked the controls into a shallow left turn. "The fucker is mine, Teemer. See him yet?"

Too busy watching the tree limbs, waiting to see which one we'd hit first, I had dropped my scan for Pyhr. Obediently, I unlocked my harness, turned, and looked out my window. He should be…shit!

"Move over!" I screamed. "He's on us!

For an instant Pyhr's face was in my window, the nostrils flared, the tar-black eyes boring into mine, then he snapped to his left and two skids flipped into my face as he and Angus both threw their Hueys into tight left turns to follow the river. I blinked, unable to shake Pyhr's glare; he was ready to kill us all, no quarter; get out of my way or we're all dying right here on the river in Hue City.

Still in our turn, the river was now a watery wall outside my window and the oil-streaked belly of Pyhr's Huey hung above me—the skids appearing to scrape our rotor disk. Neither of us could roll wings level without hitting the other. No way.

Angus saw him through the tinted green window over my head and screamed even as he took off some power to let him by. "Goddamn that son-of-a-bitch! He's grounded! I'm grounding his ass!"

Pyhr rolled back to the right as we did, sliding his tail rotor in front of our rotor disc, dropping in front of us just in time to miss slicing through a family on the riverbank who leaped into the water to avoid him. We bounced through his rotor wash while in Pyhr's open cabin, Droopy, hanging onto his M-60 with one hand, the troopseat with the other, stared at us like he'd seen a miracle.

Ahead, the trees parted again and Pyhr, the undisputed king of the playground, led us through the opening, back into the brilliant sunlight and over the dense tin roofs of the people we had come to rescue from Communism.

As the buildings, streets, and telephone wires of Hue City slid below us, I took my first full breath in minutes and released, unabashedly, a long loud sigh.

Once over the north side of the city at 500 feet, we leveled off and I turned to stare at Angus, my ear lobes burning, my mind screaming, you're an asshole, Richard P., an immature asshole!

His chin strap hanging loose, he sat hunched over the controls, the sun visor up in his helmet, the aviator shades squeezed down over his flattened nose. I agreed with Bill: Putting aviator shades on him was like putting aviator shades on a pig's ass—a waste. Not even aviator shades can make a pig's ass look cool.

He noticed me and his acne-scarred cheeks tightened to a tough-guy scowl—the combat look. He was my hero. He was everything an executive officer and gunship pilot was supposed to be—more than worthy of my worship. Angus had to be related to Wallace the suitor. Wallace didn't have a clue either.

I could refuse to go fishing with Wallace. After he ripped the bottom out of his boat and left us stranded on a sandbar for six hours, I did. Couldn't refuse to fly with Angus—never make HAC if I did that.

Two more months. Three at the most. I relaxed my hands as I remembered what Tess used to say before his revolution: "The heavies can fuck with you all they want now, but remember this: they can't stop the clock."

True. But first I had to survive my first day of Thunder Clap. With Angus.

20

Kiss His Ring

Major Pyhr, as flight leader on what Shockley had told us the night before was "the highest priority mission in the war," had our flight orbit the Green Berets' compound at 500 feet. As we circled to the right and I stretched my neck to look past Major Angus, I recalled Shockley saying this mission was not approved by the U.S. Congress. "Therefore," he had said, "if you're ever shot down on Thunder Clap, it's tough shit—Tricky Dick Nixon and the rest of our government will deny you were ever there in the first place."

Thunder Clap had its headquarters beside Marble Mountain, near Da Nang, but was conducted out of several FOBs, or forward operational bases, such as the one below us. From those bases, located near South Vietnam's borders, teams of indigenous Montagnard tribesmen, led by two or three American Green Berets, would be helicoptered into Laos for secret reconnaissance missions along the Ho Chi Minh Trail. Thunder Clap was an Army mission, but because the FOB below us was in I Corps, an area that tactically belonged to the Marine Corps, our squadron led the missions that left from there.

After all the hype back at the squadron, actually seeing the FOB for the first time was a disappointment. Located in the dusty flat land south of Dong Ha near Quang Tri, the base was surrounded by rusty concertina wire littered with bits of discarded paper and plastic. Inside the wire was a row of tin-roofed plywood huts and tents along the north side of a one-acre-square, partially-paved landing zone. Behind the huts, cut-down 55-gallon drums of diesel fuel and human waste—in the traditional waste disposal mode of every base in Vietnam—burned furiously and pushed billowing black smoke into the humid early-morning haze.

Inside the wire, on the western edge of the LZ, three Army Huey slicks had just shut down and the crews were tying blades to tailbooms. On the southern edge, two Army Cobras, sun glinting off their canopies, sat alone, blades tied.

Pyhr descended and we followed, approaching the LZ from east to west, then on short final, flying into the greasy stench and brownish haze from the burning shitters. Behind Pyhr and beside the Cobras, Angus dribbled us to a landing among the potholes and shallow puddles from an overnight rain and cut the throttle to idle.

Breathing only enough to keep myself alive, I wondered if our shitty reception was an omen. The talk around the squadron described the 15th Special Forces Group, Barry Sadler's own Green Berets, as a bunch of painted wild men who couldn't get out of a helicopter without stepping into a pile of shit. Then, inevitably, as they screamed, "Get us out of here!" we'd be pulled into the shit with them. As the engine spooled down and Major Angus applied the rotor brake, I frowned at the thought of being sucked into an over-the-border shoot'em-up today with the Bull doing the flying.

By the time Sergeant Hutchins tied our Huey's blades to the tailboom, the shitters had burned dry, the haze had dissipated, and the blazing sun was busy cooking the militarized countryside. I dumped my gear in my seat and met Major Angus by his cockpit door.

"Stay with the bird, Teemer," he said, extracting his kneeboard from the pile of gear on his seat. "I wanna talk to you when I get back."

"Yes, sir."

Angus marched through the puddles and across the LZ toward the huts. Pyhr, from his Huey in front of us, had also started across the LZ, while Rod, hustling beside him, tried to keep up.

Rod saw me and waved me over. Unable to explain across 30 meters of LZ that I wasn't invited, I raised one finger to say, in a minute. Rod responded with a thumbs up.

Angus and Pyhr's paths converged at the wooden steps to the largest hut in the compound. The size of a double-wide trailer, the plywood building featured air-conditioner units out its side and tall radio antennae from the edge of its sandbagged tin roof. On the wall by the front entrance was a large white sign with a human skull wearing a scowl and a green beret. Under the skull, black letters read, "FOB, CCN, 15th Special Forces Group."

Both Pyhr and Angus reached the door at the same time. I leaned against the nose of our Huey with my arms folded and watched as they fought over the doorknob like two kids at nursery school. I imagined Angus thinking, "I'm the XO, I should go first," while Pyhr was thinking, "I'm the flight leader, I should go first." It was over in a second. Angus, ever the self-sacrificing wingman, went first.

Rod, swinging his kneeboard like a lunch box, clumped up the two steps and into the dark interior behind them.

The door closed and I thought of Angus' orders. Did I do something wrong on the flight up here? Was he still pissed about the Silver Star write-up or the savings bonds? Did he know I'd asked Teach about the missing messages?

Laughter drifted from Pyhr's Huey and I turned. In the shade of the Huey's fuselage, Hutchins, our crew chief, stood with his back to me, laughing. Rinkes, Pyhr's gunner, sat on the ground beside him, also laughing. Smoke drifted from the cabin.

Hutchins held up a hand. "Wait," I thought he yelled, trying to catch his breath, then he said something about it getting better. He continued, making aircraft-like gestures with his hands. As he maneuvered them in the air space before him, he bent his knees and rose up and down as though he were flying. Suddenly he straightened, brought one hand on top of the other, screamed, and swiped his hand at the air. Laughter exploded from the cabin and a body with scruffy, violently kicking flight boots fell off the troopseat onto the cabin deck. Rinkes stabbed a finger at the body and fell over holding his stomach while Hutchins slapped his hands and leaned back in an even larger laugh.

I had strolled across the thinly-paved LZ by then, and now, before they realized I was there, stopped beside Rinkes.

With the sleeve of his flightsuit, eyes closed, a chuckling Hutchins wiped spittle from his pointed chin. Droopy lay supine on the cabin floor, wheezing, his flightsuit unzipped to his waist, his grimy hands on a soiled T-shirt. On the troopseat behind Droopy, the sun streaming in on his shaved head, Staff Sergeant Morchesski, our gunner and the squadron S-2 NCOIC—Scapelli's boss—sat hunched forward, shaking his head and smiling at the deck.

"What's up?" I said.

Morchesski bolted erect, Hutchins dropped his bony arm to his side, and Droopy sat upright as all three answered my question in unison. "Nothing, sir."

I stood—feet apart, hands on my pistol-belt—and looked from one to the other. "Nothing, huh?"

Droopy smiled, the matted red hair hanging over the soot smudges on his forehead, a cigarette between his fingers. He glanced at Hutchins. "We were just reviewing the flight up here, sir." He chuckled. "Hutch was telling us about how—"

"I was just telling them about how they nearly killed us in the Subway, sir." Hutchins was smiling, but he kept looking at the ground and back at Droopy.

"Shit, he's okay, Hutch." Droopy scooted forward and hung his legs over the edge of the steel deck. "Lieutenant Teemer?"

"Yeah, Droop?"

"Sergeant Hutchins says you've been ordering Major Angus around, sir."

Hutchins stared at his boots and pulled on his chin.

"I have?" I said.

"Yes, sir. I understand that when we tried to pass you guys in the Subway, you leaned out of your seat, slapped Major Angus upside the head and screamed, 'Move over, you asshole, they're on us!'" Droopy and Rinkes both fell over again in laughter.

Hutchins grinned and shrugged his shoulders. "Sorry, sir. I guess I exaggerated a little bit—kinda embellished the story you know."

Droopy sat up again. "Did you really say that, Lieutenant?"

"Not exactly." I crossed in front of Droopy so I could turn around and lean against the pilot's door. I folded my arms. "I remember what I yelled, but I don't believe I slapped anyone 'upside the head.' As I recall, I just yelled, 'Move over.'" All of them chuckled, and I said, "Yeah, yeah, I know: where was he going to move to, right?"

"Yes, sir," Droopy said, smiling. "I mean, it's not like you guys had a lot of choices—and moving over wasn't one of them."

I laughed with them. "Well, Droop, next time I'll yell something more accurate, something like, 'Begging your pardon, major, but we are being overtaken on the inside by the aircraft we are supposed to be following, sir. I recommend you reduce power while maintaining minimum clearance from obstacles on the far bank while the aircraft in question executes a passing maneuver.'" I leaned toward Droopy, eyes wide. "That better, Corporal Boufeldt?"

"Yes, sir. That should do it all right." Droopy chuckled, folded his legs under him, and pointed toward the buildings. "How come you didn't go with the other officers, sir?"

I glanced at the S-3 hut. "Well, I wasn't invited. Must be some pretty secret stuff over there."

Staff Sergeant Morchesski shifted in his seat. "No, sir, Lieutenant. There's a lot of fucked-up stuff goin' on over there, but nothin' that secret."

Every head nodded and Rinkes added, "Got that right."

"Well, I guess I'll know soon enough," I said.

I noticed Hutchins eye the partially opened case of C-rations in front of the troopseat and asked, "You guys had breakfast yet?"

"No, sir," Droopy said. "Not all of us." He reached behind him and grabbed the cardboard case by a side flap and pulled it toward him. "You want a meal, sir?"

Thinking Droopy had mistaken my question for a hint and remembering how often our crew chiefs and maintenance guys missed meals to keep our birds flying, I held up a hand. "Thanks anyhow, Droop. Maybe, if you guys don't eat it all, I'll join you later. I need to get back to some paper work."

"Okay, sir."

I walked past Hutchins and, from the other side of the tailboom, heard Morchesski call my name. We met at the tail rotor where I stopped and hung my arm over the stinger.

"Lieutenant Teemer." Morchesski stopped in front of me and put his hands on his hips. "Can we talk a minute, sir?"

"Sure," I answered. "My office, or yours?"

Under the bill of his starched utility cover, Morchesski's forehead wrinkled and drops of perspiration ran into his eyebrows. "Yours, sir."

"Okay."

We strolled toward our Huey like two good friends, which we weren't. I'd been around the staff sergeant only a few times, usually in the S-2 office and usually as a customer, not as the assistant S-2 officer. But a few times were enough. Six feet tall, shaved head, and built like the bow of a Russian ice-breaker, Morchesski was not a complicated person. He was a Marine. Period. On loan from the grunts, a loan he neither requested nor approved, he did everything hard—no frills, no comforts, no slack. As the S-2 NCOIC, he ran the intelligence shop like a boot camp. When co-pilots checked out maps for the Thunder Clap mission—like that morning for example—we got them from Staff Sergeant Morchesski. We asked for them, signed for them, and returned them by the numbers. Nobody, not even me, "Small-Shit-Dog" Teemer, sweated the small shit like Morchesski.

Shifting to my left side, the right side of the line being reserved for the senior man present, Morchesski waited until we reached the shady side of the Huey and I'd relaxed on the troopseat.

"Lieutenant Teemer, sir…PFC Scapelli says we're missing some classified messages from our files."

"Yeah, he told me the same thing. Did he tell you what happened to them?"

"Yes, sir. He said Major Angus had them." Morchesski rested a boot on the cabin deck. "Did you know another one is missing?"

Thinking that might explain why Scapelli had broken our silence, I said, "No, I didn't. You remember the date on it?"

"Three days ago, sir—the eighteenth." The staff sergeant tugged at a loose thread on the thigh pocket of his flightsuit. "Lieutenant, I'm accountable for those messages. If wing ever shows up for an inspection and our logs don't match our files, I'm up shit creek. Know what I mean, sir?"

"I think so. In fact, if that happened, I think Lieutenant Shockley and I would be in the same leaky canoe you're in. Wouldn't we?"

"Well, probably so, sir, but I don't like being up the creek. My shop's always squared away. I don't want any of us in that canoe if I can help it."

"What do you suggest we do?" I crossed my legs and hooked my hands around my knee, really enjoying myself. I was the hang-loose guy, the Bill

Catlett, and Morchesski was the uptight guy. No wonder Bill enjoyed life so much.

"Well, sir. I would like to request that the lieutenant ask the major if he would return the messages, sir."

Shit. I believe the lieutenant would sooner fall on a live grenade than do that. There must be another way.

"Staff Sergeant Morchesski, did Scapelli also tell you Major Angus doesn't know we know he has those messages?"

"Yes, sir. He mentioned that."

"So I can't just march up and demand he return them without admitting we spied on him, can I?"

"No, sir…I guess not."

"Okay, let me think a minute." I pushed my cover to the back of my head and stared at my boot, trying to imagine what Bill would do in this situation. "Okay," I said, "what are the odds that you, that is we, will ever get inspected by wing?"

"I don't know, sir, but it could happen—especially with the TTM-23 we've got."

"Okay…you're right, that damn teletype machine is a magnet. But would they just walk in unannounced or would they call first?"

"They'd probably call first, but they could just walk in. Yes, sir. They could do that."

"They could, but the odds are slim to none against it, right?"

"Yes, sir, but still…it could happen."

I uncrossed my legs and leaned forward, resting my elbows on my knees. "Do you know anyone in the wing G-2?"

Even with his spit-shined boot on the edge of the cabin deck, Morchesski had stood ramrod straight. Now, he leaned against the cabin doorjamb and relaxed his shoulders. "I have a working relationship with the gunny there. Yes, sir."

"Well, what if you told the gunny that due to a temporary situation here that was out of your control, you needed some time to get your shit in one bag and would like to be advised of any inspections pending? Would that work?"

"Well…I really don't like saying my sierra isn't in one bravo, Lieutenant. Besides, that still doesn't get the messages back."

"I know that. But if we could be assured of notification before an inspection, then we could sit back and wait for the major to return the messages in his own sweet time. If an inspection is called, then we go to the major, the squadron XO, and say something non-accusatory like, 'Sir, we have an inspection coming up and I was wondering if you would announce to the squadron that we need all S-2 material returned to S-2.' I mean, hell, he doesn't want the squadron to look bad on an inspection, does he?"

"No, sir." Morchesski's eyes wandered. He gazed at the bulkhead behind me a second, then, bringing his eyes back to mine, straightened and said, "Yes, sir, I think that'll work. The gunny's a good guy, he'll read between the lines. I'll call wing in the morning."

"Okay. Good plan." I sat erect and grinned. I'd been Bill Catlett for five minutes and I'd already talked someone into doing something they didn't want to do, plus avoided any personal involvement or responsibility in the process. Bill would be proud.

Morchesski popped to attention. "Thank you, sir." A huge globe-and-anchor tattoo on his right forearm twitched, then relaxed as he remembered he was with the air wing. We don't salute around the flight line, or in this case, the decrepit LZ. Remaining uncontaminated by our lack of discipline, he nodded, did an about-face, and in a military manner, stepped toward Pyhr's aircraft.

"Staff Sergeant Morchesski, wait a minute." I hopped to the ground and met him in front of our Huey.

"Sir?"

"Has anyone ever done this before? Taken messages, I mean. And do you know what was in those missing messages or what they were about?"

"No sir. Never happened in five months in this squadron or eighteen months in country, and no idea what they were about."

"Well, I'd like to know. How about this? There's plenty of room on the pages of the message logbook to record a synopsis of the message, and the logbook is locked away with the files, so I want Scapelli to start doing that. Have him record date, sender, and subject. That way we'll know next time. Any problem?"

"No, sir. I'll tell him in the morning."

"Thank you."

"Is that all, sir?"

"Yes…ah, no. Just one more thing. The major asked Scapelli for some maps. Did Scapelli get them?"

"He told me about that too, sir. Negative. When he called wing to ask about them, they said the order had been cancelled. The major never asked for them again, sir."

"Okay, thanks. Carry on."

"Thank you, sir."

Squinting against the sun, I watched Morchesski march toward Pyhr's Huey. No, we weren't friends—weren't supposed to be—but I admired and respected Morchesski. In contrast to Pyhr and Angus, the standards of the Marine Corps weren't going to suffer on his watch; he was one tough Marine grunt who could survive any duty the Corps gave him—even duty with the Marine air wing.

I stopped. *Three days ago.* I tapped my forehead and stared at the ground. That's what Morchesski had said; the last missing message came in three days ago. Angus had demanded to be put on Thunder Clap three days ago.

"Hey, Ross!" Wearing aviator shades and a utility cover, Rod jogged across the LZ and pointed to the sky behind me. "The circus!"

As the LZ trembled with the rumble of multiple rotor blades, the greasy underbellies of three H-34s in a tight echelon formation roared over my head—right on the deck. Rod reached my side as the leader made a right break. Dash Two and Dash Three followed at two-second intervals.

"The VNAF!" Rod removed his cover, revealing a white upper forehead above a sunburned face, and pointed. "Look at those crazy fuckers! Look at the crew chief hanging in the hatch!"

The third H-34 was in a 60-degree angle-of-bank turn. Wedged in the cabin doorway, his feet on the deck and his hands pressed against the top edge, the crew chief, in tight, tiger-stripe flightsuit and matching helmet, defied gravity and looked straight down at the ground.

"I told you about the circus, didn't I?" Rod grabbed my sleeve and dragged me around the nose of the Huey. "Well, get the hell out of the way, man!" The words were barely out of his mouth when the lead 34 glided past us in his flare, the tail wheel feeling for the ground, the blades coning upward, the rotor wash sweeping the LZ with 50 mile-per-hour winds. I grabbed my cover.

On the other side of the Huey, sheltered from the rotor wash, we watched as Dash Two flared behind the leader. Cautiously, as though he were testing a bath of hot water with a mechanical big toe, he touched the penaprime surface a few times with his tailwheel, then eased the main-mounts to the ground and squatted beside our Huey.

Behind Two, Dash Three avoided the crowded LZ and landed in the wet grass outside the wire. The entire airshow had lasted less than a minute.

Screaming above the roar from the idling R1820's exhaust stack, Rod leaned into my ear. "I told you these guys were good! I think this is the same bunch we had yesterday. If so, lead is a captain with 4000 hours of helicopter time—3000 in the same helicopter!"

I nodded. We had flown the H-34 in flight school during the advanced helicopter phase. It was a tank: clam-shell doors in the nose hiding a huge nine-cylinder air-cooled radial engine, balloon tires, pilots high above and behind the engine, integrated cabin and tailboom large enough for nine combat Marines, and a stout tailwheel. Blue Dog's own, the H-34 had been a load-hackin' workhorse for the Marine Corps for years. It was also the most demanding of any aircraft I'd ever flown, fixed-wing or helicopters. Anybody who could horse that manually-throttled monster around without an overspeed, overboost, or any of the other numerous "dumb-shit" lapses in pilot technique I feared as a student, had my respect.

By the time the pilots shut down the engines, Rod and I had moved around to the nose of the Huey. We watched as the pilot closest to us flipped some switches and yelled in Vietnamese to the crew chief standing on the ground below him.

"Suppose that was Vietnamese for, 'Gas, mags, and battery off?'" I said.

"No doubt," Rod said, laughing, combing his wind-blown wavy brown hair with his fingers—again reminding me of pictures I'd seen of World War II American soldiers going aboard troop ships: young, fair-skinned, ethnic.

I hadn't known Rod that long, maybe six months. He'd started flight school ahead of Bill and me, but because he'd received a few "downs" along the way, we'd caught up with him. I'd heard about him earlier though; he'd been a regular at Trader Jon's, and his antics were often the topic of conversation at Mustin Beach Officer's Club. The day he finally got his wings and moved on, the rumor was he was leaving behind more unpaid speeding tickets than any flight student in the history of Pensacola. I knew he'd wrecked at least one car, a new GTO, and put one young woman in the hospital with stitches in her face.

I liked Rod. He could be fun. But hanging around someone like him was like flying every day without preflighting the bird first—one day it was going to catch up with you.

Bill was just as dangerous, and that may explain why they got along so well, but Bill wasn't as reckless or careless with others as Rod. And there was one other big difference: Bill had the strength and agility to get out of the danger he created. Rod didn't.

The Vietnamese captain, who Rod confirmed was the same hot-shot from the day before, lit a cigarette and entered the Ops hut. The rest of the Vietnamese pilots headed for a screened hut beside the LZ.

Rod turned and punched me in the arm. "Hey, man. Why didn't you go to Ops with us?"

"Simple. I wasn't invited."

"Well, shit, neither was I, but that didn't stop me."

"So what's the big deal about Ops?"

"Nothin'. I just wanted to see what they had for us today."

"Did you?"

"Yeah. Piece of cake. Not half as exciting as the flight up here." Rod punched me in the arm again. "Was that Subway shit-hot or what? What'd I tell you?"

"Rod, has it ever occurred to you that Pyhr is crazy, that he's gonna get one of us killed someday?"

"Shit, Ross. Lighten up, man. Sure Pyhr's a little crazy—hell, a case could be made that we're all a little crazy to do this shit, but he's a killer, man; he's a balls-to-the-wall, take-no-prisoners, kick-their-scrawny-asses-right-back-to-Hanoi killer. I love the guy!"

I shook my head and wondered if this conversation was worth continuing.

"Forget it, Ross. Let me tell you what's going on here at the famous FOB."

"Go."

"Okay. For starters, stay out of Ops. It's a small place. They don't like crowds. Flight leaders only." Rod saw my eyebrows raise. "Except for squadron XOs, which you ain't, and unless you loosen up, probably never will be.

"Next, don't fuck with the 'yards, the indigenous, the little people. They're actually Bru, a tribe of Montagnards from near the border west of Khe Sanh, and they don't like Marines. Seems we wouldn't let 'em in the wire during the siege of Khe Sanh. They stay in tents on the other side of the Ops shack from us. Don't go down there and don't talk to the Green Berets that are with them either. Secret shit."

Rod put on his cover and stood. "Let's go talk about this in one of the 'crash shacks' and get off this LZ, man. I'm burnin' up."

I assumed he was referring to one of the screened huts. "Can't. Got to stay with the bird."

"Why? Angus say that?"

"Yep." I climbed into the cabin and sat on the end of the troopseat. "You go ahead."

Rod stepped over the skid and slid onto the deck, facing me with his back against the doorjamb and his boots pulled against his buttocks. "Nah, I'll stay here a minute. Say, you heard about Fardeau and Horsnyder, didn't you?"

"No. Who are they?"

"Shit, Teemer." Rod grimaced. "What the hell do you do at night, man?"

"Well, when I'm not flying or at the club, I'm usually in the hootch reading or writing letters. So what?"

"So, you're weird, man. If you were at the club drinkin' every night like the rest of us, you'd know about shit—new guys and shit like that. What are you readin' anyhow, Shakespeare?"

"*Catch-22*. Besides, I was at the club the night before last. The new guys should have checked in then."

Rod shook his head.

"Okay, I'm weird. So who are these new guys?"

"Well…I only knew one of 'em, Art Fardeau. He transitioned at New River. We call him, 'Art-the-fart.' I saw him light one off one night at the Air Force Officer's Club in Fort Walton Beach—dropped his trou and shot a three-foot-long blue flame at an Air Force colonel who was giving us a hard time from the next table—seems our rowdiness was bothering his wife. The MPs came and threw us out after that. Name ring a bell?"

"No." I chuckled. "Who's the other guy?"

"Horsnyder. J.E.B. Horsnyder."

"As in General J.E.B. Stuart of the Confederate cavalry?"

"No." He scowled. "As in 'Lieutenant, one each, FNG.'" Rod shook his head again and turned toward the Cobra on the other side of us.

I'd forgotten Rod wasn't a history buff—unless it was the history of sex, booze, or rock and roll. "Never heard of Horsnyder or Fardeau," I said, nodding toward the huts. "So what happens next? What are Pyhr and Angus up to?"

Rod had placed his cover on his knee. He stared toward the Cobras a second, then looked at the cover and picked it up. "We, ah...we have a brief in a few minutes. Routine extract." He tapped the bill of the cover with his knuckles. "You, ah...you pissed him off, didn't you?"

"Who?"

"Angus."

"I don't think so. Not today anyhow."

"Well, for your sake, I hope you didn't." He held his cover and leaned toward me. "Listen up, Teemer. If you've pissed him off—and the way he was stomping around in Ops, he's pissed at somebody—"

"Probably Pyhr. He's the guy who almost killed us in the Subway."

"Well, whoever. But if it's you, if you said something or did something on the way up here, then straighten it out fast, man. This is not the time to be on the Bull's shit list."

"No? Why not?"

"'Cause, numb-nuts, Borenmann's comin' back. And when he gets back somebody else has to go. That's why."

Fred Borenmann, the guy who had a place in our hootch, but didn't live there, the guy who Tess had warned me about ending up like if the majors ever thought I was smarter than they were, was on a FAC tour. For the past three months he had been in the field as a liaison officer between the air wing and the grunts—the real grunts, the guys who live in holes in the ground at night, hump 50 pounds of gear in the hot sun all day, eat out of cans when they can get them, drink water that tastes like purification tablets, and dodge bullets, hand grenades, and mortars for a living. A tour as a FAC, or forward air controller, was not a plum assignment. But, somebody had to do it.

"So, be nice to the Bull, huh?" I asked.

"You can do whatever-the-hell you want. But if you want to keep flying and keep sleeping on clean sheets, I suggest you kiss his ring and be the model hero-worshiping lieutenant—at least for the next few weeks."

"Humph!" I massaged my upper lip, prickly with three weeks of mustache growth. As much as I wanted to keep flying and be a HAC and help the grunts by doing what I do best, I wasn't going to kiss anybody's ring or anything else to insure I could do that. I'd do my job and let the chips fall where they may.

Rod watched me a second and massaged his own, clean-shaven upper lip.

"You give up on the mustache, Rodney?"

"Yeah." He looked at his lap.

"What's the problem? No hair?"

"No problem! I've had mustaches before—plenty of 'em—in college. I just decided not to grow one now."

"Gee, Rod, I recall this little mustache competition was your idea—said we needed to look salty like Teach and Padgett and the rest. Now you chickenin' out?"

"I'm not chickenin' out, goddamn it. You and your suck-buddy Catlett can go ahead and grow your fuckin' mustaches. Duppont and I are out of it."

"Duppont chickened out too? What the fuck? Over."

"Nobody chickened out, you naive piece-of-shit!" Rod's white forehead reddened.

"So, you challenged us to this contest that you didn't finish, you grew a half-assed mustache that you then shaved off, and now you're pissed at me because *you* chickened out? I don't get it?"

Rod sprang out of the cabin, turned, and stabbed his cover at me. "Teemer, goddamn it, look around, man! Do you see our XO wearing a mustache? Do you see our CO wearing a mustache? Doesn't that tell you anything?"

I shrugged. "No."

"Shit! You're hopeless!" Rod slapped his cover on his thigh, stepped over the skid, and stopped as Angus and Pyhr walked from the Ops hut.

Rod turned his head. "Hope you enjoy your FAC tour, asshole."

"Yeah, thanks," I said, watching him stomp toward his Huey. "See you later." I took a deep breath, let it slip between my lips, and slid off the troopseat onto the ground.

The sun was higher now, dominating, ruthless. I straightened my cover, shook my arms, and tried to ignore the heat, tried to look relaxed but attentive.

Weaving between the parked helicopters, Angus headed my way.

21

Taking Fire

Standing at ease, my flightsuit soaking up the heat of the sun, I watched Angus weave between the H-34s and wondered what was sloshing through that thick and battered head of his.

The normal routine on Thunder Clap was for a crew, pilot and co-pilot, to fly it two days in a row, the first day as wingman, the second day as leader. That was why to fly Thunder Clap as a HAC, the pilot had to be flight leader qualified. The schedule was designed so the leader always knew what had happened the day before, which teams were where. Three days ago, Angus designated himself a flight leader and ordered Major Lewis to put him on the flight schedule for Thunder Clap. Then he screwed up the system by skipping a day. Then last night he insisted on being scheduled today. I believed all that schedule juggling had something to do with the message he took from the files three days ago. As Angus marched toward me, head down, arms bent, and boots stomping every shallow puddle he came to, I knew nobody else would believe that, except maybe Staff Sergeant Morchesski.

Angus had said he wanted to talk to me. I had no idea why, but if it was bad, whatever had happened in the Ops hut a few minutes ago wasn't going to help my case. Mumbling angrily as he stomped across the LZ, it appeared someone from CCN Ops had just joined Bill and me on the Bull's shit list.

"Teemer!"

Damn, the man was twenty feet away and already yelling at me.

"Yes, sir," I said, snapping to attention.

"Get your shit together. We brief in ten minutes."

"Yes, sir." I turned and stepped around the Huey's nose.

"Where's that fuckin' crew chief?"

I stopped. Pyhr's Huey was unoccupied. "Don't know, sir."

"Well find him," he said, yanking his door open.

"Yes, sir." I scanned the LZ. None of our guys were in sight. As I turned to look behind us toward the last H-34, Angus pulled his helmet bag out from under his seat. He took out a thick manila envelope and his kneeboard and muttered, "Worthless Army pukes couldn't organize a gang bang in a whore house. Wrong team, my ass."

"I'll get my gear and check the crash shacks for him, Major."

"Yeah, you do that." Angus slammed the door and stomped toward the huts. "Fuckin' Green Rags."

Ten minutes later, having found and alerted Hutchins and Morchesski, I sat in a folding chair in the small briefing hut. Twenty other pilots, plus a few Green Berets, sat or stood around us. While I waited for 0900, I reorganized the papers on my kneeboard and tried to pretend I didn't feel the tension.

In front of me, Angus sat quietly, smoking, the manila envelope on his lap. To his left and directly in front of Rod was Pyhr, also smoking, his legs crossed. Protruding from the wall across the aisle to my right, a green air conditioner rattled and hummed and dripped water into a puddle on the plywood floor. Above, a fog of cigarette smoke gathered against the low ceiling and fuzzied the two bare light bulbs. A couple of Army pilots behind us whispered back and forth.

On the front row, on the aisle, directly in front of Angus, a man with a receding hairline and military buzz-cut checked his watch, stood, and stepped to the plywood podium in front of the room. His spit-shined jump-boots glistened. When he turned, I saw the muted black bars of an Army captain on his starched fatigue collar. He looked over the room. "Good morning, gentlemen. We have a ah…light schedule for you today: routine extract at 1100, maybe another this afternoon. No inserts." The captain—medium height, around 170 pounds—was in his early thirties and too heavy to have been in the field lately.

Rod nudged me and whispered, "That's Pennick, the CO."

I nodded. One thing about Rod: he forgave easily.

Without further comment, Captain Pennick introduced Captain Mendez, the Operations Officer, then Pennick clumped down the aisle and out through the door behind us.

Captain Mendez, starched and shined, stepped to the podium.

At the same time, from the back of the room, a large, stone-faced Oriental in the jungle fatigues of an American staff sergeant, marched forward to the blackboard behind the podium. He slammed a large camouflage-draped board against the blackboard rail and popped to parade rest. I figured he was the Korean-American I'd heard about—chopped firewood with his bare hands.

Rod nudged me and whispered, "Koontz. Ops NCO. Half Korean."

Captain Mendez, a small man with tight, dark skin, placed his clipboard on the podium and his hands on either edge. "Gentlemen. This morning at 1100 we will extract Team Tin Cup. Tin Cup is a six-man team that has been in the bush for four days. Originally scheduled for five days, their mission has been completed ahead of schedule and they have requested an extract. Captain Pennick has approved their request.

"We'll use the entire package: Bumble Bee, Horseshoe, Spike, and Tail Feather." The captain nodded toward a U.S. Air Force first lieutenant in the back of the room. "And of course, Beagle."

Rod nudged me and whispered, "FAC-A."

I nodded, but I knew Beagle. I knew the whole package. With over a month in the squadron, I'd heard so many stories about Thunder Clap I felt like I'd heard this brief before.

Captain Mendez gave the weather briefing, then introduced Staff Sergeant Koontz. Boots sparkling, Koontz popped to attention behind him.

Meanwhile, I glanced around the room and tried to put names with images. The VNAF or "Bumble Bee" guys were obvious. So was the Air Force FAC(A), or forward air controller (airborne)— "Beagle," the only non-Vietnamese in a gray flightsuit.

The guys in the green two-piece nomex flightsuits were Army. The slick drivers, or "Horseshoes," had to be the group sitting in the front two rows across the aisle to my right. They were all attentive, taking copious notes on their kneeboards, and there were six of them. The group of four standing against the wall behind us must be the Cobra drivers, the "Spikes." They wore shoulder holsters and held blue cavalry hats with shiny-brass crossed swords on the front.

All the Army pilots were young warrant officers except two of the slick drivers. They were first lieutenants. I noted the one with blond hair and blond eyebrows so I could find him after the briefing. The three slicks parked outside in front of us had "Nightmares" painted across their noses.

Staff Sergeant Koontz flipped the camouflage curtain over the top of his secret board—a map of the area around the LZ—and stepped to the podium.

With Angus making notes on his kneeboard, and Rod and I making notes and using the maps from our map cases, Koontz presented a textbook discussion of the friendly and enemy situation, the mission, and communications. He elaborated on enemy behavior, their tricks and techniques. He used visual aids. He repeated questions before answering. He was impressive. Then he introduced Major Pyhr, the flight leader, to brief the execution of the mission.

I looked at my boots to hide a smirk. This was gonna be good: the ol' "Stay out of my way, and stay off the radios" briefing.

Pyhr slouched to the podium, his baggy flightsuit half unzipped and the legs of the flightsuit bunched on top of his scarred and dusty flight boots. A freshly lit cigarette dangled from his lips and a styrofoam cup of coffee hung from his fingers. He dropped his kneeboard onto the podium, pulled the cigarette out of his mouth, and coughed to his left—spraying coffee spittle on the first row of officers. Without apology, he watched them wipe his saliva from their kneeboards, then raised his head toward the back of the room. Taking a raspy breath, he spoke in a high-pitched whine, "Spike, what's your ordnance?"

One of the warrant officers with the John Wayne cavalry hat answered from behind me, "32 HE, 14 nails, 3000 rounds of 7.62, and 250 rounds of 40 mike-mike per bird, Major."

"Need fuel?"

"No, sir. We're topped off."

"You understand you're not cleared on a target until I clear you on a target. Copy that?"

"Yes, sir."

"Beagle, we'll be on 34.60 fox mike and 285.5 uniform in the target area. You need to leave?"

"Yes, sir."

"Haul ass."

"Yes, sir."

The first lieutenant in the gray flightsuit slipped out the door in the back of the room. He flew the O-2, a high-wing spotter airplane with a small engine up front and another in back, a "push-pull" made by Cessna. He'd take a jeep to the airfield at Quang Tri, take off, meet us in Laos, and have radio communications with Tin Cup before we got there.

Rod nudged me, but I held up my hand and mouthed, I know. Enough is enough.

"Horseshoe." The major took a sip of coffee and a drag on his cigarette while the six Army pilots waited patiently for his next word, two of them with hands ready to shield their kneeboards. "The primary zone is a sit-down zone, but the secondary isn't. You got strings?"

"Yes, sir," one of the young warrant officers in the second row said. "Strings on both primary ships and the back-up."

"Need fuel?"

"Negative, sir."

Pyhr turned to the lead Bumble Bee pilot, the Vietnamese captain with 3000 hours in the same H-34, and briefed him on how Pyhr would identify the team and conduct the extract—apparently, the 34s were the primary pick-up birds and the Army guys were there in reserve. Closing his eyes every time he had to repeat a question, Pyhr didn't hide his disdain for the captain's lack of skill with the English language, but overall, it was a good briefing—better than I had expected.

After Pyhr had finished, Captain Mendez dismissed us.

I stood, watching Angus approach Staff Sergeant Koontz, and noticed Angus had maps in his hand. An empty manila envelope lay in his chair. As I wondered why he would have his own maps, I realized the blond lieutenant had gone. I hurried out the door and caught up with him at the edge of the LZ.

Walking with him toward his Huey, I introduced myself and described the time I was shot down with Major Hardy and how we'd been rescued by an Army slick with "Nightmares" on the nose. He confirmed that was his company. He remembered the guys involved talking about it. I asked if they had received the write-up Major Hardy and I had done for them.

"No," he said.

I stopped him. Couldn't be. I had turned the whole package over to Major Lewis a couple of weeks ago. "No?"

"No," he said, and he was sure—he was the awards officer for his company. Then he told me those guys were gone. In separate troop lifts a week apart, one was dead, the other med-evaced—severe burns. I told him I was sorry. I'd check on those write-ups. We shook hands and walked off, each toward his own aircraft. I would see Major Lewis tonight!

After the Army Cobras, or "Spikes," moved out of our way, we took off from the FOB and refueled at Quang Tri. As briefed, we returned to the FOB at 1035 and circled as the rest of the flight departed and joined us at altitude.

We flew southwest, across the Ba Long Valley south of Vandy and between FSBs Cates and Shepherd.

Later, at 2500 feet, with Angus doing all the flying, I checked the formation. Four rotor diameters ahead of us at two o'clock was Pyhr—Rinkes, Pyhr's gunner, half-visible on the end of the troopseat. Checking their Huey for oil or fuel leaks, I stopped at the "Mickey Bulls-eye" on the tail. I still wasn't used to that. At least it was a gray circle with a black number 7 in it—Mickey's "away uniform" we guessed—and not the white one with pinstripes. We talked about it less and less now, but all of us agreed—we weren't the same without the hammer.

Turning my head, I found the three Horseshoes flying above and behind us to the right, the Spikes above and behind them. Bumble Bee's three H-34s flew above and behind us on our left side. It was a gaggle, but a gaggle with a purpose, and as briefed, no one talked.

At this point in the mission, the key man was First Lieutenant Rodney Wysowski. As the co-pilot in the lead Huey gunship, "Tail Feather Lead," it was his map-reading skill that would put us in the right place at the right time. With only an hour and a half of fuel from the time we left Quang Tri, we couldn't afford to search all over Laos for Team Tin Cup. Beagle would be out there, but God forbid that as Marines we should ever ask the Air Force for directions. To do that was a "fall-on-your-sword" offense.

Before today, I'd only flown a couple of missions with Rod in the lead bird. I didn't remember any problems on those days, but Rod was the guy who told the story of taking a cross-country training flight to Phoenix, Arizona, that ended in Tucson. His instructor pilot, a bachelor captain, just sat back and watched—he didn't care. Rod realized he'd screwed up when he didn't get an answer on Phoenix aproach control frequency and the instructor suggested he try Tucson. Unshaken, Rod landed at Tucson, then saved his wayward butt by getting the captain shacked up with one of the queens behind the serving line at the Air Force Base cafeteria. The captain later referred to his weekend at the woman's trailer in the desert as his "kill in the cactus." Rod got an "up" on VFR navigation.

If the Tucson incident, which Rod called his "stumble to a tumble," suggested he wasn't an accomplished navigator, he was at least on course today. South of Highway 9, just past LZ Hawk, we were over the southern edge of the Khe Sanh plateau and headed straight for Co Roc.

I looked up from my map, again feeling an unexplained insecurity, a foreboding. The grassy hilltops and jungle-covered valleys around Khe Sanh—terrain where good men struggled to survive the night, the ambush, the point—were cheerfully warmed by the sun. But the base itself, now a flat red scar on the jungle floor, lay in a cold shadow cast by a lone cumulus cloud.

Once a quiet tea plantation, then a French airfield, Khe Sanh was the scene of a violent U.S. Marine victory. The helicopter revetments and bunkers of Khe Sanh—the only remaining monuments to the two hundred Marines who had died there—were empty. The runway, desecrated by the yellow and black shield of a U.S. Army unit painted in its center, was fractured and warped. I bounced to the beat of our blades, stared at that hallowed ground, and for the first time, appreciated the threat our Marines had faced.

At 1500 feet above sea level, Khe Sanh lay on a small plateau, a plateau surrounded by higher mountains and ridgelines—all valuable ground in a fight. Due west of Khe Sanh, I located Dong Dang mountain—LZ Fang, 2200 feet above sea level. Three clicks north of Fang was Hill 861, 2700 feet. Three clicks west of that was 881 South; two clicks north of that, 881 North. To the west lay LZs Gieger, Puff, and Shenandoah. Besides those Marines that died at the Khe Sanh Combat Base, hundreds more—grunts, aviators, and Navy corpsmen—died on and around those hills to protect the base. The politicians didn't tell us that. My Basic School instructors did. Marines my instructors described as "magnificent" won the hill fights of '67 and '68. And they paid a great price.

My mind stopped and I looked, unseeing, at my map. Maybe that was it. Dave. We graduated from Basic School together in November, 1967—good friends who shared all the hardships and red-ass the Marine Corps could lay on us. The letter he promised never came. While I enjoyed life on the beach in Pensacola in January, 1968, he stepped off a helicopter onto a grassy hilltop somewhere to my right and died. Another friend had written me.

So maybe that was it. Dave died there. Shit, I didn't know. I couldn't explain it.

With a sigh, I raised my head and confirmed we were still on course. Below us and to the right was Lang Vei, the former Green Beret FOB, the scene of the first use of tanks by the NVA—February, '68. Until they were overrun by the NVA and their tanks, the Green Berets and Montagnards based at Lang Vei could begin their missions by walking across the border. Now the FOB was 25 miles away and we were flying them in.

I turned and looked out my window at LZs Bourbon, Snapper, and Tenaru. Occupied up to a month before by the 9th Marines, they were abandoned now. Extending ahead, Highway 9, once an MSR, or main supply route, owned and operated by U.S. Marines, was now a dirt road through NVA territory. It curved off to the northwest. We pressed on to the southwest, Pyhr at our two o'clock low, radios hissing in my ears.

At the point where we would cross into Laos, the Xe Pon River—which defined the border—made a wide curve, a quick reversal, a small curve, another quick reversal, then out again in another wide curve. From altitude it looked like a huge bracket. We flew over the bracket and out of Vietnam.

As we burned fuel, we had cruise-climbed at 90 knots. Now at 2900 feet, Co Roc, at 2800 feet, was dead ahead. Angus, hunched over the controls, fidgeted with the throttle grip and stared at Co Roc. He hadn't had a cigarette since we left.

Jim Teach had described Co Roc as a "bad place." A sheer rock face soaring high above the river and stretching two miles southeast to northwest, Co Roc faced Khe Sanh like the "green monster" at Fenway faced home plate. "That's where the NVA had their big guns during the siege," Teach had said, "in tunnels in the face of Co Roc. Our guns couldn't touch 'em." Examining the mountain, I couldn't see any tunnels or NVA. But I'd never seen ants in an anthill either.

Pyhr was now at one o'clock, at least 200 feet below us, and skimming the trees of the mountain's jungle cap. He had stopped cruise climbing. Angus hadn't.

I looked back at Hutchins and out the cabin. Hutchins sat on his spare bullet bouncer and looked up at air space I couldn't see. The sky I could see was blue and empty. I swung further around and found Morchesski, the air stream rippling his flightsuit. He pointed toward the sky above and behind us and gave me a thumbs up. I nodded and turned around. The gaggle was still with us. Pyhr was the only one trying to get shot at.

The primary LZ, an isolated hilltop a few miles west of Co Roc, was advertised as secure. The team had spent four days tracing and trying to tap a telephone line spotted by photo reconnaissance aircraft. They had called in "mission complete," and requested an early extract, suggesting they had found what they came to find, and done what they came to do. I wondered if it were more complicated than that, if they had heard footsteps.

With Co Roc behind us, the ground falling away, and Pyhr unable to get anyone to shoot at him, Angus descended into position on Pyhr's left side, 2800 feet, 1500 AGL.

Below us, a large blue stream serpentined across a wide and level emerald-green plateau. Grass-covered hills jutted from the plateau floor. I would have turned due west now, but Pyhr and Rod stayed on a southwest heading. I wondered if I should say something—then Beagle, the Air Force FAC(A), appeared as a small silver speck at two o'clock.

The hissing in my ears stopped.

"Beagle, Tail Feather." Pyhr on UHF.

"Roger, Tail Feather, this is Beagle, go ahead."

"Beagle, Feather is two minutes out, say your poz, over."

"Roger, Feather, ah…you're in sight. Beagle is your three o'clock, over." There was a hesitation in the voice, as if he was thinking, I don't think they know where they're going, but I'm a lieutenant and he's a major. How do I get them unfucked without pissin' him off?

"Understand, three o'clock?" Pyhr.

"Roger, Feather. We're three o'clock and ah…got a panel out for you, over."

I smiled. Smooth, Lieutenant. Only grunts put out signal panels.

My smile vanished as Pyhr yanked his Huey into a right turn, forgetting a gaggle of nine other aircraft was flying on him.

Angus yanked and banked with him, losing the Bumble Bees on our left and causing the three Hueys and two Cobras on our right side to scatter like fragments from a bursting bomb—each one trying to avoid us and each other.

Angus glanced up at them, keyed the ICS for the benefit of his admiring crew, and yelled, "Think fast, assholes!"

When I was sure we had avoided a mid-air, I went back to my map. Rod had apparently picked out a hilltop two clicks south of the one we wanted. We were headed for the correct hilltop now, and as unhappy as I was to be flying with Angus, I was damn glad I wasn't trapped in the same cockpit with Pyhr.

"Feather, this is Beagle. The LZ is twelve o'clock. Stand by for a mark, over."

"Save it!"

"Roger."

Pyhr descended northwest, toward the hill where I figured Tin Cup, the recon team, waited for us. Seconds later, he flew over the hill, probably spotted the panel, and pulled off to the right.

"Bumble Bee, this is Feather." Pyhr.

In pidgin English, the Vietnamese captain answered, "This Bumble Bee. Go ahead."

"You got me in sight? Ready for a mark?"

"We ready."

"Beagle, is the team ready?" Pyhr.

"Affirmative." In his back seat, Beagle had a Green Beret who kept in touch with the team on a secure FM radio.

"Bumble Bee, this is Feather. Pick up my six. Here we go."

"We have you six."

Pyhr had made a wide circle to allow the Bumble Bee H-34 time to descend and pick him up. That wasn't necessary. Bumble Bee, who seemed to think those who hesitate and give the bad guys time to figure out what's going on get their butts handed to them, had started falling as soon as Pyhr had said, "Ready for a mark?"

Angus flew us over the hill at 1000 feet AGL and turned right. From the left seat, blocked by Angus, I couldn't see the team's panel—a silky day-glow red cloth the size of a pillow case—or the team.

Five hundred meters west of our team, the map showed a trail connecting two villages, one northwest of the hill and hidden by trees, the other southwest of the hill near its base. That seemed to me to be an area to avoid. Pyhr didn't agree. His circling turn took him between the southern village and the hill, possibly setting up a north-to-south final approach if they got that far. Bumble Bee was 500 feet above and behind him. Angus had us on the east side of the hill now, already out of position.

The weather briefing had said wind in the LZ would not be a factor; therefore Pyhr had briefed the approach would be made to the panel alone, no smoke. That made sense to me. Besides the risk of starting a grass fire with a smoke grenade, smoke is like yelling, "Here we come!" It wasn't always the thing to do.

"Rockets, both sides." Angus.

"Roger." I said, reaching for the armament panel.

With the panel set and the green stand-by light on, I put my map away, took the TAT gunsight off its hook, and pushed in the circuit breakers in the overhead panel. I couldn't use the TAT with the switches set for rockets, but I could be ready to switch to guns after the rockets were fired and cover our pull-offs.

Pyhr was on the opposite side of the hill from us, in a right turn inside our own, rolling onto final heading due south. Bumble Bee was in a right turn close behind and above him.

Pyhr had briefed a scenario where he would mark the LZ with a low pass, the 34 would start his approach, and Pyhr would get behind him in time to cover his landing. Meanwhile, we were supposed to be in a position to cover them both. I looked at the spacing and shook my head. Not likely.

"Bumble Bee, this is Feather…mark, mark, over." Pyhr buzzed the hilltop, pulled the Huey into a climbing right-hand turn, and flew right at us in our outside orbit. "It looks clear, Bumble Bee, negative fire, team is in the bush to the west side of the panel, over."

"O-K. Bumble Bee short final."

"You're what?" Pyhr, 500 feet below us, suddenly tightened his turn as Bumble Bee, now nose-high in his flare, was too close, too soon, and Angus, twitching with every voice on the radio, continued to hold at 1000 feet AGL and 90 knots.

I stared at him. He didn't move. Come on, damn it! He stared at the ground and continued to circle. Maybe he didn't know what to do. Or maybe he knew what to do, but didn't want to do it. Hell, maybe he just didn't know how to do it. The only one in the right place at the right time now was Tin Cup.

Below, Bumble Bee settled into his ground cushion, his tires touching the tall grass, and Pyhr hustled to get behind him, passing between Bumble Bee and us. From the tree line off the crest of the hill, a string of little green figures appeared at three-meter intervals. Moving through the tall grass like a line of beetles, they worked their way toward the helicopter. Bumble Bee, his green camouflaged fuselage standing out against the straw-blond grass flattened by the H-34s rotor wash, settled to the ground and waited. No fire.

I hung onto the TAT sight, gripped the master-arm switch, and waited.

Above us, the Cobras circled. Above them, the Hueys. Couldn't see Beagle.

In the LZ, the last of the team bunched up at the H-34's side door. Four in the bunch. Then only two. Then Angus got in my way.

On the UHF, someone said something rapidly in Vietnamese.

Another Vietnamese, more relaxed, replied, paused, then spoke in English, "Bumble Bee come out now."

Pyhr answered, "Roger, Bumble Bee, confirm six. Confirm you have six team members, over."

"We have six. We come out now."

"Roger, Bumble Bee, Feather has your—Taking fire! Break left! Break left!"

I threw the master-arm to arm, stretched out of my seat so I could see the LZ, and waited for Angus to kick us over and get on target. Below and to our right, climbing like a frightened bug, Bumble Bee headed straight for us. Angus jinked left to avoid him. The radios flared with quick voices.

"Feather's in hot!"

"West side, Feather, small arms!"

Someone filled in the gaps in Vietnamese.

Over the chatter, I turned to the major. "You're hot."

Angus yanked us to the right as Bumble Bee climbed out beneath us. "I didn't ask for hot, goddamn it!"

"Yes, sir." I switched the master-arm to stand-by. "You're cold, sir."

"Feather's off right."

"Make me hot!"

"Yes, sir, you're hot."

"Shit! Fuckin' Pyhr's in my way. Make me cold!"

"Yes, sir, you're cold."

"Bumble Bee, Feather. You okay?" Pyhr. I could hear his TAT and door guns firing when he keyed his mike.

"Bumble Bee, O-K. We O-K."

Without cover from us, but with Droopy's gun blazing back at the west side of the hill, Pyhr pulled off the target to the right and climbed north. It was a good time for the Spikes to hop in, but they had their orders. I switched to guns, put the master-arm to "arm," and swung the TAT sight onto the west side of the hill. At least I could help.

"Put that fuckin' thing away! Go cold!"

"Yes, sir." Tensing, I obeyed.

I could see the whole hill now. Clouds of white phosphorus from Pyhr's first salvo were dissipating to the west. I couldn't see any ground fire.

"Feather, Bumble Bee. We go now. We go FOB."

"Roger, Bumble Bee. Break. Spike, you go with 'em. Horseshoe, you hold south over the blue line."

"Spike, roger."

"Horseshoe, roger."

"Get over here, Two." Pyhr on FM. "It's time to punish these fuckers."

"Two, roger." Angus.

To the south, three Bumble Bees climbed against the blue sky and two Cobras fell in beside them. I eased out a breath.

Below us, the village near the base of the hill lay along the west side of the north-south trail. I'd noticed it earlier, seen the grass huts, seen the pale smoke from cooking fires, and wondered what those people—Laotian people, slash-and-burn farmers—must think of us, and of those after us, the NVA. Were they really cooperating with the NVA, and if so, had the NVA, like the Communists in Vietnam, murdered the village chief to get their cooperation? Did those primitive people even know who we were and what those strange flying machines were doing over their land?

Pyhr led us over to the village, circled it one time, then dropped in belching HE rockets.

Angus had us right behind him. "Make me hot."

"You're hot, sir."

Angus' first pass must have been confusing to the women, children, and farmers running for their lives below us. He missed the village by 100 meters, but totally destroyed a pond and the grass lean-to beside it—torched that thing.

On the second pass, with the village ablaze from Pyhr's two passes, Angus again unleased a devastating barrage of rockets. These also missed the village and impacted near the pond. A pig sty was leveled.

"Your fuckin' sights aren't worth a shit, Hutchins!" Angus climbed out to the right. "Guns, Teemer."

I switched to guns and checked my TAT. I hadn't noticed any return fire, so I decided not to fire until I did.

Back on the perch, Angus swiveled his gunsight up to the overhead, pushed the stick forward, and pointed the nose of the Huey at the village. "Fuck this thing, I'll just follow my tracers. Make me hot."

Once again we dropped in on a north-south heading, following the trail. Without friendlies to worry about, I'd been taught to vary the run-in heading. Consistently flying over the same ground—predictability—was to be avoided.

Angus had just lined up on target when I heard Morchesski on ICS and Pyhr on UHF scream, "Takin' fire!" Morchesski's gun erupted behind me. Hot brass and steel links clinked against my armored seat. Burnt gunpowder swirled around the cockpit and Pyhr yelled again, "Ten o'clock, Two, takin' fire!"

I swung the TAT sight to my left—toward a muzzle flash on the side of the hill where the team had been—and squeezed the two triggers, one in each hand. The Huey shook as flames leaped from the twin barrels below and in front of my feet and suddenly stopped. Morchesski continued firing. Angus pulled us into a climb. I squeezed again, harder, shaking the sight, clicking the triggers. Jammed.

A sharp metallic ping and clank. Vaguely, from somewhere, "Ahhhhhh!" We jerked to the right. The Huey yawed. I let go of the TAT with one hand, grabbed the cyclic, and put my feet on the pedals. Angus slumped in his seat and grabbed his leg.

"Get out of the way, Two! I'm on 'em!" Pyhr.

Over the clatter I yelled on ICS, "Major, you hit?" I let go of the TAT with my left hand and grabbed the collective. I had the controls—level at 800 AGL. Between bursts from Morchesski's gun, Angus screamed, "Ahhhh, shit!" Bent over at the waist, he held his lower left leg with both hands.

"Hutchins," I said, "check him out!"

Without an answer, I felt the Huey wallow as Hutchins rushed forward. He leaned over the major's seat, his helmet scraping the circuit-breaker panel in the overhead.

"Is he okay?" I asked. "Major, can you hear me?"

Bent over, Angus reached for the ICS trigger switch on the stick. "I'm hit, goddamn it! Get the fuck out of here. Climb!"

"Yes, sir." I pulled collective and climbed straight ahead, toward the Hueys to the south. Switching to UHF, I called, "Tail-Feather-Two is hit. Climbing south."

"Feather's off cold. What the hell you doin' Two!"

"Two actual is hit, sir," I said, looking for a sign from Hutchins.

"How bad?"

"Don't know yet."

"Hold south."

"Two, roger."

While Angus held his leg and sweat dripped from his scarred chin, Hutchins—still draped over the major's seat—turned, shrugged, and mouthed, no blood.

What? I mouthed back.

No blood!

I leveled off at 2800, looked for Pyhr, looked for the Horseshoes—the Army Hueys—and keyed the ICS. "Major, let Hutchins take a look. He's got the first-aid kit."

I glanced behind me as Morchesski took my hint, ripped the first-aid kit off the rear bulkhead, and tossed it to Hutchins. The major nodded his head and raised the leg of his flightsuit. I watched as he stopped, stared at his leg for a second, then threw the leg of the flightsuit down around his ankles.

"It's, it's okay," he said, between quick breaths. "Hutchins. Give me a cigarette."

Hutchins lit a cigarette.

Angus took it and straightened, letting his head fall back and his chest collapse. "It's okay, it's okay." He took a long drag and waved Hutchins away. "It's okay. Go back. Get back to your gun."

Hutchins stepped back and I turned to a left-hand orbit, about 500 feet below the Hueys, 1500 above the stream. Pyhr was inside my turn, flying straight at me.

"Major Pyhr's joining up on us, sir." Morchesski.

Angus took another drag and leaned forward. Expelling the smoke through his nose, he extended the cigarette toward the bottom of the instrument panel. "I'll take the—" He stopped, staring under the panel. "What the—" Bending at the waist, he looked between his legs, and reached under the collective.

I scanned the angle-of-bank and rate-of-climb, had to be steady for Pyhr's join-up, no tellin' how tight he was gonna get; and in my peripheral vision, saw Angus sit erect and examine something in his hand, a steel ashtray with a hole through it—a bullet hole.

I glanced left and caught my breath. Pyhr was closing too fast. He flared sideways, showing me his belly, and I forced myself to go back to the instruments, to hold steady.

"Two, this is Lead, I'm seven o'clock to look you over. How's your actual?" Pyhr.

Before I could answer, Angus keyed his mike and spoke like John Wayne with an arrow through his shoulder. "I'm fine, just a scratch. We're ready to get back in the fight."

"Roger. Hold what you got. You got a hole over here. I'm crossing over."

I held my breath. Hutchins said Pyhr was on top of us, moving left to right. I didn't ask how close.

"No leaks, no fires, Two. Got a hole in front of the co-pilot's door and maybe another aft of the cabin, port side, can't tell for sure. Starboard's clean. We're RTB."

"Roger." Angus shifted in his seat, sucked deeply on his cigarette, examined the wounded ashtray again, then put it between his legs. He took the controls, the cigarette trembling in his lips. "Put that worthless TAT away. I've got it."

"Yes, sir, you've got it." I held out my hands, stowed the TAT, and safed all the armament switches and circuit breakers.

"You got it back," Angus said, after I'd finished. "Keep a tactical parade on him."

"Yes, sir. I've got it."

Angus lit another cigarette. One of his. Filterless. He examined the hole in the ashtray again. Co Roc slid below us.

Ahead, baking under the noon sun, lay the route home: the bracket in the river, Highway 9, Shepherd. The FOB.

"Maybe," Captain Pennick had said at the briefing. "Maybe" there would be another extract today.

22

Mission of Mercy

The day after Angus was wounded by the ashtray, he screwed with the schedule again, didn't fly, and I flew Thunder Clap with Ono. Ono was great. No problems.

The following day I was scheduled for a "C and C," or command-and-control mission, with Jim Teach. I was on a roll—two good HACs in two days. Our secondary mission, time permitting, was to pick up the mysterious Fred Borenmann and return him to the land of flushing shitters.

"C and C" was one slick with two pilots, and usually involved flying staff officers to the different Marine positions—liaison-type work. Flying without gun cover, we would go to secure zones only. "Secure zone" was a relative term in the Marine Corps. Mutters Ridge on the DMZ was usually on our list of stops.

We took off at 0730. Jim had the radios. I had the Huey.

"Red Devil Arty, Hardball 4-3, over."

"Hardball 4-and-a-3, Devil, good mornin' to ya."

Jim smiled, the early morning sun back-lighting his mustache and turning his faded flightsuit to a coppery green. "Mornin', Devil. 4-3 for clearance: scenic Phu Bai, up the tracks to points north, over."

"4-and-a-3, Devil, roger. On the Northern-Pacific, you'll be clear of Barracuda, Bastogne, Birmingham, Brick, Rifle, aaaaand the Pistol. Stray not, however…Bastogne firing northwest, max ord 5000. How copy, over?"

"Solid copy, Devil. Catch ya later."

"Be careful out there, you guys. Devil, out."

Teach smiled again, did a drumbeat on his kneeboard, and looked to the horizon.

I banked ten degrees left. The railroad tracks were a mile ahead, leaving Hue.

I'd been flying for eight days straight and with a week still to go in July, already had 90 hours of flight time for the month. That was normal. If you didn't get 100 hours a month, you weren't hackin' the load. I was hackin' it, but my aching buns were having trouble keeping up. Bill had gotten an H-34 main-mount inner tube to sit on, a gift from the Blue Dog. The H-34 tubes were just the right size to be a hemorrhoid cushion. Bill said being just an honorary dog person probably wasn't good enough to rate an inner tube, but he'd try to get me one anyhow. As we bumped along to the beat of the Huey, I decided I needed something, a tube or maybe a cushion like Jim's, and soon.

One thing about flying with Jim: You didn't have to make small talk or pretend to be something you weren't. Some HACs thought the co-pilot was there to entertain the HAC, or be his mechanical dog in the rear window, bobbing his head up and down in agreement with everything the HAC said. I wasn't a bobbing head. Some HACs sensed that and resented it, holding a grudge like I wasn't doing my job if I didn't hang on their every word and agree with them every time they bitched about the topic of the day: the screwed-up grunts, the Army, the Marine Corps, women, Vietnamese, whatever.

B-12 was like that: Good stick, good on the radios, aggressive gun pilot, but wanted a squire for a co-pilot. B-12 wasn't with us anymore, killed yesterday. Myron Brunnengarber, the guy who turned down carrier qualification to get to helicopters faster, was gone. I didn't mind flying with B-12 because he was good, as good as any pilot I'd ever flown with, a load hacker. I could learn from him and did. But we were never close. Good thing, I guess.

Dewey Munzel was with him when it happened. They were doing their job, covering Mickey as he pulled off the target, when one round—one lousy round—got him. Dewey was taking it hard. I guess I would too if someone's brains were suddenly splattered all over my face and neck.

Dewey liked playing the squire and B-12 had been one of his favorite knights. "I was lookin' *right at him*," he had said, holding his hands out like he was begging us to understand him, understand why he couldn't shut up. Couldn't sleep either—not even the doctor's injection put him away.

"Ross, you okay?" Jim looked at me.

"Yeah…why?"

"You look…I don't know…thoughtful."

Another thing about Jim is I could tell him stuff. Even Bill would have thought I was a wimp by thinking of a dead guy. "I was thinking of B-12 and Dewey. Shake it off, right?"

"Yeah. Good advice for both of us. I was thinking of them too." He pointed to an Army Huey crossing in front of us. "Got him?"

"Yeah, got him." The H-model was at our altitude, but clear.

"Pyhr thinks it was the Dead-Eye Gooner."

"That got B-12?"

"Yeah. It was west of Con Thien. Pyhr says that's Mr. Dead-Eye's territory." Jim shifted in his seat. "That's where he got you and Major Hardy, right?"

"Well, that's where we got hit, yeah. But who knows if it was Pyhr's 'Dead-Eye Gooner' or not. I think Pyhr's full of shit."

"Well, he is full of shit—no question. But he might be right about this one. The Army lost a Cobra up there near the DMZ a few days ago. That could have been him too."

"Well, maybe so."

I followed the tracks out of Hue and dropped to 200 feet. The early-morning traffic of bicycles, water-buffalo carts, and the occasional mini-bus passed below us on Highway One, parallel to the tracks. I flew to the right, beside the highway, and enjoyed the view of cool green rice paddies and tall palms.

Jim played with the ADF radio a minute, but when he found it broadcasting an interview with a politician, he turned his mixer switch off. I did the same.

"So how'd you and Ono do on T.C. yesterday?"

"It was routine. We had one insert down near the 'Z' in the river. They must have done okay, 'cause we were released around 1700. Thought we might have to go get another team, but they broke contact or something and decided to stick it out."

"Like flying with Ono better than Angus?"

"Ah...yeah." I looked at him and we laughed together.

"What's the story with Angus, Jim? He demands to fly T.C. one day, begs off the next, demands to fly the next, then begs off again."

"I don't know." Jim glanced off to our right, probably checking for traffic, then looked to the horizon. "Granny knows him, or knows of him I guess. Let's ask him; maybe he can tell us something."

"Yeah, maybe." I thought a second. "The guy is up to no good, Jim. He's acting weird."

"Like how weird? Other than screwing with the schedule."

"Like hanging around Ops at the FOB and following the Ops NCO around—Koontz. And in the afternoon, when we had to extract another team, an emergency extract that turned out to be nothing, a stroll across campus, he left the flight—left Pyhr's wing—to go look at the area north of Co Roc, along the river, near the old French prison in Laos. The extract was just north of there, actually not too far north from where we were in the morning, but still, he left the flight. And the muttering."

"The muttering?"

"Yeah. The other morning at the FOB. He came out of Ops muttering something about the wrong team. Then—" I stopped. The whole day was fitting together; pieces fell into place even as I talked. Wrong team in the morning. Right team in the afternoon? "Then, in the afternoon, everything was cool. He wasn't happy when Captain Pennick found him down in the tent area talking to the team leader, but he left the FOB smiling."

"Talking to the team leader, huh? That's a no-no."

"That's right."

Jim pointed to an Army light-observation helicopter, a green egg with clear plastic on the big end, exhaust out the small end, and a fan on top. The L.O.H., or "Loach," flew toward us on the west side of the tracks, right on the rice paddies, hopping the dikes and weaving between the occasional palm trees.

"Got him?"

"Got him," I said.

"So, Angus is talking to Ops and the team leaders—"

"No, just the last team leader."

"—Okay, he's talking to the last team leader and he's checking out the French prison area."

"And he's got his own set of maps—the envelope, Jim. Remember when he came back from Da Nang for the parade, the presentation of Mickey's bulls-eye?" Jim nodded. "Well, he was at wing. He got Duppont—remember he flew co-pilot for him that day—he got him to sign the Silver Star write-ups, the ones we wouldn't sign, then hand-delivered them to wing *and* stopped by wing G-2 to get his maps. Duppont acknowledged all this to me last night like, 'So? What's the big deal?' And get this."

Jim looked at me and smiled. "Yeah?"

"Hutchins, when he was trying to help Angus, when he was hit by the Communist ashtray?"

"Yeah?"

"Well, Hutchins said he saw a wad of yellow paper in the calf pocket of Major Angus' flightsuit."

"Kiddin' me?"

"Nope. Kid you not. I saw something yellow myself, barely. When I asked Hutchins about it back at the FOB, he said it looked like a thick pile of messages to him. See what I mean? The guy is flying around Laos with classified messages in his pocket. He's got his own set of maps—that he keeps to himself, in an envelope—when all he has to do is get maps from S-2 any time he wants to, the way the rest of us do. He's talking to people he shouldn't be talking to. He's interested in one particular team—couldn't care less about the others—wants to be there when they come out. He's leaving the flight to check out an area we flew near but not over. And most of those messages he's packing, assuming they're the same ones he's taken from S-2, are from CCN—you showed me that! I mean shit!" I took a deep breath—hadn't planned on making a speech. "Is he weird, or is he up to something?"

"Damn. I don't know. That's bizarre behavior even for a field grade."

"Damn right." I pointed ahead to a CH-47 Chinook—a big, twin-rotor job with swollen sides and four wheels. It flew south at 500 feet. "I got him."

"Messages in the pocket, huh?"

"Yep."

"Maybe that's what saved his life, reckon? The ol' ashtray-ricocheting-off-the-messages-in-the-pocket routine."

The best I could do was a smirk. Jim laughed and I hated not to join him, but I couldn't.

"Angus and Pyhr wrote it up, you know," Jim said.

"Yeah, I know. A Purple Heart and a Silver Star. Some hero."

"I was with Major Lewis last night when Angus tried to show him where he was hit. Couldn't find it. The red mark was gone."

I shook my head.

Jim crossed his arms and leaned into the corner of his seat. "You know, I wish I could be there when Angus' kid says, 'Show me where you were wounded in the Vietnam War, Dad. Show me your scar.'"

I scoffed. "Right. Only knowing Angus, he'll probably find a scar he got somewhere else and say that was it."

"What a guy. You heard he ordered Hutchins to write him up, didn't you? He knew you wouldn't do it."

"No. I didn't. I just figured Rod wrote them both up like Duppont did the last time."

"Nope. Called the Marine to his office and ordered him to sign on the dotted line. Hutchins is upset over it. Feels guilty."

"Shit. There's leadership for you—make your Marines do unethical things, make them feel guilty."

I flew the Huey to the right to avoid a man and a water buffalo plowing a rice paddy. As I swung back toward the highway, I thought again of Hutchins and how he was so quick to help Angus when he thought the major was wounded. Then I thought of Angus again. "Jim, did Hutchins tell you about Angus crippling the Communist fish and pork industries?"

Jim laughed and slapped his hand on his kneeboard. "Yeah, I loved the way Hutch told it too—the guy can tell a story. What a fiasco! Said nobody was in position to cover Bumble Bee, but he made it without a scratch anyhow. Then Angus tried to shoot up a village that wasn't shooting at him, but couldn't hit it. Then your bird took two hits, Angus was severely injured by an ashtray, and your TAT jammed. Hey, that's a field-grade Silver Star mission if I've ever heard of one!"

Jim laughed again and I laughed with him.

"Hutchins told you about the TAT jamming, huh?"

"Yeah, I think he blamed that one on you."

"Me? Really?"

"Yeah. Said you had to fire at max deflection—not really your fault. Our crew chiefs are funny about that TAT. We're the only squadron that has that thing 'cause we're the only squadron that wants it. None of the others can make 'em work."

"Well, the damn thing has jammed on me every time I've used it."

"There's a trick to it. Droopy showed me when I was a co-pilot. It won't work unless both the crew chief and the co-pilot treat it right. Want to hear it?"

"Hell yeah, man. I don't ever want to just sit over there listening to the triggers click again. What's the gouge?"

"Count the rounds first. Cleanliness second. Minimum deflection third. Don't fire in short bursts fourth. That's it."

"That's the formula for success?"

"Affirmative."

"Count what rounds?"

"In the loops, the ammo belts. That's the crew chief's job when he arms the bird. On the ground, eye level with the bottom of the turret can, you should be able to count sixteen rounds in the belt below the can. More than that and the belt is under too much tension from the air stream. Less than that and there's too much tension from contact with the can."

"What about deflection?"

"Even though the book says—" Jim held up a gloved finger. "—even though it says you can traverse 110 degrees either side of center, 15 degrees up, and 45 degrees down, don't do that—asking for a jam."

I swung the Huey to the right, then back to the left to avoid a sandbagged ARVN position around a bridge. "So what can you use?"

"Droopy said 15 to 20 degrees left and right is max. If you can see the barrels through your chin bubble, that's probably too far. The more you twist left and right, the more the air stream screws up the belts."

"So I guess if you use it in the fixed forward mode only, keep it clean—don't taxi in dirt or near sand—and only fire one long burst, it's a winner. Wicked piece of gear."

"Hey, the Marine Corps cares about you, young man. Nothing's too good for our men in uniform."

We laughed together and I looked ahead to our left, to a huge cloud of dust on the horizon—Camp Evans. Like mosquitos, Army helicopters of all shapes and sizes swarmed in and around the cloud, coming and going in singles, pairs, and groups. It looked like everyone in the U.S. Army had their own helicopter.

"Ross. The other day. Did Angus say anything to you about Major Hardy?"

I glanced at him. On our way back from the FOB, after Thunder Clap, Angus and I finally had our talk. "Yeah. Among other things, Angus said something about 'The Hardy Boys,' as he calls us. Said we were finished. No more 'Hardy Boys.'"

"That's what I meant: us, the role Major Hardy left us. Angus called me aside too—three days ago. Said Tess was gone and I'd be next if I gave him any trouble. I think it had something to do with the new guys, didn't want us corrupting their minds."

Tess, then B-12. Only Jim and Ono left. And me. "Yeah, I got the same pitch only with a wrinkle—straighten out my attitude, which I took to mean sign Silver Star write-ups when requested, or face a FAC tour—as if that's the worst thing that can happen to an aviator. He's full of shit, Jim. I'll be a FAC. So what?"

"Well, you won't have to. Gamez volunteered last night."

"No shit? Why?"

"Just said he wanted to do it, see what it was like."

"Damn. He's about due to make HAC too."

"Something, huh?"

I nodded. Damn. Tom Gamez, the guy who told me about his friend getting killed down south. The grunts were getting a good guy.

"Did he also tell you about your write-ups for the Army guys?"

"No! I had to find out about that from Major Lewis. The son-of-a-bitch shit-canned those write-ups, Jim. Those Army pukes deserved those medals. They hung their asses out big time for us. You know one of those guys is dead now? His parents have a Purple Heart to remember him by—the same Purple Heart Angus is going to get for a bruise on his leg. What a prick! Did he actually admit doing that?"

"Not directly. I asked Lewis and he told me. Angus just beat around it. Said we weren't here to support the fucking Army or work with the fucking Army or give awards to the fucking Army. Said we were Marines. We don't need the fucking Army. Something like that."

"Well, we sure as hell needed them the day we got shot down. What a gaping, screaming, bleeding asshole! Shit!"

"Easy, Ross." Jim smiled at me, a calming smile, his head leaning to one side. "If you rip the grip off the cyclic stick, I'll have to do all the flying."

"What is the asshole's problem, Jim? I don't get it. Why the chip on his shoulder about the Army, about Hardy, about…everything?"

"Don't know. Again, Granny might help. Or maybe 'Freud' can figure him out." Jim laughed. "You're gonna like ol' Freud, Ross. He knows some shit about screwed-up people."

"Yeah?"

"You bet. First Lieutenant Fred Borenmann, a shrink with gold wings. Ever heard of such a thing?"

"Psychiatrist?"

"Psychologist. Got a masters degree in psychology from Purdue, started a doctorate program at Michigan, then joined the Marine Corps."

"Damn. He needs to see a shrink."

"Yeah. No kidding. I think he's crazy like a fox though. I think he's using this experience for his doctorate. He keeps a diary and notebooks and stuff. Talks to everybody about why they joined the Corps, why they wanted to fly. Stuff like that. Either that or he's gonna write the Great American Novel. Either way, my guess is he's not here for the flight pay."

"Borenmann, the shrink, huh? Man, have we got a challenge for him."

"Two challenges, if you count Pyhr."

"Yeah, two challenges, definitely two."

A mile off to our left, Camp Evans slid by and a fresh swarm of six Hueys descended into the dusty fog on its surface. Jim switched the UHF.

"Dong Ha DASC, Hardball 4-3, over."

"Wait one, Hardball. Break. Magpie 6-0-1, DASC. You're on mission 4-0, copy, mission 4-0. Cattle Prod 12-0 has mission 4-2. How copy? Over."

No answer.

"Magpie 6-0-1, DASC."

Still no answer.

"Magpie 6-0-1 *Dash Two*, DASC."

A loud squeal. "—ahead, DASC."

DASC called him back, but by the time they got the mission assignments straightened out, we were past Quang Tri and only three miles from Dong Ha. Jim tried again.

"DASC, Hardball 4-3, mission 8-2, Quang Tri, clearance."

"Hardball 4-3, DASC, roger, wait one."

Jim and I returned shrugs. I'd been in country long enough to know DASC didn't always have their sierra in one bravo. Not always their fault—can't know what people don't tell you—but still…frustrating. Anyhow, as long as we were on the highway and below 500 feet, we were okay.

"Hardball 4-3, this is Dong Ha DASC, over."

"Go ahead." Jim smiled.

"Say again your mission, 4-3."

Jim shook his head. "Hardball 4-3 is mission 8-2."

"Copy that, 4-3. Got pax at Owl, then pax for points west. Cleared to Owl. Contact Owl on 28.65."

"Copy that. Switching."

At Owl, the small, division headquarters LZ in Dong Ha, we landed, picked up a Navy chaplain with two enlisted men, and departed. The chaplain, a very squared-away Navy lieutenant in Marine camouflage utilities, said they wanted to go to Cua Viet, a Navy dock and Marine supply base five miles south of the DMZ at the mouth of the Cua Viet River. I did the flying. Jim worked the radios.

After we dropped the enlisted men at Cua Viet, the chaplain said he wanted to go to the *Repose*, a hospital ship three miles off the beach.

Jim looked at me. "You ever made a ship landing?"

"Not in a helicopter. You?"

"Nope," he said.

"How hard can it be? Just a floating LZ, right?"

"That's right."

"You want to take it?" I asked.

"Nah. I'll stay on the radios."

I smiled and called, "Cleared left." He answered, "Cleared right," and I pulled pitch.

The *USS Repose*, a huge white ship with a brilliant red cross on its side, rested lightly on the South China Sea—the ultimate secure zone. Jim found their call sign and frequency on a kneeboard card and dialed it manually into the UHF.

"Sea Breeze, this is Hardball 4-3, over."

No answer. Three calls and a mile later, still no answer.

"I'll try fox." Jim dialed in an FM frequency he found. "Sea Breeze, this is Hardball 4-3, over."

No answer. Two calls and another mile later, still no answer. We were almost on top of it now. I looked around for other traffic. It was quiet, not an aircraft in sight, not a ripple on the water. I swung the Huey off to the right to set up a left-hand orbit around the ship.

"Sea Breeze, Hardball 4-3." Jim looked at me. "How do you say to a ship, 'If you read me, rock your wings?'"

I laughed and shrugged my shoulders.

"Well, I give up. It looks clear. Give 'em a low pass and see if anybody's home."

In a left turn, I came around the bow and dropped to 100 feet. At our ten o'clock, painted on the deck of the fantail of the ship was a square with an "X" connecting the corners. Red fire-fighting equipment rested to the side of the square. I finished my turn, lined up on the fantail, and looked for a signal or sign of life.

Leaning out of his seat, Jim saw the man first and pointed. Against the bulkhead just forward of the square, a sailor in denim held a large white sign. Stenciled in black on the sign were "44.5" and "USS Repose." As I climbed and began another left-hand orbit, the tone in my headphones hummed then locked onto the new frequency.

"Sea Breeze, Hardball 4-3, over."

"Hardball 4-3, Sea Breeze, say state."

Jim looked at me. "Wait one." He laughed. "Okay, what the hell does that mean? I'm from Missouri, that's my state. Ah…I'm not in an agitated state. Not yet, anyhow. What?"

"You got me. Maybe he wants to know if you're in a hurry."

Jim shrugged. "Sea Breeze, Hardball 4-3, we've got a passenger for you…no hurry, over."

I could hear laughter in the background as the voice on the ship responded, "Roger, Hardball, make a port approach, your signal is Charlie, say your fuel state, over."

Jim raised his eyebrows. "Hardball 4-3 has 500 pounds, about 45 minutes, over." He looked at me again. "Why didn't he say 'fuel state' the first time? What's 'Signal Charlie?'"

"Cleared to enter the landing pattern and land, I guess. That's what it means for fixed-wing. You didn't carrier qualify?"

"No. No carriers at Army flight school. Go ahead. Land this thing. Do your 'port approach,' or whatever."

"Roger. Want me to call the ball?"

"Yeah, man. Call the ball, fill the moat, lower the portcullis, whatever it takes to make these guys happy."

"Roger. Landing check."

Jim ran down the checklist as I found the guy in denim again. This time he wore a yellow vest, eye and ear protectors, and stood at the top of the square. I followed his directions and in a minute we were safely on deck.

The chaplain asked us to be back in an hour and quick-stepped away in a crouch.

I was ready to go—Jim had already given the guy in the yellow vest a thumbs up—when a woman in white stepped from the hatch to my left and walked briskly toward our Huey. Squinting against the rotor wash, her uniform blown tightly against a sweetheart figure, she held a red can in each hand. I waved her over to Jim's side. She nodded.

Reaching Jim's window, she handed him one can at a time, pulled the brown hair from her eyes, and smiled. Huge blue eyes. He smiled back, mouthing, thank you. She mouthed, take care, patted him on the shoulder, and ran to the hatch using cute little choppy steps—elbows out, head down, then gone as if she were never there in the first place.

Jim sat motionless, staring at the hatch, holding a sweating can of Coca-Cola in each hand.

"Hey, Jim. Hello. One of those for me?"

"No, she's mine."

"The Cokes, asshole. I'm thirsty over here."

"Yeah, here are your Cokes." Jim held them toward me, still looking at the hatch.

"Thanks. You don't want one?"

"One what?" Jim looked at me, and pulled one of the Cokes back to his lap. "Yeah, you get one. Let's go. I've been in 'Nam so long I'm having visions. I swear I saw a round-eyed woman in white."

"You did. This is the Navy, man. They've got everything."

"Listen, Ross. If I'm ever hit, you bring me here. Got it?"

"No problem."

"Okay. Bumble Bee go Quang Tri now. We need fuel."

"Roger, we liftin'."

Fifteen minutes later, sitting at idle in the fuel pits at Quang Tri, we learned that "Sea Legs," the Marine Huey squadron based there, had gotten the word: They were leaving Vietnam. The lance corporal on the second nozzle said it wouldn't be immediate, more toward September-October. He also said Sea Legs had a bird shot up in the Con Thien area yesterday, five hits, no casualties. Jim listened to him, then gave me an "I told you so" look and nod. Maybe it was Pyhr's Dead-Eye Gooner, maybe not. Hell, after all those years of practice, maybe they'd all gotten to be better shots.

With time to kill before we were due back at the *Repose* and with Jim on the controls, we departed Quang Tri and flew up the Thach Han River until it became the Cua Viet. There Jim turned east toward the beach and climbed to 500 feet. "You ever done a full auto?" he asked.

"Not since primary stage at Ellyson, TH-13s."

"Never in a Huey?"

"Never in the H-34 or the Huey. They said it was too risky. Did all practice autos to a power recovery."

"Well, it's nothing. We did them all the time in Army Flight School—course we bent a few skids learning how, but the Army figured it was worth it. I figure they were right. Clear? Harness locked?"

"Roger, clear left."

Jim rolled the throttle off and we fell out of the sky in an autorotation: flight powered simply by the air rushing up through the rotor blades, spinning them.

"See that little island, or sandbar up ahead, inside the right fork in the river?"

"Yeah. I think."

"I'll land there."

I looked ahead at the flat, desolate, delta area of the Cua Viet River and tightened my shoulder straps. That was no island. It was a sandbar at best. A small sandbar.

"I'm using 60 knots, slower rate of descent. You were taught 70, right?"

"Yeah." Slower rate my foot. That sandbar was coming fast.

"Okay, as we pass through 100 feet, I ease the nose up to slow the rate of descent and bring the air speed down to 45 knots—watch the RPM—little bite of collective to hold 6600, hold it, 10 to 15 feet lower the nose, pull collective, cushion the landing." We slid one length of the Huey and stopped dead in the center of the sandbar. No big flares, no big yanks on the collective, no bounce. The big blades swished slowly over my head.

I knew some Marines had been Army-trained. Some were Air-Force trained too. With the build-up demanded by the war, the Navy flight school in Pensacola couldn't keep up. How they decided who went where was a mystery. I think they just pulled names out of a hat. For those who joined the Marine Corps to fly jets, being assigned to Army flight school was the kiss of death. They only trained helicopter pilots. On the other hand, if your name came out of the hat for Air Force training, you were a jet pilot. If you went to Pensacola, you could go either way depending on your performance, your wishes, or the needs of the Marine Corps—mostly the needs of the Corps.

Jim's auto to the sandbar was the first time I'd ever noticed any difference between Marine and Army training. Jim was obviously much more confident in his ability to handle an engine failure than I was.

The nose of the Huey twitched as Jim rolled the throttle on and the blades jumped to life. "Your turn."

I took the controls and looked around. The sandbar, 50 meters long and 30 meters wide, was really an earthbar, a tiny island. Up close I could see it had soil and weeds, even a few bushes. I wondered if it had any gooks.

I took off and climbed to 1000 feet—more altitude to work with—and lined up on the island. Damn, it looked small. "Ready, Coach."

"Make it happen, Ross. Clear right."

"You sure there aren't any gooks down there?"

"Yeah. Go man, you're gonna be too close."

"Goin' down." I did the "down, right, idle, turn" routine and centered the ball. We were too close. I "S-turned" out to the right, then back to the left. We were too short. I nosed over for 80 knots—more glide distance—then lookin' better, nosed up to slow it down. Hundred feet, raised the nose, caught the RPM with collective, held the flare, bled off the air speed. Fifteen feet, lowered the nose, pulled collective—little too late—hit, slid, crunched, lurched to a stop. A sandy dust cloud enveloped us. I rolled the throttle back on. Crunch?

"Hit a hole there, Ross?"

"Don't know." I looked down to the left skid. The tip was half-buried. The section behind the tip was suspended in midair, over a shaft, a shaft with…a rifle butt and a helmet. "Shit, Jim, hang on!"

I popped the Huey out of the hole, pushed the nose over, and kept pulling collective until the RPM sagged. Then I used beeper trim, I used right pedal—I would have beaten it with a riding crop if I had one. "Get down!" I yelled.

"What?" Jim hunched over the controls, ready to snatch them from me.

"Gooks!" Skimming the skids across the water, I hit 90 knots, cyclic-climbed up to 500 feet, then, at Jim's request, cautiously turned the Huey for another look.

"Are you sure?"

"Yeah. A rifle butt—AK, and a pith helmet, and ah...plastic. Yeah, plastic, ragged—maybe ripped away by the skid."

"Well, damn, Ross. It's probably just a storage area, a supply point. There aren't any gooks there."

"You sure?"

"Well, yeah, pretty sure. I mean, if it was an ambush site or something, they wouldn't have their guns wrapped in plastic and stuck in a hole. Would they?"

"Shit, I don't know." I looked down at the island. Didn't see anything suspicious, no movement. "Supply point, huh?" I let out a breath.

Jim leaned out of his seat, looking past me. "I'm sure of it." He stroked his mustache and stared at the island. "You know...AKs are very marketable. Good trade bait."

"Yeah? So?"

"So, you still need a fan?"

"Yeah. Either that or a new air conditioner for the hootch."

"Well, what do you think? We go back down there, lift the AKs, take one to Cua Viet and trade it for a fan, then go to the *Repose* and give another AK to that number one round-eyed vision in white."

"Give it to her? A token of your affection? Get real!"

"Trade it to her, asshole, for a case of Cokes."

I shook my head. "I don't know, Jim. What if that hole is booby-trapped?"

"If it was booby-trapped, we'd have been blown to shreds back there."

"What if it's one of those pull booby traps—doesn't go off until the line is pulled. Or lift types—doesn't blow until weight is taken off the mine." The course on booby traps at The Basic School was comprehensive. I knew some shit about mines.

"Well, they wouldn't booby-trap their own supply point, would they?"

"What if?"

"What if? Yeah, okay...what if? Give me a minute."

I couldn't believe Jim wanted to go back down there. That pat on the shoulder by the blue-eyed nurse must have really gotten to him. And that smile too.

I circled, dropping to 300 feet, then 200 feet. Jim was right: no tracks, no paths, no signs of any life. The shaft I had stumbled into was about three feet wide and probably contained a stack of helmets and at least a dozen rifles. It was in the middle of the island. I looked again…and blinked.

"Jim. Look up from the shaft. See 'em? The circles." They were faint, but distinctive—circular outlines in the ground, same diameter as the shaft, two of them, invisible unless you were looking for them, unless you knew about the first. I turned right so Jim would have a better view.

"Yeah. I see 'em. I think we've stumbled into the NVA Sears warehouse. Rifle city."

"I've got a plan," I said. "The wheels are turnin' here."

"Great. You want a fan that bad, huh?"

I looked at him, opening my mouth to say, hey, you started this, but he threw up his hands and added, "That's okay, that's okay. Let's hear it."

I looked at the island. "Okay, here it is: The VC and NVA always mark their booby traps, usually using sticks or stones. So we go back down there, check the other shafts for markings, and if none, we proceed."

"Proceed? Like how proceed?"

"If we pour enough sand or dirt into the hole to replace the weight of the AKs we remove, that should take care of the possible pressure-release type mines. I think we already eliminated the pure pressure types by dumb-ass luck."

"I roger that. Go on, go on. I can see the Coke Angel fondling my AK even as we speak."

"So the only remaining threat is the pull type, one of those rifles tied to a trip wire. I think we can eliminate that threat by tying something, rope or whatever, to the plastic bags and dragging the rifles out from a safe distance."

"Yeah, okay. You got rope?"

"Ah…no."

"Well, Master Planner?"

"Ah…got bootlaces."

"Bootlaces. Maybe five feet worth. Right."

"No, listen. This'll work. Their booby traps are usually frag grenades, small stuff, a 60mm mortar the largest. We link our four laces, and…"

Jim sat back in his seat. "And what?"

"Our flightsuits! Two flightsuits, maybe 12 feet worth, plus the laces, another five to six feet, arms length, shit, we're 20 feet away!"

"*We're* 20 feet away?"

"Okay, I'm 20 feet away. You're 50 feet away in the bird ready for a quick get-away."

Jim pulled on his mustache. "Okay. I don't think that hole is booby-trapped in the first place. Let's do it and do it fast." Jim bent down and reached for his bootlaces.

With no other helicopters in sight and no traffic on the river, I made an approach to the eastern end of the island.

Cruising past the shaft, I could see it was exactly what Jim had said: NVA supplies buried in a 55-gallon steel drum.

In a cloud of dust and sand, I landed on the eastern tip of the island with my side of the Huey facing the supplies. I rolled the throttle to idle, gave Jim the controls, and backed out of the cockpit. We were at least 50 feet away.

Five minutes later, with Jim nervously checking his watch, I walked away from the Huey in my bare feet, green boxer shorts, and pistol belt. Under my arm, I carried a bundle of flightsuits, T-shirts, and boot laces—the T-shirts were Jim's idea, another five feet.

Stalking the sandy waters' edge where the river came and went and booby traps and stickers were least likely, I didn't have a large area to search. The earth part, where the stuff was buried, was only 20 meters long and 10 meters wide and was probably the only part of the island that stayed above water during all but the heaviest rains. I walked to the other end of the island and back without finding three rocks in a row, three sticks in a row, a triangle of sticks, or other man-made signs indicating booby traps.

Still carrying the bundle, I approached the drum from the south—carefully, one foot at a time—and kneeled beside it. The soil was hot on my knees.

Our skid had ripped the steel cover off the drum and the plastic off one of the rifles. The exposed rifle butt was scarred, bare wood exposed. I could smell the oily cosmolene preservative. A stack of pith helmets, still inside their plastic bag, lay beside the rifles.

Squeezing the bundle between thighs and chest, sweat beading on my face and shoulders, I bent over the buried drum, looked for trip wires, but saw nothing suspicious: no wires, no fishing line, only dirt pushed in by our skid—enough to offset the weight of at least one rifle.

Jim and I had discussed whether to drag out one rifle at a time or go for the whole wad at once, two of them. We'd decided to go for the whole wad, but as I looked inside the crowded drum and shied from the fetid smell rising from the bottom, I realized that wasn't possible. In fact, one at a time wasn't going to be easy.

I glanced toward the Huey. Jim looked at me through my open cockpit door and tapped his watch. I nodded.

I tied the bootlace to the scarred rifle butt and backed toward the river, feeding out a line of laces, T-shirts, and flightsuits—25 feet worth. The scarred rifle probably wasn't as marketable as the others, but it was already pulled from the bottom of the drum by six inches, so I figured it would slip out the easiest. It was also least likely to still have a trip wire.

On my belly and elbows with one leg in the river and the other cocked at the knee, I held my breath and pulled. My pulse jumped as the rifle, greased by the cosmolene, slid out of the drum and dropped to the sand. Grinning, heart racing, I reeled in my catch and told myself I was a genius, a soon-to-be fan-owner and genius.

I left the rifle at the river's edge and retraced my steps to the drum. I tied the bootlace, careful not to jostle the drum's contents, to another rifle butt, this one still in a bag. After slowly and deliberately adding enough dirt to the drum to equal what I guessed to be another AK's worth, I backed off again, lay on my belly, felt the cool river water on my foot, and pulled on my clothesline.

The explosion deafened me. The heaving earth lifted me into the air and for a split second I hung suspended, arms and shoulders singed by heat, my eyes, ears, hair, and pores blasted by dirt. Then I fell, covered my head, jerked into a fetal position, and flopped onto the riverbank—breathless. I wanted to breathe, but couldn't. I struggled, my world went gray, then black.

Some time must have passed. I was wet. I was being scraped. I tasted grit, fabric, rancid water. My eyes felt full of cut glass, sharp pain. I cracked them and winced.

Over the ringing in my ears, I heard a faint voice say, "Hey, Ross. You okay? Talk to me, man."

Jim, squatting beside me, washed my face with a green cloth and held me in a sitting position, my feet still in the river.

"Ohhh, man," I said, my voice hoarse. "What a *boom*."

"Your mine-clearing technique needs a little polishing, ol' buddy. Judging by the hole, I'd say that frag grenade you expected was more like a 105 artillery round."

I sat up, supporting myself with my hands, facing the river. "I'll take your word for it. I'm too dizzy to turn around."

Jim handed me his cloth and stood. "Take your time. I've got to find our laundry."

Ten minutes later, we flew to the *Repose* with a new but dirty AK-47 rifle with a cracked stock and a butt-plate hanging by one screw. Even after I discovered he had used his boxer shorts to wipe my face, I told Jim he could have the AK. Jim, bouncing in his seat to the beat of the Huey, wore those same boxer shorts under his shredded flightsuit. The T-shirts weren't found in pieces large enough to wear.

I didn't realize I'd tied his flightsuit closest to the hole. I apologized, and he accepted. "Breaks of Naval Air," he said. Mine didn't survive unscathed either, but at least I had both arms on mine. I felt badly because I knew he wanted to look his best when the Coke Angel brought us Cokes. He was counting on seeing that angel. I was counting on the Coke. My mouth tasted like I'd been sucking on a swamp frog.

This time, Jim dazzled the *Repose* with his knowledge of shipboard operations and put the Huey right on the "X." The chaplain was waiting. He hurried over to my side of the Huey and climbed in. No angel.

Jim hesitated, waiting, watching the hatch—the Heaven's Gate for Coke Angels. When none appeared, his hairy chest, visible through tears along the front of his flightsuit, sagged with a sigh I could see but not hear. He rolled the throttle up for takeoff.

"Hold it!" The padre leaned over the pedestal panel between us. He looked at Jim, then at me. "You guys look like crap!"

"We do?" I shouted back. I guess I had hoped he wouldn't notice.

The chaplain pulled at the shredded pieces of Jim's flightsuit. He turned to me, staring at my knees. "Are you guys alright? You look like you've been blown up."

I glanced at the dirty knees sticking through the rips in my flightsuit, then my hands followed the chaplain's eyes to my face. Dirt and sand were still in the corners of my mouth and in globs in the corners of my eyes. I looked at Jim. Jim looked at me and we burst out laughing.

Jim keyed his mike. "No shit, Ross. You look like that little guy in *Treasure Island*. What's his name? Ben Gunn?"

"No kidding," the chaplain shouted. "Do you guys need attention?"

My sore eyes blinked. Attention? "Yes, sir," I yelled back. "I sure could use a drink of clean water or Coke and Lieutenant Teach really needs to see a nurse."

"Well, stay right here, Lieutenant. Lieutenant Teach, come with me."

Jim looked at me, his mouth open.

"Go, man. I've got the bird."

"Be right back."

Jim was unstrapped and out of his seat in a heartbeat. It was on his way to the hatch that he developed a severe limp.

In a minute, a skinny sailor in denim with the personality of a deck cleat delivered my medicinal Coke. It was cold, it was clean, it scoured the swamp taste away. Ahhhh.

It took 15 minutes for Jim to get the medical treatment he required. He finally returned, limp free, wearing a different flightsuit, and holding another one in his hand. I don't think he noticed the blood stains on the legs of the flightsuit.

Jim sat, strapped in, and slipped into his flight helmet. "Your turn, ol' buddy." He tossed me his bundle. "Here, see if you can keep this one in one piece."

I smiled, not moving.

"Okay, okay. Her name is Carol. Yes, she's drop-dead beautiful. No, she didn't ask to see my AK. And you are correct—I don't want you near her."

Ten minutes later, both cleaned and dressed, we departed the *Repose*. The chaplain wanted to go straight to Owl, said the guys we took to Cua Viet were going to be there all day. We complied, thinking any minute now he would ask why we had looked the way we did or how the Huey got so dirty. He didn't.

Lunch was at division headquarters: air conditioning, linen tablecloths, real silverware, cloth napkins, choice of entrees—nice life if you could get it.

We spent the afternoon along Mutters Ridge, landing and taking off in a world of defoliation and destruction: naked and splintered trees 100-feet tall, bomb craters as thick as a moonscape, makeshift landing zones with floors of deciduous carcasses crawling with tangled vines and thorns and inhabited by filthy, load-hacking Marine grunts in ripped and rotten utilities. Our cleaned, pressed, and shined passengers, a full colonel and his entourage, looked out of place. My ears stopped ringing around 1400.

By 1700 we'd been to LZs Charlie, Audrey, and Champ—as well as a half-dozen others—and the colonel was ready to RTB. We returned him to LZ Owl and told DASC we were mission complete. Time to rescue Fred Borenmann.

DASC thought otherwise. We were sent to Elliott Combat Base, the Rockpile, to work for the 4th Marines.

On a flight from the Rockpile to LZ Sierra with a captain, a lieutenant and three enlisted men—one with a PRC-25 radio, and all in flak-jackets, helmets, and M-16s—we called Fred to see if he was ready to go.

Fred, call sign "Horsehair 1-4," was so ready we couldn't get him off the radio. Located on Fire Support Base Russell, a fixed base on a 1500-foot mountain peak southwest of Mutters Ridge, he kept reminding us it was almost "nautical twilight" and there were "unstable cumulo-nimbus clouds in the western quadrant."

Jim told him we could get him on the way back from Sierra if he didn't have much gear. Fred hesitated, then explained he had two bags of gear plus his radio operator. He wasn't leaving Russell without his radio operator. He had made a promise. Jim agreed. We would make another trip.

Sierra was easy to find. Like LZ Mack, it was one of the largest scars on the ridgeline and also featured a burned-out Marine CH-46, a "crispy frog" as Shockley called them. Someone, probably Shockley, had said the 4th Marines were famous for marking their zones with burning 46s. From what I'd seen, they weren't the only ones who could make that claim.

The captain wanted stops at LZs Dodge, Catapult, and Neville, as well as Sierra and Sierra North. Neville, west of Russell, was last.

Climbing away from Neville in semi-darkness—a shadowy curtain of thunderstorms on the horizon—it was get Fred immediately or not at all. At least we were two Marines lighter—the guy with the radio and one other had hopped out at Sierra. We discussed it with the captain. He looked at the two empty spaces on the troopseat and said it was okay with him. We didn't tell him about a helicopter's reduced lift capability at altitude—seat space was not the problem.

Inbound to Russell, Horsehair 1-4 let out a less than philosophical war whoop and illuminated the corners of the steel-matted LZ for us with flashlights. Jim made the approach and landed east to west. Ahead, the thunderstorm rumbled over a parallel ridgeline, obliterating it in diagonal sheets of rain and ground-hugging fog.

Gusts of wind rocked the Huey even as we sat at idle and watched Fred and his radio operator load their gear. A flash of lightning revealed the two men struggling with two bags apiece, each man the same, indistinguishable. I figured Fred to be the one with the biggest smile, but I couldn't be sure. Both smiles were big.

Another flash of lightning. Down the steep slope in front of us, holes ringed with sandbags dotted the contour of the hill. Further down the slope, trip wires stretched between stakes in the ground, rolls of razor wire snaked among them, and a wall of triple-canopy jungle loomed in the distance. I thought I saw the tops of helmets moving in the holes. Couldn't tell for sure.

A smell like sun-baked road-kill swept over me, gagging me, and a hand slapped my shoulder. I turned. Fred leaned over the pedestal panel with one dirty hand on Jim and the other on me, his arm pits exposed.

"Driver," he shouted, turning to Jim, his smile lit by our instrument lights, "To Phu Bai! And don't spare the horses!"

Jim pointed behind his seat to Fred's helmet bag and shouted, "Plug in and get out of my face, Freud. Your B.O. is melting my avionics."

Fred slapped Jim on his shoulder and slumped onto the jump seat between and behind us. In a few seconds he was strapped in, plugged in, and calling, "Away, James."

Jim nodded as he lifted the Huey to a six-inch hover. The RPM drooped and we settled. Too heavy.

Jim nudged the Huey to the forward edge of the matting, held it there light on its skids, let the RPM recover, then waited. I released my harness lock, leaned out of my seat, and checked the steep drop below us. With the black clouds of the storm swelling over us, it was too dark to see anything. I hoped no one was in those holes.

I felt the Huey shudder with another gust of wind, sat back, and locked my harness again, knowing this was the headwind we needed.

Jim pulled the collective firmly, dropped the nose as the Huey surged off the matting, then we half-fell and half-flew into the darkness below. I scanned the air-speed indicator and radar altimeter and called, "Air speed's alive, 30 feet, 50 feet, 45 knots." The low RPM warning light and buzzer came on but I knew Jim would handle it. Then I felt the nose come up, heard the RPM build, and I called again, "60 knots, 100 feet, 300 feet, positive rate of climb." I looked up as Jim turned right. Another jagged line of lightning shocked the sky and revealed Russell, looming black against a charcoal ceiling, above and behind us.

"Shit, Freud, what's in those bags, man, soil samples?"

"No, Lieutenant Teach, just clothes, boots, and a few books. I found some interesting igneous rock specimens in a riverbed just north of Russell, but didn't think to bring any back."

"Just as well. We were one rock shy of not getting you out of there."

"Never doubted you. Can't say the same for this fine captain of Marines back here though—he jerked noticeably when you jumped off that pad. Reminded me of myself the first time I had to go out on patrol. My anal sphincter was in spasms for two days after that. Man, what a trip."

Back at the Rockpile, the captain and his fire team couldn't get out of our Huey fast enough. We left just ahead of the thunderstorm and headed toward Quang Tri for fuel and a weather report on Phu Bai. When DASC released us, it was 1930.

Quang Tri reported Phu Bai VFR, or under visual flight rules, but they forecast it to be IFR, or under instrument flight rules in an hour, and remain so for the next three hours. We could just make it.

With a full bag of gas, we departed Quang Tri and climbed to 2500 feet. Even though we were under visual conditions—we could see lights on the ground and other aircraft's lights in the sky—Jim wanted me to handle the radio so he could concentrate on flying by the instruments. "Just practicing," he said. I called Quang Tri to report clear of their traffic control, but they didn't answer. Red Devil on fox mike reported no artillery fire on our route.

One reported difference between Army-trained and Navy-trained helicopter pilots had to do with instrument proficiency. Supposedly we were better, got more training at it. To me it was like comparing a '60 Rambler station wagon to a '60 Buick station wagon. Ugly was ugly.

Like everyone else, I had been pushed through the training command and transition training at Pendleton as fast as I could go. There was a war on and "proficiency" became a relative term. The system didn't want skilled pilots, they wanted numbers—warm bodies. And instrument training suffered the most.

I tried to recall what our options were if Phu Bai went IFR before we got there. TACAN? I'd heard about a C-130 that crashed into a mountain near Chu Lai while making a TACAN approach under IFR conditions. The mountain wasn't on the charts. Sorry about that, they said. Phu Bai had a TACAN approach, I thought. I'd never seen it used though. I'd never seen anyone fly on instruments in a Huey. Not under IFR conditions. Never. Maybe they had a GCA, or ground control approach. That would be nice. Someone tells you when to turn, when to descend, what heading to use. Ah hell, maybe I was just sweatin' the small shit again. Jim had the Huey at 110 knots, flat out. We were gonna beat the weather.

Jim had flown outbound on the 1-2-0 degree radial of the Quang Tri TACAN, channel 1-0-3. Our plan was to intercept and fly inbound on the 3-1-0 radial of the Phu Bai TACAN station, channel 69. We were still in visual contact with the ground, but over a scarcely populated area. Most of the cooking fires were out. It was black down there.

Eighteen miles from Quang Tri, about halfway to Phu Bai, we were suddenly IFR, "in the soup," our red rotating beacon bouncing off the cloud and into our eyes. I turned it off. Jim lowered the collective and we descended. After losing 500 feet of altitude, the position lights on our fuselage still reflected off clouds. Then no reflection. Clear blackness.

Jim leveled off at 1500 feet with no horizon and no lights below—no up, no down—and slowed to 90 knots to lessen the effect of the beat of the blades, to stabilize the instruments. We weren't in the clouds, but we might as well have been.

After 20 miles I knew we should see something on the ground; the edge of Hue was only 25 miles from Quang Tri, and Hue was only 15 miles from Phu Bai. I gave Jim our DME, or mileage readout, from Quang Tri and a guess at where we were from Phu Bai. He wanted to try Phu Bai's TACAN channel 69 and intercept the 3-1-0 as planned. I switched.

The TACAN needle wandered around the RMI/compass rose and the DME readout had a "failed" bar across it, not the miles-to-station we needed. I switched the UHF to Phu Bai approach control and called. No answer. I watched the TACAN needle wander as I tried again, listening to the static.

We had to be over Hue, but it was black below us. Then our position lights reflected off clouds again. Jim descended to 1000 feet and the reflected light went away. The blackness remained.

I turned to the cabin. Forearms on knees, fingers locked together, Fred sat on the edge of the jump seat. He nodded, his face tense. Behind him, a dark, shapeless lump slept on the troopseat: Jimmy.

Jim had introduced me to Fred on our way from Russell to the Rockpile. Fred told us about Jimmy, the radio operator, on our way to Quang Tri. Half Cherokee and half black, two races common in North Carolina, Jimmy had enlisted in the Marine Corps to do something for his country. Also he was sick and tired of high school—it wasn't easy being mixed. Now on his way back to the world, Fred wanted to make sure he got a good start. "They don't make 'em any tougher than this kid," Fred said. "He kept my posterior afloat for three long months and is leaving this psychotic cess pool knowing he was appreciated."

I turned to the navigation radios and reset channel 69, Phu Bai. The TACAN needle still rotated against the RMI/compass rose. I looked at Jim. "Maybe it's down."

The instrument lights reflected off his face, deepening his mustache and giving his skin a pink hue. "Try the NDB and try calling Phu Bai tower. I'm worried about our UHF radio now."

Phu Bai tower didn't answer, but the ADF needle swung, then locked onto the NDB, or non-directional beacon, at Phu Bai. I got a Morse code identification to confirm it. Jim turned right to track inbound on the 3-2-0 bearing of the NDB, following the needle. The position lights reflected off the clouds again.

"Think we missed Hue?" I asked.

"No. I think there must be some ground fog or low scud down there."

I figured he was right. At first we were sandwiched between cloud layers; now we were actually in the clouds. He didn't want to go lower, and I didn't either. Not yet anyhow. Too much unknown down there.

"Try approach and tower again?" I asked.

"Yeah. Try puting the freqs in manually. If that doesn't work, squawk 7700 and get Hardball Base on the FM."

"Okay." I dialed the UHF freqs in manually, but no one answered. I switched the IFF, or Identification Friend or Foe, to 7700. That would let anyone with air control radar know we were "lost communication." J.P. Padgett answered on the FM.

Jim held up his finger as a sign he wanted to talk, so while he did, I pulled my helmet bag out from under my seat and grabbed the instrument-approach book. I found the ADF approach off the NDB for Phu Bai as Jim finished explaining to J.P. what he wanted.

A minute later, with Jim turning for what he guessed to be a five-mile arc around the Phu Bai NDB, J.P. reported back. "4-3, be advised there's a gooner in the tower and he doesn't know what the fuck he's doing."

As Jim asked, "Do you have a phone number for GCA?" I recalled a notice in the ready room saying the Phu Bai tower would be training Vietnamese tower operators. They had picked a heck of a time to let one go it alone.

"Negative," J.P. said, "and I can't get that gooner to understand who I need to talk to."

"Does he have any traffic in the pattern or on any of the approaches?"

"I'm tellin' ya, 4-3, the fucker no speaka English."

"Hardball 4-3, this is Rocker 8-0, over."

Our FM frequency was also used by the other squadrons based at Phu Bai. Rocker was the H-34 squadron and apparently one of them had heard us talking. Jim looked at me. "Take it, Ross. I'm gettin' too busy over here."

"Roger." I switched. "Rocker 8-0, Hardball 4-3."

"4-3, Rocker 8-0 is 15 nautical miles southeast of Phu Bai inbound at 4000. I've got comm with Approach Control if you need a relay, over."

Jim nodded.

"Affirmative," I said. "We're actual IFR at 1000 feet on the five-mile arc passing the 0-2-0 bearing of the NDB. No UHF, no TACAN. Squawking 7700, over."

"Roger, a gook rocket took out the TACAN an hour ago. Wait one."

A minute later, Rocker returned. "Hardball 4-3, Rocker 8-0. Squawk 1-6-0-0, ident, climb and maintain 3000, altimeter 2-9-9-0, stay on the five-mile for now, over."

"Hardball 4-3, wilco."

Jim climbed, holding the arc. I switched to 1-6-0-0 on the IFF and pressed the ident button. Meanwhile, somewhere in an air-conditioned trailer on the other side of the runway from our squadron area, a Marine or Air Force NCO watched a radar scope where the number 1-6-0-0 suddenly flashed on it—if our IFF gear was working.

"Hardball 4-3, Rocker 8-0. Approach advises they have you radar contact, fly heading 1-8-0, maintain 3000."

"Roger, 4-3 turning to 1-8-0, level 3000. Ah, Rocker, what's the weather?"

"Rocker is VFR on top at four. Phu Bai just had a thunder boomer go by a half hour ago. More in the area. Wait one."

I looked at Jim. As the Huey bumped through the unstable clouds and the genetic beat of the blades bounced us in our seats, he hunched over the controls, eyes scanning the altimeter, artificial horizon, air-speed indicator, turn-needle-ball, and RMI/compass. Working hard.

In training, instrument flying always reminded me of the guy on the Ed Sullivan Show, lying on his back on a table, with hoops spinning from his fingers, his feet, and a stick in his mouth. As soon as he would get one hoop under control, another one would be about to fall. Then he would get that one under control and another would need attention. Nerve wracking. So it is trying to keep exactly on altitude, on air speed, on heading, ADF or TACAN needle on the correct bearing or radial, and the ball centered.

Outside, the black night was tinted pink on our left side and an eerie green on our right—a reflection of the position lights on our fuselage—one instant bright, another instant dim, their brightness depending on the thickness of the clouds. And somewhere in those clouds were the mountains.

I refocused the beam of red light from the cockpit light over my head to the ADF approach plate on my kneeboard and checked the minimums. If I read it right—and I wasn't sure I had—we'd need a ceiling of 600 feet and visibility of at least one mile before we could make the approach.

"Hardball 4-3, Rocker 8-0."

"Go ahead."

"GCA advises several thunderstorm cells eight miles west of Phu Bai and closing fast. They're currently below ADF minimums and expect to go below GCA minimums shortly. They give us time for one approach. That's one approach, period—not each. Copy?"

"Roger, copy." I looked at Jim thinking we might have to go to Da Nang. Or maybe Rocker would be our radio relay, then go back to Da Nang himself. But what if Da Nang was socked in? Is anybody VFR?

"Ask if we can join up on him." Jim.

A night rendezvous in marginal VFR with no horizon, racing to beat a thunderstorm, followed by an actual IFR GCA on the bouncing rotating wing of a dissimilar helicopter? Ohhh, man. I shuddered as I keyed the mike.

"Rocker, this is Hardball 4-3. How about a section approach? We'll fly your wing, over."

"That's what I was going to suggest, Hardball. We don't have enough fuel to get back to Da Nang or Quang Tri and both are forecasting thunderstorms for the next two hours anyhow. I'll tell Approach."

"Roger."

I glanced at Fred. He wiped his hand across his mouth and shrugged.

I shrugged back.

"Hardball 4-3, Rocker."

"Go ahead."

"Approach advises climb to 4000 on present heading. You should pop out with us passing in front of you to your starboard side. We're still VFR at four, but going to four-five to give you a cushion, over."

"Roger. 4-3 is leaving three for four, heading 1-8-0."

At 3800 feet, the pink and eerie green glows on our flanks disappeared. We were on top of the clouds. Above us, the black sky to the south was clear and beautiful, dazzling with millions of glittering stars. I leaned forward in my seat, gazed at the heavens, and felt an urge to point and yell, look at that! Stupid. Position lights to bright. Anti-collision light on. Look for Rocker.

"Jim, I got Rocker at one o'clock. Either that or a flying Christmas tree."

Jim chuckled. "Roger, I got him. He is lit up, isn't he?"

I nodded. "Rocker 8-0, this is Hardball 4-3. Tally-ho. We're your four o'clock low."

"Roger, 4-3. You're in sight. Flash your landing light for positive ID, over."

Shit, I should have thought of that. That guy was good. "Roger, flashing." I flipped the switch on the collective stick.

"Good ID, Hardball. Okay, start your turn when you're ready. I'm coming back to 4000. I'll hold 80 knots then a ten-degree right-hand turn for your join-up. You tell me when. That okay?"

A flash of lightning lit a huge cloud beyond Rocker. I saw why he wanted a right turn. It would make it harder on Jim, having to look across the cockpit to his left, but Jim nodded anyhow. He knew. "Sounds good to us, Rocker."

Seconds later Jim was at the H-34's six o'clock and on his altitude. Jim nodded and I keyed the mike. "Okay, Rocker, start your turn, we're six o'clock." More lightning flashed to our left and a few seconds later, I swear I felt the thunder.

"GCA advises we've passed over the field and time's a wastin', Hardball. Can you handle a descent?"

"Affirmative." I didn't wait for Jim to nod. He could handle it.

"Okay, we're cleared to descend to and maintain 3000, leaving four, landing light and hover light going off."

We had 200 feet of altitude to get on his wing, then we'd be IFR again. Jim was almost there.

"Have him kill the anti-smash," Jim said, voice tight.

"Kill the anti-collision light please, Rocker."

"Roger."

Jim slid into a parade position with ten feet of step-up and ten feet of rotor separation just as the position lights of the 34 went fuzzy, then disappeared. My heart stopped dead. The glow from our position lights was suddenly back on our flanks. Jim flinched to the right. The 34's lights reappeared, dimly, and Jim flinched back to the left, grabbing for the lights, hanging on. I stared, holding my breath. Just lights, nothing else, lights floating in space, invisibly tied together, white light on the tail, green light on the right side, no other clues. Are we too close? Too far away? Where are our blades? Where are *his* blades? And when the lights suddenly dim, does that mean we're falling away from them or that the clouds are thicker and less light is getting through? I couldn't breathe.

"Hardball, we're gonna level off now, power coming on, holding 80 knots."

I had to breathe, had to sound cool. I sucked in some air. "Roger."

Jim hung over the controls, body rigid, and the turbulent clouds tossed us and the two faint lights our lives depended on up and down at will. Too close and we'd mesh blades and all die. Too far away and we'd lose sight of the lights and be lost, alone in the blackness with the thunderstorms all around us. The two flashlight-size light bulbs dangled in the clouds ahead and beside us and Jim fought for them.

A full agonizing minute went by, the fox mike hissing in my ears, the hum of the rotors and whine of the engine in the background. I tore my eyes from the bouncing lights and checked the gauges. Everything was good, fuel for another hour. If this approach didn't work, could Rocker still be our relay from the ground? Maybe, if the thunderstorms didn't last longer than our fuel.

"Hardball, we're gonna roll out now. We're on a right downwind for a GCA to runway 2-7. This is an abbreviated approach, and ah...GCA advises the first storm cell is two miles west, closer to the field than we are right now."

I sucked in another breath. I was representing Jim and Jim was cool. "Roger."

"Okay, we're wings level now, leaving three for two. Copy?"

"Roger, copy."

The little white and green lights ahead and to my left dropped lower and Jim dropped with them. Without taking my eyes off the lights, I keyed the ICS. "We're okay, Jim. Fuel's good, gauges good."

He didn't answer and I didn't expect him to. He was working his ass off. I remembered the landing checklist and ran through it, leaving the "harness locked" part for later, didn't want to tempt Jim to move his hands.

The hissing stopped. "Okay, Hardball, we're adding power, leveling off at 2000, and...starting a right turn...now, over."

"Roger, right turn."

The lights climbed then dropped again. Is he falling away from us or is that the right turn, a rotation in the fuselage? Jim flew up, down. The lights bobbed and weaved. Jim twitched left, right. The ICS keyed, hissing, steady hissing. What? I couldn't leave the lights.

"Ross, Ross . . ."

My hands sprang for the controls, holding them loosely. He was losing it, the lights sinking, fading away. Don't grab, ask. "Yeah?"

"Take it, take it . . ."

"I got it!" I pushed the nose over and pinched off some power. I still had the lights—dim, very dim—then they were in my face, huge, like headlights on motorcycles. I banked right, added a pinch of power and the lights dangled beside me, bouncing in the fog, fading in and out with the clouds rushing between them and my eyes.

"Hardball, we're turning onto final, gonna hold 80 knots, starting a roll-out to the left...now."

I waited for Jim to answer, quiet hissing, then: "Roger, copy roll-out."

The lights climbed, but I was ready and climbed with them. We were level now, I guessed, but my head said we were turning. I wanted to turn, I was leaning. I fought it. Believe you're level, man, believe the lights. Okay, the lights, I'm on the lights, I'm on the lights, I'm level, I'm...I'm level. I let out a breath. Almost there.

"Hardball, we're talking to the final controller now. We're on glide slope, on course. The field is 300 overcast with rain, visibility one-half mile, runway line-up lights are on bright...one mile from touchdown."

One mile. I can do that.

"Roger."

The ICS keyed again. "Ross, two clicks if you're okay."

I clicked twice. The damn lights were bobbing again, more turbulence.

"Okay, I got into some vertigo back there, okay now, it's passed. I can take it if you want me to, or need me to. Otherwise you're lookin' good, man."

"I'm okay." I thought I was okay. Hell, Jim had already done the hardest part. The lights suddenly blurred and disappeared. Damn. Then they were back. Shit. Rain. A wall of water flooded our windscreen, the lights disappeared again, then reappeared, blurred by the water. Windshield wipers? Told never use them, scratches windshield. Use them anyhow? The lights dropped, then climbed, then disappeared, then reappeared, too close! I flinched to the right, then back to the left before I lost them. The lights bounced, we bounced, wind howled through the crack in the top of my window; the clouds below brightened.

"Got the runway, Hardball, hang on a second."

The silhouette of a big black helicopter appeared in my face, an H-34, right beside me and just below me, a huge sucker with a rotor disc bigger than mine. The white light and green light I'd been chasing lit the wet tail and fuselage. The runway threshold passed under us. I took off a bite of power and eased off to the right, letting the 34 go.

"We're gonna take the Charlie taxiway, Hardball. You okay?"

Jim sighed, "Yeah, we're fine. We'll follow you, Rocker. Nice job. We owe you."

A different voice said, "You owe us not, my fling-wing brother. Though we save those who fly under the sign of the hammer—now the stupid bulls-eye—in spirit, we too are saved, Amen."

Jim and I locked eyes, our mouths open, while Fred yelled, "That Blue Dog?"

Jim smiled, nodded, and looked ahead toward the 34's blurred white tail light. "We owe you anyhow, Blue Dog. Later."

The storm lashed at us all the way down the taxiway, hurling leaves, sand, anything it could get a grip on. Along the way, I gave the controls to Jim. I was beat, eyes burning.

Jim wrestled the Huey onto the pad in the revetment, rolled the throttle to idle, and young Jimmy stirred. Fred unplugged.

I rubbed my eyes, found grit still in the corners, and noted the time, 2142—almost nine hours of flight time for the day, just another day with eleven months and three weeks to go. Rumor Control had said Tricky Dick would change the tour of duty for Marines from 13 months to 12 months soon, make it the same as the Army. I hoped they were right. I didn't think my numb ass could make it for 12 more months.

Minutes later, after the rain, wind, and my heart rate had calmed, Jim and I slung our helmet bags over our shoulders and followed Fred and Jimmy across the dark flight line. Glancing up at the low clouds, we agreed: We'd never fly IFR in a Huey again. Ever. Unless, of course, it was another mission of mercy—like bringing a Marine back to the world, or returning one of our own to the land of flushing shitters.

23

You Feel Lucky?

In PT shorts and shades, beads of sweat glistening on his freckled and lightly tanned back, Bill stood on the ladder and twisted the steering-wheel-size valve handle at the base of the water tank.

I stopped on the sidewalk below him. "Hey, Cat, you flying afternoon guns with us or what?"

"Hey, 'Small Shit Dog,' what's happenin'?"

"A brief is happenin', a brief you're scheduled for. Care to join us?"

"Can't make it. Too many other things goin' on." He put another twist on the wheel.

"What's more important than defending the 'freedom-loving people of South Vietnam?'"

Bill re-adjusted his feet, squatted on the ladder rung, and whispered loudly, "Ross, today is the day I kick Blue Dog's ass!" He made a fist with his loose hand. "Today, August…"

"24th."

"Today, August 24th, 19…"

"69."

"Yes, today, August 24th, 1969, I, the Cat's Ass, the Sun Dog, the intrepid naval aviator and steely-eyed Huey-gun pilot, will defeat the undefeated: the Hamilton Bortz, the Dog driver, the Blue Dog." He beat his chest with his free hand, stood erect again, and gazed over the tin-roofed hootches to the rice paddies and mountains on the horizon. "History will be made here today, Ross. History will be made."

"Well, that's fine, Sun Dog. Meanwhile, who flies your mission?"

Bill looked down at me with a smirk, a give-me-a-break twisting of the cheeks and an upward turn of his full-grown auburn mustache. "The new guy, Ripkevic. He's gung-ho, can't wait. I traded my afternoon guns for his slick hop with Angus."

The screened door slammed shut behind me. Granny appeared and pointed at Bill. "I hear you say you're going to Da Nang?"

Bill gave the valve another twist. "We're going wherever the Bull wants to go, I guess."

Granny paused, eyeing the line of the tank's drain pipe. He looked across the sand to the plywood-faced quonset hut 15 meters away. "Better be careful, Cat. That's a three-inch valve, lot of pressure in there, lot of water."

"I know. That's why I've got to let some out—level's too high." Bill grunted as he put another twist on the wheel.

Granny shook his head. "Okay…listen, while you're in Da Nang—I imagine you'll be at wing, Angus likes to stop there on these trips—see if you can find Tess. Hippy Dog said he saw him there a few days ago. Just check on him for me, okay?"

"No prob—" Bill grunted as he put another full twist on the wheel.

"Look out!" Granny threw out his hand as a stream of water shot from the valve, rocketed across the sand, and drummed against the door to the hut—Mickey's hut, The Bull's hut.

"Ohhhh, shit," Bill muttered, grabbing for the underside of the wheel. With one good twist, he had it under control. A faucet-size trickle ran onto the sandy ground at the base of the ladder.

"Wow!" With the back of his hand, Bill wiped his brow, laughing. "Hey, Granny, you were right, man."

Granny looked at me. "I've got a teen-age son like him— always got to learn the hard way. Let's get out of here."

As Granny and I jogged between the quonset huts, Bill hollered, "Hey, where you goin'? They're not home, man. No problem."

Seconds later, inside Hut 8, Granny, still laughing at the expression on Bill's face when the water cut loose, turned into his space. I continued toward mine, hurrying to get my pistol belt and thinking of Granny and Angus.

I'd learned from Jim Teach that Granny was a former Marine enlisted pilot. Weeks before, when I had asked Granny about that, he had said yeah, the law had once required that 20 percent of all Navy and Marine pilots be enlisted. He qualified for the program and started flight school in 1942 as a sergeant. Flying fighters during most of his career, he finished in helicopters, retired in 1967 as a warrant officer, and joined Bell Helicopter.

"No beefs with the Corps," he'd said. "They let me fly a long time and mostly gave me the duty stations I asked for."

When I asked if he had run across Angus in his career or knew anything about him, the answer was no. He said Angus was probably a senior major, in the same promotion zone as Major Hardy, but that was all he knew.

I looked toward the front of the hut and buckled the webbed belt over my flightsuit. "Granny...what does Angus do on these trips to Da Nang? Seems like he's going down there once a week."

"Don't know for sure, but my hunch is it's got something to do with promotion. Ross...who's this Lieutenant j.g. Carol Sommers that's writing Jim?"

He must have picked up our mail for us that morning. I shut my locker and walked up the aisle, adjusting the belt. "That's the Coke Angel I told you about."

Standing at the entrance to his space, Granny held a single envelope in one hand and several envelopes plus a pair of glasses in the other. "The nurse on the *Repose*?"

"Yep."

"Well, well. This may be serious. I think I feel a photograph in here."

"I hope so. She's a looker. I'll see you later."

"Wait a minute. Got one for you."

I stopped at the curtains. "Probably my mother, right? I'll get it later."

"Nope. Says here it's from—" Granny put on the bifocals. "—Mrs. Laura Catlett, Vista, California."

I smiled. "Laura's still trying to get me married. Last time she wrote she had a schoolteacher she wanted me to meet. I'll get that later too. Just drop it on my rack, will ya?"

"Okay. You keep J.P. out of trouble today, Lieutenant. Hear me?"

"I hear you, Granny. See ya." I let the curtains fall and left for chow.

I was flying with J.P. Padgett, his first HAC hop after his check ride two days before. Adam Henstrom and Dewey Munzel were now HACs as well. In keeping with Major Lewis' policy, as a new HAC, J.P. would fly only with senior co-pilots for a while. That would be me, Bill, Walt Duppont, or Rod Wysowski. I was getting there—one more month to HAC, two max.

First Lieutenant Buck Akerman, a section leader for a week, briefed the flight in the ready room. Lean and hatchet-faced, with the head posture and eyes of a hungry coyote, Akerman was tough and aggressive. Already wounded once, a leg wound with Pyhr, I knew he'd find something for us to shoot at today even if it was just NVA trees. And shooting meant we would rearm. That meant we'd have to shut down. That meant I'd get to stretch my legs and get the blood going to my now cushioned but still aching buns. Something to look forward to.

As a stick man, J.P was an unknown. He was a senior co-pilot when I was a new guy, so I'd never flown with him. Personally, other than a case of halitosis that would gag a goat, I thought he was okay.

We left Phu Bai at 1200 and were well beyond Hue—with J.P. understandably doing all the flying—before he said anything.

"Ross, you know any of the new guys?"

"I know Ripkevic, he's in our hootch, took Tess's rack. Don't know anything about O'Connor or Kerrigan."

A long white cigarette dangled from the corner of J.P.'s thin lips. "I still can't believe your dumb-ass friend Catlett stayed in the dead man's rack. He should've moved."

"Yeah, maybe. He says Tess's rack is the D.M.R.—Tess was shot down and ended up in a cast, not him."

"Well, I wouldn't sleep in either of 'em."

J.P. kept us at Akerman and Ripkevic's seven o'clock, 50 meters back, and we flew on in silence—low-leveling along Highway One. Overhead, puffy white cotton-ball clouds seeded the blue sky and their shadows blotched the rice fields and shaded us for seconds at a time. On the ADF, the Mamas and Papas sang "Go Where You Wanta Go."

After a few miles, and while passing a collapsed railroad bridge rusting in a river, J.P. keyed the ICS. "Understand Teach got you guys a new air conditioner."

"Yeah. Traded that AK we found to some Army sergeant at Camp Eagle. Brand new. Pretty good deal."

Another ICS mike was keyed, one with wind noise in the background. "That's nothing, Lieutenant." It was Earley, our crew chief, the guy with the Errol Flynn mustache, apparently listening in. "Gunny Pass traded a K-bar knife to an Army supply sergeant at Eagle for an M-21 mini-gun. Got it yesterday." Gunny Pass was Gunnery Sergeant Passamano, our ordnance chief.

J.P. twisted his pencil neck and glanced toward the cabin. "Shittin' me? What the hell for?"

"Major Angus wanted it. Been buggin' Gunny Pass about it ever since he saw the Cobras use theirs on T.C. awhile back."

"What's he gonna do with it?"

"Shit, put it on one of our birds, I guess, sir."

"As a door gun?" I asked.

"No, sir. On the change seven, like the 60s are now."

"Forward firing?"

"Yes, sir."

Humph, might as well, I thought. He can't hit shit with the rockets.

"Traded for a K-bar, huh?" J.P. asked.

"Yes, sir. Shit, sir, those Army guys have so much stuff they don't know what to do with it all. Gunny said with one more knife he could have had a jeep in the deal."

J.P. scoffed. "Those fucking Army guys. They've got every piece of gear you could ask for and they still aren't worth a damn. Fuckin' waste."

"Roger that, sir."

I ignored the ignorance and shifted in my seat. Bill had finally gotten an inner tube for me but it didn't have the right amount of air or something. It wasn't doing the job. I looked at J.P. "Anybody heard from Gamez?"

"Akerman got a letter from him sometime this week. Said he's down in the Arizona territory with the 5th Marines. Some bad country down there, lots of booby traps and shit."

"He's okay though?"

"Yeah. Says he's with a good battalion. Good people." J.P. sucked on his cigarette and exhaled slowly. "You know that fuckin' Angus won't let him come back to Phu Bai and get his flight time? I heard him talkin' to Major Lewis. 'Fuck him,' Angus said. 'He doesn't want to be in this squadron, rather be with the grunts, then let him fly somewhere else.' What an asshole."

I pointed ahead of us. Akerman had swung over to the right, heading for the Keyhole.

J.P. nodded. "Yeah, I figured he'd do this."

The Keyhole was two trees, tall palms, 50 feet apart and isolated in the middle of a large area of rice paddies. With the ball of palm fronds at the top of each tree 80 feet off the ground, the thrill was to fly between the tree trunks and below the palm fronds—through the Keyhole. Our blades were 44 feet in diameter.

I'd never been with anyone who had actually tried the Keyhole. Rod and Bill had said they'd seen Shockley do it, but he'd never done it with me. Most of our guys either ignored the Keyhole, or did the "Keyhole wave." As Akerman dropped down to 100 feet, I figured that's what he'd do—the wave. Or I hoped that's what he would do. I doubted J.P., on his first HAC hop, with two impressionable enlisted men behind him, had the self-confidence to risk the ridicule if he didn't take the unspoken dare and do whatever Akerman did.

Ahead of us, Akerman lined up on the left tree. He descended to paddy-dike altitude, increased his air speed, then suddenly banked right, then left—now aimed at the gap. I should have known. Hard not to show off for the new guy, for Ripkevic. I stiffened.

Racing at the trees, skimming the rice paddies, Akerman flew closer, closer, then pulled up sharply, rolled right, and sliced his blades between the palm fronds—the "Keyhole wave" with an Akerman twist, the low approach. J.P. followed barely 30 meters behind, dipped our blades, and clipped a palm frond with a skid. No harm done. We grinned at each other as I scratched my mustache and took a deep breath.

Forty-five minutes later, flying south of Mutters Ridge, we approached Fire Base Russell from the east. DASC didn't have any work for us and had told us to go to Vandy and shut down, remain on stand-by. Akerman had asked permission to remain on "airborne stand-by" and DASC had agreed.

The new "Horsehair 1-4," Fred Borenmann's replacement on Russell, answered Akerman's call on FM. "Horsehair FNG," as J.P. called him, said there had been a fight west of Russell on Hill 715, LZ Cougar, a few days ago, and another fight that morning just west of LZ Sierra on Mutters Ridge. Horsehair thought the situation west of Sierra was cleared up though, as all fire missions from Russell had stopped a few hours earlier. Nothing for us to shoot at. We kept flying west, toward the corner of South Vietnam formed by the DMZ and Laos.

Following the Cam Lo River valley, we passed LZ Margo along the river, LZ Cougar high on our left, and, as the river narrowed, climbed, and became the Cam, we passed LZ Catalina on a peak to our right and Catapult on a peak to our left. We were right on the DMZ. The scenery was incredible: lush tropical jungle, soaring mountain peaks with tufted white halos, misty waterfalls on every slope, mossy rock cliffs. I leaned forward for a better panoramic view, and wondered if any place on earth could be more beautiful.

Where the Cam began from little streams in the mountains, we swung left and flew south down the Ta Bang valley. LZ Green overlooked the valley from its 3000-foot mountain perch at the northern end. It passed off to our right and, like most of the others, looked abandoned.

Two of the largest mountains I'd ever seen loomed before us. Both over 5000 feet tall, the one on our right, to the west, was actually several mountain peaks together, a 5000-foot ridgeline made up of the Sa Mui and Ta Bang. The mountain to our left, at 5700 feet, was Vai Mep. I'd never seen Vai Mep up close. Visible for miles, it was the dominant terrain feature north of Hue and was perpetually crowned with clouds. On earlier missions, everyone referred to it as the "Tiger Tooth."

Alpine, another abandoned Marine LZ, appeared on a hill at the end of the valley. Beyond that, the River Rao Quan led to Khe Sanh and around the base of Hill 950, a 3000-foot observation post occupied by the 4th Marines. I was still struck with the size, sharpness, and mystery of the Tiger Tooth, and kept raising my eyes back to its shrouded peak.

"J.P., you ever seen the top of Tiger Tooth?"

"Nope, but it looks like we're gonna see it today. Check it out."

Ahead of us, Akerman was in a shallow left bank and climbing.

"It 'pears to me," J.P. said, pulling a cigarette from his lips and spewing smoke with his words, "that Buckaroo Akerman is determined to show FNG Ripkevic every square inch of this fucked-up country."

We chased Akerman up the mountain, climbing toward the misty bases of the clouds, 50 meters behind him. I smiled. Play time.

One of the incredible delights of flying helicopters is their ability to get you up close to nature. Clouds for instance. Instead of ripping through them, you can fly along beside them, nudge them, squeeze between them, fly down their valleys, through their tunnels, and hug their plump curves. Like they were in the days of Eddie Rickenbacker, clouds can be a puffy playground in the sky.

After climbing to 6000 feet, Akerman darted between two bulging walls of white and into a cumulus forest of condensed water vapor. J.P. chased after him.

"Shit, Ross, keep your eyes open. There's a fuckin' mountain peak in here somewhere."

"I've checked the map, J.P., we're okay above 5800."

"Yeah, if the map is right!"

It sounded to me like J.P. was sweatin' the small shit. I liked it. I could work with a guy like that.

With white vapor trailing from the tips of its rotor disc, Akerman's Huey led us around one protruding cumulus section, then under a ledge and into the shadows cast by yet another puffy section building off the first. I leaned forward and enjoyed the view, but kept my hands ready. Our heavy gunships were sluggish at that altitude; I could tell J.P.'s control inputs were larger and the rotor's response was more delayed.

Now completely in shadows, and with my body in goose bumps from the drop in temperature, we snaked our way between two more swollen gray walls—banking right, then left, then seeming to slow as we popped into a domed cavern. Below, veiled by thin formless clouds, a jungle protruded from the cavern floor.

J.P. glanced at me. "Is that it, the peak?"

"I don't know. Can't see enough of it to tell. The altitude seems about right."

"See any wreckage? According to Major Hardy, there's a wrecked 34 and an O-1 Bird Dog up here."

"Nope. Watch out." I pointed as Akerman's Huey, 100 meters ahead of us, dropped through a thin sheet of vapor.

"Shit." J.P. dropped the nose and dived after it.

Barely visible ahead and below us, Akerman scraped the peak of the mountain and flew down its slope through a gap in the clouds. J.P. stayed with him.

"We ever had a team or observation post up here?" I asked.

"Maybe way back. Not much use in keeping a team or O.P. above 3000 feet—too many clouds, can't see for shit."

Akerman followed the contour of the mountain down to 3500 feet where he pulled out below the cloud layer and headed east. J.P. and I glanced at each other. Is that it? End of the FNG tour? Please exit to the east?

Akerman answered by holding his heading.

Minutes later, I could see Russell again. Akerman called Horsehair 1-4 and we learned that Hotel Company, on Mutters Ridge west of Sierra, had regrouped from this morning's ambush. They'd also moved east, and needed a resupply. Akerman decided we'd refuel first, then see if DASC would let us run it for them.

We refueled at Vandy where Earley got the latest word from a lance corporal in the pits. The ambush west of Sierra had cost a platoon from Hotel Company three KIA and eight WIA. More had been wounded in a later mortar attack as they tried to recover from the ambush. After calling in artillery and their own mortars, then sweeping the area, only three NVA bodies were found. Not a good day on the ridge.

Airborne again, DASC said Sea Legs, Hueys from the squadron at Quang Tri, would handle the resupply, but we were cleared to work with Hotel 1-4 until Sea Legs and the resupply 46s arrived. Moments later, we were over Mutters Ridge with Akerman asking Hotel if they had any work for us.

"Hardball 5-7, this is Hotel 1-4. That's most affirm, sir. Wait one."

We waited, circling east of Sierra at 1000 feet above the ridge.

"Hardball 5-7, Hotel."

"Go ahead, Hotel."

"Roger, sir. Like for you to VR the slope north of our poz—got a team moving that way in a couple of mikes, over."

"Roger, Hotel. We're coming down at this time."

The Marines were located on one of those dusty stripped bumps in the ridgeline between Tiou Mountain to the west and LZ Sierra. I could tell there were people down there, but only when they moved. Otherwise they were invisible in the background of dirt and dead trees.

Akerman descended in a right-hand racetrack pattern until he headed west on the south side of the ridge at 1500 feet, the same altitude as the ridgeline. J.P. held us at 2000 feet and in a position behind Akerman that would allow us to drop in and cover his escape in case he took fire. We knew from experience what he was going to do next.

"Give me guns, both sides."

I complied, and set up my TAT switches as well.

Extending his straight-away behind the ridge, Akerman flew a few hundred meters past Hotel's position then banked hard to the right. He leveled off, flying north, and allowed his air speed to recover from the turn, then hopped over the ridge at treetop level and turned right again to sprint across the north side of the ridge just below the Marines.

J.P. cut across the ridge to get behind him. We waited, listening to the hissing in the radios, watching him run.

Just before he got to LZ Sierra, now vacant, Akerman hopped back over the ridge, did a hairpin turn to the left and roared back from the other direction, this time a little further down the slope. J.P. did a wing-over to stay in position behind him.

"Hardball, this is Hotel, got one. Gook on the run. Your five o'clock. See him?"

"Negative, 1-4, give me a mark." Akerman, just passing below the Marines, did a wing-over to his right.

I didn't see a gook; I didn't see any movement.

"Two o'clock…now twelve o'clock, Hardball. Hold it, I've lost him."

"Am I cleared to fire?" It was Akerman, an urgency in his voice.

"Negative, Hardball. No fire. No fire."

Akerman continued turning in a right-hand circular pattern. "Can you mark him for me, Hotel?"

"Negative, sir. We've got a team going down after him. Wait one."

"Yeah, Roger."

"Look at those guys, Ross." Seven hundred feet below us, four Marines from Hotel Company hurdled logs, bounced off splintered trees, and struggled through new growth of vines and brush in a race down the steep face of the ridgeline—rushing to cut off the gook's escape. "Are they crazy or what?" J.P. asked. "Crazy fuckers."

J.P. continued to turn and the four Marines on the slope were blocked from my view.

On the hilltop, standing or kneeling among the holes and stumps of a clearing, a thin platoon of men—maybe 20 of them—watched the hunt. Some were clearly exposed, standing with spread legs, open flak jackets and M-16s held casually by their side. Here we are, they seemed to say, playing the role of bait, and take your best shot, mutherfucker, 'cause when you give away your position, we're gonna kick your ass. Maybe they were crazy—all of them—but friends had died; I understood.

Down from the crest of the ridgeline, the race to the kill continued. I could see them now and wondered if this was yet another ambush, a trick like the NVA had used at Khe Sanh to lure over-anxious, aggressive Marines to their deaths.

"Hotel, left! Tell your guys left. One running. We got your people, clear me hot!" Akerman.

I still couldn't spot the gook.

J.P. stretched out of his seat and looked to his right, showing no signs he had seen him either.

"Make your run, Hardball, but don't shoot 'til cleared."

Damn. I looked for a Marine on the hill with a radio. That guy knew his stuff.

"Roger, I'm in." Akerman did a shallow wing-over to a dive from east to west while J.P. hustled to get behind and above him. "Okay, am I cleared hot?"

"Cleared hot."

All six forward firing M-60s, including the TAT, erupted from Akerman's Huey, emitting a thin stream of smoke on both sides and from under the nose. A row of dust jumped off the defoliated jungle slope.

J.P. pulled up, killing off air speed, then like a hawk before its plunge, we hung in the sky.

"He's running again, Two, you got him? I'm off."

J.P. dropped the nose. "Negative. Where?"

"My five o'clock. Below the dust." Unwittingly, Akerman had provided the screen the gook needed. I saw him now, bounding over logs like a dusty rabbit, centered in our sights.

J.P.'s head pitched forward and his Adam's apple bounced. "Got him! In hot, in hot!" Then on ICS, "Make me hot."

"You're hot, man. Stick it to him."

"Hardball, this is Hotel, we got him running east."

"No, no!" It was Akerman, machine-gun fire from his door guns in the background. "That's another one, the first one. Ours is running north. Get on him, Two!"

The deafening racket from our four fixed guns blocked out most of Hotel's next comment. He may have said, "Go cold." Couldn't be sure. It was too late anyhow. The gooner, not planning on a second Huey so close behind the first, was caught in mid-leap by J.P.'s guns. Airborne, he half-rolled, pulled his arms into his body, then sailed downhill out of control and slammed against the bleached white skeleton of a tree. Even as dust and twigs leaped into the air from rounds impacting all around him, he stuck like a mud ball and went limp, impaled on a splintered tree limb. J.P. released the firing button and called off cold.

Too low and vulnerable to spend time admiring J.P.'s success, I kept my TAT barrels trained on the slope and looked for more movement.

"Hotel, Hardball 5-7, you still got one running east?"

"Negative, 5-7, the fucker tried to move during your last pass. Our point blew him right out of his flip-flops."

"Want more?"

"Negative. We need to search those bodies first. May need you to mark yours."

"Roger. You won't have any trouble finding him. Looks like his shirt caught fire from a tracer stuck in his chest. You'll see the smoke when the dust clears."

Hotel answered on FM at the same time someone else called on UHF. On top of both, Earley screamed on ICS, "Got another one!" Then the pounding fire from his M-60 blocked out everybody.

"Where?" J.P. screamed over the noise.

"Go ahead." I faintly heard someone say on UHF.

"—in the zone," said another voice in the background.

J.P. pulled us into a right bank and screamed again as he looked out his side window, "Get him? Where?"

Earley's gun kept firing as I twisted to look back and see what he was shooting at.

Off the troopseat in a standing squat behind the gun and vibrating with the recoil of every round, Earley bobbed up and down while expended brass leaped out of the gun and off the aft bulkhead, the empty links piling up on the deck at his feet. "Run, you cocksucker!" he screamed over the noise. "Run!"

I followed his tracers to the ground where they hit further down the slope from the guy stuck to the tree, maybe 50 meters further. I couldn't see anything but flying bark and dust. In my ears, more jumbled voices on top of each other. I looked to the hilltop. Empty. I looked for Akerman. Couldn't see him.

"Shit, J.P., you got the leader?"

"Yeah, he's…damn. Cease fire, Earley. Cease fire."

The gun stopped.

J.P. rolled wings-level and climbed. He hung in his straps looking above us, then off to our right toward the empty hilltop. A voice on UHF, a voice I didn't recognize, said, "Roger, 5-7, solid copy. We got it."

"You got it."

We cleared the ridgeline. From the Rockpile, two Hueys and two 46s, the second 46 with a netted external trailing below it, flew right at us. The resupply package. A lone Huey circled east, over Sierra. I pointed. "That must be Akerman."

J.P. clicked his mike twice.

"I think I nailed that fucker, Lieutenant." Earley.

"Okay, wait a minute. Ross, where's Hotel?"

"Don't see 'em."

"They're there, Lieutenant. In their holes."

I looked at the ridgeline in time to see a puff of black smoke and orange dust appear just off the edge of Hotel's position. Then another, and another—three total. Mortars.

"More rain in the zone, Sea Legs, wait one." It was Hotel, calm, like it really was rain and not white hot slivers of steel flying around him.

"Roger."

To the south, the two Hueys broke away from the group, leaving the two 46s circling at 3500 feet over LZ Pete, a small hill down in the valley just south of Mutters Ridge. The Hueys curved around Hotel's position from the west at 2000 feet. We caught up with Akerman as he turned in behind Sea Legs. Four Huey guns on station now. That should get their attention.

Sea Legs 2-5 was doing the talking. "Hotel, Sea Legs, any idea where it's coming from?"

"Negative. We can hear the thumps in the tubes, but can't tell direction." I tried to remember the range of our 60mm mortar. Theirs were 61mm, so they could use our rounds but we couldn't use theirs. The range would have been the same though. If I could have remembered it.

"Okay, we'll back off, so you can hear better. Try to give us something to work with."

"Roger."

We climbed to 3500 feet, as high as we could go without dodging clouds, and widened our circle around Hotel's position. We held for a full ten minutes. Nothing happened.

A voice on FM broke the silence. "Sea Legs 2-5, Hotel."

"Go ahead, Hotel."

"Roger, we've got a clear LZ prepared for you. Negative fire since our last conversation. Like to try that resupply now, over."

"Roger, wait one."

Sea Legs on UHF: "Cattle Prod 7-0, Sea Legs 2-5."

"—py, Sea Legs. Have him stand by with smoke. Give us two minutes." Apparently, he'd been monitoring our earlier conversations on FM and already had the zone brief.

"Roger." Then on FM: "Hotel, this is Sea Legs, stand by with smoke."

"Hotel, Roger."

The radios hissed for a minute. We descended to 2500 while Sea Legs dropped to 2000 to pick up the 46s. Then the squeal of a 46 keying his mike assaulted my ears again.

"—'ll take the smoke now, Sea Legs. Break. Belly series, Two. I'm in first. Copy?"

"Two copies."

"Hotel, Sea Legs 2-5, pop smoke, over."

"Smoke away, Sea Legs."

I looked at J.P. "Belly series?"

"Shit, beats me." He looked off to the north. "Keep your eyes peeled for dust from the slope opposite Mutters Ridge. Those little fuckers have got to be somewhere where they can observe their fire."

Below us, the twin-rotored 46s, the number two guy with an external cargo net hanging below him, approached Mutters Ridge from the south, then turned and paralleled it heading west. Number Two appeared to continue his descent. Meanwhile, a yellow cloud formed on the ridgeline and trailed off to the west.

"Got your banana, Hotel." It was Sea Legs.

"Affirm, Sea Legs. Put it on the smoke, sir."

"Roger." Then on UHF, "Put it on the yellow smoke, please 7-0. Tally?"

"—ger, yellow smoke."

I checked our switches once again and scanned the hills looking for dust, movement, anything. When I turned back to Hotel, the lead 46 had made a lazy turn to the east. Clearly exposed, he slowed, rolled out on final, and raised his nose to slow his descent. Ahead of him, on the red dirt of the LZ, the smoke grenade spewed a final, pale-yellow mist. I stretched out of my seat, looked toward the hills again, and—

"Rain in the zone!"

I jerked my eyes to the 46 and found he'd already added power and had half-fallen, half-flown off the ridge to his right. Through the dust, the grunts dived like rats for the holes around the summit. A puff of black smoke spread among the holes, another hit on the slope, then another in the LZ—three total. I waited for number four. Quiet. Then I remembered they only fired three at a time. Usually.

The second 46, the one with the external, suddenly appeared from below the south side of the ridge and flared into the LZ. Dust rolled into a donut shape over the grunts huddled in their holes, the black net full of boxes and water cans dropped like a sack of money, and the 46 rolled out of his hover and away to his right. The dust cloud lingered a second, then three more angry puffs of black smoke erupted on the hill, more rapid than the first, more tightly spaced. Too late.

My eyes widened. The belly series—Coach Day's favorite offense. Run from the "T" formation, it was popular in the late 50s. The quarterback would put the ball in the fullback's belly, take a long side-step with him to the line of scrimmage, then when the defense went for the fullback, pull the ball out and pitch it to the halfback. Big gain. Little tough on the fullback, but when executed properly and unselfishly, it was a thing of beauty. With Cattle Prod 7-0 as the fullback, I'd never seen it done better.

"Bingo! Got a target, Hotel. Click north." It was Sea Legs. "Cleared hot?"

"Cleared hot, Sea Legs, and we'll need a med-evac when you get a chance. One with shrapnel wounds, priority."

Over the next two hours we strafed and rocketed the slope north of Hotel's position. Our flight had to rearm and refuel in the middle of it while Sea Legs kept shooting, then we went back and shot while they rearmed and refueled. Hotel didn't take another mortar round. The wounded Marine was stabilized by the Navy corpsman on the ground, then picked up by Magpie Medevac half an hour after he was hit. I don't know if we killed all the gooks or they pulled out. That was the frustrating part. Most of the time we didn't know. Anyhow, I couldn't have been much help. Even following Jim Teach's guidelines, my TAT jammed both times.

DASC released us at 1800.

Flying home down Highway One, the black mountains to the west etched in hazy gray twilight, I thought about Hotel spending another night on the ridge—another Marine short, another friend missing—and turned to J.P.

"J.P., you feel lucky…fortunate, I mean?"

"Lucky?" He took a drag on his cigarette and let the smoke trail out his nose. "No, not really. If I were an F-4 jock booming around at 30,000 feet in an air-conditioned cockpit, I'd feel lucky. Why?"

"Just wondering."

I thought ahead to the show at the club that night, the second show we'd had since I'd been in country. Australian group. Round-eyed women. I figured that was the other reason Bill didn't want to fly afternoon guns—didn't want to take a chance on missing the show. The Cat's Ass needed his entertainment.

Australian show, round-eyed women, showers, soft rack. I leaned back in my seat and adjusted my aching buns on my inner tube. J.P. hadn't asked, but if he had, the answer would have been yes. I felt very lucky.

24

Footsteps

Late for the Australian show, I sat on the edge of my rack, removed a flight boot, and looked at Bill. "Then what?"

Facing me across the aisle, seated in his folding chair, Bill leaned back against the edge of his rack and put his hands behind his head. "He took it to a house, one of those French-style houses with a red-tile roof."

"And just left it there?" Bill wasn't flooding me with information. Either he really didn't give a shit what Angus was up to or he was jerking my chain because he knew I did.

"No, asshole. You don't leave a case of Johnny Walker Red lying on the steps of a house in Da Nang—not even Angus is that stupid."

"Well, what then? Give it to someone?" I had to get what I could out of him before we left. Once we got to the club I'd be with the Cat's Ass, accomplished party animal, not Bill.

"Yeah. Gave it to an Army staff sergeant, Green Beret type."

I bent down to the other shoelace. "You see the guy?"

"Yeah, through the screened door. Angus strutted in like he owned the place, found this guy, then followed him back to the kitchen."

"See anything else, or did you stay with the jeep?"

"Shit no, I didn't stay with the jeep. I got out. Went in." He picked at a spot of dried food on his trousers.

I pulled the other boot off my foot and wondered about his attitude. Maybe he was pissed because I wanted to change my boots, keeping him from the show. "And?"

"And nothin'. It's a fucking club: bar, dance floor, lounge, pinball machines, and girls…well, one girl. The place was kinda dead at 1500."

"Hookers?"

"Entertainers, hostesses."

"Yeah, right. You make a friend?"

"Almost made a friend. I was in the middle of teaching this sweet young thing how to say 'Cat's Ass,' when another jeep pulled up with two more Green Berets aboard. She told them 'de Bull' was there and took them to the kitchen to find Angus."

"Sounds like Angus is a regular." I tossed my flight boots into the bottom of my locker and reached for my jungle boots. Lighter. Cooler.

"Yeah, I guess. You know…one of those guys looked familiar—one eyebrow missing. I've seen him somewhere."

"Thunder Clap probably. If he's a Green Beret."

"Yeah, probably."

"Then what?"

"Shit, Ross. Nothin'. I heard a lot of back slappin' and 'thanks' and 'good seein' yas' so I beat feet back to my role as the Bull's driver. We drove back to wing and turned the jeep over to the mess officer."

I straightened. Bill glanced around my space.

"Bill, think about it now. Any idea why Angus was kissing up to the Green Berets? I mean, it sounds like that's what he was doing."

He looked at my desk. "Oh that's what he was doing alright, but I couldn't tell you why. Maybe he wants them to be more excited about saving his ass if he's ever shot down on The Clap. Shit, who knows, man. Don't sweat it."

"Yeah, who knows."

Bill watched me tighten my laces, then he breathed a long sigh. "I found Tess."

"Yeah? How's he doin'?"

"Great. His arm's a hundred percent. And he's getting some flight time over at Marble Mountain with the maintenance squadron, H&MS."

He paused, stroking his mustache. "Look, Ross, I don't care what Angus has goin' with those Green Berets—he could be blowin' them for all I care—that's petty shit—doesn't affect us. But, what does affect us is why he's been running to wing every week. Tess explained that. Wanna hear it?"

I sat erect, the laces slipping from my fingers. "Hell yeah I wanna hear it."

Bill leaned forward and let the legs of the chair settle to the floor. "You know all this Silver Star shit and kissing up to Mickey?"

"Yeah."

"Well, the fucker is in the zone for lieutenant colonel and the board meets this month." Bill stood, stepped across the aisle, and leaned against my locker. "As we speak, somewhere in Washington, D.C., a group of colonels and maybe a general are sitting around a table discussing the talent and leadership ability and combat daring of Major Richard P. Angus as described by Lieutenant Colonel Donald C. Houser, combat commanding officer. What do you think the outcome of that's going to be?"

"Surely they have more information on Angus than just Mickey's report. Surely."

Bill crossed his arms. "Ross, wise up, man. I've seen this guy at work. He's a master bullshitter. I watched him kiss that wing mess officer's ass until he not only gave him a case of Scotch, but he threw in his jeep as well! He's smarter than the system, man. The fucker's a lieutenant colonel. Count on it."

"No, I'm not counting on it. I'm not ready to give up on the Marine Corps yet. Marine Aviation is a small place. Somebody on the board will know that asshole for what he is. Not even Angus can fool all of the people all of the time."

"Okay, R.T., stay in your fantasy world if you want to, but a case of beer says we're calling him 'Lieutenant Colonel Asshole' in a few weeks."

"You're on." Damn. Angus a lieutenant colonel. At least that explained some of his behavior.

I tied my last boot and stood. Bill stroked his mustache again. Mine had turned out to be somewhere between Bill's bushy and Padgett's mangy. Average. At least it was a manly black. I stepped into the aisle. "Let's do it, Cat. And thanks for waiting for me."

"No problem. I'm confined to quarters."

I stopped. "What?"

Bill hung his head. "Yeap. Seems the Bull didn't appreciate me changing the schedule, swapping out with Ripkevic."

"Well, yeah, but it wasn't the guy's first hop. He flew with Major Lewis yesterday."

"I believe I used the same argument. No go."

"Damn."

"Yeah, the Australians are gonna miss my act." Bill turned with me toward the curtains. "That's not all."

"There's more? Man, you had a big day, huh?"

"He didn't like my mustache either. Said shave it."

"Ouch. Gonna do it?"

"Don't know. Can he make me?"

"According to the *Marine Officer's Guide*, it's a tradition that sailors wear beards and Marines wear mustaches. End quote. Or something like that."

"So, he can't?"

"You have a legal right to a mustache, Marine. No doubt. However, as the squadron executive officer, he has a legal right to make your life miserable if you exercise your right to a mustache against his wishes. In other words, you're screwed."

"Fuck."

"Roger, fuck."

Bill stopped, pulled the curtains aside, peered into the front of the hut, then straightened. "Well, I'm not shaving it. I kicked Blue Dog's ass today because this mustache gives me strength. I'll trim it, but I ain't shavin' it. Fuck him."

"Kicked his ass, huh, Sampson?"

"Fuckin' A. Fifteen-thirteen, me—the Cat's Ass, the Sun Dog."

"Does that explain the mouse under your eye?"

Bill touched his fingers to the puffy skin on the lower outside of his right eye. "Yeah, he almost had me put away at ten to seven. Then I made a 'skate-save' with my face. The pain pissed me off and I started coming back. It was boss, R.T., should have been there. Hippy Dog was with me, man. We rose to the occasion. Fuckin' boss." Bill laughed. "I was screamin', 'Thou shalt not piss off the Sun Dog—commandment number six!'" He laughed again. "That fuckin' Blue Dog is a man, R.T. We went over to his hootch and poured beer on each other afterward. Drank some too, of course. He's alright."

"Yeah, I know. Look, ah…want me to stay here with you? We could write Laura. You gotta write her, Cat. Either that or I've got to stop writing her. She says she gets more mail from me than she does from you."

"Yeah, I'll write her tonight. I promise. You go ahead. Shit, actually I'm in good company. Shockley and Art-the-fart are in hack too."

"Oh, hell. Now what?"

"Morning guns. Some 46 driver got so fucked up this morning Shockley flipped out. The guy couldn't navigate, couldn't talk on the radios, wouldn't do what the grunts asked—shit, you know how some of 'em are. Anyhow, with the 46 in the zone, Shockley made a low pass across the guy's cockpit window and had Art moon them. Turned out to be a major with no sense of humor. Bad luck."

"Yeah. Bad luck."

"Shockley was given Horsnyder's duty for the rest of the night as well as the ever popular 'Confined to Quarters' tomorrow. Art's confined for the same period, Hootch 10." Bill put a hand on the back of a folding chair by the card table. "So all the cool guys are gonna miss the show."

"Yeah, well, that's Australia's loss, I guess." I turned to open the door, then remembered Granny said he would save us a seat. "Hey. Did you tell Granny you saw Tess? I think he's concerned about him."

"No. I missed him."

"Well, I'll tell him what you said…I'll see ya."

"Wait a minute." Bill strolled over, leaned against the wall by the door, crossed his arms and glanced at his dusty boots. "There's something else Tess wanted me to tell you."

I relaxed my grip on the door handle and matched Bill's posture. "You been holding out on me?"

"No. I was gonna tell you." He raised his eyes to mine. "Look, Ross, don't get carried away with this Angus thing. You don't need to fight this guy. You *can't* fight this guy. It's not your job to fight this guy. Please. Just cool it. Just let it go—like we did with the savings bond thing."

Bill's eyes were pleading, concerned. I'd never seen them like that before. "What did Tess want you to tell me?"

"Damn." He looked down, shook his head, and brought his eyes back to mine. "Tess is as bad as you are. He's spending every spare minute worrying about Angus. He's not worth all this worry, man. What is it with you guys?"

"What did he say, Cat?"

He stared at me, studying my eyes as though there was something written on them. I stared back. He blinked. "Fuck, Ross." He sighed. "He said Angus really did ask for helicopters. Then he went out of his way to get into our squadron; he picked it. Then, *after* he picked it, he found out about Major Hardy. He found out he was in the same promotion zone, everybody liked him—including the CO—and he was vulnerable."

"Vulnerable?"

"Yeah. Time in country. Apparently field grade officers are rotated out of a combat slot after six months. They can stay if they ask to, but typically they rotate. Gives more majors and lieutenant colonels an opportunity to get their ticket punched in the square labeled 'combat experience.' Tess says the war is about 'advancing careers,' not winning. Anyhow, Hardy had been in the squadron six months and had asked to stay on."

"Angus convinced Hardy to rotate?"

"Shit, no. Angus pulled some strings, convinced somebody at wing headquarters Hardy needed to rotate, and got him removed. Hardy was in his way, man."

"All this so Angus could make lieutenant colonel?"

"Yep. Like Tess says, 'If you can't defeat your enemy on the field, then make sure he doesn't get to the field in the first place.'"

"Your brother officer is the enemy?"

"This is a career officer we're talking about, Ross. A hard-core regular officer, a lifer. He's here for a lot of reasons, but defeating Communism is not one of them. Hell, if it wasn't for Communism, he wouldn't have a job."

Something bit inside me and my eyes stared hard at Bill. "*I'm* a career officer, asshole. Major Hardy's a career officer. Tess is a career officer. Angus is the exception." I could feel the heat on my face and the blood pouring into my ear lobes. My father was a career officer.

Bill's voice softened. "Okay. You guys are okay. But, really, Ross, think about it. How many Major Hardys do we know?"

I hesitated.

"I'll tell you: One. Unless you count Henry Keyser back at Pendleton, but hell, you can't count him, he's a captain!"

I turned my head and stared at the plywood door. Bill was right. Tess was right. Angus probably had done all of that: removing Hardy, accepting medals for the heroism of others and for wounds he didn't receive, changing the squadron symbol to please Mickey. All that injustice just to get himself promoted.

I bounced my head off the doorjamb, stood straight, and dropped my hands to my hips. "Anything else?"

"Nope. That's it. Tess just thought you'd want to know."

"Yeah. He was right. Thanks, Bill, that explains a lot. It helps."

Bill straightened with me, let his arms relax to his side, but gestured with his hands. "Just let it go. Okay? I'll go write Laura if you'll go get drunk, enjoy the show, and forget Angus. Okay? Deal?"

"Yeah, okay." I paused, wondering if I really could let it go, then reached for the door handle. "Catch ya later."

The spring-loaded door slammed shut behind me and snuffed out the light. I felt my way along the sandbag wall, stepped onto the sidewalk, and placed my utility cover on my head with a disgusted grunt. For me, the act of covering my head with the utility cover had always been a proud, lump-in-the-throat kind of experience. It said, "You are a Marine, one of the finest. Like your father." The Army had a nerdy green baseball cap. The Navy had a nerdy blue baseball cap. Only the United States Marine Corps had a cover that stood out as something special, something traditional, something as uniquely professional as the Corps itself. That time, it didn't stand for quite as much.

It was dark and quiet among the huts. The crunching sounds of my boots on the sandy sidewalk joined the other sounds of the night: the crickets, the generators. I smelled the creosote on the legs of the water tower as I walked by, the tower itself just a black shadow against a blacker sky, and I could already hear the band, the bass sounds moving the air rhythmically around me like a pulse. Ahead, 100 meters down the dirt road, the hooded light bulb over the main entrance to the club guided me. Good time for a sapper attack. Everybody in one place. Who guards this base anyhow?

I walked on. With each step, the legs of my flightsuit gathered dust kicked up by my boots, and I returned to what Bill had said. What if the Marine Corps, my Marine Corps, made a lieutenant colonel out of one of the most morally bankrupt human beings I'd ever met? And while Tess had explained why Angus had made so many trips to wing, why had he been kissing up to the Army, the same Army he told Teach we weren't here to support, the same Army he wouldn't let us write up for awards?

And why our squadron? He picked us before he knew the personnel. Was it really because he wanted to be with a bunch of "fighters" like he said in his speech that first day, the day he joined the squadron? I didn't believe it then and I really doubted it now. Wanting to get promoted didn't explain everything.

I was almost there, close enough to once again admire the Navy's work. The Phu Bai Officer's Club, a modernistic stone structure with exposed-beam cathedral ceiling, stood apart from the cheap and temporary buildings of plywood and two-by-fours on the rest of the base. Apparently the Navy Sea Bees who built it wanted it that way. I could imagine it speaking for them, saying, "See Vietnam, the U.S. can do solid work when it wants to."

From inside the stone walls of the club, the music pulsed louder, rhythm as well as bass—pounding. Flecks of dust, expelled from the stones by the vibrations, drifted down through the cone of light from above the door, and glittered like gold. From inside I could hear hundreds of strong voices singing along with the band's version of the Rolling Stone's "Satisfaction."

Maybe I'd get drunk, relax, and enjoy the show like Bill suggested—forget the war, the heat, Angus. No, I didn't think so. Getting drunk would mean giving up control and if you give up control bad things happen. Terrible things. No, I'd never give up control again. Once was one time too many.

I walked through a row of jeeps, stepped onto the concrete slab and walked to the door, eyes narrowed against the blinding light. Only after I'd stopped and reached for the door handle did I hear the footsteps and muted voices behind me.

25

Miss Barbie

Two shadowy figures, one tall, one of medium height, marched toward me through the darkness. Standing under the brilliant cone of light at the entrance to the club, my night vision shot, I squinted and shielded my eyes with both hands. The smaller, cockier one, the one with a diddy-bop to his step, had to be Scapelli.

"Evening Lieutenant Teemer." PFC "Vegas" Scapelli, the reflected light illuminating his white teeth, smiled big.

"What's up, Scapelli?"

Scapelli walked between the jeeps, into the light, and stepped onto the concrete slab. The taller one joined him in one graceful stride. Straderman.

"We're—that is, Corporal Straderman—is here to see Colonel Houser as ordered, sir."

I returned their salutes. "And you?"

"I'm here as an armed escort for the corporal, sir." He slapped the holstered .38 on his hip.

"Uh-huh," I said, smiling.

"He's here to see the girls, Lieutenant, but I really am here to see the colonel. Got to give him these." Straderman held up a manila folder. Yellow paper, the kind used for teletyped messages, peeked from one end.

"Messages?" I asked.

Straderman squeezed his eyes against the bright light. "Yes, sir. Routine stuff from group S-1. Lieutenant Shockley picked 'em up on his SDO rounds and told me to give 'em to the colonel. Said one of 'em is important—the colonel wanted it delivered as soon as it came in."

Scapelli had told me of Straderman's success as a high-school baseball pitcher, and as the corporal stood before me, his head held high, his shoulders and arms loose and relaxed, I could appreciate what it must have been like to face him as a hitter. "You know what that message says, don't you?"

"Ah, yes, sir."

"Care to tell me about it?"

Scapelli laughed. "You'll know soon enough, Lieutenant. I'll bet everyone in this club will know soon enough. Right, Stick?"

I followed Scapelli's eyes to Straderman. He held the folder by his side. "It's nothing, Lieutenant. S'cuse me, sir."

Straderman pulled the door open as Vegas quickly followed, whispering as he passed, "Don't go away, sir. We need to talk."

Walking in trail, the three of us crossed the foyer, passed the office on the left, storeroom on the right, and arrived at the edge of the main room in a cloud of cigarette and cigar smoke. The Beatles' "I Wanna Hold Your Hand" blared from the group of three men and one woman on the stage to our left. From the teeming mass of green-clad men jammed into the room, glasses and cans clinked, chairs scraped, and woof-whistles pierced the air. To our right, the bar was packed.

A captain with close-cut black hair and a stubby cigar in his mouth appeared to our left. He glanced at Straderman, then Scapelli, then screamed over the music, "Get the fuck out of here with that weapon. What the hell you want in—"

"Give the captain your weapon," Straderman ordered, looking at Scapelli. The captain glanced at Straderman and back to the PFC. As Scapelli reached for his belt buckle, Straderman slid in front of a heavyset bald officer standing in front of the captain. The captain spun around and raised his hand, but it was too late; Straderman was already into the crowd and the captain was left standing with his chin out and his cigar pointed at the exposed beams in the smoky ceiling.

As Straderman waded among the crowded tables and shuffling bodies, Scapelli extended his pistol belt. "Nice place, Captain. You the officer in charge of all this, sir?"

The captain took the belt and the holstered .38, stared at Scapelli a second, then looked at me. "You with these Marines?"

"No, sir. But they're from my squadron."

The captain tossed the pistol belt against my chest, took the stubby cigar out of his mouth and pointed his finger at me. "See that these Marines finish their business and are out of here in five minutes."

"Yes, sir."

"And don't give him his fuckin' weapon 'til he's gone."

"Yes, sir."

I glanced at Scapelli to make sure he understood the captain's orders, but the PFC was busy admiring the woman on the stage. I shifted my eyes to the stage as well, wondering if that was all there was, one woman.

What I saw convinced me one woman was enough. Holding a silver microphone the size of a thin flashlight, the Barbie-doll look-alike bent over and shook her long blonde hair to the rhythm of the music. White go-go boots, gold hot pants and a red sheer low-cut blouse completed the outfit—Marine Corps colors; she was one of us. She was also braless with firm, palm-sized breasts, "I Dream of Jeannie" eyes, and pouting red lips. The breasts, wet with perspiration and clinging to her sheer blouse, bounced and swayed to "I Wanna Hold Your Hand," while the adoring throng sang back to her on the chorus, "I wanna hold your glands."

Scapelli elbowed me. "Look at that, sir. Is that great or what? Man, oh, man. Australia." He shook his head. "I'm goin' there for R&R next month. They love American men, you know. Australian men treat their women like shit. Poor sex-starved little darlin's."

Miss Barbie pointed to the audience and encouraged them to sing along with her. She didn't look sex starved to me. That didn't seem possible on a tour of U.S. bases in Vietnam.

The song ended, and from the edge of the stage, the woman bowed deeply to a standing ovation from the crowd in the second row of tables—the better to see over the first row of tables and down the young woman's blouse. She stood with a big smile, throwing her damp blonde hair back over her head, and held her arms out to her sides, enjoying the applause and the turmoil in the third row after their view of her bow had been blocked by the standing second row. A table fell over, beer cans spilled onto the concrete floor, chairs scraped, some pushing and shoving, then she bowed again and the scuffling stopped—all eyes on her. She held the bow, embellished with Swan Lake hand movements, then stood, smiling, bouncing on her toes, breasts springing up and down.

"Be right back, lads! Break time!"

She pranced down the stage steps and through the emergency exit to the left of the stage, blonde hair scattered over her bare shoulders, tight little butt straining against the gold fabric of her hot pants. Meanwhile, the two guitar players and the drummer, all skinny "long hairs" with tight-fitting jeans and black T-shirts, lit cigarettes and wiped their faces with towels before following her. An armed Marine MP held the door open from the outside.

Straderman, empty handed, reappeared as some of the audience surged toward the exit behind us, heading for the four-holers on the side of the club. The three of us shuffled out with them.

Just beyond the corner of the concrete slab and outside the stream of light, I returned Scapelli's pistol belt. "Here Marine. And don't come back to Dodge without checking your weapon with Marshal Dillon first."

Scapelli smiled. "Yes, sir."

Straderman strolled beyond us a few steps and stopped, apparently waiting on Scapelli.

I glanced around to be sure we couldn't be overheard. "What's up? What did you want to talk about?"

"He's done it again, Lieutenant: another missing message, last night."

"Did you have it recorded?"

He smiled. "Oh, yes, sir. I was ready for him this time."

"Well?"

"Yes, sir. It was from 3rd Recon. About lights in the Ta Bang valley near the DMZ, west of the Tiger Tooth. Ah, two nights ago, I think."

"Lights? Truck lights?"

"No, sir. Lights in the sky."

"What?"

"Yes, sir. Probably target practice. One time I overheard a Green Beret on Thunder Clap talk about seeing weather balloons with lights sent up by the gooks—so they can practice shooting down aircraft, I guess. Big guns. 37mm, 57mm, anti-air stuff."

"Crap, Scapelli, we fly around there all the time. I was just there this afternoon. You mean we could have been in the sights of something like that?"

"Yes, sir."

"Damn. Wonder why they didn't knock us down?"

"Beats me. But they're out there, sir. No doubt."

"Yeah. Well, was that it? Anything else?"

"No, sir. That's it."

"Okay. Thanks. Carry on."

We returned salutes and parted. I walked back to the club, wondering why Angus would care about lights, target practice, in the Ta Bang valley. Maybe he was compiling some kind of super intelligence map that he was keeping to himself. Didn't trust the one Staff Sergeant Morchesski kept on the ready-room wall.

On my way through the door to the club, Fred Borenmann, "Freud," brushed past me on his way out. He told me Granny had a table in the fourth row against the far wall, near the fireplace, the "cheap seats." Granny was saving a seat for us. Freud was gone before I could tell him Bill wasn't coming.

I slipped through the crowd to the bar and bought four beers from a leather-faced Vietnamese barkeeper. At fifty cents each in MCP, military script, or "funny money," it wasn't much of a risk. There had to be at least two beer drinkers at the table.

Granny, at a table crowded with Schlitz and Budweiser cans, sat alone, facing the stage. Legs crossed, he held a can of Budweiser in his lap.

I put my four beers in front of a captain's chair beside him. "Granny. This seat for me?"

"Yeah, what say, Ross? Sit, man, sit." He looked over his shoulder, then at the bar. "Where's the Cat's Ass?"

"Can't make it—confined to quarters." I sat, my back toward an empty stone fireplace.

"Ah, shit. Angus?"

"Roger, Angus." I took a swallow of beer. It was surprisingly cold and relieved a thirst I didn't realize I had.

"I knew it. I knew he shouldn't have messed with that schedule. That was it, wasn't it? Or was it for watering down Angus' hootch?"

"No, it was the schedule. And the mustache."

"That's a bitch." Granny shook his head, finished the beer, and banged the empty can on the table.

Across the room, at a table in the center of the front row, Lieutenant Colonel "Mickey" Houser and Major Angus sat facing the stage. Walt Duppont stood beside them, distributing glasses of mixed drinks. Mickey and the Bull laughed at something Walt had just said, then Walt sat beside Angus as Captain Orndorff joined them with another round of drinks. Orndorff took the fourth chair as Walt leaned over and spoke to Major Angus. A familiar-looking manila folder lay on the table between them.

Angus, with his back to me, shook his head and extended both hands, side by side, in front of his chest. As Walt watched, Angus maneuvered both hands, "flying" one behind the other.

I pushed one of my Budweisers over to Granny. "Let me buy you a beer, Granny."

"Thank you, Senor. Muchas gracias."

"Same to ya." We clinked beer cans. "Here's to Huey guns."

"Roger, guns."

We swallowed together, and I nodded my beer can and head toward Angus. "What do you make of that?"

Walt had apparently just asked another question. Angus had his hands in the air again, this time farther apart, palms to the floor and the fingers pointed in. He flew his hands past each other and up toward the ceiling, ending with his arms and hands making a figure eight.

"Air to air, shit. Head on pass, vertical scissors."

"Something new to Huey guns?"

"I doubt it. Showin' off is more like it." Granny took another swallow, then leaned onto the table. "Did you want jets, Ross?"

I grinned. The certain question of a helicopter pilot. Hard to imagine anyone would actually ask to do what we were doing, fly what we were flying. "No, Granny. Bill did. Wanted 'em bad. But for some reason, this is what I wanted from day one."

"Bill didn't get the points?"

"Oh yeah, he got the points. The week we finished, four of us got the points. The thing is, the Marine Corps didn't have enough jets to go around. I was going to helicopters anyhow, and Bill had more points than the other two guys, so all Bill needed was one slot available. Nothing. Needs of the Corps."

"Yeah. Needs of the Corps." Granny took another swallow. "You know, Teach wanted jets too. Then Army flight school. Pisser."

Angus still maneuvered his hands, twisting one behind the other.

"What's the big deal, Granny? Is air-to-air shit that hard?"

Granny laughed. "Well, if a sergeant can do it, it can't be that hard, right?"

I smiled and shook my head. "No. What I had in mind was Angus. If he can do it, it can't be that hard."

"Well, it's like anything else. Anyone with the right training and the right attitude can do it. No big deal. Some do it better than others, of course."

"Who's the best you've ever seen?"

Granny hung his head and swished the beer around in its can for a second. "Hell, Ross, I tell ya: I've seen some good ones, some fine ones, some that aren't here anymore. But—" He sat straighter and repositioned himself in the chair. "I guess the best would have to be Joe Foss."

I knew Foss was the leading Marine Corps ace in WWII. I'd read about him. "Good guy?"

"Oh, hell yeah. Good skipper too. Myself and bunch of other young pups lucked out and got assigned to his squadron in July, '44. VMF-115. We started out in Santa Barbara, California, then after Foss got us ready, we deployed to the South Pacific." Granny laughed. "Foss was already a hero by then, got his 26 kills on his first tour as a captain. He'd been traveling around the country selling savings bonds, knew all the Hollywood folks. Thanks to him, we not only flew the hottest airplanes, but we dated the hottest women too. Great times. Joe took good care of us."

"What made him so good?"

"As a pilot or as a CO?"

"Well…both."

"Oh, I guess as a CO, the main thing was he was an example to us. We all wanted to be like him, as good as he was. And of course he looked out for us." Granny swished his beer and chuckled. "Not just getting us dates. He made sure people got a chance to lead, to fight the Japs, do the things they joined the Corps to do…and get recognition for it. He wasn't a glory hound getting all the medals for himself."

I slid my beer back and forth across a spot on the table. "Sounds good. Sounds like what I expected from my first squadron."

"Yeah. Well, that was a different Marine Corps then, Ross. And a different war."

"That's for sure." I tapped lightly on my beer can. "So what made Joe Foss such an ace, Granny? How'd he do it?"

Granny looked over his left shoulder as a group of four guys in worn khaki flightsuits walked past him toward the front. Each carried four beers stacked two on two and cradled against their chest. Pushing and elbowing their way around us, Granny barked at them as they went by and they barked back, the last guy pouring some beer on Granny's freckled balding head. Granny wiped away the beer with a napkin off the table and laughed. "Those fucking Dog People. Trouble, man. Trouble."

He wadded the napkin and tossed it onto the table. "Let's see. Foss as a fighter pilot. Hmmm. I guess his eye for the target for one thing. Ol' Joe grew up on a farm in South Dakota with a shotgun in his hands. Most good fighter pilots I knew had that bird-hunting or skeet-shooting background." He looked at me like he was searching for something. "You ever hunted?"

"No. Not really. Squirrels."

"Never bird-hunted?"

"Once. Enough to know I wasn't any good at it."

"With your dad?"

"No, with my cousin. We were about 16 then." I looked across the room for a second, watching the crowd wade back in. "I went with my dad one time when I was eight years old. Just to be with him. Saw him kill three quail from the same covey while he stepped over an old barbed-wire fence. Twelve-gauge pump, switching shoulders, bang...bang...bang. I couldn't believe it. I just stood there bug-eyed, my ears ringing. I guess he was a pretty good quail hunter."

"Yes, he was. Good fighter pilot too."

"He—" I looked hard at Granny's eyes. "You knew him?"

Granny smiled back gently. "Yeah. K.D. Teemer. He was one of those young pups in 115. We shared a Jap Zeke in September, '44. That was it for both of us for the war—one-half kill each. Hell, we wouldn't have gotten him if Foss hadn't pointed him out to us and gotten out of the way. Even then we almost shot each other down."

"Damn, Granny. How long have you known? And why didn't you tell me?"

"Well, I probably should have, Ross, but I guess I just didn't know how to go about it. I'm not good at that sort of thing. We ah...we really weren't the best of friends. You're a lot different than your dad."

I looked at the beer can in my hand. "Yeah, that's what my mother always says—I'm different."

"Did your mother want you to be a Marine?"

"Heck, no. She hates the Marine Corps. She says it's for immature, irresponsible, and reckless children like my dad." I slid back in my seat and crossed my leg. "She loved the guy, but never got over not being able to civilize him, like she had failed. At least that's what my grandmother says."

"Then why are you here?"

"I guess 'cause I fell for John Kennedy's line: 'Ask not' etc." I shook my head. "Hell, I don't know. In '65, when I committed to the ROTC program, the war was small, everybody was behind it, and I couldn't imagine not doing my part. I didn't want to be drafted, that's for sure, but I didn't want to avoid the war and ask someone else to take my place either. So, I chose to go with the finest and get it over with, maybe even make it a career. Wasn't much else to do with a degree in history anyhow."

I shifted. "Everybody thought it was a good idea then, you know, be a Marine pilot like my father and all that stuff. Everybody except my mother."

"She fought it?"

"She did at first. She asked me if I couldn't be a pilot in the Peace Corps instead." I smiled. "Then, after a while, she finally accepted it. I think her words were: 'You'll be okay. You're not like your dad.'"

"Well, I'd have to agree with that—he was a wildman."

Granny leaned forward. "Look, Ross, you may not be like him personality-wise, but there's no reason why you can't shoot a shotgun like him. Let me teach you. I've got a twelve-gauge in my footlocker. Teach and I go down to the end of the runway and throw beer cans for each other sometimes. You could join us. How 'bout it?"

"Thanks, Granny, I might like to do that sometime. But really, I'm not any good at that. I'm just a guns and rockets guy."

"Awk…guns and rockets…awk."

Granny swung his head around in time to spot Freud, four beers stacked and held to his chest. Freud reached for the chair next to Granny with the toe of his boot. Under the table, Granny blocked the front leg of the chair and looked up. "Strangle the parrot, Freud. Squawk standby."

Freud tugged on the chair, beer slopping onto his flightsuit. "Awk…squawk standby…squawk standby." When the chair wouldn't budge he looked for the reason and found Granny's leg extended. "Awk…move your fucking foot…awk…move it or lose it."

Granny laughed and released the chair as Jim Teach appeared and sat beside me.

On stage, a guitar chord was struck and reverberated around the room. A note was picked. Another. Tapping sounds from the amps. The scraping sounds and clinking-glass sounds increased as the crowd settled into their seats.

Freud turned and shouted at the stage, "Let there be music!"

From the table next to us—H-53 drivers judging by their clean flightsuits and the lieutenant I recognized—a captain screamed, "Let there be tits and ass!" The captain and his friends laughed together, mocking Freud.

I tensed, anticipating the possibility of some four versus four action, but Freud, the psychologist, jumped up, smiled, and held his beer high. "To tits and ass *with* the music!"

All eight of us sensed the moment, and with cans and glasses raised, screamed together, "To tits and ass *with* the music!"

From the second row a bunch of guys in khaki flightsuits screamed back, "Amen!" Blue Dog's crowd, Blue Dog himself in the middle.

Someone else across the noisy room screamed, "Mu-sic!" and the 53 drivers yelled at them, "Tits and ass!" and as the Dog Drivers said another "Amen," Rod Wysowski, from a table on the end of the second row, jumped onto his chair, and as though he were a conductor, pointed at Freud. Freud picked up on the rhythm of Rod's bobbing body and arm and screamed again, "Mu-sic!" Rod pointed to the 53 drivers who shouted, "Tits and ass!" and to the Dog People in khaki who shouted, "A-men!" Then Rod went around again, more coordinated this time: Freud, "Mu-sic!", next door, "Tits and ass!", Dog People, "A-men!" Again, with more tables joining in, "Mu-sic, Tits and ass, A-men!" The whole room joined in, "MU-SIC, TITS AND ASS, A-MEN!" Stomping feet, cans pounding on tables, "MU-SIC, TITS AND ASS, A-MEN!"

While conducting with one hand, Rod held up one finger of the other and watched over his shoulder as the band settled into position, microphones ready. After another chorus, Rod held a closed fist, the crowd yelled its last "MU-SIC, TITS AND ASS, A-MEN!" and Rod brought his hand down on the downbeat, the crowd exploding in laughter and applause. Wadded napkins filled the air in Rod's direction. He batted several of them away between deep bows.

The heavily amplified music rocked us back into our chairs. At center stage, the Barbie Doll moaned into the silver phallic symbol she held gently in her painted finger tips and pretended to be Diana Ross singing, "Baby Love."

The crowd quieted, but in the front row, Angus still laughed. He slapped Walt's back, and pointed at Rod, giving Rod a big acne-scarred smile and a thumbs up. Rod posed as if aloof, bowed his head, then suddenly came alive and gyrated to the music. Angus laughed again, slapping the table, and finally turned to the stage and reached for one of the many drinks placed before him.

Miss Barbie was no Diana but she was good enough. From Creedence Clearwater to the Lovin' Spoonful to the Animals and the Beach Boys she sang and jiggled through the next set and then go-goed off the stage and through the emergency exit to the pounding of drums and the clash of cymbals.

The drummer was still sending her off when bleary-eyed Dewey Munzel staggered by on his way from Rod's table to the bar. He noticed Freud and stopped, bent over at the waist, and would have stuck his nose into Freud's ear if Freud hadn't flinched. "No, shit, Freud," he slurred. "Wouldn't you eat a mile of her shit just to kiss her on the ass? Huh?"

Freud stood, grabbed Munzel by the collar of his flightsuit, and jerked him erect. Taller and heavier, Freud looked left then right as Munzel stood with slack jaw, waiting. Apparently satisfied that none of the noisy throng pushing and shoving each other around him could hear his next comment, Freud put his arm around Munzel and whispered loudly into his ear. "Listen, Munzel, can't you see the lovely young woman you're referring to has been staring at me all night? Huh? Can't you see that?"

"Goddamn, Freud. Shit, no. I thought she was staring at me."

"Well, you're wrong." Freud winked at Granny. "Not culpably wrong, you understand. A simple misinterpretation of her optical alignment is possible, nay, highly probable, given the spacial kinetics and the atmospheric conditions of this smoke-filled stone enclosure. Spatial optimecologists call that an atypical class II optical illusion. But, hey, not to worry. It was an honest mistake. Could happen to anyone." Freud looked left and right again while tightening his grip on Munzel's neck. Then he leaned back into his ear. "Yes, I'd eat a mile of her shit just to kiss her on the ass, but that's because she's *my* girl. Got that?" Munzel nodded stupidly. "But I don't want anyone else eating a mile of her shit. Got that?" Munzel nodded again. Freud slid his hand to Munzel's shoulder and gave him a rough hug. "Come on, asshole, I'll let you buy me a few beers and we'll put this little misunderstanding behind us. Deal?"

"Yeah, Freud. Deal. Come on, man. Shit, I'm sorry. Really."

"No problem." Freud looked back at us and smiled as he led Munzel toward the bar.

Granny chuckled, saluted Freud's departure with a three-finger Boy Scout salute, and slid his chair back across the floor. He rose slowly out of his seat. "Got to go get hold of myself, guys. Be right back."

I considered following him, thinking maybe I'd get a chance to ask him more questions about my dad, but I didn't. Maybe I didn't really want to know. Granny said they weren't friends. Maybe that was code for, "I didn't like the guy." He also said he was a good fighter pilot, but I already knew that. Everyone at the memorial had said that. That was the only comment I remember from that day. Men in uniform, sweaty men, smelling like cigarettes and dry-cleaning fluid, shaking my hand, telling me what a good fighter pilot my dad had been. No one said he was a good father, a good husband, a good member of the community. He may have been those things. Maybe he wasn't. Maybe "he was a good fighter pilot" was the only good thing they could say about him. I certainly thought he was a good father, but what did I know? He was the only father I ever knew. Maybe those other things just didn't mean much to the men who shook my hand. All that mattered was that my dad had been "one hell of a fighter pilot." After the attitude I saw at Pensacola, maybe that's it. "If you ain't a fighter pilot, you ain't shit." Even if he had been a good father, husband, member of the community, they wouldn't have noticed. All that mattered, the highest praise you could give anyone, was, "He was a hell of a fighter pilot."

"Ross. Hey, man, you with me?"

I looked up at Jim Teach and blinked. "Yeah. Sorry. What's up?"

"I asked about Bill. Where is he?"

For the next few minutes, I explained about Bill and Art and Shockley and their transgressions. When I got to the part about Bill having to shave his mustache, Jim unconsciously stroked his. Then I remembered the letter Granny had for him. "You get a letter from Carol?"

"Yeah, and your shit-eatin' grin tells me you know what was in it."

"Well," I said, chuckling. "Let's see it."

Jim took a zip-lock plastic bag that served most of us as wallets out of the breast pocket of his flightsuit. Smiling, he extracted a wallet-sized photograph from the bag, held it in the palm of his hand by its edges, and turned it toward me. "I think it's her commissioning picture."

The bright, smiling young woman in the photograph was exactly as I remembered her from the *Repose*. Her big blue eyes dominated the photograph. Huge, affectionate eyes. Her brown hair was flipped, the teeth bright, and the upper body trim, but shapely. She looked proud to be wearing the uniform. "She's beautiful, Jim. Really."

"Yeah. Thanks. She wants us to work out some time together at Quang Tri. She's looking for an excuse to spend a few days with the med unit there. Maybe I can get a slick hop up there or something. Meet her there."

"Wow. You must have really been working some magic in those letters of yours."

"Not really." Jim looked at the picture again, and put it back in his plastic wallet. "She's from Lawrence, Kansas. Maybe three hours from my home in Springfield."

"No kidding?"

"No kidding. And here's the best part: Her uncle lives in St. Louis and has season tickets to the Cardinals."

"Harry Caray's Cardinals?"

"Yep."

"Wow, a gorgeous baseball fan with access to season tickets. You lucky sombitch."

Jim smiled, said, "Sure looks that way," and took a swallow of his beer.

Freud appeared with four more cans of beer as Munzel staggered past our table toward the front of the room, six cans of beer clutched against his wet chest. Freud slid a beer over to me, placed another in front of Granny's chair and slid the other toward Jim. Then he sat straight and gestured with his beer toward the front of the room. "What the fuck? Over."

Jim and I turned. In front of the stage, facing the squirming audience, stood Mickey and a full colonel, both wearing utilities. I recognized the full colonel as the commanding officer of our small helicopter group here at Phu Bai. I'd met him when I checked in back in June. I remembered being amazed to learn later that he couldn't fly helicopters. The Marine Corps had given command of a combat helicopter group to an F-4 pilot. Over two months later, that still amazed me.

Mickey and the colonel held a manila envelope opened before them. Mickey pointed to something in the folder. I guessed it was the folder Straderman had delivered to him.

"What do you make of that?" Freud asked.

"Looks to me like they're getting ready to sing to us," Jim said, grinning.

"I think they're the messages Straderman delivered to Colonel Houser earlier," I said. "Maybe the war's over."

Mickey and the colonel took the stage and gathered behind the mike. It took a few minutes and some assistance by the drummer—who had led the rest of the band back from their break—before the mike was hot and the group CO's voice blasted across the room, "Testing…test." Satisfied, the colonel cleared his throat into the mike and the crowd howled in protest. He held his hands in the air, the crowd quieted, and he introduced Lieutenant Colonel Houser.

Mickey hemmed and hawed for a few minutes about how proud he was and what a great war we had, and finally got to the message he held in his hands. In our midst, he explained, were two newly selected lieutenant colonels. I cocked my head. He had the individuals stand. One was the current group operations officer, a skinny bald major wearing a set of utilities two sizes too large for him. The other was Major Richard P. "Bull" Angus. I stiffened. Mickey screamed into the mike, "Congratulations gentlemen!" Led by Walt and Orndorff and several tables of majors and lieutenant colonels in the first row, the applause swelled, but never with the enthusiasm of the officers on the stage.

Granny, Freud, and Jim clapped politely, looking at their boots, or the floor, anywhere but each other. I stared at the stage. There must be a mistake.

As the applause died and the colonels stepped down, Blue Dog stood and faced the crowd. He raised his huge hand into the smoky air and yelled, "Gentlemen, let's say hello to the new lieutenant colonels."

As anyone who had been in country more than a few weeks had heard this routine before, the crowd, sensing what was coming next, laughed, then picked up on the downbeat of Blue Dog's hand and rocked the room as they screamed, "Hello, assholes!"

The ruckus shook me from my stupor. I blinked. Blue Dog held his hand up again. "Now, my brothers, let us turn to page 69 of our hymnals and join our voices in a hymn for each of our new lieutenant colonels." The laughter resumed as the crowd got ready. Hadn't heard this one before.

Blue Dog pointed at the bald major and his huge hand dropped again. The crowd screamed as one, "Him...him...*fuck* him!" I flinched, eyes widening. Then he pointed at Major Angus, seated at the table in front of him, the smile instantly gone from the major's face. I took a deep breath, held my head high, and roared with the crowd, "Him...Him...*fuck* him!"

Blue Dog threw both arms in the air signaling a touchdown, Angus' face flushed, and the audience fell over themselves and their tables. Cans fell, glass broke, and men screamed with the pleasure of a gut-cleansing laugh. Freud and Jim and I grabbed each other's sleeves and shook them, trying to push each other out of our seats, laughing and screaming at the fury on Angus' face.

We finally released each other in exhaustion, tears rolling down our cheeks. Loud tapping sounds burst from the speakers again. The chant "Mu-sic, tits and ass, A-men" suddenly self-generated around the room.

Granny slid into his chair beside me, gasping for breath, tears in his eyes. "I love that fuckin' Blue Dog. That sombitch won't do."

A throbbing guitar chord vibrated the room, the men in the band sang, "It's Been a Hard Days Night," and the Barbie Doll go-goed around the stage, shaking her breasts to the music, and settling the crowd.

Showing her range, Miss Barbie sang for at least another hour, doing a good job with several songs by the Ohio Express, the Supremes, and even the Byrds. Toward midnight, into her final number, the inebriated crowd of swaying sentimental Marines joined her as she sang, "Leavin' on a jet plane, don't know when I'll be back again..." That's when an explosion jolted the room.

Close enough to rattle the empty beer cans and glasses on the tables and dim the lights, the sudden blast left the audience and band in darkness and stunned silence. Then a second later, the lights came back to full bright, lighting the empty tables and chairs, and a floor littered with bodies.

On my stomach under the table, head to head with Jim, Freud, and Granny, I heard Jim say, "Two mor—" He froze. I heard what he heard, a shrill whistle. We threw our arms over our heads. The second explosion was even closer, close enough to lift the table off the floor and slide its pedestal base into Granny's head. Granny yelped and grabbed his forehead as the lights came back to bright again.

"Fireplace!" Jim punched me and backed out from under the table.

The ground-level fireplace was empty, big enough for all four of us, and only five feet away. We dragged the table with us. The crowd was alive, surging for the exits and the bunkers outside. I could see Angus, grabbing people, throwing them out of his way, elbowing, shoving, tripping, fighting for the emergency exit. Another shrill whistle. Just ahead of Angus, Walt Duppont, Miss Barbie in hand, burst through the exit and disappeared into the night.

Safely barricaded in the stone fireplace, shielded by the thick table, the third rocket hit—a distant anticlimactic crack and muffled explosion. The base warning siren, slowly building in pitch, followed. "Well, hell," Freud said. "The damn rockets woke up the siren guy. I'll bet he's pissed."

After a moment of silence I asked, "Is that it?"

Jammed together like four wolf pups in the entrance to a mountain den, Jim answered, "Probably. For some reason they only shoot three at a time. But let's wait a minute."

We waited, Granny gingerly touching the lump on his head.

Carefully, the remaining members of the audience staggered to their feet. A slurred voice muttered, "Mu-sic, tits and ass, a-men." Chairs and tables scraped across concrete. Another voice yelled, "Where's the fucking band? Somebody get their asses back in here. Hey!"

A siren. But not a warning siren. A crash truck? Ambulance?

"Well, Marines," Granny said, pushing the edge of the table away, "let's go check the lines."

We dragged the table back to its place and rounded up the chairs. All around us, others, about half the original crowd, did the same. The siren got closer. With the last chair in place, Granny led us through an obstacle course of broken glass, beer cans, and drunken Marines toward the main exit.

Outside, the dirt road was lit with flickering light. Flames. My chest tightened. I broke from the group and ran. The flames rose from behind the water tower. I ran harder. An ambulance on the main road, siren wailing, slowed and disappeared behind a row of huts. I calculated where it would stop. Hut 8!

Almost to the water tower, I struggled through the soft sand of the road, breathing hard, trying to make my feet go faster. A second siren and another vehicle shot into view on the main road—a crash truck, lights flashing. It slowed. Going to beat me there. Can't be Bill. Can't be our hootch. Must be next door, Hut 10, Art. Damn, I can't wish that. Don't let it be anybody.

A second crash truck careened onto the dirt road in front of me. I leaped onto the sidewalk, turned the corner, gasping, sweat streaming down my face. A small crowd was already there, maybe a dozen people, most in flightsuits. They stood in front of Hut 10, black shadow figures, talking among themselves. I leaned back and shortened my strides. Hut 8, engulfed in flames, crackled and popped. I staggered to a stop.

Hut 10, blackened on the side near the flames of Hut 8, lay awash under the stream of two hoses. I worked my way around the right side of the crowd looking for Bill, looking for Art, knowing that the next two or three guys I came to would be them. Then, at the front of the group, flames flickered off a familiar face.

"Frankie," I said, breathing hard. "Where's Catlett?"

Franklin Ono tensed his mouth and shook his head. "Don't know." Next to him, Adam Henstrom leaned forward. "Was he confined to quarters? I just heard that."

"Yeah," I answered, looking back at the leaping flames.

Ono looked at me, his arms crossed on his chest. "Sorry, Ross."

I shook my head slowly. "Yeah, thanks, but he's not in that hootch. He's not. He's not dead."

Ono and Henstrom looked at me a second, then turned to watch the guys in the crash crew fight the flames.

"Make a hole, here, make a hole." Two Marines in silver suits and firefighter's hats walked heavily around us, dragging a three-inch black hose with a brass nozzle.

We looked at the ground and shuffled to our left, over the concrete sidewalk, making sure we didn't trip over it. The burly men brushed by me, breathing hard, and others appeared, helping with the hose. Near naked men, wet, familiar.

"Get the fuck out of the way, R.T., tryin' to fight a fire here, man."

"Cat! Art!" I picked up a section of the hose between the two wet men in PT shorts and shuffled along with them. "Where you been? What happened? You okay?"

The two silver-suited men stopped in front of the flaming remains of Hut 8 and braced their legs. We stopped with them. I could feel the heat. The hose jerked and a stream of water shot out of the brass nozzle.

"Hell, yeah, I'm okay," Bill said, looking over his bare shoulder. "Don't I look okay?"

"Yeah, but…"

Bill smiled, his bushy mustache highlighted by the remaining flicker of fire. "Come on, Ross, you didn't think I'd really stay in that damn hootch all night did you?"

I smiled back. "You're unreal, Cat."

"Yes, I am."

"So, where were you? The tower?"

"Yeah, man. I took Art over to the pit for a swim. It was great. Beautiful night."

Art interrupted from behind me, "'Til the damn rockets hit—blew my ass right off the lip of the tank." I'd forgotten about Art. "Fell on top of the Cat's Ass here and nearly knocked us both out."

Bill lowered his head. "That's a no shit! See the lump?" Without waiting for an answer, he turned to the Marines in the silver suits and asked, "You guys got it okay now?"

"Yes, sir," the smallest one answered over his shoulder. "Thanks for your help, sir."

"No problem. Just don't drain our swimming pool on that wasted hootch!"

"Aye, sir."

Bill released the hose and turned to Art. "Let's go get our towels." He laughed. "My last worldly possession."

Minutes later, as Bill and Art cleaned up, I waited outside the head in the shadow of the water tower. Out of the darkness, two figures—one a Marine, the other a female—strolled hand in hand from the club. They stopped behind an ambulance parked beside the last hootch beyond the water tower, a medical officer's hootch. The rear door of the ambulance opened. A glint of gold, and Miss Barbie disappeared. Walt Duppont stepped in behind her. The door shut.

I was about to look away when a third person appeared, thick guy—Angus. He yanked the door open. Walt reappeared, jumped to the ground, and held a salute. Angus returned his salute and stepped to the door, holding out his hand. Miss Barbie reappeared. She took Angus' hand and stepped to the sand.

Angus and Miss Barbie left Walt standing at attention by the ambulance and walked toward the upper hootches, side by side, hand in hand. I watched from the shadows as they passed the water tower. At his darkened hootch, he held the door and the faint light from the head revealed his smile.

The door closed behind them.

Hanging my head, I thought of Granny and Joe Foss. Yeah. Different war. Different Marine Corps.

"What was that?" Bill stopped beside me, a green towel around his neck. He stared at Angus' hootch.

"That? That was our executive officer in hot on the Australian show girl."

"Yeah? Well, piss on him, R.T., don't sweat the small shit. Listen, here's the plan: we're goin' over to Blue Dog's Dog Pound and break the news to him."

"What news?"

"We're movin' in."

26

The Admiral's Son

The H-34 squadron, the last of the Dogs, was scheduled to leave Vietnam a week after we moved in with Blue Dog. Unhappy about leaving when so much war was left to be fought, Blue Dog, Hippy Dog, and Hairy Dog all asked Angus for a transfer to our squadron.

Angus, probably remembering the hymn Blue Dog had led at the Australian show, rejected Blue Dog, but agreed to take Hippy and Hairy. Blue Dog took Angus' decision in stride, but the Dog People, as a family, were insulted. On the day they left, Angus returned from a morning mission to find the door to his hootch caved in, his flip-flops floating in the isle, and the water tower drained.

That was the last day of August.

On September 1st, it rained. It rained for 21 days. Four inches of muddy water covered the floor of our hootch. Meanwhile, near Da Nang, Tom Gamez was killed.

On a break from his FAC duties with the 5th Marines—flying guns with HML-567 at Marble Mountain—Tom's Huey was hit by automatic weapons fire west of Da Nang, near Charlie Ridge, and exploded in mid-air. All four crew members died.

At first, I blamed Angus. If he'd let Tom fly with us, we could have taken care of him; maybe it wouldn't have happened. Then, a few weeks later, I didn't know who to blame. Maybe it was going to happen no matter who Tom flew with. Lousy month.

On October 1st, Rod and Walt got their HAC checks. Ono said Rod was shaky, but Major Lewis signed his papers anyhow. No mention was made of when I would get mine or Bill would get his. Based on what Major Lewis had told Jim Teach, Angus was sending Bill and me a message.

On October 3rd, Angus received his silver oak leaves during yet another Friday parade, a parade remembered by the lieutenants in the squadron as the "Angus Hour." Besides a promotion, he also received two DFCs: one for his "heroism" south of LZ Hawk in June, the other for "fearlessly" attacking the Laotian fish pond and hog pen in August. Standing at attention in the rain, we were particularly impressed with the Purple Heart Angus received for his leg wound. Because of the rain, Mickey pinned the medals under Angus' poncho, out of sight. Somehow that was fitting. Walt and Rod each received a Single Mission Air Medal for their cooperation.

By October 7th, we'd received word that Mickey would rotate at the end of the month. Rumor Control claimed Angus would be our new commanding officer.

October 7th was also my day as SDO, squadron duty officer. J.P. Padgett was the ODO, operations duty officer.

By then, J.P. and many of the others had drifted away from those of us who had to move after our hootch was waxed. Originally crammed into Huts 12 and 14, Freud, Granny, Shockley, Teach, and Ripkevic joined Bill and me in Blue Dog's old hootch after the Dog People left.

Freud had said the rift between us and the rest of the squadron was natural—human nature at work. The physical separation in hootches, our hootch formerly belonging to Blue Dog, the ultimate "up yours" rebel, and most of us sticking to the Hardy doctrine while the rest had taken on Angus' attitudes, explained why we'd been subtly set apart. Even Ono, one of the last of the "Hardy Boys," had stopped hanging out with us.

By 1930 on the seventh, I'd already had chow, checked the mess hall, checked the messages at group, checked security on the flight line, and recorded my findings in the SDO logbook. Outside, it was pitch dark—raining again. In the S-2 shop, my feet propped on the desk and *Street Without Joy* by Bernard Fall in my lap, the light was good and other than the rain drumming on the tin roof, it was quiet. Earlier, the ready room had been a zoo: radio traffic, crews coming in, debriefs. Everyone had returned except Rod and Bill. Slick hop. Those were always late. J.P. was in the ready room waiting for them.

Even with the monsoons and the withdrawal of the 9th Marines and the 3rd Marines from Vietnam, we'd still been flying our butts off—mostly Thunder Clap and guns north, but guns south as well. Bill and I had over 100 hours each in September.

Our only casualty in September, even though Angus didn't regard him as such, had been Tom. Buck Akerman had taken a round in the bottom of his armored seat, but no wound this time. He was "Magnet Ass Akerman" now. For some reason Major Pyhr was still alive and Angus hadn't killed anyone. Not even any NVA.

I had started a letter to my mother, but tore it up. Too down. Wasn't sure what it was, but it had me pinned to the mat. Maybe it was the never-ending rain and gloom. Maybe it was because I was still a co-pilot.

Had to fly with Lieutenant Colonel Angus the day before. Guns south. All day west of Da Nang. Happy Valley. Charlie Ridge. Arizona. Mostly cloudy, wet, but some sunshine. I thought I was going to burn through my flight helmet one time, one of those fits of anger that had my ears on fire. Angus. We were trying to locate and extract a squad of Marines separated from their company for two days. Triple canopy. Finally made contact. The young Marine on the radio was struggling, out of food, still running from an ambush that morning, no smoke grenades, lost.

Angus couldn't find him. Kept yelling at him, "Do you hear me, goddamn it, do you hear a fuckin' helicopter?" We had two Hueys and two 46s with us. Gasping for breath, the Marine would say, "Yes, sir." Angus would scream, "Clock direction, goddamn it, where?" We'd fly to where the Marine said he was and he wouldn't be there. Angus would scream some more. I would burn. Of course the Marine heard a helicopter. We had helicopters circling everywhere. Which *one* he heard was the question. The guy didn't have x-ray vision. He couldn't see through the jungle canopy. I wanted to get everybody out of the way so he only had to deal with the sound of one helicopter.

Angus finally got so flustered he screamed, "I'm giving you five more minutes, you moron. You get your shit together in the next five minutes or I'm taking these helicopters home with me and you and your buddies are gonna fuckin' starve!"

The young man tried again. He was panting, laboring, moving as fast as he could through the jungle. "I hear you…sir. You're…close. Please wait one, sir."

Angus answered, "I better be close, you shitbird. You've got four minutes."

One of the 46s with us spotted him. We were one ridgeline off. The Marine had left his squad and wounded squad leader and struggled on his own to a narrow outcropping of rocks. There he used the inside top of an empty C-ration can as a reflecting mirror and signaled the first helicopter he saw. Pretty damn smart for a "shitbird."

Now Angus was a lieutenant colonel. Probably soon to be a squadron commander.

Major Hardy wasn't selected. Granny said he knew why. It went back to El Toro Marine Air Base, 1959. Major Hardy had been president of the accident board that had investigated the crash of an F4D Skyray. Because it had been the commanding general's decision to give a fighter squadron to an attack pilot who had never flown the F4D—or any jet—and then give the pilot three weeks to be ready to deploy aboard a carrier, and because the former attack pilot had died trying, the board found the commanding general partially at fault for the crash:

"supervisory error." The general blamed Major Hardy for the board's findings and endorsed Major Hardy's next fitness report in a way that would guarantee the major would never make lieutenant colonel. And he hadn't.

Angus. Hardy. Where was the justice? No wonder I was down.

Reading *Street Without Joy* hadn't helped. We weren't winning the war. And because our politicians and generals were making the same arrogant mistakes the French had made, we never would.

The "street" in the title of the book is the section of Highway One between Hue and Quang Tri, an area I knew well. Parallel to Highway One is the National Railroad. Every railroad bridge between Hue and Quang Tri was rusting in the river, destroyed. In seven years of U.S. involvement, at a cost of tens of thousands of American lives, the corrupt South Vietnamese government couldn't run a train from Hue to Quang Tri, 50 miles.

And Vietnamization was a joke. Half the territory we'd turned over to the ARVN—ground thousands of Marines had died for—had been abandoned to the NVA. It was a waste. A predictable waste. South Vietnam wasn't worth one Tom Gamez or one Myron Brunnengarber. Fuck 'em.

Good thing I wasn't writing my mother.

At least I'd gotten Bill to write Laura more often. With the steady rain and cold monsoon weather, there was little else to do.

I tossed the book onto the desk beside my SDO flashlight. Couldn't stand any more of that book. Maybe if and when the sun came out again, I'd finish it.

I leaned forward and rubbed my eyes. Unless Rod and Bill were staying at Quang Tri, they'd be arriving any minute. At least that would liven things up for a while. Maybe get me out of my funk.

I sighed, leaned back, slid into a slouch, and looked at the green filing cabinet to my left. Rust had bubbled the paint around its base. The drawers were locked as they should have been. Above, rain pelted the tin roof.

The screened door slammed and I heard footsteps, then voices in the ready room. I turned my head to the door as the footsteps resumed and headed down the hall toward my office. Jim Teach appeared in the doorway, water dripping from his rain jacket.

"Ross Teemer, assistant S-2 officer, junior secret squirrel, how 'bout it?"

"How 'bout it yourself, 4-3." I pointed at a spot on the floor by Scapelli's *Playboy* magazines. "Have a seat."

Jim looked at the dirty floor, tossed his wet cover onto the corner of the desk, and leaned against the doorjamb. "Thanks, but I believe I'll stand."

"So, what's up?"

"Nothin'. Just decided to get away from the rowdy poker game for a while, maybe find a quiet spot to write Carol."

"Hippy and Harry again?"

"Yeah. And Shockley. Got some recon types in the game. 'Easy money,' they said."

I scoffed, "Yeah, like the time they brought that Army Mohawk driver over from across the base. He was going to be 'easy money' too."

"Yeah." Jim laughed. "Maybe this time."

"Yeah, maybe."

"Rod and Bill aren't back yet, huh?"

"No." I checked my watch. "Any minute now."

"Good. Say, I ah…I looked for you when I got in today. J.P. said you were at the mess hall."

"Oh? Sorry I missed ya."

Jim stuffed his hands in the pockets of his jacket. "Yeah, well, I got some time with Tess while I was in Da Nang this morning. Got some word on Angus."

I scooted my chair forward and leaned onto the desk top. "Really? What word?"

"About his background for one thing. Tess has found a major in wing aviation supply who knows Angus from way back. I think he said they were lieutenants together in Korea." Jim cocked his head toward the open doorway a second, listening as if he'd heard something, then turned back to me. "Angus never flew fighters of any kind and definitely not the F-8. The only jet he's ever flown is the A-4. Was at Chu Lai for a few months in '65, then got shit-canned to wing headquarters at Da Nang."

"For screwin' up?"

"Didn't say. Just suggested they were glad to get rid of him. Anyhow, he ended up in the intelligence section at wing. Desk job. Boring desk job."

"So he was 'Super Secret Squirrel.'"

"Yeah. But while he was there he also made himself invaluable to a full colonel. The colonel later made general and was transferred to Headquarters Marine Corps. There he found Angus' bad fitness report from the A-4 squadron and removed it from Angus' jacket. You remember when Angus was visiting wing headquarters in Da Nang back in June, July, and August?"

"Yeah."

"Well, he was on the horn to headquarters getting the general to make sure all the hero stuff was in his jacket and all the bad stuff was out."

"Well, shit. That's water over the dam now. The general has fucked over the Marine Corps and the damage is done."

"Yeah, but there's more. Stuff that might at least help us understand why he's such an asshole."

"What difference does it make? An asshole is an asshole is an asshole, and Angus is an asshole!" Standing, I banged my fist on the desk, walked to the doorway, and peeked out. From behind the vacant ODO counter, the fox mike radio hissed.

Jim shifted against the doorjamb, turning to face me. "Yeah, but this may help explain some stuff. He's the son of a retired admiral."

"Yeah, that explains a lot. Probably an academy man."

"Well, I don't know about that, but the admiral never married Angus' mother. He left them to fend for themselves. Knocked her up while he was an ensign in flight school. Pensacola. 1930."

"So?"

"So, Angus grew up near the docks of Mobile, Alabama. His stepfather, who his mother married when Angus was an infant, was a longshoreman. Mean bastard. Beat Angus and his mother."

"According to who?"

Jim tensed his mouth. "Look, don't get mad at me. I'm just the messenger here."

"Well, message some good news. I don't want to hear any excuses for Angus. How the hell does this supply guy know all this intimate shit about Angus anyhow?"

"I don't know, but if you want to, I know how we can check his facts."

"You do?"

"Sure. Follow me." Jim bounced off the doorjamb, but stopped with his hand out to me. "Don't say anything to J.P. If he comes down the hall, we're just checking our logbooks."

"No problem."

In the S-3 office at the end of the hall, Jim walked to the S-3 clerk's desk and opened a drawer. I stood in the doorway.

"Here it is." Jim opened the small blue logbook with Angus' name and rank stenciled on it. He turned to the latest entry and worked backwards. "Huey, Huey...R4D, Quantico." Jim looked up. "How 'bout that? A multi-engine driver."

I made a "hurry up" motion with my hand and looked over my shoulder toward the ready room.

"R4D again. Must have been a staff puke. R4D, R4D...A-4E, Kaneohe." Jim looked up again. "Must have had a tour in Hawaii after 'Nam. Tough duty."

I glanced over my shoulder. "Come on, man, pick up the pace."

"R4D, Da Nang...here we go. A-4E, Chu Lai, May...through August '65." Jim looked up. "Okay, that checks." He shut the book and slipped it into the drawer. "Next."

"Next? What next? Call his mother? Ah, Mrs. Longshoreman, this is Jim Teach, Hardball 4-3, calling. I'd like to know if in fact your son, Bull, is illegitimate."

Jim frowned. "Cute."

"Well?"

"His OQR, man."

"His officer qualification jacket doesn't have his birth certificate in it."

"Well, it'll have his place of birth and date. Isn't that good enough?"

I shrugged. "I guess."

"Okay, I'm going into the S-1 office and—" Jim pronounced the words carefully, as if reading me my lines in a script. "—get a pencil and paper to write a letter."

"Roger, pencil and paper."

I returned to the S-2 office and waited in the doorway.

A few minutes later, Jim returned with a pencil and paper and a satisfied grin. He slipped past me, punching me on the arm as he went by. He sat at the desk. "Mobile, 1931."

"And his father was an S.O.B.?"

Jim threw up his hands. "Man, you're in a shitty mood tonight. What's the problem?"

"Ah, crap, I don't know. Bad day at the office."

Jim sat there, watching me.

I leaned against the wall by the *Playboys* and stared at the floor. It had stopped raining. Water dripped from the roof into puddles outside the screened side of the hallway and for some reason, I wanted to scream, "Shit!" as loud as I could.

Jim slid into a slouch. He tapped his boot against the base of the filing cabinet. "What's the latest on the missing messages?"

Without looking up I answered, "Two more missing."

"Really? Know what they were about?"

"Yeah."

"Well?"

I looked up, shifted my weight to the other leg, and pointed to the 1:50,000 topographical map on the opposite wall. "Both were on the same day, September 19th. Third Recon reported some rotor sounds south of LZ Fang heading west. The other was from SOG. Their radio relay on Hill 950 reported hearing rotor sounds around Khe Sanh."

"Get the times?"

"No. Scapelli just recorded the basics."

"What do you think?"

I shook my head. "I don't know what to think. I've been over it and over it, but nothing makes sense. What's the big deal? We've got helicopters all over the place."

"Well, I don't know either. But there must be something to it or recon and SOG wouldn't have called it in. Think it could be one of theirs?"

"What? The rotor sounds from one of theirs?"

"Yeah."

"Shit, Jim. The NVA don't have helicopters. Do they?"

"Well, I've heard rumors."

"Really? You serious?"

"No shit. Just rumors though. Never seen one or talked with anyone who has."

"Well, hell, even if they did, they wouldn't be flying them into our territory, would they? And even if they did, why would Angus care?"

"Got me."

Jim picked at his fingernails, and I stared at the map. Target shooting in the Ta Bang valley, rotor sounds around Khe Sanh, rotor sounds south of Fang. That would have been near Highway 9. Heading west. I pulled at my mustache, then thought of something Bill had said. "Jim, what do you know about a SOG Green Beret with one eyebrow missing?"

"At the FOB?"

"Yeah."

"There's an E-6 or 7 that used to work the radio room at the FOB. He was missing most of one eyebrow. I think he's on Hill 950 now. SOG put a radio relay up there after the 4th Marines moved out a few weeks ago."

"This one-eyebrow guy. He's a radio operator?"

"Well, I think he's more than that. Seems like they have some super gear up there. A portable radar for example." Jim pointed at me. "Now that's a good piece of gear. Picks up moving targets: troops, trucks—even gives you coordinates for artillery. Wicked. Marine Corps doesn't have it."

Jim dropped his arm. "Then they have a bunch of radio intercept stuff. In fact, I think this one-eyebrow guy—seems like his name is Wicken or Wickman or something—is some kind of language guru. Speaks several dialects of Vietnamese. Or maybe he can interpret several dialects. Anyhow. He does something like that."

"Language guy, huh?"

"Yeah. Ah…why you ask, over?"

"Bill said Angus was buddy-buddy with a Green Beret with a missing eyebrow. Saw them together in Da Nang."

"Angus hangin' out with the Green Berets, huh." Jim shook his head. "It's gettin' weird, Ross."

"Yeah. Weird. Really weird."

Jim stroked his mustache while I stared at the top *Playboy*. On the cover was a head-on shot of a nude Miss April riding a huge stuffed grizzly bear. She wore a Davy Crockett coonskin cap and held a muzzle loader. The cap reminded me of Davy Crockett's motto—or the Disney version of the Davy Crockett motto: "Make sure you're right, then go ahead." As a kid, I'd spent a lot of time playing Davy Crockett with my cousins. I wondered if it would be "right" to search Angus' office.

"Hey, Jim."

Jim looked up at me, smiling. "Yes?"

His look caught me by surprise. I bounced off the wall. "You thinkin' what I'm thinkin'?"

"Maybe," he said, smiling. "What are you thinkin'?"

I laughed. "I need to go into S-1 and get a pencil and paper. You keep an eye on J.P. for me."

Jim laughed. "Yes, I believe I am thinkin' what you're thinkin'." He walked to the door and grabbed me by the sleeve, pushing me into the hall. "Where's Cat's Ass, the Cat Burglar, when you need him?"

A good question.

A few minutes later, after making desk sounds in a darkened S-1, I eased down the hall and slipped into Angus' unlocked office. I shut the door behind me, switched on my flashlight, and flinched at the yellowish beam of light. Should have used the red lens filter.

I kept the beam low and stepped toward the coat rack on the wall, the plywood floor creaking beneath my jungle boots. The room seemed larger than I remembered and stunk of cigarette and cigar butts damp with humidity.

At the rack, I pulled on the arm of a flightsuit and winced at the ammonia odor. One thing for sure: If the gooks ever shot Angus down, they wouldn't have any trouble finding him. I shifted the flashlight to my left hand and hurried through the flightsuit's pockets.

Without finding any maps or messages, I left the rack and tip-toed toward the desk. The floor squeaked with each step. A gust of wind whistled through the window screens to my left. From behind the door, another squeak and I froze, mid-stride, snapping off the light, straining my ears. Another gust of wind in the screens. The roof groaned and popped with each gust. Outside: quiet, no footsteps. Probably nothing. Just in case, I waited, barely breathing, while over my head, sporadic raindrops plunked onto the roof. A minute later, I let out a breath, snapped on the light, and stepped to the desk.

The football-size ceramic bull, bloody red, gaudy yellow and green even in the reflected light of my flashlight, stared at me from the corner of the desk top, watching while I checked the three stacked baskets, the folders on the desk top, the center drawer and side drawers. No messages. I stared back at the bull a second, gave it the finger, and tried the baskets again.

Finally, shaking my head, I straightened. Avoiding the window and the door, I moved the beam around the room one more time. Maybe I'd overlooked something. I didn't see anything worth examining and eventually came back to the desk.

I pulled the center drawer out again. The floor creaked. I didn't do that. It creaked again. I snapped the light off, held my breath, and stared at the door. It moved. I pushed the drawer in, squatted, and twitched as the drawer hit the stops with a loud clunk followed by another clunk. I was dead!

"Pssst. Ross."

Jim? I raised my head to look over the desk. A dark shadow of a man's upper body hung suspended above the doorknob. The head turned slowly, left and right, blind in the darkness. Jim's head.

"Over here," I said. "Close the door."

The shadow slipped into the room and the door squeaked shut.

I switched on the flashlight. "What are you doin', man? You scared the shit out of me!"

"Got worried. You okay?"

"I was. Now I'm shaking so much I can't hold the light steady."

"Sorry." He walked to the desk, reached out, and picked up something the size of a long wallet. It came from under the ceramic bull. "What's this?"

Oh, shit, I've broken the damn bull. I raised the light and let it bounce off the desk. "I don't know. Let me see."

Jim handed it to me.

Heavy and cool to the touch, the thin, slightly curved piece of ceramic had two beveled sides and no rough edges, like a panel. At least I didn't break anything. I blinked. "Hey. Who's guarding the fort? Where's J.P.?"

"Oh, yeah." Jim backed toward the door. "He went down to the line shack to get some Cs. Hungry." He cracked the door and peeked out.

I set the flashlight on the desk—the beam paralleling the back edge—and picked up the bull. Had to get that thing back together and get the hell out of there.

"Go on back," I said, "I'll be right th—" Paper. There was paper in the bull. "Jim."

"Okay, I'm goin'."

"Wait a minute. Just a minute." I eased the folded paper out of the hollow bull, my hands still shaking. A newspaper clipping, *Baltimore Times*, May 1966.

"Got something?"

"Just a minute." A photograph with a story. An older stocky man in a suit and a younger man in a Navy officer's uniform. A medal hung over the officer's breast pocket, below his ribbons, below his gold wings. The caption: Retired

Navy Admiral Richard J. Nunnally, Naval Academy class of '29, congratulates his oldest son, Navy Lieutenant Richard J. Nunnally, Jr., USNA class of '61, on his Navy Cross for heroism." The proud father was shaking hands with his son. The hand was thick. The man was thick. The man was Angus with gray hair.

"Come on, Ross!"

"I'm comin', I'm comin', just a minute." I scanned the article, my eyes straining in the dim light. Faster. Wow. I finally finished, folded the paper, slipped it into the bull, popped the panel into place, and set the bull down as I remembered finding it. "Okay, we're out of here."

The screened door to the flight line opened as we strolled into the ready room—Jim's stroll smooth and flowing, mine stiff and measured. J.P., a fresh cigarette hanging from his thin lips, stepped through the door dripping water from the bill of his cover. He held a carton of C-rations. I turned down the hall to S-2 as Jim stopped at the ODO counter.

"Heard from 'em yet?" J.P. asked.

"No," Jim said. "They're probably at the club at Quang Tri by now."

"Well, I'm calling DASC and Quang Tri. If those butt-wipes have stayed up there without calling me, I'm gonna have their ass."

Back at the desk in S-2, I put my head in my hands and tried to think. The article said the retired admiral had finished flight school in 1931 and served as a carrier fighter pilot in WWII and Korea. Had two kills in an F6F in 1943. The admiral's son, Lieutenant Nunnally, had gotten the Navy Cross for shooting down a MIG-17 over North Vietnam in July, 1965. The kicker was he did it in an AD7, a Skyraider, an air-to-ground prop airplane. The MIG jumped him and his wingman and the lieutenant got the kill. Good flying. Probably good enough to induce a jealous rage in the half-brother who was never recognized by his biological father. A jealous rage that might have been a factor in his dismissal from his A-4 squadron the following month.

Minutes later, still trying to find a place in the puzzle for my new information, I heard footsteps in the hall.

Jim stopped just outside the doorway, his hands pressed against the doorjambs. "Ross. Got a problem."

"What? Listen, have I got some news for—"

"It's Bill and Rod. They're missing."

27

River Rats

On October 8th, 1969, First Lieutenants Rodney Wysowski and William Catlett were officially listed as MIA, Missing In Action.

Jim Teach, J.P., and I had done all we could the night before to locate them. They'd just disappeared. For some reason I was angry at Bill. I couldn't sleep or eat I was so angry. Here we go again, I thought. He's gotten himself into a jam, worried everybody, scared the shit out of me, then he'll come waltzing into the ready room tomorrow whistling "Semper Fidelis" and asking why everyone is so uptight.

For a while, the official announcement and Captain Orndorff's request for me to write his wife and family and get his gear together replaced the anger with fear. When Angus refused to search for them the next day, the anger returned.

"Let the Air Force Search and Rescue do it," Angus told us. "That's why they're here." I considered slitting his throat, stealing a Huey, and searching for them myself, but the attitude of the rest of the lieutenants in the squadron intervened. For the first time since Angus was selected for lieutenant colonel, we were one. The word spread among us. We'd search anyhow.

Meanwhile, I had to write Laura. That was the hardest thing I'd ever done. I think we were all prepared to die doing what we did. And our wives and families must have known that was a possibility. But I don't think any of us ever seriously considered the consequences to our families if we were missing—not alive, not dead, just not there anymore. How do you grieve, mourn, and put it behind you if the one you love isn't there, but isn't dead? How do you deal with thoughts of him suffering, a fugitive, maybe a prisoner, maybe injured? How? I did it by slamming my fist into something and screaming at him, "You asshole! You're alive and you're jerkin' me around, and you're pissin' me off!

Shit!" But I couldn't write Laura that. "He's alive," I wrote. "And if he ever isn't alive, I'll tell you."

Inside Blue Dog's old hootch on the night of the 8th, all the lieutenants, even Walt, met to look over the next day's schedule and formulate a plan. Jim Teach and Buck Akerman were in charge.

Akerman had written the schedule to maximize lieutenant with lieutenant crews, some guns, some slicks. It hadn't been easy. On the 7th, before anyone knew Rod and Bill were missing, Angus had ordered Akerman to start scheduling him and his select crews on Thunder Clap. He wanted Duppont as his wingman, and Kerrigan and O'Connor, two good friends known collectively as "The Irish," as their co-pilots. Angus wanted one day on T.C. then one day on afternoon guns, then T.C. again—a screwed-up schedule contrary to previous procedures. Angus was getting weird again, but I was too concerned about Bill to give it much thought.

Akerman had managed to work around Angus' orders and put lieutenants on two slick missions plus the sniffer package (two gunships, one sniffer). I wanted to be with Akerman in the sniffer bird; we'd be through with the mission by 1100, have maximum time to search for Bill, and when we found him, no matter how dangerous it was, there was no doubt in my mind Akerman would go get him. But I wanted to be there to make sure. Teach and Ono would fly the guns.

It rained on the 9th and the sniffer was cancelled. Can't smell urine in the rain. Angus was gone on T.C., Major Lewis was on R&R, so we launched the package anyhow. I figured I knew where they were. It pissed me off when I thought about it, but I had a hunch. Either the Keyhole or the Ba Long River valley.

Rod and Bill, "Hardball 4-0," were last seen leaving Vandy heading south toward Ca Lu and the Ba Long valley around 1740. DASC had released them at 1735, early. Sundown was at 1812. The Ba Long valley led southeast from Ca Lu to the foothills south of Quang Tri, a dangerous shortcut to Highway One we used regularly in guns, but not when alone in a slick. I figured Rod had taken it anyhow, intercepted Highway One, then wrapped his Huey around a tree at the Keyhole showing off for Bill. That was where we'd find them. The Keyhole. Banged up, but alive.

In spite of the rain and the cancellation, we took off from Phu Bai at 0730 and headed north. Dewey Munzel was the ODO. He was to claim he didn't know about the cancellation until the crews had launched and were out of radio range.

After a long day of low clouds, rain showers, and miles and miles of wet green leaves, muddy rivers, and flooded rice fields, we returned. We didn't find Rod and Bill at the Keyhole, or in the Ba Long valley, or even in the Subway. And Angus wasn't buying our excuse for launching. He knew. An AOM, all officers meeting, was called for 2000 that night.

At 2010, with Mickey seated at the first picnic table, Angus stood in front of the ODO counter in the crowded smoke-filled ready room and glared at us. Cigarette smoke trailed from his nostrils and perspiration filled the acne scars on his flushed face. His neck swelled as he stabbed his stubby finger at us and threatened us, screamed at us. His point was this: the missions of the squadron came first; we were there to support the grunts, not run our own rescue service. From then on, we'd use our aircraft on assigned missions only and those who disobeyed that order would have their HAC papers taken, be grounded, or worse. He was serious. We were to ignore losses and press on like Marines.

If that speech had come from Major Hardy, I think we could have accepted it. It didn't.

The lieutenants met again that night. We'd keep a lower profile, but we'd keep looking, keep using the Ba Long valley at every opportunity. They were alive and we'd find 'em.

Another frustrating day passed. We didn't find them and the ax fell on Akerman for continuing to try; Angus grounded him for two days and busted him from flight leader to wingman. Jim Teach called off the search, but privately told those in our hootch to press on. Hippy and Hairy—who'd made HAC right after Rod and Walt, another message to Bill and me—were included. Still no luck.

On the 13th, on Angus' orders, I flew guns south with Akerman. Akerman said that was to keep us from searching up north. It had been a week of frustration. Only "nothing yet" from the Air Force. Akerman told me I looked like shit—bloodshot eyes, getting wrinkles in my forehead. I told him I'd always had wrinkles in my forehead. I guess the eyes were from lack of sleep.

Akerman also told me Angus had changed his scheduling orders. Angus wanted two days off then Thunder Clap on every even-numbered day. That evening in the head I asked Walt and the Irish about the change, but they weren't talking. Thinking there might be a connection, the next morning I asked Scapelli and Morchesski if there were any more messages missing. None were.

The new Angus schedule had also pissed off the crew chiefs and gunners. Droopy's bird had been selected as Angus' personal gunship, so Droopy had the M-21 minigun to care for. That meant humpin' six times the ammo and cleaning three times the barrels. He didn't mind it at first, but doing it day after day, then maintaining the bird night after night had become a problem. Droopy wasn't an Angus fan anyhow. He still remembered what Angus had done to his hammer symbol.

Also on the 13th, we had our first casualty of the month. While flying wing on Major Pyhr west of Con Thien, Hippy Dog was hit in the face. The round glanced off the windscreen post, shredded his cheek, and ripped through his flight helmet. Art-the-fart was with him. Art said he felt the jolt, grabbed the controls, and turned to see a bloody face with one eye looking at him—no nose, blood everywhere. While he stared in disbelief, Hippy's hands slammed into the sides of his helmet and snapped it back into place to expose his nose and other eye. "Didn't hurt," Hippy said, yanking the controls from Art. "Where's that son-of-a-bitch?" Art barely got him to the med facility at Quang Tri before shock set in. Hippy was medevaced the next day, the 14th.

On the night of the 14th, Hairy Dog got drunk at the club and broke his arm jumping from one table to another, a compound fracture. He was medevaced on the 17th, the day I finally got my HAC check and the day after Major Lewis returned from R&R. Major Lewis was desperate for HACs.

On the night of the 17th, I was scheduled as Major Pyhr's wingman for the next day, afternoon guns. Seeing my name in print for the first time as a HAC wasn't the thrill I'd anticipated. Bill had been missing for eleven days. Still no word from the Air Force.

Late that night, 0200, still wide awake in my rack, I gave up on sleep, dressed, and left the hootch. In light rain, I slogged through the wet sand for an hour or more—wandering, working up a sweat. I finally stopped, leaned against a wall, and unsnapped my rain jacket. I was behind the club. Breathing hard, the anger suddenly swelled again. "You ass-hole!" I screamed, "you gaping, screaming, hot-doggin', ass-hole!" A stray raindrop hit me on the forehead. I let it run between my eyes as I raised my fists to the sky and screamed at him again. He was alive, he was screwin' around, and he was pissin' me off!

I hung my head, took a deep breath, and listened to raindrops plunk into the puddles at my feet. That was stupid. Accomplished nothing.

Back at the hootch, I returned to my rack. It rained harder. I apologized to Laura again—I'd made a promise and I wasn't doing a good job of keeping it. I said I'd keep trying. I took a deep breath and sleep finally came.

That afternoon, J.E.B. Horsnyder would be my first co-pilot. Over six feet tall, broad shoulders, dark complexion, a pale scar under his right eye, "Hoss" was from an old Virginia family. Solid guy. Looked like he might have played some football.

We met Pyhr and Ripkevic, "Rip," at early chow. Based on Pyhr's brief, there would be no time to look for Bill. When we got a chance, we'd work the northern edge of Leatherneck Square until we found the Dead-Eye Gooner. I'd have to hope for a slick hop the next day. I'd talk to Akerman. I thought of the stories I'd heard of guys E&Eing, escape and evading, for as much as two weeks before being found. Bill could do that.

DASC sent us to Dong Ha mountain, LZ Fuller, to escort an H-53. The 53 was to remove a few of the older 105 howitzers from the fire base. The 4th Marine Regiment, the last of the 3rd Marine Division, was leaving Vietnam.

En route to Fuller, the 53 had mechanical problems and had to return to Phu Bai. DASC told us to refuel and stand by at Vandy while another 53 was launched. By then it was 1510 and Pyhr was snapping at everyone on the radio. I wasn't surprised when he ignored DASC and led us to Con Thien.

Con Thien was a sea of mud, a mosaic of war litter and mud puddles. Pyhr contacted the ground unit there, but was asked to "wait one." They had an air strike in progress. We switched to the UHF frequency of the OV-10 controlling the strike and backed off to the southwest to watch. A flight of Marine A-4s with napalm and snake-eye bombs were to drop on a target two clicks north of us. As we waited, circling at 1500 feet, I remembered being taught the bombs should be dropped first (to open the holes), then the napalm (to burn 'em out). It wasn't done that way. I'd heard jet pilots explain why. "You get rid of that jellied gasoline hanging from your ass first. *Then* you drop the bombs."

The A-4s put on a good show, especially Dash Two. "No doubt he's a lieutenant," Hoss explained, pointing at the climbing A-4 after his first pass, a napalm run. I had to agree. Told to drop 100 meters short of number one's hits, Two got right down on the deck and appeared to scrape the napalm off his wings with the tree limbs. Great hits. He was just as good with the snake-eyes, the hard bombs. Minutes later, we decided the number two guy hung it out enough to be acceptable to us as an "Honorary Huey-gun Driver." We laughed together as Hoss described the scene at the awards banquet where we'd present the award, an inscribed tail-rotor blade, to a Marine officer with a bag over his head—too embarrassed to be mingling with helicopter pilots to show his face. Good pilot though.

After 15 minutes of work, the A-4s climbed above the clouds and Pyhr tried to get Mustang Chip, the OV-10 driver, to clear us onto the target. Chip said the target had been a "suspected ambush site" and he was sure the A-4s had taken care of it. Also, the 1st ARVN Division was already on the move, sweeping the area on foot. To the east I could see six Army Hueys flying toward Con Thien in trail. Two Army Cobras, like olive-drab sharks, cruised the hazy skies beyond the Hueys.

After some persuasion, Chip agreed to stay on station for 15 minutes and help us find another target. Five minutes later, with rockets and guns, we attacked a "suspected enemy bunker complex." No return fire. I enjoyed the shooting and as I had promised myself in June, I let Hoss make two runs.

We refueled and rearmed at Vandy, then returned to LZ Fuller, Dong Ha mountain. The replacement H-53 finally joined us and lifted the three 105s. We bored holes in the sky and watched.

With the last 105 hanging beneath the 53 and safely on its way to Quang Tri, Pyhr had us refuel again, then return. Once more circling Dong Ha mountain, he worked the fox mike radio until he found a platoon from Golf Company on a patrol east of LZ Fuller. They needed a VR, visual reconnaissance.

The area they needed checked was in "Helicopter Valley," so named years before when several H-46s were shot down there in one day. We flew east to have a look.

North of LZ Fuller, the Khe Chua River ran east out of a gap between Mutters Ridge to the north and Dong Ha mountain to the south. Spilling out of the high country as a fast-moving stream, it turned southeast at the foothills, slowed, widened, and slithered into Helicopter Valley, a wide green valley of elephant grass and scrub brush.

The Marines from Golf were following a ridgeline to a finger that extended to the edge of the valley. They were to set up there for the night and wanted us to make sure they were alone.

I asked for guns, both sides—quicker response, wider coverage—and flipped my sight down from the overhead.

A thousand feet below me, to my right, Pyhr leveled off at the treetops and ran down the finger. I followed, trying to stay in position to protect him. Dropping into the valley floor, he curved north. The valley itself, already half in shadows from Dong Ha Mountain, looked harmless, mostly grass, no visible trails. Turning around at the mountains, Pyhr flew down the valley, up the finger, and back around again.

"Get down here, Two." Pyhr.

I looked at Hoss. He shrugged as I answered, "Two, Roger."

I dived to Pyhr's altitude and joined up at his five o'clock, loose parade. We hit the valley floor again, skimming it, skids in the grass.

Hoss, with the TAT sight in his hand: "What the fuck? Over."

"Don't know."

We kept flying: across the river, across the grass and shrubs on the other side, and into the rolling hills of the next mountain range—low level, hugging the ground, heading back toward Con Thien and right through the NVA's front yard.

We flew for three minutes on a heading of 0-3-0, back to where we were earlier, the sun setting behind us. A mile or two ahead, a pair of Army Hueys circled at 1000 feet. Must have been a good-size operation up there.

Then Pyhr banked left, hard. From his right side I banked harder, cut behind him, and settled on his left flank. We were going back, heading 2-1-0, flying toward thick luminous clouds, trimmed in silver, lit by a sun hidden by mountains.

Leaving the ridges, still hugging the ground—100 knots, hissing radios, high-pitch whine from the transmission—I realized I was hanging over the cyclic stick and shook my shoulders to relax. Cool it, I said.

Then we were completely in the shadows. Wide valley ahead. Deep green. Not a word from Pyhr. Now over a still and silent sea of grass, skimming its surface. Ahead, in the shadows, I could make out the finger of high ground with the Marines on it, but couldn't see them—too far away. Then the river, suddenly exposed, flashed under us, and we hugged the grass on the other side—both low, nobody covering anybody, two hunks of meat on a stick—shishkebob without the supporting onions, tomatoes, and peppers. Too quiet.

I whispered, "Make me hot, Hoss. Guns."

Two clicks on the ICS. A hand to the master-arm switch.

The valley floor ahead…moved! More movement! Everywhere! Pyhr's rocket pod shot flames and rockets leaped ahead of his Huey, one after another, spewing fire then smoke. I squeezed. Hoss squeezed. The noise rattled me. I stayed with Pyhr, not aiming the Huey, just keeping the ball in the middle. Helmeted NVA ran everywhere, their grass-covered backs to us, rockets and tracers landing among them, some turning around—just clumps of grass with faces and legs. We couldn't miss. No need to aim. Now flying right over them and through a cloud of smoke. Acrid smell. Flashes by my windscreen, streaks of green. Pyhr turning, door gun blasting, brilliant red tracers. Then streaks of green all around him too—had to be taking hits. I released the trigger and turned with him, feeling the bouncing in my buttocks. Hoss hung in his straps, working the TAT. Both guns hammered away in the back and I pictured Sergeant Hutchins off his bullet bouncer, dancing behind his flame-spitting gun, working it left and right.

Pyhr held his turn, hugged the grass, then rolled out and headed up the valley parallel to the river. I let out a breath and glanced quickly to the ground behind me, then back to Pyhr. We were clear. Hutchins and the gunner, a new guy, black kid named Jennings from the paint shop, stopped firing.

"You guys okay back there?"

"Yes, sir," Hutchins answered, breathing hard. "You got a starboard gun jammed, Lieutenant."

"Okay. We'll clear it when we get a chance. Cold, Hoss."

Two clicks.

Hutchins would have to get out on the skid to clear the gun. I would have to slow down to 50 knots to make it as easy as possible for him. We had gooks in the open. No time to slow down. "Switch to rockets, both sides."

I couldn't believe we didn't take any hits. Impossible. I knew we'd surprised them, but shit. How could they have missed? Maybe they didn't miss. Sometimes you couldn't tell. I checked the gauges and caution panel. Okay.

Ahead and to my right, Pyhr eased his Huey into a climbing right turn. I climbed with him. Thank goodness he was going back with altitude. Now I'd get a chance to aim and nail 'em—to do what Hardball 3-3 does best. At 1200 feet, we rolled out over the river, heading back toward the gooks.

"I'll cover you, Two. Make the first pass. You've got the lead." Pyhr.

"Two, roger," I said. "I've got the lead." Shit. What the hell was he up to now?

I held my heading. Pyhr eased his nose up and slid behind us, left side. Pyhr wanted to be the wingman? I looked at Hoss. He watched the ground. Jennings called Pyhr at seven o'clock.

I lined up on the part of the valley floor between the finger and the river. Man, what a great target for artillery: troops in the open; the guys on Dong Ha Mountain would foam at the mouth if they heard that. But they wouldn't. Major Warren Pyhr had dibs on those gooks and—wait a minute. My eyes widened. Were we the bait?

Shit. "Make me hot, Hoss."

"You're hot, man. Get some."

I keyed the UHF. "1-9 Dash Two's in hot."

The valley floor filled my sight ring, dark green and still; nothing moved. No wind, no clumps of grass like a minute before, no real target. Smart gooks. Centered ball, 85 knots, squeeze. The Huey flinched and flames shot by me on either side. Still no fire from the ground. Squeeze again, and again. The last two rockets streaked by and I pulled, 110 knots, 500 feet, and turned, the beat of the blades pounding me into my seat. Hoss's hand darted from master-arm to select switches, then his TAT shot flames below me. Both door guns erupted in the back.

I keyed the mike. "Two's off cold."

Halfway into my turn—tail toward the river—a noise, not really a noise, more like a feel in my butt and ears at the same time, a thump that slipped through the clatter of the guns. I shot a look at the caution panel—no lights. The gauges—okay. Hoss—still looking through his TAT sight, firing. I spun my head left, to the cabin. Jennings, squatting behind his gun, still firing, brass clattering at his feet. There, on the steel deck—a bare bullet bouncer, Hutchins' butt plate, like an upside-down turtle shell, spinning, a spent round also spinning on the deck beside it. Damn. At least one hit that time, but where'd it come from?

Vibrating in my seat, climbing past 700 feet at 80 knots, I looked for Pyhr. Through the yellowed plexiglass window, raised to keep out the burning rocket propellant, I found him in a shallow dive, ahead of me, opposite direction and at my altitude—pairs of rockets flying from his pods one after another, way early. Why was he so low and so...flat? And why was he aiming at the riverbank, not the grasslands. Nobody shooting back. Was that where my hit came from?

Hoss stowed his TAT. Must have jammed. Jennings stopped firing. Hutchins continued, his tracers pouring into the valley floor and walking toward the riverbank where Pyhr's rockets were hitting. Good job of cover. I went back to the horizon, pulling all the torque I could get out of the Huey, and glanced at Pyhr.

He'd switched to guns, the muzzle flashes on the Huey's sides and under its chin pulsing bright yellow in the dim light. He was too close, pressing, the red tracers pouring from his guns and ricocheting wildly off a berm of dirt and short grass on the bank of the river: a berm whose base suddenly exploded in muzzle flashes and returned a straight spurt of green tracers. The tracers ripped past the incoming red ones and washed over Pyhr like a stream of water from a high-pressure hose. His Huey shuddered and fish-tailed and shedded pieces of plexiglass that disappeared in the slipstream. His guns stopped. But his last burst of fire found the base of the berm. Grass and dirt leaped into the air around the muzzle flashes and the green tracers ceased. Stillness. Pyhr continued in a shallow dive, no more than 100 feet off the grass.

Meanwhile, I'd pulled the Huey into a perch position—65 knots, 20 pounds of torque—and nudged the nose over. "Make me hot."

Pyhr was twelve o'clock, in my sights, a dark green shadow flying low and slow over the silent target—no smoke, no fire, but no turn or climb either. Enough of that shit. I squeezed the mike. "1-9, this is Dash Two, you okay?"

Quiet, then, "Hydraulics." Ripkevic!

"Cold, Hoss."

I pulled power and leveled off at 800 feet. In the fading light, a tiny, khaki-clad torso lay exposed against the dark earth of the berm ahead. Still no fire from the grasslands. "Rip, understand hydraulic failure?"

"Roger." His voice was strained, breathing hard, like he was in a tug-of-war.

"Okay, we gotcha. Keep it level, keep it slow, and ah…70 knots—lookin' good." The E-model Huey had a 540 rotor head—big, heavy, couldn't control it without hydraulics. Had two primary systems plus an accumulator, an emergency backup worth three pulls on the collective. Both primary systems must have been shot out. "Pyhr?" I asked.

"Dead maybe. Nothin' left, Ross…goin' in."

Damn. Should've had something left, should've had the accumulator. I looked ahead. At least it was flat. "Get on guard freq, Hoss, then go to DASC." I switched to fox. "Okay, Rip, we're gettin' some help. I'll be on fox mike for you. You copy?"

"Mayday. Hardball 1-9 Dash Two on guar—" I switched off my UHF mixer switch.

"Rip. You copy on fox? I'm with ya."

No response. Ahead in the shadows, Pyhr's Huey flew into the tall grass beyond the berm, bounced back into view, settled again, dribbled, then shuddered to a stop. Only the white-striped blades and his red anti-collision light remained visible. I glanced at my navigation instruments, TACAN and DME. The number two needle wandered and the DME had a bar across it. Too low. I looked left and right and tried to get a line between two terrain features, a fix. I decided on the hook in the river, and climbed as I flew over the crash site, invisible below me. At least it wasn't burning. Spray the gooks? No. Didn't know for sure where they were. Conserve. I started a right-hand orbit.

"Hardball 1-9, this is Golf 1-4, did you call us, sir?"

The grunts on the finger. Forgot about them. "Negative, Golf. Got a bird down. Be advised that valley is full of gooks and they're movin' your way, over." Hey, maybe the grunts could get to Rip? No. No way. Not with a company or more of NVA between them.

"Copy that, 1-9. Interrogative, sir. How many?"

"Hundreds, 1-4."

"Roger, sir, copy hundreds."

Nine hundred pounds of fuel. Too heavy to lift four people with no wind to help, even if I jettisoned the rocket pods. Maybe if I shit-canned everything: weapons, ammo, bullet bouncers, all that shit Hutchins kept under the troopseat. Maybe if I left Pyhr. No. Marines don't leave Marines. But it's Pyhr, damn it. He probably had his hydraulics shot out on the first pass; that would explain the shallow approach on the second pass, using his accumulator. Suicidal prick. Save Rip and the rest, fuck Pyhr.

"Ross, you copy?"

"No." I flipped my UHF mixer back on. "Guard?"

Hoss was already talking: "Affirmative 5-2-0, come up the valley from Cam Lo. We're at 1500 feet, position lights on bright."

"Copy, Hardball, we're two minutes out, 1000 feet."

Hoss: "Roger."

"Whatcha got?" I asked.

"Army Dustoff en route from Con Thien to Camp Evans."

"Outstanding."

"Maybe, but DASC wants us to use the 46 medevac package out of Quang Tri."

"Okay." Even better. Two more guns and two 46s. "Where are they?"

"They're launching them now. Not airborne yet."

I shook my head and looked to the ground. "Don't think we can wait that long." It was dark down there. Rip had shut it down, no lights, no moving blades. I could make out the river, but not the crash site. It might take the gooks two minutes or twenty minutes to get to our guys. I had no idea how close they were.

"Hardball 1-9, Golf 1-4." The grunts.

"Go ahead," I said.

"Hardball, my six advises we're in position to adjust fire, and a fire mission is on its way, over."

Oh, shit, they were going to shoot artillery. "Negative, 1-4, negative fire mission. We're trying to rescue a downed crew here. Check fire."

I looked at Hoss. Pink instrument lights reflected off his clear visor. "Did you give 5-2-0 our FM freq?"

Hoss nodded as a breathless voice broke the silence on UHF, "This is Hardball 1-9. Two, you there?" Rip on his survival radio, guard frequency.

I switched to UHF. "We're here 1-9, you're loud and clear. How me?"

I could hear the relief in his voice. "Loud and clear, man, lima charles."

"Okay, 1-9, we got helos comin' from everywhere for you. What's your situation?"

"Pyhr's dead. Everybody else can walk."

"How 'bout the LZ?"

"Swampy. Grass. No trees."

"What can you use to mark it?"

"Flashlight, strobe."

"Okay. Don't forget the blue cover for the strobe if you use it. Save your battery now, we're only minutes away."

"Two?"

"Yeah."

"I hear sloshing sounds."

Damn. That trail of smashed grass they left behind. "Move toward Dong Ha Mountain. Can you see the mountain?"

"Negative," he whispered. "We're movin'."

A flash of fire on the ground. Artillery. Damn it! I switched my transmitter to fox, took a breath to yell at the grunts, and heard, "Hardball 1-9 Dash Two, this is Dustoff 5-2-0 on fox."

"Hardball 1-9, Golf 1-4, you call me, sir?" The grunts on the finger.

"Negative 1-4, but shut off the damn artillery, we got friendlies down there!" Shit! "Break. 5-2-0 this is Hardball."

"Roger, Hardball, we've got lights ahead. That you?"

"I'm flashing the landing light, 5-2-0, on a 1-4-0 heading."

"Roger, you're in sight. We're eleven o'clock low."

I found the Army Huey's anti-collision light and position lights at eleven o'clock just as the ground below me flashed red and yellow followed by a concussion wave that shook us. Pyhr's Huey had exploded in flames. No tracers, no muzzle flashes. Rip must have blown it.

"Hardball, Dustoff 5-2-0. What the hell was that?"

"Tell him that's our way of marking zones," Hoss said, smiling behind his clear visor.

I shook my head. I was running out of ideas and Hoss was making jokes. Another flash on the ground, artillery again.

"5-2-0, this is Hardball. Stay east of the river, and south of the hook in the river at 2000. That was our crash site exploding and we've got artillery impacting to the west, over."

"Roger. We're climbing." The voice had a "Yes, sir" tone to it. Made me realize my voice was up an octave and sharp. Had to calm down, be cool.

Another group of three artillery rounds, their flashes reflecting off the mountains, fell into the valley north of the burning Huey. If that was where they were gonna land then to hell with 'em. "5-2-0 this is Hardball, go Jack Benny, minus ten, plus Joe Dimaggio on fox, copy?"

"5-2-0 copy J.B., minus ten, plus Joltin' Joe. Switchin'."

That guy was good. Thank God. Hoss made the switch.

"5-2-0's up fox."

"Hardball's up. Thanks, 5-2-0. Here's the brief: Three down crew men moving from the burning Huey. Direction unknown. Monitor guard and this FM. How much time you got?"

"Twenty minutes."

"Copy, that. Wait one." Man, I thought. What do I do now? I switched to guard. "Hardball 1-9, if you read me come up voice, if you can't talk, key your mike twice."

No response. Damn.

If they had walked west toward Dong Ha Mountain like I told them to do, they would have headed toward drier land, friendlies, and a clear landmark, but they would have also been heading for a trail I suddenly remembered seeing marked on the map. Not good. Trails had gooks. Also, they would have been closer to the artillery. I shouldn't have told them that. Dumb. Okay, knock it off, think positive. Rip was the co-pilot, he had the maps, he would know the trail was there. Maybe. I keyed the mike. "One-Nine, this is Dash Two, if you read me, go east toward the river. Acknowledge with two clicks."

Nothing.

"Hardball 1-9, this is Dong Ha DASC on guard, switch to alternate frequency. Leave primary guard frequency open for other emergencies. DASC out."

I looked at Hoss. "You think Rip could switch freqs?"

"Don't think so. I think he's running for his life—in the dark. Fuck DASC."

"Roger, that." I looked to the ground. The flames from the Huey had died down and the fires the explosion had started in the grass were out. Corporal Cobb, Pyhr's crew chief, had probably put a thermal grenade in the fuel tank.

More flashes in the valley floor, a steady barrage, a "Fire for effect." Close. God, I hoped I hadn't made things worse.

"Two, you there." A whisper.

I squeezed the trigger switch and pulled the Huey into a steep right turn, back to the northwest, looking almost straight down. "Yeah, man. Where are you?"

"River."

Of course. Bill had told me Rip had been a swimmer for Chico State. Of course a swimmer would head for water. "In the river now?"

"Opposite bank. Got a bird ready?" Still whispering.

"Affirmative. Got a place to land?"

"Affirmative. Clear, but wet. Hover only. Ready to mark."

"Wait one." I switched to FM. "5-2-0, Hardball, you copy?"

"We copy, Hardball, and we're ready for the mark."

"Okay, 5-2-0, look southeast of the hook in the river, on the east bank, maybe 500 meters down from the hook." I looked up to my right and found a flashing anti-collision light above me, alone against the black sky.

"Roger."

Back on UHF, I called Rip. "We're ready, 1-9. Mark it."

I heard two clicks, then a small white light appeared in the blackness below, east of the river, only 200 meters below the hook and 400 meters below the gooner that killed Pyhr.

"Shit, they're close." Hoss.

"Roger, that." I called Rip: "Tally-ho steady white, 1-9."

"Affirmative." A whisper.

"Hardball, 5-2-0 is in on the steady white, goin' lights out."

"Copy that, 5-2-0. Give me a short-final call if you will."

"Roger."

The flashing anti-collision light arched downward and disappeared. I flew northwest of the hook in the river to give him some room and to get in position to cover him. A long minute ticked by. I turned east, staring at the blackness below.

"Hardball 1-9 Dash Two, this is Sea Legs 6-2 on guard, say your working freq, over." The Marine medevac package.

"Squadron Common fox," I answered sharply, then told myself to cool it. They were only trying to help.

I listened to the radios hiss and the faint whop-whop of my Huey's blades, and finished a turn to the southeast. They should be just about on final. I raised the nose to slow down, 70 knots…65.

"Hardball 1-9 Dash Two, this is Sea Legs 6-2 on fox. Say your poz, over."

Damn! "Hold over the end of Helicopter Valley, Sea Legs, and please stay off—" Muzzle flashes! East bank.

"Make me hot." Two clicks. I dropped the nose, set 20 pounds, and…no, no tracers, just flashes. Maybe our guys. Couldn't see the flashlight anymore. Where was 5-2-0?

"We're takin' fire, Hardball. Comin' out southeast."

Comin' out? Hadn't called "in" yet. Did they get close?

Red tracers, Dustoff's door guns, appeared along the east bank of the river, starting from space and spewing northwest toward more yellow flashes on the ground. I put my sights on the flashes and squeezed. Flames shot by me on both sides and a shower of sparks engulfed the Huey, destroying my night vision. I squinted my eyes and squeezed again, blindly, then pulled and climbed, watching the rockets flash on the ground below. Close enough to rattle their cage, but I doubted if I hit any. Good thing Sea Legs was there. The gooks knew where Rip was now.

"Hardball, Dustoff 5-2-0 is clear southeast. Got three green river rats with me. Where do you want 'em?"

"Hot damn, Rosser!" Hoss shook his gloved fists in the air. "We got 'em, man! They did it!"

I sucked in a huge breath, released it with a "Wow," and raised a thumbs-up. Ahead of us, an anti-collision light flashed on, climbing. I climbed behind it. "Dustoff, this is Hardball. We'll follow you to Quang Tri and pick them up from you in the fuel pits. Unless they need medical attention, over."

"Negative medical, Hardball. My medic is giving me the okay on all three. See you at the pits."

"Roger, that. Thanks, guys. Hell-of-a-job."

I heard two clicks from 5-2-0, then, "Hardball 1-9 Dash Two, this is Sea Legs 6-2, over."

"Sea Legs, Hardball, go ahead." God, I couldn't believe it was over. We got 'em. I let out a huge breath and relaxed the grip I had on the cyclic stick. My gloves were wet, my hands ached. Hoss safed all the switches and circuit breakers, smiling.

"Hardball, this is Sea Legs 6-2. Interrogative. You need us, or you just get us launched so we could fly around and jerk off while you work with the Army?"

I pulled my sliding window down, felt the cool air rush in, and looked at the four circling anti-collision lights off to our right. Did I hear him right? "Sorry, Sea Legs. Dustoff was available and our guys were in deep shit. I used what I had, over."

"Well, we don't appreciate being rushed out here for nothing. I'll see that your CO hears about this."

I looked at Hoss.

He keyed his ICS. "Let me talk to this prick, Ross."

I shook my head and looked at the lights, now in trail, heading toward Quang Tri. "Appreciate your help, Sea Legs. We were a gnat's ass away from turning over a real shit-sandwich to you. Thankfully, it wasn't necessary."

I waited, but he didn't respond. I guess he'd already switched frequencies.

28

Worthy of Respect

True to his word, Sea Legs 6-2, a major with the Huey squadron at Quang Tri, called our ready room the evening we rescued Ripkevic. Captain Cain took the call. The irate major reported my unwillingness to work with his flight of Marines, Cain went straight to Angus, and my fate was sealed without a hearing. I was grounded for the following two days—the 19th and 20th—assigned as SDO for the 19th, and busted to co-pilot.

Seeing Ripkevic's smile on the 19th was the only bright spot in a lousy day as SDO. I sat with him in the back of the ready room for a few minutes before he got started on the write-up he was doing for the Army Dustoff crew. Hoss and I had already collaborated on a write-up for Rip and his crew.

During our conversation, Rip said their hydraulics had been shot out on the low-level pass, the one where we caught the gooks in the open. He said Pyhr had noticed movement in the field during the VR, then led us away to make the gooks think we had left. He tried to sneak up on them when we returned low-level. Pyhr knew the hits that took out their hydraulics had come from behind him, but didn't know it was from the berm by the river. He learned that when my bird drew fire on the first gun-run from altitude. We really were the bait. By then Pyhr was down to just the fluid in his accumulator. He used it to set up his last shallow dive at the berm, adjusting his fire to the bunker at its base. Pyhr was convinced it was the Dead-Eye Gooner—he finally had him in his sights.

When I asked if it really had been the Dead-Eye Gooner, Rip said, "Who knows? The guy was a hell of a shot whoever he was—Pyhr's head looked like a smashed tomato." Corporal Cobb had been unstrapping Pyhr's body when Rip heard the sloshing sounds. The body was still in the seat when the Huey blew.

After I left Rip to finish his Dustoff write-up, I tried again to get the Air Force SAR on the telephone. I got through, but the news was not good. All search and rescue had been cancelled for Hardball 4-0. They'd given up. Adam Henstrom, the ODO, avoided my eyes as I hung up the phone.

Squeezed by a sudden need to get away from everyone and clear the area, especially the area near the cubbyhole with "1st Lt. Catlett" stenciled on the red vinyl flap, I snatched my cover off the counter and marched down the hall.

The screened door to the squadron building slammed shut behind me. It sounded so good I wanted to go back and slam it again. I didn't. I marched across the sand, my gut burning, shoulder muscles in knots—angry as hell at every one of them. They'd given up. They'd quit. They were getting on with it, the missions, the duties—as if two more guys weren't really missing, as if it didn't matter.

I hadn't given up, but hell…who was I kidding? I'd carry on too. Coach Day taught me that on the first morning of two-a-day practices. Guys fell out in the heat of August, guys came up lame with blisters, but the rest of us played on. That's what real men do—keep going, and ignore the fallen because they were stragglers. "When the going gets tough…" Right. The next letter to Laura was going to be a bitch.

I marched straight ahead, kicking the clods of mud defining the ruts in the road. It was early, so I took the long way to the mess hall, a sandy trail that led past the two-story enlisted barracks, then left across a field to the dirt street that fronted the last row of NCO hootches—plywood huts with tin roofs—then back up a side street to the mess hall. Bill and I would take that route when we had some time to kill. The loose sand of the field provided good exercise and reminded us of the sand-based obstacle course at Pensacola. Bill liked exercise, but didn't care for that obstacle course—said it was too easy. For us, it was. We had our orders.

I didn't know Bill until that first day, the day we gathered in a large room of an old wooden one-story office building across from the PX at Pensacola. It was January, 1968, crisp, clear blue sky. The man standing before us in a Winter Service Alpha uniform with four rows of ribbons, gold wings, and a set of full colonel's eagles on his shoulders, was the commanding officer of the Marine Aviation Detachment—our boss.

The colonel was an imposing figure: tall, straight, trim, close-cut gray hair. Every crease in his uniform was perfect. The shoes glistened like polished black marble. He spoke for an hour, routine stuff, administrative stuff: pay, housing, speed traps on Santa Rosa Island. I don't remember everything he said, but I remember how he finished, a discussion of the training we would receive and the traditional role of Marine Aviation in the history of the Navy's flight school. He said from First Lieutenant A.A. Cunningham in 1921, to Major John Glenn, the first American to orbit the earth, Marines had always set the pace at Pensacola and been an example to the Navy. Now it was our turn. His last statement, a command actually, said it all: "Gentlemen, because you are Marines, you *will* do better than the Navy. You will kick their ass in the classroom, in the cockpit, and on the PT field. They expect that, and you better damn well believe *I* expect that. Is that understood?"

As one, the sixty of us screamed, "Yes, Sir!" By then, we were so pumped one flick of the colonel's finger would have sent us tearing through the walls to get at the obstacle course, the classroom, the nearest cockpit, or the Navy itself if that's what the man wanted. And the tall guy in the chair in front of me, the guy with the bulging neck and freckles flushed with blood, would have led the charge. His name was Bill Catlett. God, was he tough. For Catlett, every new day was an opportunity to serve his Corps and kick the Navy's ass. And he did, dragging me along with him, maxing the Navy's physical fitness test, maxing the Navy's obstacle course, and acing the Navy's flight program. Proud doesn't begin to describe how we felt. The tradition of Marine aviation at Pensacola was in good strong hands.

I smiled at the memory of Bill bounding up the rope hanging from the ceiling of the old seaplane hangar, how he would slap the wooden disk at the top, slide down, and walk away before the Navy ensign on the rope next to him could get one body length off the floor. No contest.

I shook my head, clenching and unclenching my fists as I trudged through the wet sand. The cool wind ruffled the lapels of my utilities and the low clouds, dark and swollen, drifted by. Bill was hell on wheels. He had to be alive.

By the time I reached the mess hall, the ruts and mud clods had taken the brunt of my anger. My hands hung loosely at my sides. Even the tension in my shoulders and the pain in my gut had eased. Ahead, the door had just opened and the line of slouching, smoking Marines moved inside.

I joined the Marines at the stainless-steel serving counter, picked up a metal tray, and side-stepped down the line. I wasn't hungry, but I'd eat anyhow.

Sergeant Rappo, Bill's friend, watched me from the doorway to the kitchen. Tight-lipped, wiping his hands on his soiled apron, Rappo nodded. He knew Bill was missing and he cared, but a nod was all the caring he could show and still be a Marine sergeant. I nodded back and turned for the tables behind me.

The mess hall was busy: people in flightsuits and people in utilities coming and going, pushing and shoving, laughing and complaining. Steamy warm. Flies. Puddles on the concrete floor left over from that morning's wash-down. I found an empty picnic table in the back and sat. For a minute I stared at my tray of creamed corn, weiners, and a peach half. A slice of white bread was already half-soaked by the peach syrup. I poked at it with my fork as a young red-headed Marine in utilities sat at the opposite end of the table. He was pale, freckled, thin as a rifle barrel, and alone. He laid his cover on the table and ate from a tray piled with food, enough food for two men. I watched him, and wondered if Bill would be that pale and thin by now. The Marine never looked up, ate everything on the tray, and left. I opened the waxed carton of milk and drank.

After chow, I went by the base post office to inspect packages, a duty I detested, made me feel like a peeping Tom. I guess it was necessary—didn't want guys sending grenades back to their sweethearts. But I didn't find any grenades or drugs or stolen government property, just junk: Vietnamese dolls or wood-carved water buffalo or small silk purses—trinkets that some Marine paid good money for that some girl in Chicago or New York or Denver would toss in a drawer and forget. Maybe. What did I know? Laura probably would have loved something from Bill just then. Even junk.

I was relieved as SDO the next morning, the 20th, by a new guy named Laker, Army-trained. He had a white bandage on his forehead, the result of a fall he took trying to get to the bunker the night before during a rocket attack. The rockets hit in the ARVN compound on the north side of our base. They actually took more rockets than we did. I didn't even bother to get out of bed anymore.

That afternoon, around 1400, I walked back to the squadron building. I thought Staff Sergeant Morchesski would know how I could check our intelligence system for word on Bill and Rod. Maybe they had a way of identifying who had been captured. In the ready room, Bill's and Rod's cubbyholes had been reissued to Laker and another new guy. The pain in my gut returned. I didn't find Morchesski.

In the S-2 office, Scapelli, sitting on the floor reading his latest *Playboy*, said Morchesski had caught a ride on a supply run to Da Nang—a message had come in on the TTM-23 he wanted to follow up on—and he would be back that afternoon. Scapelli didn't know how to check on POWs and didn't know what was in the message that sent Morchesski to Da Nang. When I asked him for the list of missing messages, he said Morchesski had taken that too. I sat at the desk, checked my watch, and laid my head on my crossed arms. Tired. Morchesski must have made a connection between the new message and the ones Angus had taken. I'd wait for him.

Time passed. I slept. In a place I didn't know and for reasons I didn't understand, I was in my underwear on a campus, sitting on a bench by myself, trying to figure out why I wasn't dressed. How could I be so stupid? I stood to leave—late for a class I hadn't attended all semester—and spilled a piece of cake on the carpet…carpet, not grass. I didn't realize I had a plate in my hand. Wedding cake. Other students with books in their arms passed by, staring at me. I tried to pretend I wasn't aware of my nakedness. Then a faint, but familiar voice called my name, hollow, as if from one end of a culvert under a road. I didn't see a road.

"Hey, Ross."

I raised my head. "Yeah?" I was back in S-2, Phu Bai, Vietnam. Freud, six feet tall, small shoulders, stood in the doorway, survival vest hanging low around his waist, making him look heavier than he was. My watch said 1510. "What?"

"You asleep?"

I sat straight and wiped my face with my hands. My hands smelled of eraser dust. Scapelli was gone. "Yeah, I guess. What's up?"

"Well, I've got a bit of news for you." Freud unzipped his vest and tossed it onto the desk. "Nothing big, just a crumb. About Bill." He pushed his vest aside with his hip as he sat on the corner.

I put my hands on my knees. "Speak to me."

"I flew morning guns today with Jennings. We just got in. You remember him?"

"Sure. He was with me the other night, the night Rip was shot down with Pyhr. Good man. Did a good job."

"Well, he works in the paint shop and he remembers Rod Wysowski coming in early in the morning on the 7th and asking for cans of spray paint, green paint." I nodded as Freud continued. "Rod told him his crew chief needed it."

"Rod and Bill didn't have a crew chief that day."

"That's right. So why did Rod say that?"

"I don't know. Did Jennings give it to him?"

He nodded. "Gave him two cans."

"I guess if Rod was lying about who needed it, he didn't tell him why he wanted it, did he?"

"Nope. Any guesses?"

I shrugged. "Hell, I don't know. Rod could have been selling them on the black market for all I know. I wouldn't put anything past him. What's Jennings telling you this for anyhow? Why didn't he tell me the other day?"

"I don't know. Maybe he didn't get a chance, or didn't know you guys were close. He only told me after we got to shootin' the shit about the squadron." Freud smiled. "You know me. I was givin' him the old 'Why did you join the Marine Corps routine' and one topic led to another." Freud leaned forward. "Research, my friend, like camouflage, is continuous."

I faked a smile. "You're weird, Freud."

"I prefer 'colorful,' but you can use 'weird' if you like."

"Colorful then." I leaned the chair backward, resting it against the teletype machine, and shifted my eyes to the map on the wall behind the stack of *Playboys*. "Whatever."

Freud cleared his throat. "Henstrom said the Air Force had called off the search."

"Yep."

"You okay with that?"

"What do you think?"

"I think not. But that's okay. Look…talk to me, Ross. Tell me what you're feeling."

I let the chair drop forward, stood, and leaned toward him, my fingers on the desk, eyes on fire. "I'll tell you what I'm feeling—I'm feeling like ripping your damn head off. How can you sit there and shoot the shit about Bill and Rod when you could be out there doing something about it? I'm stuck in this fucking office, useless, grounded by the most worthless human being to ever wear the uniform of a Marine. You're free to come and go in your own government-issue Huey and you choose to sit here in this office and shoot the shit. Where's the 'Esprit de Corps' I've heard so much about? Where's the 'Marines don't leave Marines,' where's the 'Look out for your people?' Was all that just so many piles of bullshit? Lies?" I straightened, stabbing a finger at him. "That's how I feel. I feel like ripping your head off and I feel like shit!" I grunted, looked at the plywood ceiling, and added, "A worthless pile of shit. Worthless." Releasing a deep breath, I collapsed into the chair, leaned forward, and put my cheeks in my hands. I took a few more breaths, the last coming more easily than the first.

Freud sat quietly.

"He's alive, Freud. He's alive, probably hurt, and he's wondering where the fuck I am, why I've abandoned him." I rubbed my forehead with my finger tips. "He deserves better than this."

Freud watched me, I guess waiting to see if I was finished, then stood, reached over, and gripped my shoulder. He shook me gently, then backed up and sat on the floor by the *Playboy* magazines. He rested his arms on his knees and cleared his throat. "I made a pass down the Da Krong valley today. We had a little time between resupply missions. I figured I'd work west from the Ba Long, one valley at a time, just in case."

From behind my palms, I squeezed my eyes shut. I'd screwed up again, accused the wrong guy. Then I pictured the Da Krong valley, a bad place, and a long way by foot from the Ba Long. No reason for them to be there in the first place or for Bill to go there after a crash. Freud was grasping at straws, but at least he was doing something. "Look, Freud…I'm…I'm feeling all kinds of things here. Mostly I'm feeling…failure. If you can help me figure this out, find Bill, then I'm all ears. Lay it on me."

"Ross…" He leaned over and flicked some sand off the toe of his boot. "Look, I'll keep searching for Bill every chance I get, but listen. There's more to this than finding Bill. He's one issue. Your welfare is important too. I'd like to see both of you come out of this okay."

"I'm okay, damn it. It's Bill that needs help. And it's Angus and the Marine Corps and this fucked-up war that aren't okay."

"Well, I'm not defending Angus or the Marine Corps or the war; I'm trying to help *you*, help you put it in perspective, so you don't blame yourself."

I shook my head and crossed my arms. "Damn. Why do I feel like the next thing you're going to say is, 'Don't sweat the small shit?' Is that it?"

"No. That's not it at all. Losing Bill and Rod is not small shit. But it's out of our control. That's the point. Don't let things that are out of your control destroy you."

My hands dropped. "But we do have some control, damn it. We don't have to just sit back and accept this. How many times in history has the world been changed by people who kept going, kept trying to change things after others had given up and accepted the status quo? Sheep do that, damn it. Not Marines."

"Well, I think you may have hit on the problem now. We are Marines and we've been taught to do impossible things, meet impossible standards. In a sense, we've been set up for failure."

"How the hell do you figure that? Marines aren't failures."

"No, of course not, not by any normal criteria. But consider the Marine Corps standards, our creed, our traditions. Consider the code of conduct for Marines in combat: 'Marines don't leave their dead or wounded comrades on the field,' 'Marines will do anything to accomplish the mission, even charge into certain death,' 'Marines will do anything to save their buddies, even fall on live grenades.' These are impossible standards—illogical, irrational standards. Maybe one guy in a thousand can meet those standards and survive while the rest of the survivors are doomed to feel like failures, guilty."

"But enough guys have met those standards to keep our country free. It works." I leaned back. "Anyhow, I didn't join the Corps looking for low standards."

"Yes, it works. It's effective. And if we were actually defending the United States of America, if the gooks were in the wire on the beaches of California or the Carolinas and we were fighting a black-or-white, live-or-die war with the survival of our society on the line, then placing black-or-white, illogical and irrational standards on our country's finest young men would be necessary and worth the price. Laying a guilt trip on thousands of Marines who did the best they could, but still left one Marine on the field, or had the good sense to jump out of the foxhole instead of falling on a live grenade, would be an acceptable price to pay to save our society. But that's not the case, man. This war is London-fog gray—thick, murky; and contrary to what our lying politicians have told us, this war has nothing to do with saving the United States of America."

He ran his fingers through his hair: light brown, thinning, longer than regulation, but he got away with it. "So here we are, brain-washed with black-or-white standards and fighting a London-fog war, solid gray. There is no black, no white, just solid depressing gray. It's not worth it, man. We're squandering our finest—getting them killed or maimed or laying guilt trips on them—for some worthless politician's ego. Just isn't worth it."

"Well, the damn war may be gray, but Bill's life isn't. His survival is a black-or-white issue if I've ever seen one. And right now, as we speak, he's out there wondering where the Marine Corps is in his hour of need." I thumped my chest. "Where *I* am in his hour of need."

"Shit, Ross. Haven't you been listening to me? It's not your fault, man. You didn't lose Bill. Don't waste yourself on some guilt trip." He paused. "Guilt, Ross, is a disease that will destroy you. Hey."

I looked up from the desk and found Freud looking at me, firmly. "What?"

"Your father was killed in Korea, right?"

"Right. So what?"

"You were—"

"Eight."

"Eight. And you had a younger sister?"

"Yeah, and a brother on the way—miscarriage."

"Oh, I didn't know about the brother. Sorry. Where's the sister now?"

"Don't know."

"Hasn't written?"

"Hasn't written, hasn't talked, been…three years."

"Something happen between you two?"

"Yeah, you might say that—she trusted me and I let her down." I leaned forward. "Look, man, I've got enough to worry about without dragging this one out of the closet. What's done is done."

"Well, I won't push it if you don't want me to, but it sounds like it would help you to talk about it. You know, if we get this one behind us, the rest could fall into place too."

"I don't want help, damn it."

"What did your father say to you before he left for Korea? His last words."

I looked away. "I don't remember."

"I'll bet you do. You're seeing him off. Family there?"

"Of course." Once again the scene re-appeared—vague, like an incomplete watercolor.

"And what did he say?"

"A lot of things. To all of us."

"But what did he say to you? Be a good boy?"

"No."

"No? What then?"

The scene sharpened: my family, the concrete, the airplane. "He didn't talk to me. He talked with my mother—house stuff, who to call for medical, etcetera. He didn't even look at me, he…"

The scene shook, then roared. The transport's starboard engine rumbled to life and blue smoke drifted by us, toxic, like being behind a bus. After that it was too loud to hear what he said…until he kissed my mother and sister goodby and ordered me—yes, he ordered me—"Come here, Tiger"—to go with him. Looking up at him, I stretched my legs to get in step. He was six foot two. I always wanted to be that tall.

"Well?"

I stared at the floor, close-mouthed. Marine cargo flight. My father was the only passenger. At the airplane he had me climb the ladder to the door while he stood on the concrete. When I reached eye level, he leaned into my face and I tensed, not knowing what he expected, not wanting to disappoint him.

Sighing, I remembered the smell of his Old Spice aftershave and tobacco breath, remembered how the bright sunlight glinting off the white fuselage hurt my eyes. And I felt it again—the fear, my stomach drawn up in knots. Standing on that ladder at attention, my lower lip trembling, I was ready to cry and scared to death I would. That would have crushed my father—having a crybaby for a kid. What a disappointment. Marines don't cry. Then he gave me my orders. I heard his words. Again.

"Well?" Freud said.

"Well nothing." I folded my hands over my belly button and massaged my burning gut.

"He didn't say anything?"

"Yeah. He said a few things. Personal things."

"You don't want to tell me?"

"No. You don't have a need to know."

"I do if I'm going to help you understand why you feel guilty about Bill when nobody else does."

I snapped my head up and stretched toward him. "I feel guilty about Bill because I'm the only one who promised his wife I'd take care of him. And maybe because I'm the only one who feels like a Marine, any Marine, is my brother."

"Ross, did you promise your father anything?"

I banged my hand on the desk. "Hell, yes. He was my father. He told me to promise him something and I did."

"What?"

"None of your business." The promise was bold in my memory now, as well as the feeling—how my chest tightened, my throat swelled. Standing on that ladder, I just wanted to please, not to disappoint.

"Ross, you remember Jimmy, my radio operator on Russell?"

"Yeah." I massaged my gut again. Burning. Damn, it hurt.

"Well, before Jimmy, I had a young kid named Miguel, a Puerto Rican-American from New York." He laughed. "Actually, he'd be ticked if he heard me say it that way. He told me one time he was *American* of Puerto Rican descent—American first. He said he'd been to Puerto Rico and that was not his country. America was his country. Proud kid. He was the oldest of six children. Father died when he was twelve, pneumonia. His father told him on his deathbed to take good care of his brothers and sisters. He did, for as long as he could. Finally after working two jobs, one before and one after school, he dropped out and joined the Corps the day he turned seventeen. He sent every penny he made back home. Great kid." He paused.

"Well, what happened? And what's this got to do with me?"

"I'm getting to that." He shifted on the floor. "Well, Miguel had been a point man in a rifle platoon. Good man. Reliable. Conscientious—the type that ends up with the most dangerous and demanding jobs. Anyhow, he got burned out—too many ambushes, too many close calls, too many buddies killed and wounded. He took it all personally, as if he should have kept them all alive. He got shaky, hollow-eyed, couldn't eat.

"Finally, his platoon leader saw what was happening and found him another job, with me. The next day, the new point man was killed. Miguel never got over it. No matter what I said, he was convinced it was his fault. Miguel stayed with me for no more than a month, then went back to his platoon. A week later he was badly wounded in a fire-fight—suicidal charge on a fortified position. Guilt is debilitating, Ross. It warps your mind. It destroys. I saw it in Miguel. I see it in you. You don't have to tell me what your father said. I know. It was something like, 'Take care of your mother and sister for me. You're the man of the house now. I'm counting on you.'"

I stiffened. Exactly. Practically word for word.

"I'm right, aren't I? I can see it."

"So, what if you're right? What if he said that? What's that got to do with Bill?"

"You are not Bill's keeper, and yet you *feel* like you're Bill's keeper. You're one of those conscientious types, you were born that way. Then your environment, your childhood, reinforced that trait, built on it, developed it until you got so eaten up with responsibility that now you no longer have any perspective on what's really your responsibility and what isn't. I don't care what you promised your father. You were not responsible for your mother. She was an adult. She was responsible for herself. You weren't responsible for your sister. Your mother gave birth to that child; that was her responsibility. And you sure as hell weren't responsible for that fetus. You were not a man. You were not a Marine. You were *eight years old*, Ross. A child!"

"You don't know shit, Freud. I *was* responsible. Especially for my sister."

"Bullshit. I don't even know the story, but I know, just by knowing you, that you were not responsible."

"I was."

"Convince me."

I looked up at him. He sat there, studying me, head cocked to one side, eyebrows raised. Smug son-of-a-bitch. I knew he was goading me, but...what the hell. Maybe it was time to talk about it. I leaned forward again. "Okay, but I swear, Freud, if you ever—"

"Hey, man. I'm a professional. Please."

"Okay." I pointed at him. "But I'm warning you—"

He held his palm to me, shaking it. "No problem. Tell me what happened."

I dropped my hand and cleared my throat, listening for signs of life in the hall. Nothing. I started slowly, thinking back. "My ah...senior year, Sally, my sister, had been buggin' me about coming to the university for one of our fraternity parties. Football weekend. Big deal. So, I finally agreed. I got my girlfriend to set her up at the dorm, got her a date with one of our pledges, a freshman that I didn't know very well, but seemed okay, and I went home to get her. Anyhow, the game was great, the party was goin' good, and Sally was having fun. She's a much more outgoing person than I am. Well, I didn't usually drink. As you so smugly pointed out, I was the responsible one, always trying to be a good example to my fraternity brothers. So...with Sally there, I guess I wanted to play the role, the macho fraternity man, you know, show my little sister how grown up I was. I ah...I decided to loosen up. My girlfriend and I hit the beer keg and kinda lost track of Sally and her date. When the party was over Sally was gone, but I didn't notice. I'd passed out. Haven't seen her since."

"Well, what happened? Why?"

"I don't know. All I know is the pledge said he had her back to the dorm at twelve o'clock. The party was still going, but as a pledge he had to get back and clean up. My date said when she and another girl got back to the dorm, Sally wasn't there. Supposedly someone saw Sally on the dorm fire escape around 12:30, leaving. There was a guy, just a shadow really, in the trees waiting on her, like it was planned." I shook my head. "My mother said Sally got home on a bus, just before daylight. She stayed in the shower for most of the morning, then left." My eyes dropped to my hands. Thoughts of my mother's voice on the phone, sobbing, hysterical, stopped me. My eyes watered, as they did every time I thought of her crying, and I recalled how helpless I felt, how...guilty.

"Ross...was she raped?"

I sighed. "I guess. We don't know. I got rid of that damn pledge, black-balled his ass. Shit, I even feel guilty about that. The records at the dorm said she was back by midnight and the guys said the pledge was back at the house cleaning up. He probably had nothing to do with it. It was my fault."

"I disagree. And you haven't spoken with her since?"

"Nope. She finally called my mother, but wouldn't tell her where she was. My mother was frantic. Cried for weeks. Sally calls her about three times a year now, I guess. Takes my mother about two days to get over each call."

"Your mother let her go to this party? Gave her blessings?"

"Oh yeah. Told me to take care of her, that she trusted me."

"She didn't tell your sister to take care of herself, that she was responsible for her own behavior?"

"No. Said listen to your brother." I hung my head. "Me, Ross, the party animal."

"Ross, when you were seventeen, who did your mother tell to take care of you?"

"Well, nobody. I took care of myself."

"Was your sister impaired in any way, mentally retarded?"

"Shit no. She's bright. Smarter than I am for sure."

"Then why couldn't she take care of herself the way you did?"

"Because…well, because she's a girl, I guess."

"Girls can't tell right from wrong? Safe from dangerous?"

"No. I mean yes. Sure they can."

"So, if Sally was capable of knowing right from wrong, safe from dangerous, and smart enough to take care of herself, why are you beating yourself to death over this? Doesn't it follow that if she got into trouble, it was her fault, or the pledge's fault, or anybody's fault but yours?"

"Wrong. She depended on me. She heard me promise my mother I'd look out for her. That took the monkey off her back and put it on mine. She was there to have fun, not sweat the small shit. That was my job. And I failed."

"I'm going to have to start calling you Miguel. You are determined to condemn yourself." He pointed his finger at me and made a jabbing motion. "Now, listen up. I didn't spend two summers in a VA hospital listening to survivor-guilt stories for nothing. I know some shit about guilt and I know some shit about psychology and personality. You're a hard case, but common. Hear that? Your story is *common*. I've heard it over and over. You may think you're the only one to have things like this happen in your life, but you're wrong. It happens every day. And every day good people like you destroy themselves over things that are out of their control."

He paused, looked at the wall, and back to me. "Okay, here it is." Freud was getting worked up, his breathing rapid. He leaned toward me. "Your father had no business telling you to take care of the family. That's absurd. You didn't have the power to take care of the family. Giving someone a responsibility without giving them the power to carry out that responsibility is stupid. And another thing. Children believe everything their parents tell them. Literally. Until they've been out in the world long enough to understand the nuances of jest, ridicule, humor, satire, exaggeration etcetera, they are vulnerable to literal interpretation of whatever the parent says. For example: If the parent says the grandmother doesn't love the child because the grandmother only visits once a year, then that's a fact—grandmother doesn't love the child. If the parent says the grandmother *does* love the child, and offers as evidence the fact that grandmother visits them every year, then that's a fact—grandmother loves the child. The physical evidence is the same, one visit a year, but one child is loved by their grandmother and one isn't because of what they are told.

"Now, your sister. Teaching children responsibility is good, but teaching one and not the others is a mistake, a common mistake. And, believe me, the younger siblings resent it when it's done. They resent it and they get even. I think your sister unconsciously set you up, Ross. People do amazing things, or rather their subconscious does amazing things on their behalf. In my experienced professional opinion, she resented the fact that you were always the leader, Mr. Responsibility, and she was always the little sister, forced to follow you and do what you said. She had a mind of her own and she wanted to use it. Mom and Dad, then Mom, wouldn't let her. Did she ever get you into trouble when you were kids?"

I swallowed, facing him. Freud was on a roll, and his words were hitting home like darts in a bulls-eye. "Sure. All the time."

"Okay. If something happened that night after the party, it was the culmination of well-meaning but misplaced parenting and poor judgement on the part of a seventeen-year-old girl who may subconsciously have been trying to prove that her brother wasn't capable of taking care of her, and she should be given the responsibility and the mandate by her mother to take care of herself. She hurt herself to hurt you and your mother, to punish you. Notice how effective that punishment was."

"Why didn't she just say something?"

"She doesn't understand it herself. She has no idea. The subconscious is a powerful force, Ross. It's programmed without us being aware of it, and it takes action without us being conscious of it. Accidents are not always accidents. Fate is not always fate. The human mind is deeper than we know or understand."

I sat quietly, looking at my lap. I wanted to believe. I felt the weight on my shoulders shift, but not fall. Almost as if I wouldn't let it fall. Didn't dare.

He glanced toward the doorway. "Let me try to wrap this up for you, then chew on it awhile and get back to me. Okay?"

"Yeah...okay."

"Okay. Because of your genetic disposition toward responsibility, you soaked up the responsibility given to you in childhood, your environment. You feel toward Bill the same out-of-balance sense of responsibility you feel toward your mother and sister. You're predisposed to and conditioned to worry about stuff you can't control. In addition to that you are a judgmental person, naturally, born to it. You see and identify right from wrong, good from bad, beneficial from harmful before 90% of your peers. Your environment also built on that trait. I'm willing to bet there was a person close to you, probably your mother or grandmother, that was critical or judgmental of others. 'He shouldn't do that.' 'She shouldn't be that way,' etcetera. And that's not all bad. I mean, shit, where would we be without judges, or safety inspectors, or engineers—people who can tell right from wrong, safe from unsafe, efficient from inefficient? But, when it begins to dominate you, get out of balance, then it's a problem. You lose perspective. Everything becomes black or white. No gray. See the parallel here? Your genes and your environment prepared you for a society of black-or-white issues when in fact they're mostly gray. The Corps prepared you for a black-or-white war then sent you to the London fog of 'Nam. You've felt like you've failed your family and now you feel like you've failed a Marine—Bill."

He pointed a finger at me. "You're too hard on yourself, Ross. Your type always is. Carl Tess is like that. Hell, Major Hardy is like that. You guys are never satisfied with yourselves. Good is not good enough, excellent is not excellent enough; you've got to be 'outstanding' at everything or you're a failure. I suspect your family promoted that attitude and I know damn well the Marine Corps, your current family, does. Like I said earlier, the Marine Corps says these are our standards, and if you don't meet these impossible standards, you're not a good Marine, you've failed, and here's the kicker: You're guilty. See? There's that word again. Listen—" His eyes widened. "I remember, when I was at The Basic School, I read the *Marine Corps Officer's Guide* from cover to cover. I came across quotes like, 'And remember: whenever the Marine Corps is impoverished by the death of a tradition, *you* are generally to blame.' Did you ever read that book?"

"Cover to cover."

He smiled. "I thought so. You know how it should be done, Ross. You know what makes a good Marine and what doesn't—instinctively you know." He paused, made a fist, then thumped it on his knee. "I'll bet Angus is driving you nuts."

"You know damn well he is. He's screwing up my Marine Corps on my watch. He's 'impoverishing the traditions,' or whatever. And hell, Freud, guys like Walt Duppont, the academy man, just go along with it, let him lower the standards for awards, for leadership. I can't stand it."

"Well, back to what I said before. Don't get wrapped around your rotorhead over things you can't control. That quote I just gave you didn't ask you to control the colonels and majors. It just asked you to control what you could. You can't control Angus. You can't control Walt. And remember this too: This is Angus' Marine Corps as well. Just like your mother is your sister's mother as well. If your sister wants to screw up your mother's life then so be it; that's not your problem or within your control. She has the right to make your mother miserable if your mother lets her. Angus has a right to screw up the Marine Corps if the Marine Corps allows it. They promoted his ass, not you."

"Yeah, they did. And we're the ones who are suffering for it—not the assholes who promoted him."

"Well, it's possible they just made a flawed decision while doing the best they could in a flawed system."

"Then fix the fucking system, man! What the hell are generals for?"

"Okay, okay. Enough. I'm not about to defend our generals. That would be like trying to defend our politicians—very damn difficult and beyond the scope of my training."

"Well just tell me this: If you can dissect my persona so well, then tell me why Angus is such a prick. Explain the Bull to me."

He smiled and folded his arms over his knees. "Well, funny you should ask. I've been trying to figure him out ever since I got back from Russell. I don't have a concrete diagnosis yet, not ready to claim success, but at least I've arrived at a possible hypothesis, a 'working hypothesis,' if you will." He cleared his throat. "Angus…is a bully."

"Well, no shit, Sigmund. A bully. Why didn't I think of that?"

Freud chuckled. "Well, maybe I've over-simplified the answer. I'll try again." He scooted his buttocks closer to the wall and crossed his legs Indian-style. "Angus, as I touched on earlier, like all of us, is a product of his genes and/or his environment. There are various schools of thought as to which is more important, or even if both play a role, but those are the two basic theories. In other words, most professionals generally agree that you are what you are, but what you are can be modified or shaped by your environment. Okay?"

"Most? Generally? Doesn't sound like you guys can make up your minds."

"Well, no. It's kinda like the way we Huey-gun drivers argue over the best way to cover the 46s. Probably a lot of ways will get the job done. There isn't a single best way."

"Yeah there is."

He shook his head, smiling. "There you go again. What'd I tell you about that black-or-white routine?"

I laughed. "Okay, there may be more than one way. But…maybe not."

"Shit, Ross. I'm not giving up on you, man. You're gonna see some gray in this world before I'm through with you, somehow, someway."

"'Maybe.' I said 'maybe,' didn't I? That's some gray."

"Okay, a tinge of gray there." He chuckled and looked at the floor. "Anyhow, people are predisposed to some behavior patterns: some selfish, some generous, some leaders, some followers, some confident, some not, some accepting, some judgmental—" He looked up. "Like Ross Teemer."

"Hey, enough already."

He grinned. "Okay. Now, Angus' behavior, the bullying. The bullying suggests Angus is not a naturally self-confident person. So if he were raised in an environment that belittled him, made him feel inadequate—and usually guilt is involved here also; that is, people like that feel guilty because they're inadequate, or think they're inadequate—then yes, his lack of self-confidence would be a problem. But not the major problem. The big one, the feeling that pushes people over the edge, is a lack of love. If that were the case—if he were made to feel small, inadequate, *and* unloved—then he would need to build a defense against those things to be a functioning adult. For one thing, he would give up on being loved, and develop ways of replacing love with a substitute: respect."

I thought about the newspaper article I found in Angus' ceramic bull. The article only mentioned one son. Apparently that was all the admiral wanted to acknowledge. Angus knew who his father was, so someone must have told him. His mother?

"Ross, you with me?"

"Yeah, just thinking."

"Okay, the bully needs respect to replace the love he feels he doesn't deserve or can't get. He gets respect by creating fear in others, intimidation. It's a poor substitute, but effective."

"And what better place to intimidate people than the Marine Corps."

"Exactly. The boy is in his element. He's a functioning adult in this environment."

"You saying Angus was born to be a bully?"

"No, not at all. He may have been born to have trouble with self-confidence, but in the proper environment, self-confidence may have never been a problem, never a factor."

"How proper?"

He looked at me, his head tilted a degree to one side. "Why? You know something?"

"I know a little bit, plus I've heard some other stuff." I shifted in my seat. "Okay, Mr. Shrink, let's say patient A is the illegitimate son of a very successful man, a professional in a macho, aggressive profession. Let's say the father never acknowledges the son. The son grows up in a bad neighborhood with a difficult stepfather. What's the result?"

"The result isn't certain."

"Shit, Freud, don't go leather couch on me now. Do we end up with Angus, or don't we?"

"Depends on the mother, maybe even the grandmother. Maybe others. But the mother is a big factor."

"Well, I don't know a thing about his mother. What would she be like to get an Angus?"

"Well, with all the other environmental factors you mentioned, if a given mother was strong, high self-esteem, confident—which she probably wasn't based on the scenario you've given me—then the child could be fine, loved and felt loved."

"But?"

"But if she wasn't, if she felt sorry for herself, reminded the child of his father's rejection, reminded the child of how mistreated they were by the father, by society, by the school system—whatever—then the child would grow up feeling unloved, unworthy, and that the world was against him." He smiled. "Mothers and grandmothers are incredibly powerful creatures in the life of a male child. They can make 'em, they can break 'em."

I pressed on. Something was taking shape. "Would he go through life trying to prove he was worthy of his father's love?"

"Maybe. Or at least prove he was worthy of his father's respect."

Damn. Maybe all that medal stuff wasn't just for promotion. Maybe he was after the big one, the Medal Of Honor. That would top the half-brother, that would get him in the papers. "Freud, how possessed can these Angus types get?"

Freud stood, brushed the seat of his flightsuit, and reached for his survival vest. "You mean, Patient A? To what lengths will he go?"

"Yeah."

"Well." He threw the vest over his shoulder and stepped to the doorway. "It's hard to say. Depending on the individual, it's possible he could go all the way to self-destruction."

Heavy boots crunched toward us from the hallway, long strides.

Freud glanced out the door. "You've got company, Ross, and I've got to go. See you back at the hootch."

As Freud disappeared, a gruff voice in the hall greeted him with, "Good evening, sir."

A second later, Morchesski stopped in the doorway—a manila folder in one hand, a starched cover in the other. He glanced after Freud, looked at me, and tapped the folder with his cover. "Stand-the-fuck-by, Lieutenant. You're not going to believe this shit."

29

One Lousy Transport

The information Morchesski brought back from Da Nang completed the puzzle, at least the puzzle as I knew it.

Later that night, after Morchesski and I had finished comparing information and playing "What if," I arrived at our hootch at the same time as the next day's flight schedule. Jim and I were scheduled for morning guns; Freud and Ripkevic would be our wingman.

I took the schedule to Jim's space and we talked about looking for Bill. Then I told him about Morchesski and the last message, the one that had sent him to Da Nang. As Jim sat at his desk, I explained how Morchesski had used his NCO connections in Da Nang to go over the files at Wing G-2 and 1st Force Recon and how he'd found copies of the messages Angus had taken from our files; how he'd picked their brains for related information and gotten the rest of the puzzle. Jim knew NCOs ran the Marine Corps and wasn't surprised Morchesski could get information Tess or I couldn't.

I explained that Angus didn't have the last message, the one that sent Morchesski to Da Nang, because Angus had been forced to RON at Quang Tri due to weather. I explained that all the messages Angus had taken from the files dealt with one subject and one geographic area. I got to our conclusions: The lights reported in the Ta Bang valley two months ago weren't from target balloons, the rotor sounds reported around Khe Sanh and Fang last month weren't from our helicopters, and the next day could be the day Lieutenant Colonel Richard P. Angus, rejected son of Admiral Richard Nunnally, set himself up for the Medal of Honor and his father's recognition by winning the first helicopter air-to-air engagement in history.

I waited for Jim's reaction. He shrugged, his square jaw set. "We'll run our missions, then search for Bill and Rod," he said. "Let Angus do whatever he thinks he has to do."

"Okay," I said, and for the time being, I let it go. Even though I thought we should at least get Angus on the radio and warn him, I could see the other side too. I mean, how hard could it be to shoot down one NVA helicopter? Probably be easy with two Huey gunships on your side, especially when one of them was armed with an M-21 mini-gun that fires 6000 rounds a minute. Even easier if the target were an MI-4 "Hound," a 1950s helicopter with performance similar to our old H-19, a predecessor to the H-34, and armed with door guns only. A piece of cake, a slam-dunk, even for a fighter pilot who wasn't.

But just in case, just to make it even easier, Angus had a radar site just above Khe Sanh on Hill 950, a site we now knew could track low-flying helicopters as well as moving trucks and troops. And the radar came complete with a Green Beret who liked Angus' Scotch. The Green Beret could use his radio monitoring and interpreting skills to tell Angus in advance which day the Hound would make its run, and on that day, give him a call when the Hound crossed the DMZ and made its dash down the Ta Bang valley at sundown for the French prison and "abandoned" French airfield in Laos, north of Co Roc—the Hound's destination.

To set it up, to make it happen, Angus had gotten himself scheduled for Thunder Clap every other day and afternoon guns on the days in between—probably so he could check in with his man on the hill often and be in the area every evening. That's when we figured it would happen, at dusk, and only one day a month—usually in the third week when the messages had suggested the Hound's logistics and high-priority medevac run was scheduled. With everything in place, including a hand-picked and hand-trained crew and wingman who would write Angus up for anything he asked, Angus could pounce on the unsuspecting Hound and get the kill—maybe not a Medal Of Honor, but certainly a Navy Cross and his name in the headlines. The admiral was a reader, wasn't he?

Angus was a reader. He hadn't read the last message though, and that was why I had a problem with Jim's "let him do what he has to do" position. The message said a recon team from the 101st Airborne had found a Soviet-made North Vietnamese helicopter in the DMZ just northwest of the Tiger Tooth at the head of the Ta Bang valley. The wrecked helicopter, a victim of bad weather or mechanical failure, had been there a month or more. No bodies, no weapons. But there was a problem: this Soviet-made helicopter wasn't an MI-4 with light door guns. It was an MI-8, a single-rotor helicopter as big as our CH-46. Fast. And the door-gun mount suggested a larger gun, a 12.7mm, or at least a .51 caliber similar to the .50s on our 46s.

Angus' kill wasn't going to be so easy after all. But the Bull didn't know that. The Bull was looking for a sure thing, the same old MI-4 they'd been using since 1965 when he first discovered their existence while working at Wing G-2 in Da Nang. Then the NVA logistic and high-priority medevac run was just a single component in a plan under development for Angus. The key component, four years later, would be an assignment to the only Marine squadron in Vietnam that would give him the weapon and the opportunity to make history—HML-467, "Hardball," Huey guns with the TAT-101 chin turret and the Thunder Clap mission. Too bad the TAT was a piece of junk. He'd scrounge a better system, the M-21, and congratulate himself for his ingenuity. Angus was armed and on the mission of a lifetime: win the admiral's respect—make headlines.

With Jim's lack of concern, I returned to my space, but later, after thinking it over, I came back and asked him to at least discuss it with Freud. In our flip-flops and underwear, we walked to Freud's space and told him the story.

"Not our problem," Freud said, looking up from his paperback, his camouflage poncho-liner tucked under his bare arms. "Besides, if what Morchesski's report says about the MI-8 is true, the damn thing can outrun his ass—Angus'll be left sucking wind and out of range."

Jim sat backwards in a folding chair, his arms resting on the seat back, quiet.

"But if we're right," I said, my foot propped on the end of Freud's rack, "if this really is what he's up to, then shouldn't we tell him, shouldn't we find him tomorrow and tell him what he's up against?" It sounded strange to hear myself defend Angus. I guess I was trying to do the right thing again, the black-or-white thing. Freud was thinking gray.

"Listen, Ross—" Freud snapped off his words. The book was *Lolita*. Maybe he was at the good part and resented our interruption. Or maybe he was frustrated because he thought he had me straightened out and now I was showing signs of regression. He flopped the book onto his stomach. "Angus' personality type doesn't handle being helped very well. It's insulting to them. It reinforces what they secretly think about themselves—that they're incompetent and worthless. Forget it."

Freud flipped the book to his face and focused on the words.

I waited a second to make sure he had said all he was going to say, then looked at Jim. "Jim, how 'bout it? You sure you don't want to tell Angus what he's up against?"

Jim stroked his mustache and watched Freud read a few more lines. Finally, with a grunt, he stood, grabbed his chair by the seat back, and tilted it onto its front legs. "He's right, Ross. Even if you and Morchesski have got this thing figured out and Angus really is going to run into an MI-8 instead of an MI-4, Angus wouldn't thank us for telling him. And I'll bet it wouldn't change his plans either—he'd lose face if he did that." He lifted the chair and walked across the aisle. I followed as he turned and pointed a finger at me. "But on the other hand, if you're wrong and we go to him talking about messages, MI-4s, 8s, well, he'll see it as a bunch of lieutenants looking over his shoulder—an insult. He'll have our ass."

Jim placed the chair by his ammo-box desk and propped one foot on the seat. "You said the MI-8 is delivering mail and passengers to the French prison and airfield in Laos, right? Then extracting medevacs—colonels, generals, stuff like that?"

"That's what Morchesski was told in Da Nang. They've never been able to pinpoint when or by what route before, never really cared. They've just monitored the French prison with SOG teams to check on what was coming in and what was going out."

"But Angus knows."

"Yeah, I guess he's the only one that wanted to know. With all those messages together—all those sightings, sounds, radio intercepts—it's pretty obvious they're using the Khe Sanh plateau as a shortcut, and they've been doing it regularly, for years."

"Well, if wing doesn't care, why should we?"

I shrugged. "I don't know."

"I don't either. Look." He leaned toward me over the chair back. "This MI-8 is trying to get from point A to point B. He's not looking for a fight. He'll see Angus and haul ass, lose him. We're really at more risk by telling Angus we know about it than Angus is by finding an MI-8 instead of an MI-4."

I nodded.

"Besides, if two Marine gunships can't handle one lousy troop transport, they don't deserve wings. Imagine how pissed those crews would be if we suggested they couldn't hack it."

I nodded again, and that was where we left it.

30

Cheap Shot

Early the next morning, in the dark, Jim and I walked down the main road to the mess hall. I'd reluctantly agreed with him the night before, but now I was sure he was right. Telling Angus what we knew was a no-win deal.

I blew into my cold hands, raised the zipper on my leather flight jacket, and felt a fresh bounce in my stride. The stars were out and the air was crisp and clear. A break in the monsoon could be an omen; this could be the day I found Bill.

In the brilliant starlight, Jim smiled, probably thinking of Carol. She almost had an assignment to Quang Tri the week before but it hadn't happened—cancelled at the last minute.

We walked on, caught in the headlights of a passing jeep.

My grounding had ended, but so had my status as a HAC. Art-the-fart and Hoss Horsnyder would get their HAC checks and pass me by. Angus had spoken: I would never make HAC again as long as he was in the squadron. As his coronation as commanding officer was the next Friday, I was looking at another six months as a co-pilot. That was a downer, but I remembered what Freud had said about worrying over stuff I couldn't control and forced a bounce into my step. This too would pass.

Beside me, Jim took a deep breath, walked through a puddle, and sighed long and loud. I grinned. The boy had it bad—love sickus extremus.

Lovesick or not, he was still the best pilot in the squadron and I felt lucky to be flying with him. Plus we were on a mission that would allow us some free time to search for Bill, morning guns. And as of late last night, I had a plan. We turned off the road and walked toward the smell of fried bacon.

An hour later, I met Corporal Cobb at our Huey. Cobb, a rugged farm kid from Ohio with small eyes, thick skin, and straight, almost bristle-like brown hair, had everything but clean underwear stuffed under the troopseat. He said the next time he got shot down he was going to be ready. He had extra gun barrels, cleaning kits, a case of frag grenades, a case of smoke grenades, an M-16 with eight full magazines taped two together, an M-79 with HE, gas, and smoke rounds, a machete, pop-up flares, two claymore mines, four canteens of water, and a case of C-rations. He even showed me a pair of high-top tennis shoes he'd dyed black. Said those steel-toed flight boots were too heavy in the mud—couldn't run, couldn't swim. The first thing he was going to do next time was change shoes.

Scapelli arrived late, diddy-bopping out of the darkness, an M-60 balanced on his shoulder. I wasn't surprised it was him. The crew members needed five hours of flight time a month to get flight pay. As of the day before, Scapelli had zero for October. I didn't get a chance to ask him if he'd seen the last message or talked with Morchesski.

In the next revetment, Sergeant Whipple and a gunner I didn't recognize armed Freud's Huey.

At 0615, Jim squeezed the start trigger, and by 0630 I had the controls and was taxiing out of the fuel pits, skipping the skids along the steel matting.

Departing Phu Bai, we flew along the Perfume River past Hue, then cruised at 500 feet along the east side of Highway One. To our right, the sun, a shimmering orange ball, broke from the South China Sea and lit the thin gray clouds to the west. The clouds stretched over black mountains, mountains humped like dark sea serpents, and followed them north. I paused. Bill was out there somewhere, probably still in darkness.

Freud's Huey suddenly dropped between our Huey and my view to the west, three rotor-diameters away, the gun barrels and rocket pod glistening in the sun and the anti-collision light flashing red against a purple sky. The Huey's position lights also flashed at me, a ground signal that should have been changed to steady bright at takeoff. Freud wasn't sweating the small shit. He wasn't in position either—should have been at seven to eight o'clock, not nine.

"4-3, Dash Two on fox." It was Freud, a lightness to his voice, coy.

"Go ahead, Two."

"Hey, man. Come up ADF."

Jim grinned. "Roger."

I reached beside me and flicked my ADF mixer switch. Jim did the same, then turned the tuning knob to change the static in our ear phones to the clear sound of the Armed Forces Radio Station…and the Beatles.

I glanced over my right shoulder and saw Cobb reach to the overhead, to his switches, and smile.

"Hey, 4-3. How 'bout a join-up?" Freud again.

Looking across me, Jim clicked his mike twice.

Freud, his hand on the window edge, rose with his Huey and disappeared above and behind us. Rip had the controls.

Their Huey reappeared on our right side, settling like a cruising mallard into a perfect parade position, four o'clock, and silhouetted against the huge orange sun. Smooth. The position lights on steady bright.

Now together above the rice paddies, flying in the soft morning air, we listened to John, Paul, George and Ringo, and I banked the Huey lazily to their rhythm, to their gentle chant, their da-da-da das.

Just beyond our cabin doorway, Rip banked with me. I grinned and swelled against my straps. We were one: the Ripper, the Beatles, and me. And Jim, smiling behind his lip mike.

In the cabin, on the troopseat, Cobb and Scapelli swayed with us—their hands in the air like witnesses at a tent-camp revival. They made the peace sign with their fingers and Scapelli, already wearing his aviator shades—his white teeth glowing in the darkened cabin—pointed at Freud's Huey.

Freud's crew members, Whipple and his gunner, rode the air above and beside us, framed by their cabin doorway, two synchronized black silhouettes with large rounded heads connected to the overhead by thick coiled wires. They swayed in rhythm with Cobb and Scapelli, with our banking Hueys, with the Beatles, and, with peace signs in the air, their lips moved to the words of the lieutenants' and junior enlisted men's favorite song, for some reason unannounced, unrecognized, but still understood as ours—"Hey Jude."

We continued that way for miles, flying together like two mechanical birds in a mating dance, warmed by the glare of the rising sun, and I smiled as the lyrics of Paul McCartney spoke encouragement to me. Another omen. On this day I would succeed. I would take a sad song and make it better. I would find Bill Catlett.

DASC had other plans.

With the Quang Tri air group and Huey gunship squadron busy packing to leave Vietnam, our flight of two was the only pair of Huey guns not already assigned to recon or medevac. DASC kept us busy.

By late morning we'd finished escorting a section of "Cattle Prod" CH-46s on resupply for the 2nd Battalion, 4th Marines operating north of the Rockpile. Then, because Vandy was shut down and being leveled by Marine engineers, we refueled at Quang Tri. Arriving back in the 4th Marines' area, DASC sent us to escort a section of "Magpie" 46s on a troop lift near the Khe Gio Bridge east of the Rockpile on Highway 9. After that we did a VR for a company of 4th Marines operating north of Helicopter Valley. We stayed busy, but it was quiet. No fire.

At 1310, DASC released us. Angus and Walt Duppont had already checked in on afternoon guns. Jim said we'd refuel at Quang Tri, then head west to look for Bill. Two days of wondering why Rod wanted cans of spray paint would pay off—I knew where to look.

While at idle in the fuel pits at Quang Tri, two of our gunships appeared, hovered off the runway, and landed by the fuel nozzles ahead of us. The closest Huey was stitched with at least a dozen holes—one through the pilot's door—but no one looked hurt. I held the controls while Jim hopped out, walked forward, and leaned into the pilot's window.

Jim returned with the co-pilot's green vinyl map packet—a Thunder Clap packet. After connecting his pig-tail mike cord, he held it out to me. "Akerman's bird is down. They left a team in deep shit. Ono's going to lead us back." I squeezed the cyclic between my knees and took the heavy packet with both hands. Jim put his hands on the controls. "I've got it."

For the second time that day, Jim took off and flew down the side of the runway near the medical facility, staring out his window, looking for a nurse we knew. Later, we joined two Army slicks and two Cobras, and headed west. Bill would have to wait.

Jim gave me the highlights en route. The story was fairly typical. I didn't know who thought up the missions for those recon guys, but the crazier the mission the more they seemed to like it—Green Beret and Marine. This one involved inserting a twelve-man "dragon" team using Army Hueys (no ARVN H-34s) near a rest stop on the Ho Chi Minh Trail. They were to assault the unsuspecting rest stop at night, snatch one of the rest-stop managers and be picked up in the morning with their prisoner. Contrary to their usual mission, this time they were going in looking for a fight. Unfortunately, a fight found them first.

Put into a one-bird LZ by two Hueys, one at a time, the second bird had lifted when the lead element of the team triggered an ambush. The team immediately called for an extract. The Huey pilot heard their call and aborted his takeoff, but in sliding backwards into the zone, he caught his tail rotor on the ground and spun in. That closed the LZ.

With no place for a pick-up bird to land and a fire-fight in progress, Akerman tried to cover the team and Huey crew as they moved downhill toward the alternate LZ. That's when he got stitched and immediately lost his radios. Ono took over. As Beagle, the O-2 spotter airplane, called for the Air Force A-1Es from Thailand, Ono had the Spikes, the Cobras, cover the team on the ground while he and the remaining slicks escorted Akerman to Quang Tri. The Cobras, faster than the Hueys, were to return to Quang Tri for fuel after the A-1s arrived to help Beagle cover the team. "Magnet Ass" Akerman landed with no radios, a shattered altimeter, and low transmission oil pressure.

Akerman had told Jim we should get back to the team about the time the team got to the alternate LZ. That was *if* they had successfully broken contact from the ambush. He figured we were thirty-five minutes away.

Using the grid coordinates and maps Jim gave me, I found the team's location. It was well into Laos, north of the DMZ and west of the North Vietnamese border, an area known as "the Karst." I'd been there a couple of times before. Laotian Route 92, mostly invisible, snaked through it.

The Karst was a combination of limestone sinkholes, ridges, and steep spikes. Some spikes, like 500-foot limestone apartment buildings, jutted straight out of the valley floor. Hollowed out, and covered in moss and ferns, the spikes were the garages, storage areas, and shelters for the NVA troops and vehicles moving south—impossible to attack from the air. I got butterflies in my stomach just thinking about it.

On the way out, we passed over the Rockpile, the Gurka Valley, and across the bottom of the Ta Bang valley. The Tiger Tooth appeared off to our right and Khe Sanh off to the left, too far to the left to check out my theory on Bill and Rod. I wanted to ask Jim to swing closer, but I knew what he'd say, and I agreed. Our mission was to get that team out of Laos. Other things, including Bill and Rod, would have to wait.

Five minutes across the border, we flew under a 3000 foot layer of broken cumulus clouds. Beneath the clouds, haze and smoke reduced our visibility to five miles. On the horizon, we could see an occasional flash of yellow on the ground and black smoke from burning napalm, then twice, the flash of silver as an A-1's wing caught a shaft of sunlight. My crisp clear day had deteriorated in more ways than one.

Once in the area, we learned the team had to move across a valley and uphill to reach the LZ, but they had broken contact. At Ono's request, Beagle made a low pass to mark the zone—an old slash-and-burn clearing on the side of a mountain bordering the Karst. Too steep for the Hueys to put more than one skid on the ground, it could at least handle both birds at once.

Twenty minutes later, when the exhausted team and downed crew crumpled to the ground on the edge of the clearing, Ono took control. As the slicks made their low-level approach along the slope, Ono had the Cobras fire half of their fleshette rockets—2.75-inch warheads packed with a hundred steel darts—into the trees on the three sides of the LZ around the team, a preemptive strike against another ambush.

After the edge of the jungle leaped into the air from the last salvo of fleshettes—the air now thick with splinters and dust—the slicks flew through the debris and settled into a one-skid hover. Ono and Jim and I were right on their butts. Freud was supposed to be on our six to cover us, but he ended up high and sucked out of position.

It didn't matter.

As the team and crew scrambled aboard, the one gooner who opposed the landing was blown away by the door gunner in the second slick—no hits, no sweat, a shit-sandwich that wasn't. One more tense orbit around the LZ and we departed.

Amazed it had been that easy, I took a deep breath and put my TAT away. Maybe we could check out the Khe Sanh runway on the way back. I checked the fuel. Five hundred pounds. Maybe not.

"Jim?"

Hunched over the controls, his lip mike pressed up under his mustache, Jim kept his eyes on Ono and keyed his mike. "Yeah."

"How 'bout a low pass down the Khe Sanh runway on the way back?"

"What?"

"Got a plan."

"No. Your last plan cost me a flightsuit."

I laughed. "Yeah, but it found you a Coke Angel too."

"True enough, but the answer's still no. Let's get these guys back to the FOB. If they don't need us again, we'll come back."

I figured that's what he'd say. Didn't hurt to ask though.

"What kind of plan you got, anyhow?"

Ah. I grinned. "Well, you know that gaudy-ass Army unit symbol on the runway at Khe Sanh?"

"Yeah."

"Well, if it shows signs of being erased by spray paint, then I'm right—Bill and Rod have been there. We search there and the route they would have taken to and from there."

"Huh?" Jim looked at me. "They'd be that stupid?"

I shrugged. "You know 'em as well as I do."

Jim looked at Ono's Huey and crinkled the corners of his eyes. "Yeah," he said, "I guess so. They'd do that."

Thirty minutes later, released by DASC, we sat at idle in the fuel pits at Quang Tri.

Once refueled, Ono taxied toward HML-667's old flight line to pick up Akerman and his crew. The lance corporal on our fuel nozzle turned his back to the rotor wash from Ono's Huey as it taxied by, and held out a clipboard for Cobb to sign.

A minute later, our blades back at flying RPM with everyone aboard, Cobb plugged in. "Lieutenant Teach," he said, his words rushed.

"Yeah."

"Got some news."

"What's that?"

I finished the takeoff checklist, listening in.

"The guy in the pits, the lance corporal?"

"Yeah?"

"Well, he said the medevac package had just refueled here. Said the 46 crew chief said they'd picked up a guy about three or four clicks southwest of the Rockpile. A pilot he said. Spotted him in the river. Just happened to fly over him en route to somewhere."

Jim and I looked at each other.

"Alive?" Jim said.

"Yes, sir."

"Name? Unit?"

"Don't know, sir. Said they took him to Lima Med."

I stabbed my finger at the long tin-roofed building in the distance. "Check complete, man. Let's go."

"We're liftin'!"

A minute later Freud landed with us in a field beside the helo pad at Lima Med. Jim shut down the Huey as I unstrapped. I kicked the collective stick trying to get out, then nearly choked myself on my bullet bouncer trying to get it over my head. I kept telling myself it might not be him. Wrong place. Could be some jet jockey who punched out and landed in the river. Could be anybody. Needed to check it out fast, though. If it wasn't him, we were wastin' daylight.

I was the first one to the door. I stepped into a white hallway with office doors on both sides and large double doors at the end. A Marine in utilities sat at the desk to my left.

The Marine raised his hand as I walked past him. "Sorry, sir. You can't come in here."

Jim came through the door behind me.

I glanced at Jim and stepped to the Marine's desk. "You receive a Marine pilot here a little while ago?"

The Marine glanced at Jim, and down to a clipboard on the desk. "Yes, sir."

Freud and Rip stepped inside the door and crowded behind us.

The Marine glanced down the hall and blinked. "Please, sirs. I can't let you beyond this point without approval from a doctor."

I leaned toward him. "I just want his name and condition, Marine. Can you do that?"

"Yes, sir, if you'll—"

"Jim?" The voice—soft, with a thrill around the edges—came from down the hall.

Jim leaned backward and looked around me. "Carol!" He pushed me against the desk with one hand, pushed Rip toward the far wall with the other and as if parting a curtain, stepped between us. "You're...you're here!"

She shut a door behind her and turned toward us. She wore green—a surgical gown, a surgical mask, and had blood on her gloved hands and sleeves. But the eyes. The blue eyes were Carol. No doubt.

"You got my message. Thank goodness." She reached up and pulled the mask to her neck. Big smile.

Jim hesitated. "What message?"

"I sent a message over to the Marine helicopter guys here," she said, peeling off her gloves, tossing them into a waste can along the wall, walking toward us, "ah…air group, or—"

"Whoa." I reached over and grabbed Jim by the sleeve. "We're here to find Bill, remember? Otherwise we need to press on." I probably pulled on his sleeve harder than I meant to, but Jim didn't seem to care.

He cleared his throat, never taking his eyes off Carol. "Carol—" They were face to face now, Jim's hands hovering in front of his pistol belt, hesitating, as if he wanted to touch her but didn't know if he should. "Did they bring in a Marine pilot a little while ago—maybe a big guy, freckles, mustache?"

Carol grinned. "Yeah. Cat's Ass." She smiled at the rest of us. "I was leaning over him getting some leeches off his chest when he opened his eyes for the first time. His lips and tongue were swollen so I can't be sure, but I think he said something like, 'Hi, I'm Cat's Ass, Marine pilot, how do you like me so far?'" She laughed. "You guys know him?"

I stepped up beside Jim. "Darn right we know him. Can we see him?"

We could. He was behind the double doors, on a white bed in a long row of white beds, and along a white wall with windows and white curtains. Air-conditioned. Jim and I went in together. Freud and Rip waited with the Marine at the desk. I took one look and stopped breathing. Four rows of beds, half of them occupied, occupied by men in casts and bandages, men missing limbs, missing faces; tubes hanging above them, below them, fluids clear or colored, flowing in or flowing out; the hum of machines beside them, clicking sounds, a smell of Lysol disinfectant—a scene forever stitched, taped, and plastered in my memory. We followed Carol to Bill's side. He was asleep. He was whole. I breathed again.

His thin arms, streaked with scabs and splotched with red welts, lay outside the top sheet—his bare chest beneath it. From the inside of his left arm a tube of clear fluid entered his body. His neck was small, not Bill-like at all, with more scratches and welts, and pale. His beard, ragged, auburn colored, was almost as thick as his mustache. Eye lids swollen and closed. Only one tube. He looked good.

Carol took the clipboard from the foot of his bed and scanned the information clipped to it. "He's got dysentery, dehydration, cellulitis, and a slight fever, but otherwise he's okay. You can have him back in a week or so."

Jim put his arm on my shoulder. "You really want this guy back?"

I looked at Bill and nodded, thinking I could now, finally, write Laura the letter I'd been waiting to write. "Yeah. I want him back." I turned to Jim, grinning. "You really don't want him here harassing Carol, do you?"

"No. Definitely not."

"Well, okay."

Carol stood at the foot of the bed, the clipboard pressed to her chest. I looked at her. "Carol, you may not remember me from the *Repose*. I was the dirty one. I'm Ross."

"Aw geez, Carol, I'm sorry." Jim hung his head and held his hand out to me. "Carol, this is Ross Teemer. Ross, Carol."

Carol put those big eyes on me and nodded, smiling. "Hi."

"Hi. Look, I...I really appreciate you letting us in here. Bill's been a friend for a long time, and...well, anyhow, he's a good friend, good guy." I looked at Jim and back to Carol. "Anyhow, I was wondering if...if I could just kinda stay here with him a minute. You know. Maybe you guys could go get a cup of coffee or something." I smiled and winked at her. "Okay?"

Jim looked at Carol. "Yeah. Good idea. Can he do that?"

Carol let her arms fall to her sides and looked up at Jim. Her eyes were unbelievable, sky-blue jewels radiating warmth. "Sure."

Carol pulled a chair over for me, eased the clipboard into its tray on the footboard, then the two of them walked toward the front. As the doors swung shut behind them, a voice whispered, "Hey, R.T. What the fuck? Over."

I turned.

Bill looked up at me through reddened eyes. He tried to smile, but grimaced. Sores in the corners of his mouth.

I yanked the chair to his side and sat. "Hey, asshole. Can't say I'm surprised to find you skatin' around in some air-conditioned hootch full of soft racks and pretty women."

"Yeah. Some shit, huh?"

"How ya doin'?"

"Doin' fine, man. How do I look?"

"You look like shit."

"Yeah? Nah, man. The Cat's Ass can't look like shit. Impossible." He reached up and stroked his gaunt face with a trembling hand. "Just need a shave, that's all."

I chuckled. "Yeah. My mistake. You look great, man. You look great."

He tried to smile again. "Yeah. I do. I look great."

We sat silently for a few seconds, then Bill closed his eyes, opened them again, and looked at the ceiling tiles. "Rod didn't make it, Ross. The son-of-a-bitch quit on me."

"You don't have to talk about this now if you don't want to. I can wait."

"No. Hand me that water will you?"

I held a glass of water by his mouth and helped him get to the straw. He took three short pulls and dropped his head back onto the pillow. "I had him. He was alive. He could have made it, but the fucker quit on me. Damn, Ross." Tears pooled in his eyes.

"Hey. It's okay. If he didn't make it, he didn't make it. It's okay."

"He could have made it, man. He could have."

"It's okay."

Bill turned his head and squeezed his eyes shut. He took short rapid breaths as the tears ran into his beard. I waited. His breathing slowed. Finally he rubbed his cheek on the pillow and turned his head to me. "You know that fuckin' Army pukin' symbol on the runway at Khe Sanh?"

"Yeah." I smiled.

"Well, Rod decided for his first HAC hop he wanted to do something special. He talked me into going out there with him to paint over that fucker."

"Talked you into it, huh?"

"Yeah." Bill tried to smile again then grimaced in pain. "Okay. So he didn't have to do a lot of talking." He pointed a thin finger at me. "That's Marine Corps property, goddamn it." His hand settled to the sheet on his chest. "I'm glad we did it, or tried to do it. Shit. Rod was glad too. He told me so before he died." He looked at the ceiling again and sighed. "I may try it again."

I started to say something, but decided to let it go.

"Ross?" He still looked at the ceiling.

"Yeah."

"We were shot down by a helicopter, man."

I eased forward, catching myself with my hands on my knees. "What?"

"Yeah. There were two of 'em. Big fuckers—as big as a 46."

"Two of 'em? You sure?"

He turned to look at me. "Hell yeah, I'm sure. It was almost dark, but I saw 'em."

"Well…how? What happened?"

"Let me have another sip of water. I'm dry as a bone."

I held the glass for him again. A nurse walked by in a white uniform, several folders in her hand, sour expression. Bill swallowed, and sighed. "We were on the runway. Rod had given me the controls. Facing runway heading…northwest, I think. The sun was gone, overcast, about a 2000-foot ceiling but the clouds still had some light."

"You're in the left seat?"

"Yeah. Rod was digging in his helmet bag for the paint; I was looking out my window to the west. It was eerie, man. That Khe Sanh is a spooky place."

"Yeah, I know. The helicopters. You saw them coming?"

"Yeah." Bill coughed, and cleared his throat. "They were southwest of us, near Highway 9. You know where Fang is?"

"Yeah."

"Well, they were passing Fang when I saw them. At first I thought they were 46s. I remember thinking, Damn, they see us. Hope there isn't a major in that flight." He tried to laugh, then coughed again.

"So they spotted you right away?"

"Yeah. Almost like they knew where to look."

"No shit? Then what?"

"Well, one more glance told me they weren't 46s. They were wide like a 46, but only had one rotor. Anyhow, I wrapped on the throttle and yelled at Rod. He dropped the paint cans and buckled up as I pulled pitch, hauled ass.

"I took off on their heading, maybe due north, trying to keep whatever separation we had. I got to the base of Hill 950 and tried to cut the corner into the Gurka Valley, thinking they wouldn't chase me once I got that far. Was gonna head for the Rockpile. Anyhow, I was barely into the turn when the tracers went by and we got waxed, or hammered. That's what it sounded like anyhow. Big hammers."

"See the guns?"

"No, they just looked like transports to me. Had door guns of course. I remember that from the first look—another reason why I thought they were 46s, looked like .50s in the doors." He motioned for more water and I got it for him.

I checked my watch. 1615. "How bad were you hit? Could you still fly?"

He took another sip and swallowed. "It was like instant engine failure, man—zap, no more engine noise. I got into an autorotation. Chased the big needle at first, then realized the little needle was the rotor needle and it was in the green." He chuckled, coughed, and cleared his throat. "Anyhow. Did the auto into what I thought was some tall grass, pretty dark. Good auto, man—zero ground speed, level skids, swish." He shook his head. "No grass. Those trees sucked us up like a rock hitting a pond. Lights out."

"But you were okay?"

"Yeah. Pretty much. Rod had taken a round across his shoulder, right at the tip of the shoulder joint. And his insides were fucked up, forgot to lock his harness. Anyhow, I had a kneecap out of joint and a gash on my leg. I got the knee unfucked, but it swelled on me. Neither of us could move around very well for a while."

"Stayed with the bird?"

"Yeah. No choice really. Couldn't move."

"Radios?"

"The FM was crushed in the crash." He paused a second as if considering his next words. "Ross. This is just between me and you, right?"

"Sure."

"Well, Rod had left his survival radio in the pouch on his bullet bouncer, and left his bullet bouncer in the cabin. Slick hop, right? What can happen?"

"Lost in the crash?"

"Yeah."

"And yours?"

"In my survival vest."

"Which was?"

"Hanging on the back of my armored seat."

"Lost in the crash?"

"No. Swung up and around my neck. Nearly knocked me out."

"Well?"

"The battery was dead."

"Battery was dead. Small shit. Getting your battery checked on schedule is small shit, Bill. Don't sweat it."

"Funny."

I shook my head. "Sorry. Couldn't help myself."

"Well, I knew no one had seen us, 950 was socked in, no Marines in the area. I knew no one knew where we'd gone. I knew the next day that no one could see the wreckage if they were looking for us. So, I concentrated on getting us ready to move on our own." He coughed again, more forcefully that time. Perspiration showed on his forehead.

"Look, Bill. Maybe we better do this later." I held the glass for him again. "I'll get you a fresh glass of water and check back with you. Okay?"

He took a sip and closed his eyes as he swallowed. The swelling was brutal—like he'd been the main course at a mosquito convention. "Yeah. Good idea, man." He opened his eyes and held out a trembling hand to me. I took it and he squeezed. Not a handshake. A squeeze. "Thanks, Ross. Thanks."

"No problem, Cat. I'll be back." I set his hand by his side and pushed the chair away. I got his water from a fountain in the corner, then left through the double doors thinking of those MI-8s. Angus was in way over his head.

I passed Jim and Carol in the first office, a makeshift staff lounge with a small table and four chairs. Freud and Rip rose from their chairs in the hall and walked toward me.

"How is he?" Rip asked.

"He's okay. Be a hundred percent in a couple of weeks."

"Rod?" Freud asked.

"Dead from internal injuries and a shoulder wound."

"Wound?"

"Yeah. We need to talk. Just a minute." I stepped back to the doorway of the lounge and knocked. They held hands across the table. Jim looked at me, saw me tilt my head back, and stood, patting her hand as he let go.

"What's up?" he said, joining us just outside the door.

"Bill and Rod were shot down."

"So?"

"They were shot down by MI-8s armed with .50s."

"What? You sure?"

"I'm sure. Angus is up shit creek, guys. He's gonna blunder into *two* MI-8s, and they're fighters, not runners."

Freud forked his fingers through his thin hair and leaned into the circle. "So-the-fuck-what, Ross? He started this shit. It's his problem."

I leaned into his face. "I don't give a shit about Angus, Freud. If he were by himself in his piss-ant A-4 or his make-believe F-8, I'd say, 'Go for it, and excuse me while I cheer for the North Vietnamese.' But he's not! He's about to get Droopy and the Irish and a few other good guys in a three-layered shit-sandwich."

Freud leaned right back at me, his voice raised. "Still not our problem, damn it. They'll handle it!"

I stood erect, sighed, and looked at Jim.

Jim leaned against the wall, one arm across his chest, the other hand stroking his mustache. His brow wrinkled. "You sure? Two of 'em?"

"Yes, two of 'em. They ran him down, chased him into the Gurka Valley, and shot his butt out of the sky. They're fast. They're aggressive." I crossed my arms. "Look, if we do this right, and it's a false alarm, Angus'll never know we were there. If it isn't, then maybe we'll be at the right place at the right time and save a few good Marines."

"Or get our asses wasted." Freud scoffed. "Have you considered that?"

"No, I haven't. Is that the damn gray area I'm always missing?"

"Yeah. Maybe it is. Listen to me, damn it. Pay attention here. What you're suggesting is not reasonable. You want to endanger our lives in an unauthorized and unnecessary mission. I think you're letting emotion take over. I think you just want revenge for what they did to Bill and Rod."

"I want—"

"Hold it." It was Jim. He looked at me. "You got a plan?"

"Well, yeah. Sorta."

"Sorta?" Freud tossed his hands in the air and turned away. "Sorta? A sorta plan?"

Jim persisted, quietly. "What's the plan?"

I scratched at my mustache. "Well, I figure Angus thinks he'll intercept his 'MI-4' just below the DMZ, north of Khe Sanh, somewhere near his Green Beret buddy on Hill 950. So, we come up Highway 9 to the south edge of the Khe Sanh plateau about twilight—" I checked my watch. 1635. We would need to leave in the next 15 minutes. "—from there we'll be able to see what happens and help if needed or duck back down Highway 9 if not."

Freud turned his face into mine. "And what if we are needed, Einstein? Do we arm our imaginary 20mm cannons, go to imaginary burner, and pretend we're in F-4s? These guys are faster and they have bigger guns. Doesn't that spell 'suicide mission' to you? You want to die to get a prick like Angus out of trouble?"

Jim held up his hand again. "Hold it." He turned to Rip. "How do you feel about this?"

Rip shrugged his broad shoulders. He looked like a swimmer, body shaped like a wedge. "I'm flying with Freud, so I guess I'll do whatever he says, but..."

"But what?" Jim asked.

"Well, I'd hate to see something happen to Droopy and Rinkes and Sergeant Earley...and the Irish. You know. Maybe Angus is about to fuck up some good guys. Course, maybe he'll skate too. False alarm. I don't know."

Meanwhile I'd been thinking. Maybe Freud was right. Maybe my emotions were taking over for my good sense. I really was pissed about Bill. I could feel the blood going to my ears every time I visualized those two MI-8s hosing down an unarmed Huey. Cheap shot. I hated cheap shots. But it could have been the Marine training talking too. Or even Coach Day. Whatever it was, or whoever it was, had a strong message and it was getting through.

Jim continued, turning to Freud. "Whipple's guns are usually bore-sighted good. You haven't fired any today, have you?"

"No."

"We haven't either. Better clean 'em good anyhow, and fast."

Freud slapped his palms against the side of his head. "What? You're going to do this?"

"Yeah, I'm going to do this. With Angus and Walt we'll have them outnumbered four to two and we'll have surprise on our side. Besides, we're Marines and they aren't. Let's go."

31

Balls of Fire

Jim led us past the front desk and stopped. He turned toward the lounge.

I passed him and held the door open as the others filed out, Freud mumbling, the scalp beneath his thin forelocks bright pink.

Carol stood in the hall, close enough to have overheard. Hands to her mouth, eyes wide, she blinked as Jim jogged to her, then she raised her hands as he stopped and lifted her into his arms and onto her toes and hugged her, hugged without hesitation, without doubt—as though it had always been that way. Carol clung to him, pressing her cheek into his and squeezing her arms behind his neck, eyes closed, lips trembling.

He whispered and she nodded, rocking her chin into his shoulder. Then she opened her eyes and looked up at him as he let her down slowly, slipping his hands into hers. He whispered to her again, she whispered back, and he walked away. I followed him out the door and down the steps.

Jogging with Jim across the steel matting of the helo pad, I looked to the west. The weather was still good, a broken layer of puffy rose-tinted cumulus clouds at three to four thousand feet, sky hazy, but at least three to five miles visibility. And I had another idea.

As we left the matting, Freud was waiting for us. Forehead glistening in the light of the setting sun, he pulled Jim aside and stood in his face. I kept jogging, up to where Cobb and Scapelli sat on the edge of the deck of our Huey.

Cobb stood first. "Which one is it, Lieutenant? I figured it must be one of our guys or you wouldn't have stayed so long."

I stopped by the skid. "It's Lieutenant Catlett. He's okay—weak, dehydrated, but gonna be okay. Lieutenant Wysowski is dead."

"Oh. Sorry, 'bout Wysowski, sir."

Scapelli stood, dropped his cigarette into the sand, and rubbed it out with his boot. "I knew it was Lieutenant Catlett, sir. That guy's a survivor." He showed his white teeth in a smile. "Like me."

"Well, Mr. Survivor, I hope so 'cause we're about to go get the asshole that shot him down."

Scapelli's head dropped forward. "Say, what?"

"No shit, Lieutenant?" Cobb's eyes brightened.

"That's right. Let's get to work."

I told them the story and briefed them on what we were going to do while Cobb helped me clean the TAT and readjust the ammo links. Meanwhile, Scapelli cleaned and oiled the fixed guns. As we worked, Cobb pounded his fist on his knee and repeated, "Hot damn, hot damn." Scapelli just listened. Jim joined us in a few minutes and helped Scapelli finish the guns.

At 1655 Jim hit the start trigger. The compressor blades spun up, the igniters popped, and the little turbine engine roared to life. I rocked in my seat as the big rotor blades accelerated over my head, then I completed the checklist and keyed the ICS. "Jim, can I make a suggestion?"

Jim's easy movements and relaxed face made him appear buoyant, almost happy. He laughed. "Uh-oh. You're not going to blow yourself up again, are you? Maybe a diversionary technique?"

"Hope not. Once was enough. Listen, I think we should rearm, swap these HE heads for some of those Army fleshettes."

"Really?"

"Yeah. If we do end up in an air-to-air situation, we'll have shotgun rockets instead of these wayward bullet rockets. Granny says you're good with a shotgun."

He pulled the Huey to a hover, called Quang Tri tower, then air-taxied ahead to the matting and awaited clearance. "I was just going to use the fixed guns."

"Well, I'm just thinking ahead here, you know, just wondering. If…if we really do come up against an MI-8, then he can use his .50s on us long before we can get in range with our piss-ant little M-60s. Right?"

"Yeah. Guess so."

"Okay. Shock effect. You've heard of that, right? Like with tanks?"

"Yeah."

"Well, we get together, flight of two, parade, and if they turn on us, both of us fire a pod of fleshettes at them, seven shots each. You know, the first punch, the first hit. A couple of thousand steel darts flying into his face should screw up his sight picture pretty good. My football coach always said the first hit of the game on the guy across from you was the most important. Rattle him. Okay?"

Jim glanced at me, smiling, shook his head, then answered the tower's call and took off. Turning toward the Army rearming pit across the runway, he keyed his mike. "That's crazy enough to work, Ross. The problem is it's just going to be us, no wingman."

Jim was right—Freud didn't show. We departed Quang Tri as the sun dropped behind the mountains, alone. Freud had made a stand for the color gray. I couldn't believe he'd quit on us, but on the other hand, I had to admire his self-discipline; neither peer pressure, nor blind obedience to his leader was going to get him to do something he didn't feel was right. And legally, he was correct. We weren't exactly on an authorized, legal mission. The butterflies in my stomach took flight again.

"Ross, go squadron common fox and UHF." I made the switch as Jim leveled off at 2500 feet. Ten minutes later, Ca Lu, covered in shadows, slipped below us.

Jim had thought ahead as well. When we rearmed with fleshettes, he had Cobb leave all his excess weapons, ammunition, and grenades behind. Jim wanted us to be as light and fast as possible. He didn't plan on getting shot down and needing that stuff. I liked that.

At LZ Hawk, Jim climbed as high as he could and still be VFR. Our rotor blades scraped the clouds at 2900 feet, the broken layer now an overcast. Still nothing on the radios.

"Go Sea Legs squadron common UHF and the FOB radio relay FM we used today on Thunder Clap."

"Roger."

Jim turned north and I looked for Khe Sanh in the shadows on the plateau ahead. Hill 950, rising into the clouds, was beyond Khe Sanh and to the right. To our left, the sun had set. On the horizon, only a faint sliver of light and a few charcoal-fired clouds remained. Then Khe Sanh got to me again—a chill, goose bumps, a crawling in my skin. I pushed my window up, then remembered I might need the visibility. In an air-to-air engagement, the guy who spots the other guy first is usually the winner. Read that somewhere. I pulled the window back down.

Even if both of those MI-8s showed up again, we'd still have them three to two. Good odds. Well, good odds if we were together—Angus, Duppont, and us. Hadn't considered what we'd do if they caught Jim and me by ourselves, alone.

The hissing in the radios stopped, a faint voice called, "Two, go spread."

A faint reply, "Two, roger."

Jim looked at me, the clear visor in front of his eyes reflecting the instrument lights. "That's them."

Jim had guessed right. Angus and Walt were using the UHF frequency that had belonged to Sea Legs, the Huey squadron formerly at Quang Tri.

"Lights out, Ross. Set up guns, both sides."

"Guns?"

"Yeah, ah…yeah, guns."

"Roger." Guess he didn't like my plan for the rockets after all. I switched off the position lights and anti-collision light, then set up the switches and got my TAT sight down from the overhead. I cycled the arming switch to charge the guns, then changed my mind and put the sight away. I switched the TAT to fixed-forward. Jim would have six forward-firing guns now.

Jim rotated his ring-sight down from above his windscreen. "Okay Cobb, you and Scapelli keep your eyes moving back there, scan left, right, up and down. We're looking for our guys and we're looking for a Soviet-made helo the size of a 46. Give me a clock direction on anything you see, copy?"

"Yes, sir."

I looked over my shoulder at Scapelli. He sat on the edge of the troopseat, facing outboard, the legs of his flightsuit rippling in the slip stream and his face reflecting the pale light from the west—no smile, tight lips. He held the cross he wore on a gold chain in one hand and his M-60 grip in the other.

"Got him! I'm in!"

It was Angus. I leaned into my straps and tried to see him in the gray dusk ahead. Jim followed the river gorge behind Khe Sanh, our blades scraping the cloud base above us. Altitude. The guy on top first is usually the winner too.

"There they are." Jim calmly raised a gloved finger and pointed. "Eleven o'clock."

I saw them, three miles ahead, just as the Huey, probably Angus, opened fire. It looked weird. A steady stream of tracers poured from the M-21 on his right side, a rope of red-orange flame, while his left side and nose put out a thinner stream.

Brilliant in the semi-darkness, the tracers seemed to curve, missing their target. I could see it now, a big, serious-looking black helo, definitely not an MI-4 "Hound." It churned our way but would pass a mile off to our left, in a shallow right turn. Angus was in a hard left turn from an initial 90-degree intercept position, still firing, still missing short and not really in range. Losing ground. I couldn't see Walt.

The MI-8 suddenly fired back. Tracers, like glowing jade-green baseballs, reached across the sky and streamed beneath Angus' Huey—Droopy's Huey. Huge tracers. I squeezed my fists, waiting for the MI-8 gunner to adjust upward, just one twitch upward, one twitch would do it, couldn't miss. Angus stopped firing and broke away, climbing to his left, now just a faint shadow without the muzzle flashes from his guns lighting him. The green tracers followed him for a second, and stopped. I let out a breath.

More muzzle flashes, steady, another Huey, this one closer to us, two miles, ten o'clock low, his tracers reaching out ahead and under the MI-8, closer in. I figured it was Walt, in a left turn, another near 90-degree intercept.

Jim on ICS. "Just see one?"

"Yeah. One MI-8. Think that's Walt firing now."

"What happened to Angus?"

"He's running, sir. Heading down the Gurka Valley toward the Rockpile." Cobb.

The gun on the MI-8 erupted again, this time at Walt, balls of green fire pouring across the sky. Walt banked harder, closing, his red tracers seeming to curve around the green ones and down, arching past the big dark helicopter, both of them missing low, but Walt adjusting, now pulling the stream of his tracers up and into the front of the running helicopter, finding it. The explosion lit the sky like a bolt of lightning; flaming pieces of helicopter flew on, unpowered, separated again, and fell into the darkness. The stream of tracers from the doomed MI-8, cut short, arched harmlessly past Walt's turning Huey. I watched Walt's anti-collision light flash on and imagined him yelling at Kerrigan in celebration. I sucked in my breath and wanted to yell too. Man, what a sight.

Walt continued his turn toward us, our nine o'clock low, a half mile. I watched him, smiling, then blinked, wide-eyed, mouth open, stunned at the sight of more tracers—green, like a long thin frog's tongue reaching out in slow motion, coming from the semi-darkness to the southwest, behind and beside us, then sailing past Walt in a thin stream, adjusting left to right.

"Eight o'clock, eight o'clock!" Scapelli.

I spun my head past the faint gray light on the horizon and froze, gripping the sides of my seat. Not one but *two* of the ugliest damn helicopters I'd ever seen in my life—huge black monsters, protrusions like catfish whiskers on their nose, parade formation, dim position lights, one mile and closing, the leader pouring a stream of tracers right past us. I jerked back into the armored seat.

"Make me hot!" Jim threw us into a steep left turn, max torque. The Huey shuddered and dribbled us in our seats.

I flipped the master-arm switch. "You're hot, guns."

"No. Rockets."

"Roger, rockets." I shook my head as I changed the switches, puzzled, then realized he was avoiding continuous muzzle flashes by going to rockets—plus they weren't close enough yet. Damn close, but not close enough.

Jim snapped us wings-level. The grotesque pair of MI-8s were at twelve o'clock, slightly low, head-on, still firing at Walt. Jim squeezed, our Huey jerked and flaming rocket-motors leaped in front of me, one after another, dusting us in sparks, bathing us in brilliant yellow light. Blinded, I slammed my eyes shut, paused, then opened them in time to see faint puffs of smoke from the exploding fleshette heads. I imagined thousands of steel darts the size of construction nails forming a pattern as large as a drive-in movie screen flying at the MI-8s as the two helicopters scattered—one pilot yanked up, the other yanked right and down. Walt passed below us, sinking fast, lights out, maybe sparks in the cockpit but couldn't be sure. Still flying.

The lead MI-8, the one that broke upward, passed right through the bulk of the fleshettes. He wallowed, some pieces fell away, then he disappeared into the clouds.

Jim broke left, 100 knots, diving for the other MI-8. I found it in the shadows, a half mile ahead and 200 feet below us, rolling to its right, now yellow muzzle flashes from its fuselage. Several tracers, like headlights on speeding trains, ripped by us. A flash of light, we lurched, dust and flying plexiglass filled the cockpit, I snapped my eyes shut, was tossed in my straps, then slammed back into my seat. I cracked my eyes to find us diving at the ground.

I grabbed the controls and pulled. Jim was beating at flames by his side. Thin smoke swirled around me, the smell of scorched fabric burned my nose, and the MI-8 gunner suddenly appeared centered in my windscreen, now distracted, pulling his gun to my left as streaks of tracers—red tracers!—flew from behind us to beneath the MI-8. The MI-8 gunner fired at the tracer's source, muzzle flashes lighting his face, a Caucasian face—not Vietnamese.

The Huey pounded me, bouncing, 120 knots and slowing as I got the dive under control, now as close as I was going to get, 50 meters, the big MI-8 pulling away. I switched to fixed guns and pressed thumb to firing button, turning left to get my curving red stream of tracers ahead of him, then easing back to the right, leading him as if he were a wide receiver on a corner route, trying to hit him in full stride, muzzle-flashes from the TAT lighting my feet, ears deafened by the clatter of the guns.

Frantically, the MI-8 gunner pulled his gun back toward me, dragging the stream of tracers across the dark sky, but as the balls of fire reached me and streaked past, my rounds knocked him away from the gun and continued down the side of the helo, past the red star on the fuselage and into the fuel cells. The explosion lit the sky.

I pinched my eyes to slits and rolled right, peering at my instruments, looking for the artificial horizon, the RMI, turn-needle-ball, altimeter.

"Holy mother of God! You got him, you got him, you flamed that fucker!" Scapelli. I could hear Cobb screaming a war whoop and both of them pounding their feet on the deck.

"Hold it down, hold it down! There's another one out there somewhere. Not over, yet."

Still smelling burned fabric, I glanced at Jim. Slumped, he struggled to sit up straight, his left hand pressed into his upper right arm. The right side of his seat was scorched around the armored side panel and seat back.

"Jim, you okay?"

He nodded and flopped his helmeted head back against the seat, his face distorted.

I stayed in a right turn, climbing, looking for Angus, looking for the other MI-8.

"Five o'clock low!" Cobb.

I twisted to my right and saw it: position lights, an anti-collision light, and flying right at us. Angus? Walt? Another MI-8? "Hold your fire, Cobb, maybe one of ours, probably can't see us anyhow." I climbed for the black clouds above.

"4-3, this is Dash Two on guard. If you read, come up squadron common, over."

Freud? I leveled off at 2800 feet and switched to button six, squadron common. The bird with the lights on was still below us, turning to the east.

I called, "4-3 Dash Two, this is 4-3. If you read, flash a light, over."

"Roger." The position lights flashed.

Freud! "Tally-ho position lights."

"Affirmative."

"Where'd you come from? Was that you firing back there?"

"Hell, yeah, that was me. I missed, didn't I? What's your poz?"

"Just a minute." I switched on our position lights and anti-collision light. "I'm level 2800 feet, heading 0-3-0…your ten o'clock. And be advised there's at least one more of them out here somewhere, and listen…if he shows up again, I'm out of here, man, I'm doin' the actual IFR routine to Quang Tri. Copy?"

His position lights went to steady bright. "Copy that. We'll be right behind you. You're in sight."

"See anybody else? Walt? Angus?"

"Negative."

"Roger. I'll hold 0-3-0 'til you get joined up, rotator coming off again. Takin' my actual to Lima Med. And, hey…let your TAT operator fly, will ya?"

A different voice answered, "I'm already flying. No sweat."

"Good."

"I resent that." Freud's voice. "I save your sorry ass, and this is my payback? Insults? Hey, is the actual okay?"

"Yeah. Just an excuse to see that nurse again." I glanced at Jim. A weak smile, head shaking slowly, sitting tall.

"Roger that."

God, it was cold. I just realized I was soaked in perspiration, chilled. I reached to raise my window, but it was already up. I shivered, checking the gauges. Other than the golfball-size hole in the windscreen in front of Jim, everything looked okay. "Jim, you sure you're okay? Need the first-aid kit?"

Jim, his face twisted and pale in the glow of the instrument lights, took his hand off his arm, reached out to the cyclic stick with a wet glove, and squeezed the mike trigger. "I'm mostly just burned I think…maybe some gauze to help with the bleeding…Walt?"

"Don't know. Still flying the last time I saw him." I squeezed the mike trigger all the way in. "Two, go Sea Legs fox mike." I hadn't heard anything on the SOG FM freq so maybe Angus and Walt were on Sea Legs FM as well as their UHF.

"Two, switching…and we're aboard, right side."

I answered with two clicks and glanced through the cabin doorway. Rip was in a loose parade position. In our cabin, Cobb unzipped the first-aid kit. I started to reach for the FM control panel, but Jim reached out with his bloody glove and switched for me. A tone, then…

"—should have me in sight. Move it." It was Angus.

"Roger, sir, roger that, ah…got some lights now, sir. You're at the Rockpile, right, sir?" Kerrigan, little Kerrigan. Never seen him in a flightsuit that wasn't too big for him. His voice was strained.

"Yes, Rockpile, damn it. I just told you that. Right-hand turn, 2000 feet…say no electrical, just battery?"

"I guess so, sir. Just battery power."

"You guess so. That's great, Lieutenant—you 'guess so.' I'm goin' to Dong Ha at 90 knots. Put it down there. Rollin' out. You on board yet?"

"Negative, sir. Not yet."

"Shit!…Get on board, goddamn it!"

"Yes, sir. Almost there. We're nine o'clock, sir, 'bout two miles."

"Close enough. I'm rollin' out, heading east. Any casualties? Need a corpsman?"

"No, sir…I mean, yes, sir."

"Well, which is it, goddamn it?"

"Lieutenant Duppont, sir—" The voice was pinched now, pinched from fatigue, fear, or just plain anger. I'd known Kerrigan long enough to feel sure it wasn't fear. To me it sounded like barely bottled up, barely controlled Irish anger. "Lieutenant Duppont…*sir*…is dead."

32

The Decision

Another Friday, another parade. Maybe the last. With my leather jacket squeaking in protest, I leaned against the steel, rain-slicked revetment wall and wiped the mist from the face of my watch. 1615. Fifteen minutes to "Adjutant's Call."

Off to my left, across the wet flight line and behind the wooden pallet reviewing stand, a general-purpose tent stood beside the squadron building. Inside the tent, under a single bare light bulb, a full colonel, a couple of lieutenant colonels, and several majors gathered in a cigarette-smoke haze. Like politicians meeting to congratulate a newly elected member of their inner circle, the COs and XOs of the neighboring squadrons smiled, laughed, and shook hands with Mickey and Angus. In less than one hour, Lieutenant Colonel Richard P. "Bull" Angus, the man I'd seen abandon his wingman and run for his life three nights before over Khe Sanh, would officially be the new commanding officer of HML-467.

All the award write-ups from that night were in and Mickey couldn't stop smiling. According to those write-ups, Mickey's executive officer, a man he'd personally trained in the art of combat helicopter flying, Lieutenant Colonel Angus, "—while doing a visual reconnaissance in Quan Huong Hoa Province, was attacked by two heavily armed, determined, and hostile MI-8 North Vietnamese helicopters. In spite of deteriorating weather, darkness, and faced with an overwhelmingly superior force, and with total disregard for his own safety, Lieutenant Colonel Angus was steadfast and resolute and determined in his defense of his aircraft and his wingman." Then there was the usual crap about "bringing deadly and accurate fire to bear," and "in the finest traditions of the Naval Service," followed by, "recommended for the Navy Cross."

The key write-up had come from the Green Beret on Hill 950, the staff sergeant with one eyebrow. According to Kerrigan, the guy really was a radar and linguistics expert. He had identified the correct day for Angus, and when the time came, picked up the MI-8 on his radar and used his FM radio to tell Angus where it was. When the shooting stopped, Angus called him on the FM and told him Angus' version of what had happened. Hill 950 was in the clouds that night, so the staff sergeant never saw the fight, nor could he really tell what was happening on his little radar. But a deal is a deal, he really had enjoyed Angus' Scotch, so he wrote what Angus told him to write.

After the fight, Kerrigan said Angus had sequestered the crews at Dong Ha until he was satisfied they had the story straight. From there on, it was in the bag. When the write-up comes from the Army and your commanding officer wants to believe it, who among the ranks would say it ain't so? Who would call a lieutenant colonel a liar? Who wanted to be the next Carl Tess or the next Ross Teemer?

I sighed, crossed my arms, and watched the squadron gather two by two, forming platoons of young men in damp rain gear, some in leather flight jackets.

Directly in front of me, the officer's platoon took shape—a captain here, a few lieutenants there, most of them friends of mine and yet, lately, strangers.

Secrets breed strangers. Freud-the-shrink knew that. But Freud had said it had to be that way and Teach had agreed. Actually, after hearing Freud's argument the night we delivered Teach to the hospital, we all had agreed. What we'd done earlier, over the Khe Sanh plateau, what we'd seen, never happened. No one suggested we lie about it, but unless pointedly asked, Freud said we'd be better off if we pretended we hadn't been there. He felt sure Angus would never bring it up. He hadn't.

Ahead, Kerrigan and O'Connor, "The Irish," stepped into the ranks. While thanking Rip and me earlier, O'Connor had told us what Angus had really done over Khe Sanh: how he'd shit bricks when that MI-8 fired at him, how he'd turned and ran, and how he'd seen Walt get hit. He'd seen Teach scatter the MI-8s with our rockets and the second MI-8 explode too. Then he'd heard Freud use our call-sign on guard frequency. Angus knew.

I looked up as the mist thinned and a cold wet wind blew across us, ruffling the colors beside the empty reviewing stand. Turning up the fur collar on my flight jacket, I crossed my arms again. Overhead, the wispy clouds, a drifting gray ceiling, pressed down. Sighing, I thought of the letters I'd received from Major Hardy.

Major Hardy wanted me to save the write-ups we had done for the Army guys who had rescued us back in June, the write-ups Angus had trashed. "Be patient," he wrote. "The time will come." I'd also saved the write-ups Rip and I had done for the Dustoff guys. Angus had trashed those too.

I grunted and shifted shoulders against the cold steel of the revetment.

Across the matting, Captain Orndorff stepped onto the reviewing stand and stopped behind a plywood podium. He held his head as if reviewing the papers there, maybe rehearsing. Behind him, in the haze of the wrinkled tent, Mickey and Angus laughed at something said by our group commanding officer, the full colonel, the fighter pilot who commanded helicopters but couldn't fly them.

Behind me, from the runway 100 yards beyond the steel revetment wall, I heard the dull roar of reversing propellers— someone had beaten the weather and made the instrument approach. I scratched at my bare upper lip and figured it was the general. Angus had made everyone shave their mustache for him. Be a bummer if he didn't show.

I shook my head. The general had decided Richard P. Angus would command our squadron. Obviously, he hadn't asked for my opinion. Wouldn't accept it if offered. I could tell him though. The Marine Corps had taught me how to recognize a good leader. My father had taught me how to recognize a man of character. Wallace, my stepfather—the man who divorced my mother when I was fourteen so he could marry the daughter of a local judge—had taught me about losers. I had learned well. I could tell the general about the man he had chosen to be responsible for the lives of 200 mothers' sons. But he wouldn't ask. And even if he did, he wouldn't listen.

Walt wouldn't listen either, hadn't wanted the truth to interfere with his career. That night over Khe Sanh, Walt had died within seconds of being hit. Half the side of his head and all of his right leg below his knee were gone. His mother and father would have a Silver Star to hang by his photograph in the den. Their son was a hero; he had died supporting his leader's victorious attack against a larger, faster, superior Communist helicopter. A Marine lieutenant colonel had said so.

Kerrigan, O'Connor, Droopy, Earley—all good Marines, all had done what they had been ordered to do, so all would get a Distinguished Flying Cross. Droopy had told me his medal would never see the light of day, but I'd told him to wear it and wear it proudly—he'd earned it on earlier missions and it wasn't his fault the Marine Corps didn't have their priorities straight.

In front of me, Dewey Munzel and Warrant Officer Glazener, the old guy with the thick black-frame glasses, arrived to fill in the last rank. Munzel jumped into one of the beach-ball-sized puddles and splashed water over Hoss Horsnyder and J.P. Padgett—the guys on either side of him. Hoss, his white scar shining from his perpetually tanned face, snatched Munzel into a head-lock and held him while bare-lipped J.P. (my only consolation for the loss of my mustache was to see J.P. without his, a major improvement) held Munzel's arm behind his back and threatened to set fire to Munzel's hair with his cigarette. Munzel stomped on J.P.'s toes. Captain Cain, from the second rank, ordered

Hoss and J.P. to knock it off, then ordered Munzel up to the second rank, beside him. Bill was missing it. He enjoyed a crowd, and of course, he loved parades.

Everyone else looked forward to Friday evenings without the Mickey Mouse parade routine. Granny had said the first thing a new commanding officer did was change the things that made the command look like the last commanding officer's command. So most of us figured Angus would give up the parade and find some other form of entertainment. Shockley figured we'd have a "bull fight" every Friday evening. He said Angus would put a water buffalo in a ring, piss him off, then throw a South Vietnamese civilian into the ring to be gored. I could see that.

Granny also had said Angus had his friend at wing assign most of our frag orders for the day, our missions, to HML-567 at Marble Mountain. Angus wanted us to fill out the ranks—big show. I'd heard some of the guys in maintenance grumble about that, made them look bad to the maintenance guys at 567, as if our guys couldn't hack it, couldn't keep the birds flying. They were proud people. Unwise to suggest they couldn't hack it.

Freud was flying Thunder Clap, his first time as flight leader, and would miss the parade. He wasn't happy about the promotion. The night before, after a few beers, he'd said, "I joined the air wing for flight pay and a clean rack—not to get my ass shot off on some worthless Army mission—that kind of research I don't need."

Freud would do alright though. He liked to play the role of the liberal academic, but he was still a Marine, still as affected by Marine Corps training as the rest of us. After the fight over Khe Sanh, after we were back in our hootch, I had asked him why he'd followed us. He smiled and said, "Freudian slip. Won't happen again."

There was more to it than that. I'd asked Rip about it.

"Yeah, he changed his mind alright," Rip had said, "but first he had to give me his black-or-white speech, you know, Marine Corps codes and standards being unreasonable for anything but the most desperate situations. You heard it?" I nodded and he said, "I just listened for a while, then pointed out what I thought he'd overlooked." I asked him what that was and he said, "You guys. Before you guys left, it was pretty simple for Freud. The Marine Corps' code said 'go,' but the Marine Corps' orders said, 'don't go'—not our mission. He couldn't be faulted for not going. But once you guys left on your own, all that changed. Now both the code and the orders said 'go'—Freud was a wingman, and a wingman has standing orders to follow and protect his leader. Now he could be faulted for not going. Leaving his leader was a crime very few lieutenants in this squadron would forgive. That's all I had to say."

I'd said I was surprised Freud hadn't continued the argument, used another angle that would cover him. Rip had smiled and said, "You know, I think that damn Freud just plain wanted to go. He gives us all this high and mighty book talk, reasonable shit, but when you strip that away, you find a guy just like the rest of us; he wants to help. It's a human weakness I guess is how he sees it, but hell, he's human. Yeah, Freud wanted to go. I just stripped away all his educated excuses, then he made the human decision. Freud's okay. He can't fly for shit, but he's okay."

I'd thanked Rip again for coming to our rescue, for drawing the MI-8's fire, so I could get close enough to get my guns on him. He said no problem, he owed me one anyhow; the night he went down with Pyhr, the gooks were searching both sides of the river—not waiting on the medevac package from Quang Tri had saved his butt.

I smiled as I recalled the scene over Helicopter Valley and remembered the feeling of exhilaration and relief when I heard Dustoff say, "got three green river rats." All three of those "rats" were cleaned, dried, and in formation in front of me.

Another gust of wind blew across us and I lowered my head, touching the bill of my utility cover, proudly.

The wind abated, the mist thinned again, and our new major, the new operations officer, wearing a field jacket and a starched utility cover blocked like a blunt-nosed bullet—very uncool—walked toward us. The old Ops O, Major Lewis, the Elmer Fudd look-alike with the Bing Crosby pipe, would now be Angus' executive officer.

The new major was tall and heavy like a former football player gone soft: big head, fat hands. He stopped in front of the platoon and assumed a parade-rest position as platoon leader. His name was Biggerstaff, Dean Biggerstaff. The first words out of his mouth the week before, the day he checked in, had been, "Get a haircut, Lieutenant." He had addressed Ken Shockley. "Shit-Hot Shockley" later named him "Biggerprick," or "BP" for short. Shockley was on Thunder Clap too, wingman for Freud.

Carl Tess, banished from the squadron after his untimely revolution back in July, was not part of the parade—not invited, no longer in Vietnam anyhow. The original "bandaged lieutenant" had finished his thirteen-month tour two weeks before. None of us had gotten to see him off or even knew when he was leaving. One day Ono returned from a slick hop to Da Nang and said Tess was gone. I think Ono was disappointed. They had been close.

Ono, the last of the thirteen-month-tour guys, would leave Vietnam the next week. He'd received orders to Camp Pendleton. President Tricky Dick had finally made the Marines' tour the same as the Army's—twelve months.

That had worked out well for Jim Teach. Because his twelve months would end that week, he'd have another couple of days in the hospital at Quang Tri with Carol, then he'd be transferred to the Huey squadron at Camp Pendleton. His recovery would be followed by the Navy Hospital there.

Carol had been trying to get her orders changed from Norfolk to Camp Pendleton or San Diego. She had another month left on a six-month cruise. I'd seen them together only once since the first time, the day Bill was found. It was hard to tell who had it worse. They were like a couple of high-school kids, holding hands, brushing up against each other when they walked—embarrassing.

Bill had been doing fine. A couple of accounting types from the CIA who carried leather briefcases and wore wire-frame glasses had interviewed him about his experience. They told him not to say anything to anyone. Bill knew stuff that could help other downed pilots, but they wouldn't let him talk about it. What a way to fight a war— "We've met the enemy and he is us." Shit. Bill told me the story anyhow.

He said he and Rod had lived off of a single B-1 C-ration unit for a couple of days, then beetles, other bugs, and an occasional grub worm. Rod refused to eat the worms. Bill said he didn't want to try fish from the streams or anything that would mean exposing themselves, or make noise, or leave waste—a trail. His plan was to reconnoiter each move by daylight, then move at night. With no clearings or former fire bases in the valley, they had only the Rockpile as a destination, nine miles of jungle away.

They spent the first night at the crash site. The next day Bill went out alone, then returned in the afternoon. They made good time that evening, but did less and less as Rod got weaker and weaker. He died the eighteenth day. Bill figured it was pneumonia; it had rained for seventeen of the eighteen days and Rod had such a high fever he was convulsing. To avoid any burial signs or smells, Bill sunk Rod's body in a stream and covered him with rocks. A recovery team found the body a few days later, right where Bill had said it was.

I didn't have much time with Bill, had to get back to a slick mission, but I can't forget his summary: "We're losing this fucking war, Ross. They're out there by the thousands, man, truckloads of them. I saw lights and heard voices almost every night. They're everywhere." He'd also said he would never again be without fresh batteries for his radio. "Those assholes in flight equipment are going to get tired of looking at me," he said. "Tired of looking at 'us' you mean," I said. He had smiled. "Yeah, 'us.'"

The day after Bill was found, I got through to Laura on a MARS call. I'm still not sure how that worked, but it involved some HAM operators around the U.S. Somehow the military would patch in to a HAM operator who would patch in to a local telephone call. I woke her in the middle of the night and the call was garbled, but the message that Bill was alive and well got through. She sobbed, thanked me over and over, made me promise again to take care of myself, then our three minutes were up. I wrote her a long letter after the call.

I sighed as a hand-signal from Rip got my attention. I adjusted my cover, bounced off the revetment wall, and stepped toward the end of the second rank of the platoon.

Off to my left, down the mist-shrouded rows of Marines to the last platoon, PFC "Vegas" Scapelli had made airplanes out of his hands and was dog-fighting with them, telling the story one more time; how he had flown to the rescue of his friend Droopy and his friend Earley, saved them both. Not the official version, not Angus' version, but closer to the truth. I'd told Scapelli not to tell that story, but I couldn't stop him. He needed to tell it, especially the stern summary: Scapelli was a Marine, and Marines don't leave Marines.

I smiled and settled into a relaxed parade-rest beside Rip. The platoon quieted, all cigarettes out. Major Biggerstaff turned his broad face back to us, nodded, and returned his eyes to the front.

Across the flight line, on the muddy road leading past our squadron building, a jeep with a canvas roof bounced and swerved around the potholes disguised as puddles. With headlights illuminating the mist, the jeep left the road and turned toward us, toward the side of the tent. Inside the jeep, in shadows, a driver and four passengers rocked side-to-side, clinging to the seats and roof supports around them. The jeep ground through the soft sand and slowed.

A loud scratching sound jumped from the speakers behind the screens of the ready room. Visible under the lights in the ceiling, Adam Henstrom hunched over the record player. He stood erect and the scratchy recording of a bugler blowing "Adjutant's Call" rolled across the flight line and over our damp formation of Marines. In reply, Captain Orndorff, in wilting utilities, marched onto the steel matting, snapped to a halt in front of the reviewing stand, swelled his chest and commanded, "SQUADRON...AH-TENNN HUT!"

One hundred pairs of boots popped and one hundred pairs of eyes snapped to a straight ahead and locked position. Instant silence. My eyes, from the safety of the second rank, wandered to the jeep. Empty. The reviewing stand behind Orndorff was also empty. The seats beside the reviewing stand were filled with officers, their heads turned toward the tent.

Inside the hazy tent, in the glare of the light bulb, a general and a captain wearing the braid of a general's aide-de-camp halted in front of Mickey and Angus. Into the shadows stepped two men in civilian suits, white shirts, and ties. Angus and Mickey, their backs to us, held their covers and shook hands with the general.

"REPORT!" barked Orndorff.

I snapped my eyes to the front.

Turning his head toward Orndorff, Major Biggerstaff barked, "OFFICER'S PLATOON, ALL PRESENT OR ACCOUNTED FOR!" The Staff NCO, maintenance, and shop platoons all responded in order as the major returned his eyes to the front and mine wandered again.

The civilians were small and thin, one balding and one with thick dark curly hair—both bookish, like accountants. They had moved and were doing all the talking, their backs to us, one on either side of Angus who faced the general. The general was silent. Mickey, his New York Yankee cap rolled and gripped tightly in his hand, stood aside, out of the light.

On a fresh gust of wind, the mist turned horizontal to the steel matting and the colors fluttered, briefly, then fell limp as the breeze passed.

Orndoff swelled again. "PRE-SENT...ARMS!" Every right hand in the formation snapped to a salute. Orndorff, his shiny chin held high, did an about-face, snapped his hand to a salute, and froze. The words, "Sir, the parade is formed," never came. No Mickey. Silence.

From under the bill of my utility cover and my right hand, my eyes wandered again. The seated officers turned and stared toward the tent. The tent emptied. Angus walked between the two civilians to the squadron building where all three entered, one at a time. A stiff, silent Henstrom held the screened door. The civilians carried leather briefcases. They wore wire-rimmed glasses. The general and Mickey followed.

In front of the formation, Orndorff waited—rigid, the right hand quivering by his right eyebrow. Behind him, standing as his command had left us, we saluted an empty reviewing stand.

The screened door squeaked open and Adam Henstrom reappeared, alone. He jogged down the two steps to the steel matting and straight toward Captain Orndorff. Orndorff's hand fell to his side. No way was he going to appear to be holding a salute to a lieutenant.

Henstrom saluted the captain, said a few words which we couldn't hear, then saluted again and marched back to the ready room. Orndorff listened with stretched neck between salutes, did an about-face as Henstrom departed, and barked, "OR-DER...ARMS!"

Orndorff paused as I heard mumbling from our back row. Captain Cain, the squad leader at the end of our rank, turned his head and growled, "You're at attention back there!" The mumbling stopped.

I glanced at Orndorff. His stiff body faced the formation but his head was turned, eyes staring at our platoon. He swelled again. "Lieutenants Teemer, Ripkevic, O'Connor, and Kerrigan, report to Lieutenant Colonel Houser immediately after being dismissed!" He returned his eyes to his front and took another deep breath. "PLATOON LEADERS...TAKE CHARGE OF YOUR PLATOONS...AND DISMISS THEM!"

Major Biggerstaff did an about-face, dismissed the platoon, and searched the crowd of lieutenants as if looking for the ones named Teemer, Ripkevic,

O'Connor, and Kerrigan—the ones getting all the attention. Rip and I ignored him and stepped toward the ready room.

Ahead, through the fine mist and fading light, Orndorff, the career officer who wouldn't fly combat missions, had no such problem—he knew who we were. He stared at us, hands on his hips, the scowl lines on his face asking, why do you get to see the CO?

I didn't know why. But without Teach who was in the hospital, and Freud who was on Thunder Clap, and Walt who was dead, our group of four plus Angus were the only guys involved with the MI-8s. My mouth tensed as I walked. If our audience with the CO was about downing those MI-8s and serious enough to stop a change of command, then somebody was in serious trouble. Angus? No. He claimed the MI-8s at first, but he wouldn't claim them now, not if there was a problem. With Walt dead, there was only one of us left who actually did shoot down an MI-8, and Angus wouldn't hesitate to expose him—me.

A few minutes later, Rip and I and the Irish were seated along the plywood wall on the S-1 side of Angus' office, ordered there by Lieutenant Colonel Houser. I sat at the corner of the wall, next to the hallway to the XO's and CO's offices. Corporal Straderman's desk was in front of me, his silent blue-bladed fan guarding the papers on the desk top.

Straderman had gone down the hall to Mickey's office with two cups of coffee and hadn't returned. Major Lewis had followed a few minutes behind Straderman, also holding two cups of coffee. I figured the general was with Mickey, and judging by the way both Straderman and the major slowed on their way by Angus' office—their heads cocked toward the closed door—the two civilians were with Angus.

Against the wall, Rip and I sat with our arms and legs crossed, bodies turned as if we were half-looking at each other. Rip offered me a stick of Juicy Fruit but I declined, didn't want chewing sounds to keep me from hearing through the bare plywood. Wasn't having much luck as it was.

At first, all I heard was an unintelligible monotone. One voice. Then another. Neither of them Angus. Occasionally a chair would scrape, a cigarette lighter would click, a man would cough or clear his throat. I pictured the two civilians, one balding, one curly-headed, seated in metal chairs across the desk from Angus. Angus probably glared at them from behind a curl of cigarette smoke. I imagined the bloodied ceramic bull with the trap door in its belly also glaring at them.

The two civilians could have been the ones Bill had described to me at the hospital, the ones who interviewed him—same glasses, briefcases. Was that what the discussion was about? Bill? Maybe, but I doubted it. The Irish had nothing to do with Bill. Neither did Rip. But Bill had been shot down…by an MI-8. That was the thread. It had to be about the MI-8s.

Rip stopped chewing and whispered, "What's he saying? Who the hell are those guys anyhow?"

"Can't tell. Maybe CIA."

Across the dusty S-1 office, poorly lit by two bare light bulbs in the ceiling, Warrant Officer Glazener, his profile to us, hunched over some papers on his desk. Beyond him, outside the screens, darkness had settled in.

O'Connor and Kerrigan leaned forward, looked around Rip, and stared at me with raised eyebrows as if to ask if I'd figured out what was going on. I shrugged, held a finger to my lips, and pressed my ear against the wall. I was already in trouble. Who cared if I got caught eavesdropping? Rip nodded and pressed his ear into the wall.

As soon as Rip touched the rough plywood, a loud indignant voice—Angus' voice—screamed, "A fucking what? A goddamn Russian? So what the hell is a goddamn Soviet deputy ambassador doing on a logistics run?" The monotone voice answered. Angus boomed back, "Hell, I just guessed it was a logistics run—it was a goddamn transport—what else could it be? Anyhow, it was going away, so I let it go."

The monotone voice resumed, softly, slowly at first then building, still unintelligible. Angus again: "Bullshit! That's all bullshit! You want to know what happened? Okay, goddamn it, I'll tell you what happened." A chair squeaked and Angus' voice faded to conversation level. He continued, but I couldn't tell what he said. Rip glanced at me, eyes flared. "Russian?" he whispered. I nodded.

After a few minutes of mumbling, I heard a thump and a ka-clunk, probably a fist on the desk top, then Angus' voice continued, loud enough for me to hear again. "Wouldn't fucking answer me." Then, "'Cease fire,' I screamed." Another thump and ka-clunk. "Fuck! No answer!"

The original monotone voice resumed, briefly, and Angus responded, "It was fuckin' Duppont, goddamn it—a fuckin' dumb-shit lieutenant. He disobeyed my direct order. If he hadn't been killed, I'd have court-martialled his ass myself." The monotone resumed, and Angus interrupted again, "No, damn it. The lieutenants you're talking about, Teach and Teemer, are another couple of dumb-shits. You guys don't know what I have to put up with in this squadron. Most of these fuckin' lieutenants are fuckin' reserve officers. They aren't professional Marines, they're wartime fuck-ups. If you guys only knew the shit I have to put up with."

There were a few seconds of silence. Someone breathed out forcefully, maybe expelling cigarette smoke. I thought I heard paper. A throat was cleared. Then the monotone resumed, slowly, patiently. Suddenly, a chair scraped loudly and two thumps landed simultaneously accompanied by another ka-clunk. "So what! The fucking boat school graduated a shit-bird that's all. Regular commission or not, Duppont was a fucking shit-bird and disobeyed my direct order to cease fire."

A second chair scraped less emphatically. Footsteps moved toward the door. I snapped my head away from the wall and whispered, "Did you hear that?"

Rip bobbed his head once. "Lying asshole."

Around the corner and behind me I heard the door to Angus' office open and footsteps continue down to Mickey's office. A few seconds later, heavy boots jogged toward me from the end of the hall. Straderman, with loping strides, turned toward the ready room. He returned a few seconds later with a folder in his hand and reentered Mickey's office. A second later, the civilian with the curly hair, his head down, his blue tie loosened and collar unbuttoned, strode out of the office with the folder in his hand, and reentered Angus' office.

I turned to Rip as he pulled his ear away from the wall. "Did I miss anything?"

"Nothing I could make out."

We leaned against the wall again. More snapping paper sounds, as if with emphasis. The monotone resumed, measured, maybe reading something lengthy.

"No!" Angus screaming again, "You fucking guys just don't get it. Award write-ups like that are mostly bullshit anyhow. You can't believe that shit. I've already told you what happened. Shit. That son-of-a-bitch Duppont shot him down after I told him to cease fire, I told you that. Listen, I didn't shoot anybody down, I tried to prevent it. That's what happened. That, that write-up is worthless paper…bullshit…means nothing."

The monotone asked a question.

"Fuck no!"

The monotone asked another question.

"No, goddamn it! When are you fuckin' white shirts going to start payin' attention? I'm a lieutenant colonel, a United States Marine, a commissioned officer serving the President of the United States, and I say I didn't do it. You have my word on that. Get it? My word. On my honor, two goddamn lieutenants—"

A loud thump. "Shut up, Colonel!" The monotone was loud and firm.

"But—"

"Shut up!" A violent thump, a clunk, then a crash, like dishes on the floor. "Shut up and don't move. Sit!"

"You—"

"One more word, Colonel. One more word from your foul mouth and I'll have the general in here watching me put you in handcuffs. You hear me?"

A mumble.

Paper slapped together.

A throat cleared.

"Now here it is, Lieutenant Colonel Angus, Marine officer, serving the President—" The voice was hot, vehement, no more mister nice guy. "I think I can speak for my colleague here when I say our investigation, which may end here or with the interview of four more of your 'dumb-shit' lieutenants, has, to this point, given us one of two conclusions. First: either you are a *cowardly* liar who instigated an illegal mission that resulted in the death of one American officer and several Soviet officers, including the deputy ambassador to North Vietnam—in which case you will be arrested, court-martialled, and imprisoned, *or*...now listen carefully, Colonel, listen very carefully...you're just a well-meaning Marine officer, too aggressive for your own good, who should be immediately transferred out of Vietnam as a statement of apology to the Soviets. No command. No medal." A pause, then, "Your choice...'sir.'"

"Holy fuckin' Christ! I don't believe you guys. You want my command *and* my Navy Cross? All over some piss-ant Soviet politician? You shittin' me?"

"Make a decision, Colonel Angus. Court-martial or go quietly with the DFCs you have now. Make up your mind."

"Fuck you! I earned this command and that goddamn Navy Cross—got the write-ups to prove it. Maybe I didn't shoot anybody down, but I risked my life to prevent it from happening. That Navy Cross is mine, and no fuckin' CIA spook in a shirt and tie is going to take it from me. It's mine!"

"Make a decision, Colonel."

"You son-of-a-bitch! Listen to me, listen just one fuckin' minute here. I—"

"I repeat, Colonel. Court-martial or go quietly. *Or* we get the general." A chair scraped. A pause.

"Okay, okay...wait a minute...okay, take the command, fuck it. But not the Navy Cross. You can't take—"

A squeak, metal scraping metal, chains. "We can and we will. Get the general, Ken."

"Wait a minute, wait a fuckin' minute...shit!"

Footsteps toward the door.

"Okay! Okay...okay." A muffled statement.

"Very good decision, Colonel. Stay right here." Another chair scraped and two pair of footsteps moved toward the door.

I peeked around the corner in time to see the curly-headed one drop a pair of handcuffs into his suit pocket and walk toward Mickey's office. The balding one, his back to me, closed Angus' door and waited, his hands at his side, a large gold academy ring on his ring-finger.

Inside Angus' office, a chair squeaked. Footsteps. A stomping, smashing sound like a boot on dishes or pottery or...ceramic.

I put my ear to the plywood and heard heavy, erratic breathing. Loud grunts. More smashing. A pause, then the heavy scrape of moving furniture, a deep shuddering sigh, a rustle of paper, a frenzied ripping of paper. A low moan.

I straightened and looked at Rip. Holding his chewing-gum between his fingers, Rip pulled away from the wall.

"Did you hear that?" I whispered. "Is he leaving?"

He nodded. "The asshole is history, man. He's outta here."

"Are we next?"

Rip's jaw dropped. "Oh, shit. Hadn't thought of that. Did he say we wasted a Soviet deputy ambassador?"

"Walt did. We must have gotten one of their two escorts. Maybe all Soviets."

Rip shook his head. "Not good, man. Our candy-assed government is scared to death of the Soviets."

"Yeah, I know. Maybe one lieutenant colonel's scalp will be enough to cool it. Reckon?"

Rip opened his mouth to respond, but an explosion cut him off.

All four of us hit the floor at the same time—one big dusty thud. Rip groped for the pistol belt that wasn't around his waist and whispered, "Jesus, the son-of-a-bitch is trying to shoot his way out!" I held my hand up to him and crawled to the corner. I didn't think so. I'd heard another thud.

The two men in white shirts ran into Angus' office and I knew I was right. I guess if I'd kept my ear to the wall, I could have anticipated it. Maybe I'd have heard the footsteps going across the room to the coat rack, or the unsnapping of the fastener, or the metallic scrape and clunk of the slide chambering a round. As it was, all I heard was the explosion of a .45 in a confined space—probably Major Hardy's .45, the one Angus took after he had Hardy transferred—and a heavy thud on the floor.

Our flight surgeon, already in the ready room with the rest of the officers, ran by me and into Angus' office. Later, when he stepped into the hallway, I overheard his conversation with the general. Angus had placed the point of the barrel between his eyes—execution style—pulled the trigger with his thumb, and blown the back of his head off.

Fifteen minutes after the suicide, still in the S-1 office but now standing, Rip and the Irish and I met with the two civilians and Mickey. While the curly-headed one spoke to us, I heard the heavy pounding of thick rotor blades against the night air—two Huey guns, probably Freud and Shockley. Across the flight line and revetments, the blue lights along the taxiways and white lights around the control tower across the runway were crisp and clear, mist free. The swollen clouds had lifted.

The two civilians turned out to be CIA officers from Saigon. They had been to see Bill, they had been to see Teach. They had asked pointed questions. The curly-headed one spoke of placating the Soviets. The Soviet deputy ambassador was ambushed by Angus while on his way to a routine annual inspection tour of North Vietnamese supply points in Laos. His government was so incensed over his death that World War III wasn't out of the question.

I listened as the Hueys, visible only as two red flashing anti-collision lights above pale green position lights, air-taxied off the runway.

The balding one, the one with the academy ring, explained that step one had been to get Angus quietly out of country. That had failed. His suicide would please the Soviets, but not change step two. All of us, including Freud, were to be transferred as well—to Okinawa. That stopped me. What about Bill?

The balding one continued to explain the timing and logistics of the transfer, his voice fading as the slapping heartbeat of a taxiing Huey grew closer.

I raised my head, feeling the vibrations in the air. The tin roof over our heads rattled and the smell of jet exhaust blew through the screens. The CIA men and Mickey looked over their shoulders.

In the blackness of the revetment area, a Huey—identifiable only as an anti-collision light, a position light, and a steady white landing-light—bobbed and weaved forward, searching like an alien UFO for an empty space between the high thin walls of steel and sand. It found one, turned sideways, and inched forward, fighting the turbulence off the walls as it entered. I'd heard Freud say taxiing a Huey into a revetment at night was like trying to circumcise yourself blindfolded—a painful, potentially life-threatening, and probably unnecessary experience. My hands tensed as I watched him fight it.

The curly-headed one took over, shouting above the scream of the turbine engine and clamor of the blades outside. It would just be a routine transfer he yelled, no recrimination, nothing in our records to suggest we'd been transferred for cause. But it had to be done—no options.

He stopped and looked over his shoulder again, distracted by the din between the steel walls beyond our screens.

Outside, the Huey's anti-collision light floated above the revetment wall like a drunken firefly, bobbing, weaving. Finally it dropped, bounced, dipped, dropped again, and steadied as the Huey squatted onto the matting.

The screaming engine changed to a dying whine, and the curly-headed one turned. After a final statement, he shook our hands and walked away. Freud had not just survived another circumcision, he'd survived his last combat mission.

We'd leave on a C-130 the next afternoon.

33

The Emblem

The next morning, Rip and I gathered the copies of the write-ups we'd been saving and marched to the squadron to find Major Lewis.

In the ready room, slipping into his survival vest, the major stood by his cubbyhole with an extinguished pipe in his teeth. He smiled when he saw us enter.

"Hold it," he said, observing our stern faces. "Before you guys open your mouths, let me show you something." He reached into his helmet bag, extracted a large manila envelope, and thumbed the papers inside—our original write-ups plus Colonel Houser's endorsements. "I'm on my way to Camp Evans right now. The 'Nightmare' crew who rescued you, Ross, and the Dustoff crew you wrote up, Rip, will get their medals. I promise."

Rip and I glanced at each other, then the floor, then said together, "Thank you, sir." The major laughed, shook our hands, then Rip excused himself to go check on our C-130.

Major Lewis, still smiling, pointed at my cubbyhole. "I left you a note, Ross. I want you to do something for me."

"Yes, sir."

The major struck a match and put it to his pipe. "Want you to…to do me a favor when you get to Okinawa." He blew a stream of blue smoke toward the ceiling, whipped out the match, and dropped it into an ashtray on the cubbyhole shelf. "There's a new unit forming there, a detachment of Marine Cobras. Their mission will be to experiment with different tactics and types of ordnance and weapons—Zuni rockets, 20mm gun, TOW missles—and to train new guys headed for Vietnam." He smiled. "They'll need a few combat-experienced HACs; they'll need a few Dead-Eyes. I submitted your name."

I smiled, but had a sudden thought, and the smile faded.

"Yes, Lieutenant," the major said with a chuckle. "I submitted Catlett's name too."

"Thank you, sir."

He shook my shoulder. "Glad to do it, Ross. Oh, and by the way, the new CO of this detachment is a friend of ours."

"Sir?"

"As I said in my note," he nodded toward the cubbyhole again, "when you get to Okinawa, I want you to ask for a Major Ben Hardy." The major smiled. "I sent him a message last night. He's expecting you."

Later that afternoon, our Marine C-130 climbed into the muggy air, groaning with the effort of retracting its wheels and shuddering from the strain of its four engines.

Seated in a troopseat, facing a porthole in the opposite side of the cabin, I watched South Vietnam fall away, each flooded rice paddie a mirror of the scattered clouds and bright blue sky above. Beside and across from me, the others either covered their ears or pretended the roar of the engines and vibrations of the cabin weren't bothering them. I readjusted my ear plugs, grinned at the thought of Granny insisting I take them with me, and remembered the mail he'd given me—a letter from my mother.

"All is well here," she wrote. "The store is adding a new wing to the women's department and I'll be the new department manager. Going to Myrtle Beach this weekend to celebrate. Aunt Martha will drive. Hope you are warm." At the bottom of the letter was an "I love you" note from my grandmother.

I opened my briefcase to confirm the letter was still there and smiled, thinking of my grandmother, my childhood advisor, and all the questions she had so patiently answered for me, including the big one.

"Why are we here," I asked her after a neighbor had died. "Why are we alive, on earth?" It was a fresh summer morning and we were hanging wet clothes on the line behind her house. I held the heavy basket for her—man's work. She wore a cotton dress, winged collar, and had her gray hair braided and coiled around the back of her head, pinned there.

I remember she never paused, never batted an eye. She took two wooden clothespins from the pocket of her apron and another heavy white towel from the basket, and said in a matter-of-fact tone, "We're here to make a difference, Ross." She held the corner of the towel in place on the line, pinned it, then stretched and pinned the other.

"That's it?" I said.

A quick breeze popped the sheets at the end of the clothesline and rustled the new leaves on the tall oaks in front of us. She laughed, roughed the close-cut hair on my head with her freckled hand, and picked up another towel. "That's it, my boy. If, before we die, we're considerate of other people, we help more than we hurt, we give more than we take, then we lived a good life—we made a difference."

Inside the dim belly of that shuddering, deafening, Moby Dick of an airplane, I closed my briefcase, smiled again, and savored my grandmother's wisdom.

Across from me on the other side of a long, narrow, and netted pile of duffle bags and B-4 bags, the Irish played chess from a board on the seat between them. Kerrigan's sweat-stained khaki shirt hung on him like a pajama top. O'Connor, high-and-tight haircut, bars and brass shining, studied his next move.

Ripkevic sat beside O'Connor, reading a paperback, legs crossed, jaws working his gum. Rip had told me his specialty had been the butterfly and he'd been an alternate on the '64 Olympic team. His shoulders confirmed that, broad and square even when seated on a troopseat.

Ripkevic, O'Connor, Kerrigan.

I looked at the overhead, remembering Kerrigan's voice on the radio, struggling in the dark with a damaged helicopter, electrical failure, splattered with blood from his dead HAC, and how he had gotten his aircraft and his crew back safely. And Rip, making quick decisions, the right decisions, moving his crew at night through a swamp of elephant grass and across a river, evading the NVA, then cool on the radio, "Two, you there?" I could feel my heart rate jump as I visualized the lights of the Dustoff Huey climbing safely above the blackness of Helicopter Valley. Man, what a thrill that had been.

And Freud, seated on my right, what a shock it had been to find him with us over Khe Sanh. He had probably saved my life that night just by showing up, having the courage to get in the fight. He was quiet now, reading a stereo equipment catalog, running his hand through his thinning hair, convinced that after talking with me until two o'clock that morning, he really did have me straightened out. And maybe he did. I felt less guilt now about leaving after only four months. As he'd said, "You did your job for as long as they asked you to do it. That's enough." Like Jim Teach, Freud had made a big difference in my life just by being there, being a friend.

I took a deep breath, leaned my head against the bulkhead, but pulled it back when the vibrations rattled my teeth.

I scanned the cabin again and felt an inward smile. Those guys, plus the guys we'd lost: Wysowski, Duppont, B-12, Gamez—all those guys, and the guys we flew with too: Droopy, Earley, Whipple, Cobb, Rinkes, Jennings, Morchesski, Scapelli—all of them, all of those load-hacking Marines, all had taken care of each other, taken care of the grunts, the frogs, the dogs, and especially the Marine Corps. By any definition, they had given more than they had taken and had helped more than they'd hurt. Those guys had made a difference.

I chuckled and looked at the slumped, khaki-clad body to my left. Even the Cat's Ass, that emaciated shadow of a Sun Dog asleep in aviator shades beside me, that asshole who'd staggered aboard at Quang Tri after the rest of us had waited for him in the sweltering C-130 cabin for 30 minutes, then laughed at us because he was the only one who still had a mustache, yeah, even Bill Catlett—the guy who kept Rod alive for 18 days, then made sure his body could be recovered—even he had made a difference.

My ears popped, my body weight lifted, and I settled as the C-130 leveled off at altitude.

I sighed and looked to my lap, at the khaki cover lying there, and the blackened Marine Corps globe-and-anchor emblem affixed to it. I slipped my fingers under the emblem and traced my thumb along its face, along the rope that fouled the anchor and the wings of the eagle atop its globe. I didn't know what I'd do with the rest of my life, but for now, where I was wasn't so bad. I was with the finest, the first string. I was with guys who cared enough to take a sad song and make it better. I was a Marine…and I was proud of it.

Acknowledgements

Of the many who encouraged and assisted me during the years it took to write this story, none was more steadfast than my wife, Linda Reeves Crew. Known in our Marine Corps days by the call sign "Lima-Lima," she has always been the best of friends, the sexiest of companions, and the brightest of advisors. Without her, this book wouldn't be a reality.

Ed Watson and Greg Duesing, two of the finest Marine officers to ever enter a ready room, were a huge help. Also helpful were my friends in the South Carolina Writers Workshop: Russ, Gene, Khris, Sue, John, Harry, Steve, Doug, Pat, Frankie, Mindy, Anne, Meridith, Tom, Allison, Bob, Steve H., and Phil. Valuable assistance also came from Dave, Jerry, John, Manny, Joey, Chrys, Susan, Nancy, and of course, Alice.

From beginning to end, the Gower family of The Open Book, the number one family-owned bookstore in South Carolina, was a kind and generous friend. Tom, Tommy, Duff Bruce, and staff personify a community and neighborly spirit that has endeared The Open Book to the people of Greenville for generations, and nurtured my writing for four years. I am one grateful customer.

The final critique of this novel was provided by my son, Phillip. A discriminating reader, Phillip provided the precise insight I needed for the finishing touches.

The voice in my head that told me I could write this book belongs to my mother, Martha Bell Crew. "You can do anything," she would say. And for some reason, I believed her. Whatever I have achieved in life, or will achieve, I owe to her.

For the background information I needed on the senior characters in this story, I would call the finest Marine officer I've ever known, my father, Colonel Erskine B. Crew. His voice is in my head as well. "Always do more than you promise," the voice says, "and remember: your men eat first—you eat last." As surely as this book deals with character and moral courage, my father's contribution is on every page, and even though he passed away in 1995, I will say now, as I've intended to say all along, Thanks, Dad. In a special way, this book is for him.